RHUBARB

M.H. VAN KEUREN

For Dexter and Michael

PART I

1985

A shape extruded from a swirling green event, pouring into real space like a stretching cheetah on a moving sidewalk. The green event plipped away as queerly as it had popped, leaving a complete and coherent object drifting with silent purpose on a background of stars—a ship.

The vessel was immense and segmented. Two sections were nearly identical cylinders of pitted chitin. The third section, the front—or perhaps the rear—clearly the business end, bristled with antennas, sensors, and receiver dishes. Bits, certainly involved with propulsion, protruded at ungraceful angles. In its entirety, the ship could have been a thing of chthonic wonder, like an unholy trinity of sea cucumber gods, but for the corporate logo emblazoned on every facet. City-sized renderings blanketed the principal sides, block-sized versions adorned the lesser edges, and bumper sticker-sized ones decorated parts that no one but a mechanic would ever see.

It had a history—the logo, not the ship. A four-day symposium had been held to select the aspect ratio. Two new colors had been invented for its design. Evolutionary algorithms had been used to breed the font that would best convey the company's reputation for quality. The company behind this logo hired hip young beings on hundreds of worlds to normalize its name as a verb, an adjective, and an interjection. The marketing department had been mandated to make customers want to tattoo the logo unironically on their external surfaces.

At the front—or maybe the rear—of the ship, a single window the size and shape of a minivan windshield glowed just below an Olympic swimming pool-sized logo. Inside, a single being ran his tentacles over a wraparound touchscreen and brought the vessel to a halt. He then coaxed it backward, slowly and carefully, between a pair of not-entirely-similar vehicles bearing different logos. A dozen warning icons flashed as one of the ship's segments drifted out of alignment, and he had to stop—muttering words that would have puckered his mother's suckers, if only he'd known which of the several billion females had deposited his particular egg on his father's reef that season—and pull forward to make another attempt. When he had successfully parked the ship, the being let out a visible blubber of relief.

Moments later, an airlock door opened near the bottom—or the top—of the hull, and a secondary vessel emerged, this one about the size of a whale. It headed directly for one of the chunks of ice for which this region of space was known. There wasn't anywhere else to go. The nearest star, though a significant object in the sky, offered little in the way of light or heat this far from its significant planets.

As the vehicle approached the lonely berg, its headlights revealed an installation, bigger than a house but smaller than an airport. At the tap of a tentacle, a bright white point flared from the installation and then burst wide, like a toilet bowl filled with electric-blue plasma, flushed in reverse. The swirling well opened wide enough to swallow ten more whales and the school buses used to measure their lengths. The vehicle accelerated, even as a tongue of blue light shot out and sucked it in, extruding it to a single line. Then the light collapsed into darkness, and the vehicle was gone.

A few minutes later, a semi-trailer—about the size of a whale, and with sizable chrome exhaust pipes sticking up like a bull's horns—rumbled to a stop in a gravel parking lot. It resembled the dozen or so other trucks parked in the yard or fueling at the diesel pumps, except that its rear mud flaps featured the silvery silhouette of what appeared to be a squid.

A man climbed down from the cab. He was thick rather than tall, with an even thicker mustache. He wore grubby jeans, a flannel shirt open over a Harley-Davidson T-shirt, and a tweed pork pie hat.

Bells jingled as he entered the truck stop. The elderly man behind the store's register gave the trucker a manly little wave and returned to stocking cigarettes. The trucker headed straight for the men's room. A few minutes later, he took a seat at the diner counter, grunted a greeting to a couple of other truckers a few stools down, and plucked a menu from between the napkin dispenser and the ketchup bottle. Country-western music warbled from a jukebox in the corner, but something else screeched from a cheap radio in the kitchen.

"Well, hiya, Glen. Ain't seen you in ages."

A waitress sauntered behind him in a mustard-yellow, knee-length dress with a white apron. She was blond, in the loosest sense of the word, and wore too much lipstick. He checked out her rear as she walked past and rounded the counter.

"Linda, lookin' prettier than ever," he said.

"Now, don't you go flirtin' with me, Glen," she said. "You told me last time about that sweet wife and kids of yours back home."

"Did I?"

"Yes, you did," she said. "Besides…." She patted her belly.

"What's that mean?" the trucker asked.

"It means, dearie, that I am going to be a mother. And I don't need you ogling me like you just did," Linda said. Then she winked.

"Well, congratulations, I suppose," said the trucker.

"So what you haulin' that's got you come all the way through Herbert's Corner?"

"Oh, you know. A little of this, a little of that," the trucker said.

She turned over the cup waiting on a paper doily, filled it with steaming coffee, and took a pen and pad out of an apron pocket. "Now, what can I get ya?"

"You got any of that rhubarb pie?" the trucker asked.

"Fresh made this morning," said Linda.

The trucker ate a buttery Reuben sandwich and french fries before Linda brought his pie. He quivered a little as she set it in front of him and then devoured it as if he hadn't eaten in days. He ate a second piece with deliberate relish, slicing off tiny fork-fuls and taking sips of sweetened coffee between each bite. He watched the third piece arrive like a drunk watches his bartender pour. Linda refilled his coffee.

"Can't get enough of this pie," he said.

"Best rhubarb pie in Montana," said Linda.

"Montana, hell. Best rhubarb pie anywhere."

"I'm glad you like it."

"You make it?"

"My mother's recipe," said Linda. "God rest her soul."

The trucker paid the check with cash on the counter. Outside, he adjusted his hat against the wind and sun and rounded the building toward the yard. Linda was leaning against the wall near the back door of the kitchen, one forearm across her waist, the other raised, a cigarette between her fingers. He gave her a wave.

"You have a safe drive, now," she called.

"Thanks," he replied, and hesitated.

"I know, I know," she said. "I shouldn't be smokin' with a baby goin' on, but it's so hard…"

"Probably would be a good idea to quit," said the trucker. "Hey, Linda, you ever think of selling that pie recipe of yours?"

"Selling?" she said. "What's to sell? Anyone can make pie."

"I don't know. Something about yours. You know it's kinda famous."

"I've heard tell," said Linda. "But it ain't famous among no one but you long-haul boys. They ain't servin' it to Ronald Reagan in the White House." She took a final drag on her cigarette, dropped the butt into a pickle bucket full of sand, and then shook a fresh one out of the pack. She offered it to him, but he wrinkled his nose and shook his head.

"Even so," said the trucker, "seems you sell that recipe and you'd do all right."

"I don't know what there is to sell," said Linda, lighting the cigarette with a pink disposable lighter.

"I know some folks that might be interested."

Linda laughed, blowing smoke out her nose. "Well, you tell 'em to come on up here to Brixton, Montana, and we'll see what we can work out."

CHAPTER
1

Just past mile marker 241 on Highway 360, a white ambience grew over the crest of the hill, glinting off insects and limning the roadside weeds like crystals in the moonless night. Maybe, just maybe, Martin thought as he switched off his high beams. Maybe he'd come over the hill and there'd be a craft swooping up the road on a blinding shaft of light. He'd slam on the brakes, skidding his truck sideways like they do in the movies. He'd get out as the craft stopped directly overhead, and then it would shoot straight up into the night. The only sound would be the sonic clap as air rushed in to fill the void. There'd be no time to take video, no time for a phone call. But he'd finally have a better story to tell than the time he rounded a corner and broke up two coyotes fighting over a dead snake.

At the top of the hill, the approaching headlights dimmed. A semi roared by, dwarfing his own truck as it passed. Its brake lights winked out of sight on the other side of the hill, leaving the night darker than before.

Martin switched his brights back on and sucked down another gulp of Diet Mountain Dew. The commercial on the radio ended with a satellite blip. After a few moments of silence, a familiar crackling static faded up, followed by a voiceover:

"From Virginia Beach to Yreka, from the Rio Grande to the Upper Peninsula, from Boston to Yuma, from Sequim to Key West, from Mauna Loa to Mount McKinley…" Martin unconsciously recited the montage, mimicking the various voices: "My fellow Americans, ask not…One small step for man…noises from the room where she died…Back and to the left, back and to the left…nothing to fear but fear…You want the truth?…Military cover-up…the question is whether you're paranoid enough…I deny…disappeared…No comment…totally exsanguinated… they came in low over the hangar…What are they hiding? What are they afraid of us knowing?…I want to believe. I want to believe."

Martin shivered at the final whispering voice. He had heard that very "best of" show. A woman had called in claiming to be haunted by the ghost of her husband mouthing a message and holding a ghost baby she didn't recognize. Martin sighed, relieved, not for the first time, that his company truck had no back seat. It was bad enough to be out here alone—no sign of civilization—without having to worry about a disembodied spirit popping up in his rearview mirror. They'd find him mangled in the wreckage, eyes wide with fright even in death, his hair turned white, and a terrible load in his pants. Thankfully, Lee Danvers did ghost episodes only a couple of times a month. But seeing a UFO, that would be another thing altogether.

The montage ended with fading, squelching radio feedback.

"Welcome back to *Beyond Insomnia* on the Weirdmerica Radio Network. I'm your host, Lee Danvers, coming to you from the always-on-the-move BI Bunker. Whether you're on a long haul or cleaning a mall, I've got the talk to keep you awake.

Doesn't matter if you're a tweeker or a seeker, we want to hear from you. Call 1-800-555-WAKE. 1-800-555-W, A, K, E.

"We've been talking with Dr. Calvin Atford, author, researcher, and lecturer. He's a noted international expert in the history of UFO phenomena and the author of the recent book *The Shepherd Hypothesis: Ancient Aliens and Human History*. He's graciously agreed to stay with the Waker Nation for a second hour from his office in London. Welcome back, Dr. Atford."

"Thank you, Lee. It's been my pleasure."

"In a few moments we'll get to listener calls. But before we do, Dr. Atford, where can listeners go to find your books?"

"All my books are available online, both print and electronic. There are links on my website…"

"Which Wakers can find a link to on the BI website, wakernation.com. Now, Dr. Atford, I've been fascinated to hear about some of the lesser-known instances of UFO activity in history. You talked about the records from the Zhang Dynasty and the twelfth-century journals of Abbott Dmitri of the monastery at Saratov, but are there more recent cases?"

"Of course, Lee. One of the more interesting cases—which many of your listeners may not be familiar with—is in your own country. Have you ever heard of Brixton, Montana?"

"I remember hearing murmurs about it many years ago…"

"No way," said Martin, turning up the volume.

"Wasn't it revealed to be a hoax?"

"Perhaps, but there's some compelling evidence, nonetheless. The stories were declared a fraud after the death of Herbert Stamper, the owner of a well-known truck stop at the junction of U.S. Highway 15 and State Highway 360. He opened the gas station after World War II, and it became known as Herbert's Corner. After he died in 1986, the Great Falls Tribune reported that he had paid people to claim sightings and UFO-type phenomena for almost forty years."

"What types of phenomena?"

"Low-altitude aerial objects, strange bright lights over certain geological formations, those kinds of things. Particularly in spring and early summer. Brixton is less than two hundred miles from Malmstrom Air Force Base, home of a large portion of the United States' land-based nuclear missile inventory, and no stranger itself to these kinds of unidentified aerial events."

"I think we all remember the reports from the fall of 1998."

"Oh, yes. But the Brixton story has a strange angle that distinguishes it from the Malmstrom events. Herbert Stamper claimed that aliens actually frequented the Herbert's Corner truck stop, eating in the diner and shopping in the convenience store."

"Incredible. He claimed to interact with them?"

"Yes. I visited Brixton in the mid-nineties. The new owners of Herbert's Corner had made an effort to distance themselves from the diner's past. But I met a woman, whom I've agreed to keep anonymous, who had been a waitress there for more than thirty-five years. She had salvaged many of the photos and memorabilia from the diner after Stamper's death. She showed me several photos of Herbert with people he claimed were alien visitors."

"The aliens looked like people?"

"The photos appeared to be of truck drivers and other travelers. Their pictures had been framed and hung in the diner for curiosity-seekers."

"Did this woman believe Stamper's claims?"

"I can't say for certain, but she admitted that the diner had a reputation for odd clientele. Whether deserved or manufactured, I couldn't confirm."

"Is there any other evidence, besides Herbert Stamper's

rumors, that shed any light on what might have been going on in Brixton?"

"The most compelling evidence for me, as you might expect, comes from historical documents. Early French trappers reported that both the local Assiniboine and Blackfeet people called the area around the current town of Brixton by the name of 'Big Thunder Valley,' because it was known for strange sounds, odd weather, and unusual light events. One tale refers to 'nights with many sunrises.' Trapper Gustav Cuilliard wrote in his journal that he had been told of an existing trading post in Big Thunder Valley, and that there had been others there like him, by which he assumed other Europeans. But when he arrived, he found no signs of other people or a trading post. Well into the eighteen hundreds, settlers reported that the buffalo herds avoided the area. These kinds of reports provide some anecdotal suggestion that something strange indeed was going on in and around what became the town of Brixton."

"Were there similar reports from later settlers?"

"None that I've found. The situation seems to have quieted until Herbert Stamper came along in the 1940s, and then the rumors stopped again after his death in 1986. One must keep in mind that he ran a traveler-dependent business as Interstates 90 and 94 were built across the southern part of the state. Was Stamper simply playing off local legends to boost tourism? Or did alien visitors frequent his truck stop?"

"Fascinating, fascinating. Once again, we're talking live with Dr. Calvin Atford about his research into historical UFO sightings and his book *The Shepherd Hypothesis*. We have to break, but when we return, we'll get into some of the details of your book and take calls from the Waker Nation. Stay tuned. This is *Beyond Insomnia*."

Lee Danvers, now as a recording, began to shill for a company offering non-genetically-altered seeds. Martin had stopped at an intersection, left turn signal on. He barely remembered driving the last few miles. Across the highway, the gas pumps of Herbert's Corner glowed under their canopy. The little neon sign in the window of the convenience store blinked Open, Open, Open, not quite in time with the blinking red light over the junction. A few semis were parked in the gravel lot behind the building. At this hour, truckers would be sleeping in their cabs after a shower on the second floor, but a few might still be inside nursing coffee and waiting out their legal rest periods. The twenty-four-hour diner was the only place in a hundred-mile radius to get halfway decent coffee, eggs, bacon, and hash browns. Or chicken-fried steak, or a burger, or fried clams on Friday nights. Martin had heard that they'd never installed locks on the doors of Herbert's Corner, even as they'd remodeled over the years. They'd never planned to close. Martin was tempted to cross the intersection to see if that was true, among other things.

A cattle truck rumbled through the intersection, heading west along Highway 15. Martin turned to follow. A minute later, in Brixton proper, Martin slowed to a strict twenty-five miles per hour. The sheriff set his deputies out to make money for the county from every speeding scofflaw they could catch. A few pickup trucks were parked rakishly around the front and side of the bar. On the other side of town, Martin rolled into the parking lot of the Brixton Inn.

Martin shut off his engine before *Beyond Insomnia* returned from commercial. He got out and stretched. No strange lights tonight, only the constellations he'd never learned the names of. And no big thunder in Brixton. Only a little wind, some insects, and the distant chug of a truck slowing down on the other side of town.

🐛 🐛 🐛

Wake Up to the Perfect GOLDEN SUNRISE™ Waffle!

Step 1: Fill cup to line with GOLDEN SUNRISE™ waffle batter.

Step 2: Spray top and bottom of griddle with GOLDEN SUNRISE™ Griddle Spray.

Step 3: Pour batter evenly onto griddle.

Step 4: Close griddle and Flip! Fun!

Step 5: When timer signals, open griddle and remove waffle with spatula.

Step 6: Enjoy with GOLDEN SUNRISE™ maple-flavored syrup or your favorite toppings.

Caution: Griddle surfaces are extremely hot and may cause injury, including burns. Improper turning may cause wrist strain. Children under the age of 15 should operate griddle with supervision. Cooking time should not exceed three minutes. Use at your own risk.

"Good morning," Cheryl said, and plunked a variety pack of General Mills cereals on the counter. Martin started. He hadn't heard her come out of the pantry. "Need any help?" she asked with a polite smile.

She'd have recognized him, of course. How could she not? He'd been staying at the Brixton Inn about twice a month for the past few years. Its rooms weren't as good as the Comfort Inn in Glendive, but they were a far sight better than the Highline Lodge along the train tracks in Glasgow. It didn't have HBO, but it got the Billings and Great Falls stations well enough over antennas, and it usually had hot water. Most importantly, it served a complimentary breakfast, an absolute requirement for the savvy business traveler. All in all, his favorite place to stay in the state.

His second favorite had been the Hampton Inn in Great Falls, until FastNCo.'s latest budget cutbacks.

"I'm good," Martin said, pointing to the red placard dotted with happy waffle-faced suns. "Just reading the directions." Cheryl had her nametag pinned to her red hooded sweatshirt. She wore the sweatshirt unzipped, practically falling off one shoulder. Her polyester maid's uniform underneath might have been gleaned from the clearance rack at a nurses' supply store, but she made it work. She gave him another weak smile.

Martin lifted the handle of the waffle mix dispenser, and the batter oozed into the plastic cup. Cheryl tore into cellophane. Martin popped the lid off the waiting can of Pam and sprayed the griddle. An even, circular, instantly bubbling layer on the vertical surface, and then on the horizontal surface. Cheryl filled a wire rack with single-serving boxes of Honey Nut Cheerios, Wheaties, Total, and Lucky Charms. Martin poured his batter onto the griddle, finishing with a thin, dripping flourish like that guy with that show on the Food Network. He closed the griddle and flipped it. The red digital timer began its countdown.

2:30

2:29

2:28...

"Do you get those from Costco?" Martin asked.

"What?" asked Cheryl. "Oh, the cereal? No, they come with the food delivery."

"Oh, I wondered, 'cause they sell packs like that down at Costco," Martin said.

"Oh," Cheryl said, crumpling the cellophane and heading to the little storeroom.

Martin swore silently at himself. *They sell those at Costco,* he mouthed, letting himself hear the inanity. He peeled apart a pair of paper plates and checked the timer.

1:56

1:55

1:54...

And why hadn't he greeted her by name? In the afternoons, Cheryl worked as the cashier at the co-op. When he came in, she always called up to the office, "Lester, Martin Wells from FastNCo. is here." Then she usually said something like, "You can go on back," or "He'll be right down. Hondo got into a scrap with a porcupine and he's been on the phone with Dr. McFrain all morning." Why hadn't he said, "Good morning, Cheryl," like he'd said to the mirror a few minutes ago? Maybe because a few weeks ago he'd choked out a "Good morn, Churl" and hadn't yet found the courage to try again.

He selected a pastry off a chromed tray with plastic tongs. It felt a little crunchy around the edges, probably day-old, but the red goo in the middle and the lace of frosting glistened appetizingly enough.

1:28

1:27

1:26...

Cheryl returned with a box of individual Splenda packs to restock a little bowl. Martin pressed the top of an airpot, and coffee squelched into his Styrofoam cup. He added half-and-half, two Splendas, and a red stir stick.

0:52

0:51

0:50...

An elderly couple, the only other breakfasters up this early, had taken his table. The one near the windows. The one with the best view of the breakfast counter and the pantry door.

"With those BNSF crew trucks in the parking lot, I was afraid it'd be crowded this morning," said Martin.

"Brenda said they got in real late last night," said Cheryl, nodding her head toward the woman behind the desk on the other side of the lobby. She tucked the box away in a cabinet under the counter. "She said you got in pretty late, too. Didn't think I'd see you up this early."

Interesting. Cheryl had actually thought about him, had had a conversation about him with the night clerk. Probably only a few quick words over a clipboard showing which nine or so of the forty rooms needed to be cleaned later, but at least she knew he existed.

"Yeah, I thought I'd get in a run before I got over to the co-op," said Martin. What? A run? What had possessed him to say that? He'd bought those Asics on sale at Sports Authority almost a year ago, and his quisling tongue picked now to commit him to jogging? Had he even packed that Under Armour he'd gotten to go along with the shoes and the good intentions?

"I didn't know you were a runner," said Cheryl.

"Just getting into it," said Martin. His waistline belied any other reply. He didn't belong on *The Biggest Loser*, but he ate too many motel breakfasts, too much fast food, and more than his share of convenience store snack packs and microwavable meals. The Diet Mountain Dew—it did nothing.

"Good for you," said Cheryl. "Should be a nice morning for it."

"Yep. Spring's here," Martin said, and stuck his hand into a bowl of ice to avoid saying anything else asinine. He emerged with a foil-topped cup of orange juice and shook the freezing water back into the bowl.

Beep beep beeeeeep. Beep beep beeeeeep.

The waffle stuck to the top of the griddle but fell free with a gentle nudge from the spatula. Martin plucked two gold-foiled pats of butter out of a bowl and took a pack of Sysco breakfast syrup from the top of a neat stack. Cheryl crossed the lobby, chewing on a fingernail as she rounded the wood-paneled front desk, and disappeared into the back office hall that led to the housekeeping room.

Martin ate at the table with the words "Brixton" and "Sux" scratched in the laminate—the "Sux" intersecting the name of the town like a Scrabble play. He forced himself to read yesterday's Billings Gazette—he didn't want Cheryl to catch him looking for her to return—but only the doleful mounted head of a measly four-point buck looked his way.

CHAPTER
2

The rumor wasn't true; the doors of the Herbert's Corner Convenience Store, Diner, and Trucker's Lounge had locks. Martin had never known them to be used, but there they were. They probably had to put them in to get insured or to keep the Health Department placated.

The diner's unnaturally brown carpet couldn't be called anything but "colorless" in polite company. Beyond the "Please Seat Yourself" sign, six tables filled the floor between the eight stools at the counter and a U of ten brown upholstered booths. Sunlight peeked through one small window in the narrow vestibule near the till, but otherwise the diner's only lighting was fluorescent. Was it brunch or midnight? The Pepsi clock behind the till stayed out of the argument. Not that it mattered—the whole menu was always available.

Five men were seated in the diner, reading newspapers or filling out paperwork amid their dirty dishes. A pair of ranchers dropped their check and some cash next to the register and squeezed out past Martin.

"Yo, Screw Man," called a familiar voice. Jeffrey Scarborough waved from the far corner booth.

Jeffrey was a candy guy. Those no-brand candy packs that hang on hooks to the left of the candy bars and gum, and to the right of the nuts—those were him. Cellophane packs of gummy worms, candy corn, Jordan almonds, chocolate pretzels, butter mints, wax colas, licorice—all the candies people sort of like, but not enough to brand. Jeffrey was probably the biggest seller of carnauba wax in the Northern Rockies. Martin had tried a few varieties after meeting Jeffrey, shortly after signing on with FastNCo.—what, five years ago?—but found them a little off-putting. He imagined ungloved, unwashed workers scooping candies out of bins at the maws of filthy machines. Martin had seen enough of that Food Network show about snack factories to want to know where his junk food came from. But everyone stocked Jeffrey's stuff. Somebody must buy it.

Jeffrey sported his usual ironed shirt, open collared under a tailored jacket. FastNCo. insisted that Martin wear khakis and scratchy blue embroidered polo shirts, which never seemed to fit quite right. He felt like a gadget salesman without a Best Buy.

"Thought I saw the ol' Screwmobile parked at The Brick Mattress this morning," said Jeffrey. Martin waved to Eileen, who was chatting with a truck driver at the counter, as he slid into the booth across from Jeffrey. "Why do you still stay there? It's only two hours from Billings."

"Two and a half," said Martin.

"You could have slept at home and gotten up here by now, no problem," said Jeffrey. "Look at you. You look like hell. Like you're about to have a heart attack or something."

Eileen arrived and poured Martin a cup of coffee.

"The number four, and some water, too, please," said Martin. "I went for a jog this morning."

Jeffrey laughed. "A jog? You? You're kidding."

"What? What's wrong with wanting to get in shape? You're in shape," said Martin.

"I'm blessed with a naturally thin physique, and I do taekwondo."

"You do not."

"I do, too," said Jeffrey. "And let me guess: You were trying to impress what's-her-name and told her you're training for an Ironman." Jeffrey stretched his arms across the back of the booth. "Does that mean you actually talked to her instead of drooling all over yourself?"

"We exchanged a few words," said Martin. He peeled open a pack of half-and-half, dribbled it into his coffee, and stirred it in. "And don't be a jerk."

"Just trying to give you a nudge in the right direction," said Jeffrey. "If you like this woman, you've got to make a move sometime. You can't waste your whole life being afraid to talk to her. You might call it being a jerk, but I'm looking out for you."

"You know it's not that easy," said Martin. Eileen arrived with a tall, sweating glass of ice water and Jeffrey's meal. "Eileen," said Martin, "did you know Herbert Stamper?"

"Before my time," she said. "You must have heard BI last night. Everyone was talkin' about it this morning."

"Any truth to it?" asked Martin.

"Strange stuff happens around here every day, but I don't need flying saucers to explain any of it. Just a restaurant full of boys like you comin' in off the road," said Eileen.

"BI? You still listening to that crap?" Jeffrey asked.

"Are you about to give me more advice?" Martin asked, then turned to Eileen. "The guy on the radio said he interviewed a woman who used to work here."

Eileen laughed. "Probably Doris Solberg. She lives out on

McMasters Road now. Used to have a thing with Herbert, and that woman can talk. Yours'll be up in a minute." Eileen reloaded her tray with dishes from another table on her way back to the counter.

"Danvers talked about Brixton?" asked Jeffrey.

"And Herbert's Corner. Apparently this very diner used to be the aliens' favorite truck stop," said Martin.

"And of course you believed it, hook, line, and sinker," said Jeffrey.

"Wouldn't it be cool, though?" said Martin and scanned the diner. The last of the other customers was settling up with Eileen at the till. "Eating lunch with extraterrestrials."

Jeffrey rolled his eyes and plucked the frilled toothpick out of his toasted club sandwich. "Audiobooks," he said. "That's what I listen to."

"Gotta keep awake somehow," said Martin.

"You working the co-op this afternoon?" Jeffrey asked through a half-swallowed bite. Martin nodded. "Then I suggest you take the opportunity to ask her out."

"We're still talking about this? What about your adventures? Still seeing the assistant manager at the McDonald's in—where was it? Columbus?"

Jeffrey shook his head and wiped his mouth with a napkin. "Focus. It's a big day for you."

"I can't just ask her out. I don't want to end up like Frank Odessa. Remember him? The paint and stain guy? He asked her out and Lester practically had him arrested."

"Odessa didn't ask her out, he grabbed her ass," Jeffrey pointed out.

"Plus, I heard she punched the homecoming king in the balls for doing something similar, and that he pretty much had to leave town after that," said Martin.

"I doubt that happened," said Jeffrey. "Look, she's the town daughter. How many other women stick around a place like Brixton after high school? Of course people are going to look out for her. But if your intentions are noble, no one's going to stop you."

"I'm at least five years older than she is," said Martin.

"You're talking yourself out of this before you've given yourself a chance," said Jeffrey. "Who cares about age? You're what thirty-three, thirty-four? So what? Besides, she probably likes older men."

"I'm twenty-nine," said Martin. His food arrived, and he thanked Eileen.

"You're not going to do it," said Jeffrey, sliding the bottle of Heinz ketchup across the table without being asked.

"It's more complicated than that," said Martin.

"Whatever," said Jeffrey. "Maybe I'll ask her out."

Martin shook his head and poured ketchup on his hash browns as Jeffrey laughed.

♪ ♪ ♪

Out in the parking lot, Martin put on his sunglasses and watched Jeffrey turn out onto Highway 360 on his way to sell more lame candy to every store in Montana. Jeffrey liked to go on at length about how his Lincoln Town Car was the only car for the traveling salesman. Roomy, powerful, floated like a cloud. "It's like flying a leather sofa," Jeffrey always said. "You oughta get yourself one."

That was easy for him to say. He didn't have to carry inventory. He had one of those cushy jobs where he just went from store to store writing up orders. He didn't use paper, or even a PDA with a UPC wand and a docking station. Jeffrey had an iPad app. Martin had seen him work. Jeffrey spent about two minutes checking the inventory levels of no more than twenty products, then spent the next fifteen minutes glad-handing owners, shooting the breeze with assistant managers, or chatting up cute cashiers. He'd upload the order on the stroll back out to his flying couch, via some kind of always-on 3 or 4 or 5G wireless. The order was probably boxed up and loaded on a UPS truck before he even got to his next account.

That was not the life of a FastNCo. area account representative. No cushy Town Car for him. Instead, Martin drove a Ford E-250 Super Duty Cutaway, a pickup truck cab and chassis with a custom payload box on the back. Every FastNCo. truck in the country was identical, thanks to some company bean counter. When fully loaded, the four hundred different cabinets, drawers, and compartments contained more than a ton of nails, screws, nuts, bolts, washers, and staples. The fleet-style cab had been stripped of anything that might make a Ford truck a pleasure to drive. That bean counter—who probably commuted a half-hour to and from work in an Acura with heated seats somewhere in Ohio—never conceived of the distances and conditions that the reps out West had to cope with.

Martin had outfitted the gray-on-gray interior with a steering wheel cover, a back-supporting seat cushion, a cup holder stuck in place with double-sided foam tape, and a Garmin GPS unit he'd bought with his own money. Martin had tried to get a couple of different places to replace the AM/FM radio, but no one would touch it because he wasn't the official owner of the vehicle, not even when he offered the guy at Radio Shack forty bucks. Instead, Martin had mounted a SiriusXM radio and speakers in a homemade plywood box, held together with various FastNCo. fasteners, that sat on the passenger seat. Martin had had to do a little tinkering with the truck's electrical system to make it work, but he could disconnect it in four minutes flat if his district manager ever showed up.

Martin rolled into the parking lot of the Brixton Co-op shortly after one o'clock and stopped along the side of the building where Lester liked vendors to park, under the Purina and Monsanto signs. Martin loaded his folding cart with a couple of boxes each of 425s and 10478s. Ranchers chewed through those by the pound to repair fences, and Lester always needed more.

The doorbell jangled as Martin wheeled the cart through the door. Cheryl glanced up from her paperback behind an enormous mechanical register. She still wore her red hoodie, but she'd changed into jeans. Lester didn't make her wear a nametag. "Hey there," she said. "How was your run this morning?"

"Pretty good," said Martin. He would have liked to go into detail, but he doubted that the mile or so of sweat, panting, and fending off an unfenced blue heeler would impress. She picked up the phone on the pole and pressed a number. Across the store, on the second floor, Lester turned around at his desk, peered down, and waved through the window.

"Martin Wells from FastNCo. is here," Cheryl said when he answered his phone.

On a rack next to the register, near a spinner of cowboy-themed greeting cards, hung a dozen varieties of Jeffrey's candy. Martin imagined Jeffrey smarming over the counter, showing off his whitened teeth and bragging about his prowess at taekwondo. Martin exchanged another polite smile with Cheryl. Jeffrey probably would have had her agreeing to an evening down in Billings, maybe Red Lobster, a 3-D movie at the new Shiloh 14. He'd arrange a room for her at the Crowne Plaza. Martin told himself to stop it. She'd never agree to that. Not with someone like Jeffrey. Not with anyone. If she could be wined and dined, someone would have done it by now.

Cheryl went back to her book, but Martin couldn't see the cover. He hoped he hadn't left anything weird in the room for her to find—yesterday's underwear, an unflushed toilet, kinky hairs in the shower. He could never be sure whether Cheryl, Pam, or Vonnie would clean his room, so he always rinsed out the tub, double-checked for belongings, hung his towels, and took his food trash out to the can in the lobby. He didn't want Cheryl finding out how many Pop-Tarts or Pringles he ate in the middle of the night. But he also worried that she'd find him too neat, oddly fastidious, or serial-killerish. So he always made sure to leave the bed a mess, and to toss the TV remote casually on the nightstand.

Lester, so bowlegged he walked with a cane, had been running the store longer than Martin had been alive. He liked to think he was one of a kind, that he ran the tightest ship around, but to Martin, he was one of a score of rural old-timer retailers still running ahead of the actuarial odds as if too busy for a funeral. Lester had bigger fish to fry. "I got a few returns," he said, leading Martin away from Cheryl. "Ronnie's boy Mike came in here last week with a couple bolts, heads broke clean off. Says there weren't no torque on 'em at all."

"I'll take a look," said Martin. "I'm sure we can get you a credit."

"I'd appreciate it," said Lester.

The FastNCo. setup took up more than a third of one aisle with its array of little drawers, each with a picture and a list of specs on a card on the front. A few bins near the floor contained high-volume products and a scoop on a chain. A set of shelves held the boxed items. Lester tapped a few drawers. "I ain't moved none of these in a few months. Maybe you got something else we can put in there instead?"

Martin agreed to figure something out, opened the first drawer, and unholstered his PDA and scanning wand.

From the FastNCo. procedural manual for area representatives:

1. Make contact with the account holder. If the account has invoices outstanding, confirm that a payment plan has been established.
2. At FastNCo. installation, take a general survey of the product presentation. Is the area tidy and organized? Is it free of competing products and easy for a customer to use?
3. For each drawer:
   a. Scan product code into FASsys.
   b. Confirm that product matches PIC card. Remove inappropriate items and return items to their correct drawers.
   c. Weigh contents. (For products 1264-2350, hand count must be taken.)
   d. Record weight (or count).
   e. Restore product weight (or count) to specified inventory level for bin size.
   f. Confirm restoration of inventory with FASsys.
4. For bulk products:
   a. Scan product code into FASsys. ...

Martin rose stiffly from neatening the hundred-count boxes of screws on the lower shelves and rubbed the small of his back. His early lunch had long abandoned him. Even Jeffrey's no-brand candy sounded appetizing. Martin made a final check for loose product, hanging PIC cards, and general debris. He topped off the tray of paper sacks and hung a fresh pen on the string by the digital scale.

"I suppose you need my signature," Lester called from the end of the aisle, appearing as if he'd been watching Martin work. Which he probably had been.

"The ol' John Hancock," said Martin. He'd printed out the long tape of the order on the little portable printer back in the truck. On his first visit, he'd tried to get Lester to sign on the PDA's screen with the stylus and have an invoice emailed to him, but Lester had declared he'd be damned before he'd sign anything but paper.

Lester scanned the three feet of receipt tape. "Six hundred and change. Sounds about right," he said. He signed the bottom of the tape with his own pen on a nearby shelf. "I suppose you heard that fool on the radio last night."

"I did," said Martin.

"Well, don't you go believin' a word of it." Lester traded the signed tape for a copy for his records. "Sure, Stamper built the truck stop after the war and made it a success, but he made the whole lot of us look like nincompoops—all that talk of aliens and flying saucers."

"So you've never seen anything strange?"

"Bah," said Lester, waving off the thought of it. "I only bring it up 'cause Cheryl doesn't need the attention. She and her step-father doin' fine now."

"Churl?" Martin asked. "I mean, Cheryl?"

Lester nodded gravely and lowered his voice. "Her mother used to work for Stamper at the diner. She got caught up in his tales. Right after Cheryl was born, she left Stewart and ran off to California with Cheryl's real father, some deadbeat vagabond, traveling shyster salesman—no offense. She came back a couple years later, all messed up on drugs and who knows what, claiming she'd been abducted by Stamper's aliens. A complete disgrace. God bless Stewart Campion. He settled in and raised Cheryl like she was his own. Now you see why I don't want rumors getting started up again."

"No business of mine," said Martin.

"Good. Good. Where you off to now?"

Martin tugged his emptied cart past the register as Cheryl cha-chinged up an order for a woman in mud-splattered boots. Who am I to her? Martin wondered. I'm the modern equivalent of the shyster who seduced her mother and ruined her life. I'm the guy she's staying in Brixton to avoid. And what do I have to offer her that's better than this? A one-bedroom apartment in the Billings Heights and twenty-four nights out of thirty out on the road? Plus, she had her stepfather to care for. Martin had heard that he was fighting cancer or something. He'd seen him in the co-op, carrying an oxygen tank with a—what was it called?—a cannula cinched around his ears and under his nose.

The doorbell jangled as Martin left, but Cheryl was busy punching numbers into the till. It was just as well.

CHAPTER
3

"You're listening to the best of *Beyond Insomnia with Lee Danvers* on SiriusXM Channel 162. If you hear phone numbers in this rebroadcast, please do not call. *Beyond Insomnia* is broadcast live from 10:00 p.m. to 2:00 a.m. Eastern Standard Time, Sunday through Thursday and 10:00 p.m. to 3:00 a.m. Friday and Saturday."

"Welcome back, Waker Nation. Lee Danvers coming from the BI Bunker somewhere out there. It's been a strange show so far. Not at all what I had planned. Stepped out during the last break to see if it was a full moon. Feels like one of those nights. To fill you in, this strangeness started when I took a call from Frank in Joplin, Missouri, who announced that his name is not really Frank, but Tootex, and he's a visitor from a civilization in the Rigel Cluster, an observer of our planet, and he has been compelled to break cover to warn us about the self-destructive path we're taking as a species. An interesting conversation, to say the least. And he's informed us that there are many other visitors on Earth right now. So I've tossed my plans for tonight's show out the window and have opened the phone lines to visitors only. Any and all aliens, extraterrestrials, dimensional travelers, and time travelers are asked to call. We have a lot of questions for you. But be prepared. I want to know exactly where you're from, how you arrived here, and the true purpose of your visit. 1-800-555-WAKE.

"We'll go right to it. El Cajon, California, you're Beyond Insomnia."

"Hello, am I on?"

"You're on, caller."

"Oh, cool…"

"What's your name?"

"Dennis. At least that's my Earth name."

"Where are you from?"

"A planet in the Pleiades. It's called Klipthon."

"Klipthon?"

"It's hard to say it right with a human mouth."

"You're not human?"

"I have a human form. But my people are more like lobsters."

"Lobsters."

"You could learn a lot from the lobsters here on your own planet."

"So how did you get to Earth, Dennis?"

"A ship."

"You'll have to be more specific than that."

"It has a muto-fission drive."

"Can you explain that?"

"It's powered by mutating living fissionable matter. We breed it on Klipthon for ship fuel and to provide energy to our planet."

"Okay, we'll go along with you on that one for now. Is that why you've come? To bring us this remarkable source of energy?"

"No. We're breeding you humans as food."

"Oh, my. That's not very nice, Dennis. You know that we

humans don't take being eaten lightly. How many of you Klipthonians are here?"

"It's only me for now."

"One Klipthonian?"

"When there are ten billion of you, the harvest will begin."

"And if we resist?"

"Resistance is futile."

"Uh-huh. It's my opinion that Jonathan Archer was undoubtedly the best captain of any Enterprise."

"You're crazy, Lee. Archer and his cheese-farting beagle aren't fit to lick Picard's boo…"

"And goodbye, Dennis. Nice try. Little Rock, you're Beyond Insomnia."

"Hi, Lee, this is Naomini. And my home world is actually in another galaxy. It's called Monhonia, and we are descendants of what you would call Atlanteans."

"As in people from Atlantis?"

"Yes, that's right. They left Earth almost fifteen thousand years ago and resettled on Monhonia. But before that they lived in a different galaxy."

"So how do you travel between galaxies?"

"Reincarnation, Lee. It's the only way. These other callers claiming they have ships are lying to you."

"So you have to die, and then what?"

"Focusing crystals guide our souls to their next life. It's so beautiful."

"You were born human?"

"When I turned twenty-four, I became aware of my nature."

"It's a one-way trip then? Or do you have a focusing crystal here on Earth to guide you back to your home world?"

"We have a few crystals here."

"So there are more of you?"

"I think there's a few hundred of us, Lee. But most of us are pretty reclusive. I've never met any others, but I can feel them."

"And what are you doing in Little Rock? What's your purpose for being on Earth?"

"When our culture left, we accidently tore a hole in Gaia's soul, allowing evil to take hold. It's irreparable, but we meditate every day to keep evil from completely destroying all life here."

"Let me be the first to thank you for doing that."

"You're kind to say so, but it's what I was born to do."

"Are you married? Do you have children?"

"Two beautiful little girls. I'm very blessed."

"Are they Atlanteans also, or Monhonians?"

"No, they're human. I'm the only one in my family."

"You say you can feel the others. Is there anyone we might be familiar with who is also a Monhonian?"

"I've never met her, but I'm pretty sure Angelina Jolie is one of us."

"I don't think I'd argue with that. Thanks for calling, Naomini, and thanks to all your people for holding the soul of our planet together. More wake-up calls after this break."

♪ ♪ ♪

Martin tucked his phone between his cheek and shoulder and opened his freezer. The cool air felt good. He'd spent the afternoon loading a new shipment into his storage unit and restocking the truck. He'd rather be in the shower than talking to Rick, but when Rick called, Rick—the FastNCo. district manager for the Pacific Northwest and Northern Rockies—must be talked to.

"Got to talk to you about your expense reports," said Rick. "Now, I'm talking to everyone, not just you. But the fact is you've got one of the highest sales volume to expense ratios, not just in my district, but in the whole company."

"I've also got one of the lowest-density territories in the country," said Martin. "We've discussed this. Other reps get three, four, accounts in one town, with towns a half-hour apart. I get one account per town, towns two hours apart. It's simple math."

"I know, I know," said Rick. "But management's coming down on everyone…" Martin dug a box of DiGiorno Rising Crust Pizza out of the freezer and shut the door with his elbow. He tore off the perforated strip and shook the disc onto his counter. "…wanting to cut overnight stays by forty to fifty percent across the board."

"Impossible," said Martin, setting the oven for 400 degrees. He ripped open the plastic wrapper. His cookie sheet was still in the sink from his last meal at home. He gave it a quick wipe with a paper towel. "They can't reasonably expect me to drive home every night, or even half the nights. If I'm lucky I get to three, maybe four, accounts in a day outside the Billings, Bozeman, and Great Falls areas. If I have to start out from home every day, that number drops to one, maybe two. It can't be done. Perhaps back East they don't understand that this is a huge state. Can we explain that a town like Plentywood is a seven-hour drive from Billings?" He slammed the oven on his pizza.

"I'm sure we can trim some fat. I'm reviewing your March expenses now. You spent three nights at the Brixton Inn, but you only called on the Brixton Co-op once."

"It's a junction town, Rick. It's a central starting place to cover a lot of the northern and eastern part of the state. It's also about half the price of places in Great Falls. Don't the money guys take that into consideration?"

"I don't know what to tell you, Marty," Rick said. Martin

cringed. Rick was the only person in the world who called him "Marty." "Something needs to give."

How about the fact that if I drove a big rig, I'd be violating federal law with the hours I put out on the road for you and FastNCo.? It might not be constructive to say that out loud.

"Any cutback means I get into accounts less frequently. I'm already pushing it to stay on a forty-day cycle," Martin said.

"If a few more of your accounts would commit to the Triple-P installation, maybe we could stretch that out to a fifty- or even sixty-day rotation." The Premiere Product Partner rack took up ten more linear feet and pushed six inches deeper into the aisle than the traditional unit.

"I hard sold it to everyone," Martin lied. He hadn't even bothered to mention it to most of his accounts. "But these are small stores. Tight aisles. They can't give up any more floor space."

"Do you have your expense reports handy?" asked Rick.

When Rick had been finally, albeit temporarily, placated, Martin closed his laptop, stripped off his damp, stiff clothes, and got in the shower. A few minutes later, he heard the beeping.

Smoke billowed out of the oven. Water dripped on the linoleum. He had to let his towel go to use both hands to take the battery out of the smoke detector. After he got dressed and opened some windows, he dumped the charred pizza in the trash and dropped the trash in the Dumpster on his way to Sonic, or maybe Wendy's. No, Sonic had those giant slushes.

☙ ☙ ☙

"Randy Coburn is a physicist and author who worked with JPL on the Voyager missions and has consulted with NASA on several projects, but he's known internationally for his recent research on the Nazca Lines of Peru. Welcome, Randy Coburn, to *Beyond Insomnia*."

"Thank you, Lee. It's an honor to be on the show."

"I had the pleasure to introduce you at this year's WakerCon. And we had a great response from your talk there. So it's great to have you on now, and I hope we can get you back to WakerCon next year in Cincinnati."

"Wouldn't miss it, Lee."

"At the con you debuted your new book, *Lines of Sight: A New Perspective on the Construction and Meaning of the Lines of Nazca, and What It Means for Us Today*. How have you been received with these new theories?"

"Lee, the response has been overwhelming. I can't tell you how many letters, emails, tweets, and even telegrams I've gotten from supporters."

"Now, you spent a lot of time in the field while doing the research for this book."

"Six trips to Peru in as many years, Lee. I made thirty flights over the lines and many overland visits. We're still waiting to get special dispensation from the Peruvian government and UNESCO to do more accurate surveys."

"For those who haven't read the book, can you give us a brief synopsis of your theories?"

"Absolutely. Reiche believes that the lines and figures were entirely the creation of the Nazca people as a religious astronomical calendar. And of course von Daniken theorizes that the lines were a landing field for ancient astronauts. I fall somewhere in between. The problem, Lee, is that the figures and lines don't correlate with anything we know in our own sky, even when we roll back the star positions a few thousand years. Nor do the figures correlate well with the common religious imagery of the Andean tribes at that time."

"That leaves us with a bit of a mystery, doesn't it?"

"I postulate that the lines are actually a map, created by the Nazca people at the direction of extraterrestrial visitors. It's not a map reflecting the sky of Earth, but the sky of the visitors' home world. The lines are meant to orient and provide spatial coordinates. The figures are constellations seen in that other sky, but rendered as local animals as a mnemonic device."

"So it's your assertion that if we locate these constellations, it will reveal the visitors' home."

"Exactly. I'm working on a computer program that will…"

♆ ♆ ♆

Thank you for stopping at Lockwood Town Pump Conoco.
Step 1: Select Pay at Pump/Credit or Pay Inside/Cash.
Step 2: Swipe card.
         Credit, Debit, or Fleet Card? Enter fleet card PIN.
         Would you like a receipt? Y/N
         Would you like a car wash? Y/N
Step 3: Select grade.
         85.5 Regular Unleaded
         88 Mid-Grade Silver Unleaded
         91 Premium Platinum Unleaded
Step 4: Lift handle.
Step 5: Begin fueling. No smoking. Do not top off. Report
         spills to attendant.

A little after five in the morning a few weeks later, a familiar Lincoln Town Car floated into the gas station. The driver's-side window rolled down. "Yo, Screw Man, I got one of your nails in my tire," Jeffrey called. He got out and swiped his card in the opposite pump.

"Morning, Jeffrey," Martin said with a yawn.

Jeffrey set the nozzle in his ride. "You working Billings today?" he asked.

"No, I gotta do Columbus, Absarokee, Red Lodge, Joliet, Bridger, and maybe Laurel if I can get there."

"That's a lot for you, isn't it?"

Martin rolled his eyes. "Company's pushing me on expenses."

"Sorry, man. Too bad. I'm heading up to Molt for lunch. That café up there. Have you been?" Martin shook his head. "Great place. Hey, how'd it go with that Brixton chick? You talk to her?" Martin gave Jeffrey a sour look. "Sorry, I shouldn't pry."

Martin watched his expense dollars drain away into his deep and thirsty tank. If he called a couple of accounts and arranged to come in over the weekend, he could probably swing lunch with Jeffrey. And Rick could bite him. "What time are you going to lunch?" he asked.

※　※　※

The waitress should have been pledging a sorority rather than taking orders at a quaint café in an old general store with nothing but high prairie for miles around. She set their meals down with a smile and spun on the spot to take the order of a couple at the next table.

"Looks good, no?" asked Jeffrey. He indicated the waitress's jeans and winked.

"And here I planned to scarf down a Subway sandwich on the road," said Martin, keeping his eyes on his food.

Martin was about halfway through his meal when Jeffrey asked, "Why don't you tell me what's on your mind?"

"Is it that obvious?" asked Martin.

"You look like you've been carrying that truck around on your back," said Jeffrey.

"I'm thinking of getting out. Company's pushing for more and more with less and less. I work seven days a week. I spend more than forty hours a week in that truck."

"I thought you enjoyed it, especially with Lee Danvers there all the time," said Jeffrey.

"I'm being serious," said Martin. "I don't know if I can keep doing this, but I also don't know what else I'd do. I'd love to get on with a bigger company, something with a little more recognition than FastNCo., but the job market now scares me to death. And this whole thing with Cheryl up in Brixton has gotten me thinking. I don't even have time in my life for her. All I have time to do is work. And for what? To pay for the crappy apartment I never sleep in? To afford the two-week vacation I don't take so I can make bonus? To make the payment on the Subaru I never drive? What can I offer her that's anything like a normal relationship?"

"You own a Subaru?" asked Jeffrey.

"How do you do it?"

"Who says I do?" said Jeffrey. "Maybe I'm just as angst-ridden as you."

"You seem to have it all together," said Martin.

"It's my naturally cool demeanor," said Jeffrey. "Plus, I'm a workaholic."

"Have you heard of any openings anywhere?"

"What makes you think another company is going to be any better?" Jeffrey asked. "I'm getting all kinds of pressure from the head office now. The grass isn't going to be greener anywhere else, just a different shade of brown."

Martin sighed. "I gotta do something. One of these days I'm going to hit a deer, or go sliding off in a snowstorm, and I'm going to die out on these roads. And for what? So FastNCo. can meet analyst expectations for the third quarter earnings reports?"

"You're not going to die," said Jeffrey. "Stop being depressing. I'm trying to enjoy my catfish."

"Sorry. I'm definitely going to start searching for a new job."

"I'll keep my ear to the ground for you," said Jeffrey.

Martin shifted in his seat. He couldn't believe he'd poured all that out in front of Jeffrey. How did it come to be that his best friend in the world, his only confidante, was a smarmy candy salesman he met around the state a couple of times a month? He didn't know his neighbors. All his high school and college friends were off having lives with wives and kids, at least according to Facebook. I can't even get a dog, he thought. I'd be hunted by the ASPCA.

"You still jogging?" Jeffrey asked.

"Not really," said Martin.

"I suppose we make the time for the stuff we really want to do."

"Is that meant to be insightful?"

"It's meant to be an excuse to get dessert," said Jeffrey, waving to their waitress.

CHAPTER
4

"But how can we trust the CIA about what's really going on over in Iran? You know they lied to us about the assassination attempt on the pope in '83."

"Did they?"

"Of course they did, Lee. They wanted Pope John Paul II dead because he was reaching out to the Eastern Bloc. The CIA was actively trying to start World War III. That was their job. They couldn't have the pope preaching peace and understanding to the commies."

"Do you agree with that, Colonel? Was the CIA involved with the attempt to assassinate the pope?"

"That's a new one to me, Lee. As far as I'm aware, the CIA never had any active operations targeted against the Vatican or the pope. The pope was an outspoken critic of the communists and their treatment of the church in his native Poland. I doubt the CIA would have wanted to do anything to hinder him getting his message out."

"Thank you, caller. Next up, Charleston, West Virginia.

You're on with Colonel Timothy Mumford, author of *The Secret History of the CIA*."

"Wow. Hi, Lee. Longtime sleeper, first time awake."

"Glad to wake you up. What's your question for Colonel Mumford?"

"Sure. Um, Colonel, I was wondering about the fact that the Reptoids of the Babylonian Brotherhood have taken control of the CIA in order to bring the United States into the New World Order, and if your access to the archives gave you any additional insight into this?"

A car had pulled over on the side of the road, hood open, with its flashers blinking red into the night. Martin moved into the other lane to pass, as FastNCo. policy forbid him from offering roadside assistance in the company truck. Then he caught a glimpse of a red hoodie by the front bumper. He slammed on the brakes and caught his makeshift radio before it slid off the seat. In the back, the full load of fasteners shifted noisily.

"…when George H. W. Bush became president, but that didn't materialize. The archive referenced several documents, but I wasn't able to loc…" Martin turned off the radio. The person in his side mirror was definitely wearing a red sweatshirt, but was it her? Now that he'd stopped, he couldn't just drive off. He levered his truck into reverse.

He stopped twenty yards away. The truck's exhaust billowed into the dim extent of the stranded car's headlights. The roadside at night felt like an alien world, something meant to be streamed by at seventy-five miles per hour. He shouldn't have been walking along the corroding edge of the asphalt. He shouldn't have been able to see individual tufts of grass. He shouldn't have been able to touch a reflector post. The insects should have been splats on his windshield, not noisy, living things, drawn by the light.

"You need help?" he called.

"There's no cell coverage out here," she called back. Cheryl. Not at the store, not at the motel. But out here. Martin checked his own phone. Not only were there no bars, but the phone helpfully added, "No Service."

"Me neither," said Martin.

"It'd been making a funny noise for a while," said Cheryl. "Then I came around the curve there, and it made this horrible sound, then just stopped wanting to go. The engine revs, but it doesn't drive."

"Hate to say it, but it sounds like a transmission problem," said Martin, wondering if he'd oversold his masculinity. "But you probably shouldn't take my word for it."

Cheryl sighed. She lifted the hood, took out the brace, and snapped it carefully back into place. Then she let the hood down easily, letting it drop only the last couple of inches. "Poor little thing," she said, putting a hand on her white Pontiac Grand Am. "I suppose I need a ride. Do you mind?"

Martin thought in mumbles and sputters but somehow managed to say, "No problem."

"I need to bring a few things," she said. She popped the trunk. A dozen green oxygen tanks had been laid out on towels. "I have to go to the clinic over in Lewistown to have them filled every couple of weeks," she said. They loaded them into the back of his truck.

Martin invited Cheryl into the cab, in flagrant violation of FastNCo.'s policy. Only the plywood radio box separated them. If he drove his usual five miles over the speed limit, they'd be in Brixton in twenty minutes. He set the cruise control for a safe and legal pace.

"I'm glad it was you, and not some stranger," said Cheryl. "Are you staying in Brixton tonight?"

"Yeah."

"You can just take me to the motel, then."

"I'll take you home," said Martin. "It's no problem. How's your stepfather?"

Cheryl sighed. "So stubborn. I've tried everything to get him to go down to Billings and get checked out by real doctors."

"But he won't go?"

"Says it won't do any good," said Cheryl. "I've spent so much time on WebMD, they should give me a medical degree."

"He's lucky to have you around," Martin said, instantly regretting it. But Cheryl didn't seem to take it as any sort of double entendre.

"Yes. He is," she said.

"How's Lester doing? Has he upgraded that mechanical till to a computer yet?"

"Are you kidding?" said Cheryl. She began to dig in her purse, a cloth thing hung around her neck and shoulder. Oh my god, she's looking for pepper spray, Martin thought. Or a taser. Cheryl popped the lid off a tube of ChapStick and quickly smeared a bit on both lips. She snapped the lid back on and zipped her purse closed. Martin felt as if she had tased him, but he had no time to sort out the implications of her lip moisture. She poked at the plywood box with her elbow. "What's this thing?"

"Satellite radio," said Martin. "Company won't let me install the upgrade, so I had to make do." Don't ask me what I listen to, Martin prayed. Don't ask me what I listen to.

"What do you listen to?"

"Talk, mostly."

"Stewart listens to *Beyond Insomnia* religiously," said Cheryl.

"Who? Oh, your stepfather?"

"You ever listen to it?"

"Will you hold it against me if I say yes?" asked Martin.

"As long as you don't believe all the crap."

"I take it you don't."

"If even half of the stuff were true, we'd all be neck deep in weirdness. And that Lee Danvers, you can tell he's laughing all the way to the bank."

"He's always said he's a skeptic," said Martin.

"Skeptic. Don't give me that," said Cheryl. "And Stewart buys anything that man advertises, like a sucker."

Garmin GPS, national sponsor. The caffeine pills in the ashtray, frequent advertiser. The wind-up emergency radio behind the passenger seat, Lee Danvers recommended. The shake-up LED flashlight in the glove compartment, no Waker should be without one. Had she noticed? "It's a funny show," Martin offered. "And Lee's one of the last guys who really knows how to do radio, you know?"

"The fastener guy before you, he definitely belonged in the tinfoil hat crowd. He'd come in talking about conspiracies. The *guv'ment's* out to get us. Lester told him off one day. You came along a couple months after that."

That had been five years ago. That meant that Cheryl had registered his presence, had mentally tied it to a positive, albeit inconsequential, change in her life. And in those five years, he'd managed to become "not some stranger," but a regular and slightly welcome presence.

"No tinfoil hat for me," said Martin. "I *want* them to read my thoughts."

Cheryl smiled at this, and laughed briefly. And then after a silence, she asked, "How much do you think a transmission repair costs?"

About a mile south of the co-op, before the pavement ran out, a tiny cluster of lit windows and porch lights appeared amid the black fields. Cheryl had Martin rumble across a cattle guard into a gravel court of about a dozen mobile homes and pull into the third driveway on the left, behind a beat-up Buick Skylark.

As Martin got out, the door of the trailer opened, and a large, hunched form filled the aperture.

"What's going on?" the man called in a gravelly voice, and then coughed.

"I'm fine, Stewart," said Cheryl. "The car broke down. Martin Wells picked me up and drove me into town."

"FastNCo.?" Stewart asked, leaning over the rail of the little porch of untreated lumber. Martin stepped into the light so Stewart could see him. After a strained breath, Stewart greeted him with a begrudging nod.

"Hello, sir. The car's about twenty minutes west, up 15," said Martin.

"I'll call Hank, get his rig rolling," said Stewart.

Martin helped Cheryl carry the tanks into the trailer. Stewart had settled into an ancient plaid recliner with a phone pressed to his ear. On a table beside the chair, among magazines and newspapers, a portable radio played *Beyond Insomnia*. The TV flickered a detective show, muted.

"Why didn't you do the dishes, Stewart? Or take out the trash?" said Cheryl. She tutted over the empty Keystone Light cans on the kitchen table as she took the last of the tanks from Martin.

"Thank you again. Can I give you some money for gas?" she asked, following him out.

"No, no. It all goes on an expense report," he said.

"Okay," she said.

"Good luck with your car," he said.

The truck was idling, but he'd never wanted to get into the cab less than he did at that moment. "Cheryl?" he heard himself say. He stepped back into the porch light. "I know this is kind of out of the blue, but I wondered if I could take you out sometime." He almost said more but found the sense to keep it simple, mature even, wrapped in some shred of confidence.

"That's very sweet," she said, "but I don't think it would be a good idea." She wagged a thumb behind her, but whether she meant to indicate her mobile home, her stepfather, or her life in general, Martin couldn't say.

"Okay," he replied.

"I'm sorry. Thanks again, though," she said, and left Martin alone in the driveway.

♪   ♪   ♪

Wake Up to the Perfect GOLDEN SUNRISE™ Waffle and the Woman Who Rejected You But Still Made You Breakfast!

Step 1: Eschew self-pity in favor of masculine self-confidence.

Step 2: Fill cup to line with GOLDEN SUNRISE™ waffle batter as if nothing were awkward or amiss.

Step 3: Don't ask for GOLDEN SUNRISE™ Griddle Spray, which doesn't seem to have made its way to the counter this morning. Trust that your waffle will peel right off the residue of a thousand previous waffles.

Step 4: Pour batter evenly onto griddle.

Step 5: Close griddle and Flip! Feel white-hot presence of woman dropping individual yogurts into bowl of ice!

Step 6: When timer signals, release INNER CLUTZ™ to scrape stuck waffle from griddle with plastic fork. Burn finger.

Step 7: Pretend that GOLDEN SUNRISE™ maple-flavored syrup over your waffle doesn't taste like the ashes of your self-esteem.

Caution: Heating surfaces are extremely hot. Do not add alcohol. Accidental glances may cause flight response. You probably should have stayed in your room and finished off the Pop-Tarts. Cooking time should not exceed three minutes. Is this really the story of your life?

"Did you get your car towed in okay?" Martin asked.

"I've been told as much," Cheryl replied.

"Good to hear," said Martin. He gathered his breakfast and took his usual spot, a choice that required an embarrassingly long mental decision tree. In the end, the appearance of normalcy won out over the instinct to hide.

The Great Falls Tribune had a very informative article describing a state utilities commission hearing concerning a new transmission line project. As he ate, Martin focused on becoming concerned, but torn. The proposed electrical transmission line would mean jobs and growth. But property rights and the environment should be protected, too. The in-depth analysis of the hearing melted into gibberish as Cheryl slipped in and out of his peripheral vision. Martin forced the words back into English as she filled a Plexiglas breadbox near the toaster, so close he could have touched her. Then she was at his table. If he'd been taking a sip, coffee might have snorted out his nose.

"Hi," said Cheryl. Martin wiped his mouth with a napkin. "Stewart says I was rude to you last night, and that I should thank you properly for your assistance."

"Oh. You don't…not…"

"No. He's right. Would you like to come over for dinner some evening?"

"Um…sure…that sounds great…"

"Are you going to be in town tonight?" she asked.

"Yes" would be a lie. He'd have to skip his afternoon appointments, and that would bump the rest of the week. FastNCo. would get back on his case for spending consecutive nights in Brixton. He didn't want Rick flying out here to evaluate his routing plans, as he'd hinted at during his last phone call. Plus, sounding desperate—bad.

"I doubt I can do it tonight. Let me look at my schedule. You going to be at the store later?" She nodded. "Okay. Thanks. I'll let you know."

Martin felt like jogging, or having another waffle, or waffle jogging, an amazing new sport sweeping the globe. If the utilities commission put him in charge, he could have built that transmission line, protecting all the species and becoming a hero to the landowners. Governor declares statewide Martin Wells Initiative. Details at ten.

♪ ♪ ♪

Martin swaggered into Herbert's Corner with a date, a time, and an actual solid, real plan to share a meal with Cheryl. Not Cheryl of the Brixton Inn. Not Cheryl, cashier at the Brixton Co-op. But Cheryl, host for dinner Thursday evening next. He needed to go to City Vineyard down in Billings and pick up a really nice bottle of wine. Nothing too pretentious, or with too weird a name. Nothing in a box. It should have a real cork.

"Lorie and I were wondering if you'd show your face around here today," Eileen said as Martin took a stool at the counter. She called to Lorie, the other waitress, who unceremoniously dropped a couple of burger baskets in front of a pair of truckers and scurried over.

"Okay, boy, you need to tell Lorie and Eileen absolutely everything," said Lorie, matching Eileen's mile-wide grin.

"Everything," Eileen agreed.

"What? Oh my god. Don't people in this town have anything better to do?" asked Martin.

"Not right now," said Lorie, loud enough for all the other diners to hear. "Milton told us that Laura saw you propose last night on Cheryl's doorstep."

"I most certainly did not propose," said Martin.

"You met Stewart, though?" asked Lorie.

"We spoke briefly about her car."

"And then you popped the question?" asked Eileen.

"What? No. Can I get a country omelet, hash browns, and sourdough toast?"

"But she turned you down," said Eileen.

"And a coffee," Martin said.

"And now you're going to dinner at her house?" asked Lorie.

"How do you—? Forget it. I don't want to know," said Martin. It could have been Brenda at the front desk of the motel, or anyone at the store.

"It's like that movie," squealed Lorie. "She's Reese Witherspoon, and you're that boy with the sideburns and back muscles." Eileen agreed enthusiastically.

"I have no idea what you're talking about," said Martin.

"Oh, yes, you do," said Lorie. "Everyone's known for years that you've had your eye on her."

"We've all been dyin' to see what you'd do," said Eileen.

"Oh, have you? Look, it's a thank-you dinner. She didn't even want to do it. Her stepfather suggested it."

Lorie and Eileen shared a look, then rolled their eyes back to Martin. "Well, that explains it," said Eileen.

"What explains what?" asked Martin.

"Stewart knows full well that girl can't cook," said Lorie. "He tells everyone that she's the worst cook he's ever known."

"Summer potlucks, we all just sign her up to bring paper plates and cups," said Eileen.

"She's almost burned that trailer down twice…"

"Until they got that Radar Range…"

"The Radar Range," Lorie agreed.

"So what does that explain?" Martin asked.

"He is a thick one," said Eileen. A diner called to Lorie from a booth.

"Hold your horses, Gene," Lorie called back. "It means that Stewart's trying to shake you off. Inviting you over for a taste of life with Cheryl taking care of you."

"That's ridiculous. I don't need anyone to take care of me," said Martin.

"Well, Stewart's an old man," said Eileen, and tapped her hairnet. "Thinks like an old man. And it also means that if you hurt her, her cooking'll be the least of your worries."

"Duly noted," said Martin. "Now, I think we've discussed this quite enough. A country omel…"

"One Romeo special coming up," said Eileen.

The women hurried away. A trucker looked at him from two stools down. "Brixton busybodies," said Martin, shaking his head.

The trucker lifted his coffee cup in agreement.

CHAPTER
5

Martin had heard that an ocean once covered Eastern Montana. The water had receded as North America drifted and swelled into roughly its current shape, leaving the sandstone of the Billings Rims and other bluffs and buttes full of seashell fossils. Then for a while, dinosaurs called Eastern Montana home, grazing, hunting, laying eggs. If that dinosaur movie was to be believed, they evolved into Western meadowlarks—squeaky little bastards, but at least they didn't hunt you in packs. During the last ice age, mile-thick glaciers had crushed and scraped their way into Eastern Montana and then retreated, dropping mammoth carcasses and Canadian rocks as they melted away. And then, in another stretch of geologic time, Martin counted down the week until his dinner with Cheryl. A new age dawned as he knocked on her door.

As he waited on the steps, Martin didn't see any binocular glints or stirring curtains, but that didn't mean the neighbors weren't watching.

"Hi there," he said, when Cheryl answered the door.

"Hi. Come in," she said. She'd done something different with her hair, but Martin lacked the vocabulary to explain it. Her red hoodie had been replaced by a blouse. A mouthwatering smell wafted out around her.

Stewart rocked in the recliner where Martin had last seen him a week ago. He lowered the volume on *Wheel of Fortune* and waved Martin inside. The place had been cleaned up. A vacuum lurked in the hallway leading back to the bedrooms. Countless copies of *Awake*, the official companion magazine of the *Beyond Insomnia* radio program, had been stuffed into a rack beside Stewart's recliner. The table had been set for three.

Stewart stood with effort, trailing a clear plastic line from a humming, bubbling appliance by the television. He donned a large pair of sunglasses that fit over his prescription glasses, and extended a large, age-spotted hand toward Martin. Stewart had once been a tall man, probably fit, certainly strong, but he had been crushed from below by long hours in the recliner's gravity. He wheezed as he studied Martin for a long moment. Oxygen hissed from the cannula under his nose. Gray hairs tufted from his ears, which hadn't shrunk with the rest of him. "Whadja bring us?" he asked, letting go of Martin's hand.

Martin slipped the bottle out of the brown paper sack and handed it to Cheryl. "I didn't know what we were having, but they told me that this would go with almost anything. Whatever's cooking smells good."

"Thank you," said Cheryl. "And what are you wearing, Stewart? Take those off."

Stewart took off his sunglasses and guffawed. "That's the broasted chicken from the market," he said. "If Cheryl was cooking it, you'd be reaching for a gas mask."

"I'm sure that's not true, Mr. Campion," said Martin.

"What's this 'Mr. Campion'? Call me Stewart."

"Dinner'll be ready in ten minutes," said Cheryl, and took the wine to the kitchen.

"So, you get much of that rain we had last week?" Stewart asked, gesturing for Martin to take a seat on the couch.

Fifteen minutes later, Martin accepted a foil tray and chose a piece of chicken. He already had a healthy scoop of mashed potatoes and a ladle of gravy. He'd taken a large spoonful of the canned green beans, with every intention of eating them and offering genuine compliments. Cheryl poured the wine into glass tumblers, but Stewart refused, shuffling into the kitchen and returning with a beer.

"So how's FastNCo. holding up through this economy?" Stewart asked.

"We've tightened our belts like everyone," said Martin. "But we're well positioned. Not dependent on the big box stores."

"Good to hear it," said Stewart.

"What did you do, Stewart? Before you retired. I mean, I assume you're retired."

"Look at me. Of course I'm retired. I did whatever I could. A little construction. Worked out at Gephardt's chicken farm. Stacked lumber for Lester. Even drove the school bus for a while. And took care of baby Cheryl. Poor kid; don't know how you survived," said Stewart. "County probably should have taken you away from me."

"The county should probably take you away from me now," said Cheryl. Martin sensed an inside joke.

"You know the story of Cheryl's mother?" asked Stewart.

"Martin doesn't need that sordid tale," said Cheryl.

"I've heard the basic story," said Martin.

"Most likely from Eileen and Lorie down at the Corner," said Stewart.

Cheryl shook her head. "I think we can talk about something else," she said.

"How's your car?" Martin asked after a long pause.

"Still waiting for parts from Billings," Stewart said.

"Should've had someone other than Hank work on it, Stewart," said Cheryl. This was clearly another sore subject. Martin prepared to crawl under the table if the dishes started flying.

"Everything's really good," he said, waving at his half-eaten portions with his fork.

"You live down in Billings, Martin?" asked Stewart, breaking another long silence.

"I do. In the Heights," said Martin.

"Awful long drive. But you're probably not there much, are you? What with driving all over the state. Do you cover Northern Wyoming, too?"

"I don't work Wyoming, no," Martin replied.

"That's good. I can't imagine. Sleeping every night in a different fleabag motel. But, boy, I've heard some tales from the salesmen who come 'round town. Most of them not fit to tell in front of the lady-folk, eh, Martin?"

"Oh, for heaven's sake, Stewart," said Cheryl. "No one wants to hear your lecherous old stories. We're trying to eat."

"Just trying to make conversation," said Stewart.

And shine a harsh light of truth on my job, thought Martin. He hoped that Cheryl could see he didn't chase women in every port of call. But to openly defend himself might insult Cheryl's real father—a hit-and-run, up-to-no-good salesman, if the rumor was true—and Cheryl's mother, who by implication must have been a bit…scarlet.

Cheryl rolled her eyes, and Martin gave her a weak smile. The mashed potatoes were too thin to be anything but instant, the gravy too thick to be anything but canned, and the silences too long to be anything but uncomfortable. Martin groped for some subject, some question to break the frost. Unable to think of anything better, he opened his mouth to ask Stewart if he'd heard last night's BI when Stewart shoved his half-eaten meal away, drained his beer, and got up with an epic wheeze, dragging his oxygen line into the kitchen.

"What are you…? Stewart?" Cheryl asked.

He opened a cupboard, took out a crinkling package, and shuffled back to the table. He took several Oreos out of the blue wrapping, then tossed the pack in the middle of the table. "Dessert," he said.

"I got ice cream," said Cheryl. "You said you wanted ice cream."

"Maybe I should go," said Martin.

"Sorry, we couldn't be better company," said Stewart, wiping little black crumbs from the corners of his smile. "I gotta get going, too. It's bingo night at the Grange."

He headed to the hall, muttering about shoes.

"Dinner really was good," said Martin.

"You're kind to say that," said Cheryl.

Stewart returned, shod in loafers slightly more substantial than his slippers, jingling a ring of keys, and with a portable oxygen tank slung over his shoulder.

"Ready to head out?" Stewart asked.

Martin opened his mouth to answer, but Cheryl spoke first. "Martin's going to stay. We're going to have some proper dessert and enjoy the nice wine he brought."

Stewart looked at Martin, then at Cheryl. Martin looked from Cheryl to Stewart. Cheryl kept her glare on Stewart.

"You run along to bingo," she said.

"Can't argue with you any more than I could your mother," said Stewart. "You all have a pleasant evening."

At the sound of Stewart's car on the gravel drive, Cheryl shook her head and blew out a sigh. "You're not compelled to stay," she said.

"I'd like dessert," said Martin. She began to clear the table, and Martin helped.

"I'll dry," said Martin, yanking a dishtowel off the handle of the oven, and Cheryl smiled.

"That man drives me absolutely crazy sometimes," she said. "I'm so sorry. This was supposed to be a simple meal."

"Simple's boring," said Martin. "Don't worry about it."

A few minutes later, the dishes done and the leftovers stowed, Martin folded the dishtowel and set it on the counter. "You said you had ice cream?" he said. "Might go good with these Oreos."

"No," said Cheryl. "Everything else has been a mess. I'm going to make you a proper dessert. But it'll take a while. How long can you stay?"

"Long enough to make your neighbors wonder what's going on over here," said Martin. Please take that as a joke, he begged silently as soon as it fell out of his mouth.

A mischievous grin slid across her face. "Good." She turned on the oven, adjusting the temperature precisely, and then dug a huge knife out of a kitchen drawer. "Wait here." She grabbed a flashlight from a charger by the front door and left. Was this how she'd almost burned down her house? Twice?

Martin peered through the kitchen window but couldn't make out anything in the night. A few minutes later, Cheryl returned with an armful of thick stalks topped with wide, dark-green leaves. Each one looked like the forbidden love child of a celery stalk and a lily pad.

"What is that?" Martin asked.

"Rhubarb," said Cheryl.

"Is that really a thing?"

"You've never heard of rhubarb?"

"I mean, I have. I've just never…experienced rhubarb."

"So you've never had rhubarb pie?" she asked.

"I've never even seen rhubarb in a store. It's weird that you can step outside and come back with rhubarb. 'Rhubarb.' Even the word is weird."

"Well, first of all, rhubarb is not weird. And second, who would want to buy rhubarb from a store when it's best right out of your garden? It practically grows like a weed. Pops right up every spring."

"In that case, I apologize. By all means, let's have some rhubarb pie."

"What you don't know is that I'm making this pie to spite Stewart," Cheryl said as she started in on the rhubarb, washing it and chopping away the leaves.

"He likes your pie?" asked Martin.

"Are you kidding? He hates it. My mother used to make it all the time, but he claims I can't do it justice," said Cheryl.

"If she taught you, it can't be that different," said Martin.

"That's what I think."

"So maybe it's something else. Maybe it reminds him too much of her." The rhythm of her chopping changed slightly. "Sorry. We don't have to talk about her."

Cheryl scraped the rhubarb chunks into a large bowl and added some sugar and flour.

"Oh, we might as well. Before those waitresses at the Corner sink their teeth into you. You said you've heard the general story?" Martin nodded. "That she got knocked up by some random dude from out of town?"

"Heard that."

"That she'd been seeing Stewart at the same time even though he was about twice her age?"

"Figured that."

"Well, she ran off with said random dude, and Stewart took care of me. But she came back. Showed up one night. No call. No letter. Just walked in."

"Okay, now you're getting into new territory. Except—I should warn you that now I'm expecting to hear something about an alien abduction."

Cheryl hung her head over the bowl of chopped rhubarb. Martin held his breath, but she laughed and said, "Says the Waker with bated breath."

"Don't blame Lee Danvers," said Martin. "Blame the Brixton rumor mill."

"Hold that thought," said Cheryl. She dug an ice tray from the freezer and cracked it over a towel. She wrapped up the cubes and pulverized them with the rolling pin. Then she shook the shards into a cup and topped it off with cold water.

"Is that a warning not to gossip about you?" asked Martin.

"Damn straight." Cheryl dumped Crisco, flour, and salt into another large bowl. "I was four when my mother came home," she said, mashing the ingredients together with a fork. "So I never knew her any different, but she suffered from a serious mental illness. I mean, I wouldn't have called it that then. I really didn't figure it out until later. She died when I was sixteen. Lung cancer. The woman smoked like a chimney."

"I'm sorry," said Martin.

Cheryl tossed a handful of flour on a clear bit of counter and spread it out. She poured the ice water into the bowl and mixed the dough with her hands. "Stewart tried to protect me from the worst of it. She'd have long spells. I remember her crying all day, screaming in the night. She'd go wandering on the roads alone."

"Did she get help?"

"She'd go on meds for a while, then she'd stop. She had periods of lucidity, where I got to know her for real. That's when she taught me how to make pie. It's actually my grandmother's recipe. My grandmother and mom used to bake it up at Herbert's Corner, and truckers would drive hours out of their way for it. My grandmother taught her, and my mom wanted to teach me, even though Stewart would tell her it was a waste of time. I never knew my grandmother. She died in the late seventies. Lung cancer, too. You'd think Mom would have learned her lesson."

Cheryl stretched the dough into two rough circles with short, deft strokes of her rolling pin. She draped the first gracefully into a pie plate, trimmed the edges, poured in the red and green filling, and then blanketed everything with the other crust. In seconds, the pie was vented, crimped, and vanished into the oven. Like a magic show, Martin was sure he'd missed some sleight of hand.

"You know, everyone told me you have no idea how to cook." Martin handed her glass of wine over, and poured her a little more. "You've been holding out."

"It's easier to let everyone think what they want to think," said Cheryl.

"Why don't you bake for the diner?"

"One, screw the diner. Two, Stewart says my pie's nothing like Mom's. Three, he won't let me work anywhere near Herbert's Corner. Thinks I'll wind up like her."

She sipped her wine and stared at a cupboard. Martin sipped his own and tried desperately to produce a less prickly topic of conversation.

"Fine," she said. "Yes, my mother claimed she was abducted by aliens. She had this elaborate story, all about how they poked and probed her. The tale got more vivid and ridiculous every time she told it. As a kid, it didn't even occur to me that she was making it all up. Now, do I believe she was abducted? Absolutely not. But do I believe her? I do. I think she sincerely believed she'd gone through all those things."

"I'm sorry," said Martin.

"Now, fair's fair. I want your most sordid family secret," said Cheryl.

"What's to tell? We're a pretty normal bunch," said Martin.

"Nope," said Cheryl. "Start spilling."

"Okay…before I was born, my dad totaled a brand-new car. So he went back to the dealership and bought another one. My mom still doesn't know."

"You can do better," Cheryl said. "This pie's going to be in the oven for forty-five minutes."

By the time the timer beeped, Cheryl knew exactly why Martin's family had been thrown out of SeaWorld. And she was now the only other person in the world who knew that it was Martin's Welsh terrier who had torn up and fouled the First Lutheran nativity scene during that fateful December walk when he was eleven. Martin finished his last story as she returned to the oven.

"…what could I do? I waited by the back door with a shotgun. Dad took the front door. I don't know what he was expecting. As if civilization would melt down instantly. Like, three…two… one…Happy Looting Zombies! My mom shouted Dick Clark's countdown up from the den. Worst New Year's Eve party ever."

Cheryl brought a sweet scent from the kitchen as she set the pie on a hot pad on the table. Steam vented from the slits in the golden-brown crust.

"State fair. Blue ribbon. Right now," said Martin.

"It's got to cool a minute," said Cheryl.

"Don't you usually do that on a windowsill or something?" asked Martin.

"Only if you like bugs."

Martin couldn't believe Cheryl had created this pie for him, from scratch, with her bare hands. She hadn't burned it, or burned anything down. Instead, she'd brought warmth and a sense of contentment to this little home. Martin felt as if she had set out the Brixton Inn breakfast for him alone. And yet, in his wonder at the moment, Martin felt like he deserved to be with her. There was no ego in it. He knew that he was the one who understood her, who understood that she didn't want worship or pity, who understood that she didn't need to be taken away from anything.

Martin prided himself for figuring all this out as a scoop of vanilla ice cream melted white into the thin syrup of the rhubarb filling. The first bite was hot and sour, but lingered as sweet. "I didn't expect it to be so tart, but wow—just, wow," he said. The tender crust gave him something to sink his teeth into. The rhubarb itself almost dissolved on his tongue.

"It's not bad for such a quick job," said Cheryl.

"If this isn't as good as your mom's pie, I don't know if I'd even want to try hers," said Martin. "It might ruin every other dessert for me forever."

"Give me a break," said Cheryl.

"Seriously. Your mom could have been the next Mrs. Fields."

"Mrs. Fields bakes cookies," Cheryl said.

"Your mom could have had a rhubarb pie empire."

Cheryl wrinkled her nose. "Have you ever eaten a frozen pie?"

"Sure. That's what we always had."

"Chewing-gum crust. Waxy gelatin goo for filling. They're all chemicals. Oh, and good luck finding a frozen rhubarb pie."

"I like 'em okay."

Cheryl shook her head. "Poor thing. Are you staying in town tonight?"

"No, I need to get back to Billings," he said. He'd deliberately not booked a room, ninety-nine percent in case of an evening so disastrous that he could never eat breakfast at the Brixton Inn again, and one percent in case the evening went extremely well. Well, maybe ninety/ten. But by luck or instinct, he'd made exactly the right decision. Not needy, not expectant. Mature. Employed. "I have to work Bozeman tomorrow."

Martin thanked her as she took away the empty plates. Her home felt different now. Cozy, not cramped, with a bit of the mystique—if one could use that word in a single-wide—peeled back.

At the door, she presented him with the leftover pie, foil-topped and on a dishtowel.

"I insist," said Cheryl. "I don't need to eat the whole thing. And if Stewart finds it, he will literally dump it in the trash. Take it. Bring the plate back next time you're in town. Careful though, it's still hot."

"Thanks. For dinner, for this. Everything."

"Thanks for bringing the wine. That was a treat. And, of course, the roadside assistance."

"No problem," said Martin.

On the first step down the porch, he turned and said, "I feel like I've got a second chance here, so I'm going to take it. I'd really like the chance to get to know you better. I know you've got a lot going on, and I do, too. But who knows? This is Brixton, after all. Weirder things have happened."

She sighed, but it sounded friendly, harmless. He steeled himself to be rejected again, and resolved to be okay with that.

"Hold on," she said, and ducked inside. Martin shifted the pie on his scorched palms. She returned and set a little scrap of paper on top of the foil.

"Call me," she said. "We'll see."

"Thanks. I will," said Martin, maneuvering a thumb over the paper to keep it from blowing away. He crunched down the gravel drive, surprised with every footfall that his feet were touching the ground.

*. *. *.

A few minutes later, as Martin filled a 54-ounce cup with Diet Mountain Dew out of the fountain at the Herbert's Corner store, Lorie appeared, her eyebrows leaping off her forehead.

"Stewart at bingo. You two alone for almost two hours," she said.

"Oh, no, you don't," said Martin. "I was a perfect gentleman, and that's all I'm going to say."

"Uh-huh," she replied.

"Don't you have some waitressing to do?" he asked, jamming a big straw through the lid. "Sorry, Lorie, but there may be some things you will never know."

"You go on believing that," she called after him as he headed to the register. He turned, threw his arms wide in triumph, and they both laughed.

CHAPTER
6

"…and paralyzed. I was conscious. I felt several presences in the room with me. I wanted to scream, to call for my husband, but I couldn't make a sound."

"That must have been terrifying."

"At first, but then I not so much heard as felt a voice in my head, telling me that everything was going to be all right."

"Can you describe the voice?"

"I remember it being masculine, but also soothing, almost motherly. I'm not sure that it spoke English, but I understood everything."

"Now, you didn't stay in the room."

"All that first part, the lights, the waking, and the helplessness, was as if I was being prepared to be taken somewhere else. And then came a very bright light. I couldn't close my eyes, and I remember the voice urging me to ignore the pain. It would be over very soon."

"Your husband didn't experience anything?"

"Nothing. They must have done something to keep him asleep, or he's the heaviest sleeper in the world, Lee."

"After the bright light, where were you? What did you see?"

"Someplace very cold, and hard. I felt naked, but I couldn't move, couldn't see my body. There were devices above me, like you might see at a dentist's office, but none of them made any sense."

"What about the presences? Did you still feel them?"

"I could. But more concrete, like they were in the room with me, not like spirit presences anymore. I don't know how long I laid there until finally they looked down over me. They had gray skin. No hair. And their eyes were large, silvery things."

"On the video of your session under hypnosis, it seemed like the fear returned at this moment."

"It did. The voice told me that they had to do some tests, and that they were necessary. And the devices on the ceiling began to move toward me."

"Could you communicate? Did the presence listen to your thoughts or sense your fear?"

"If it heard me, it did nothing to help me. I felt a pressure on the sides of my head, and I heard a very high-pitched sound, like a dentist's drill. And I felt them doing things to various parts of my body."

"Was any of it painful?"

"I sensed that it should have been, but I didn't feel any actual pain. Still, I begged them to stop in my thoughts."

"How long did this go on?"

"It's impossible to say. Minutes? Hours? I remember feeling relief when the machines lifted away. And then I woke up in my own bed."

"Now, you didn't realize right away what had happened."

"I woke up exhausted, but at first I had no memory of the event. Then I began to have nightmares, these terrible images in my head. These recurring feelings were so powerful that I was sure that something had happened to me."

"And that's when you discovered regressive-hypnosis therapy and Dr. Yeardley?"

"I'd never heard about it before, but I did some research online and called her. After only a few sessions, she helped me remember clearly what happened that night, and also to recall that I'd been taken many times, as young as eight years old."

"Incredible. Incredible. When we come back we'll hear more of Carrie's story. And joining us later will be Dr. Marsha Yeardley, a psychotherapist and noted expert on alien abduction. And we'll ask Carrie the question, 'Why her?' Stay tuned, Waker Nation. This is Lee Danvers. And you're Beyond Insomnia."

🌑 🌑 🌑

"Who's this idiot?" Martin asked himself. A car was approaching in his lane, passing a semi, and rapidly running out of space on this two-lane road. Martin backed off the cruise control, but it wasn't going to be enough. He hit the brakes. Too close for comfort, the car swerved back into its lane. A familiar Lincoln Town Car flashed by.

"Jeffrey," Martin cursed. The semi roared by, clearly annoyed, if Martin cared to anthropomorphize.

Martin's phone warbled. He let it ring as he got the cruise control back up to speed. "Nice driving, Candy Man," he said when he finally answered.

"Don't give me that. I moved over in plenty of time," said Jeffrey. Martin pictured him, reclined, a single wrist on the steering wheel, his irritating Bluetooth glowing in his ear.

"What do you want?" Martin asked.

"Long time no see. How's the job hunt going?"

"Poorly," said Martin.

"Well's dry, man. No one's hiring. And no one's quitting. Someone's going to have to die for you to get an opening."

"Keep driving like that and I can have your job," said Martin.

"Funny. And speaking of funny, I heard something else hilarious," said Jeffrey.

"What's that?" Martin asked, bracing himself.

"Heard you got lucky in Brixton a couple weeks ago."

"I did not 'get lucky.' And please don't be spreading that around."

"So what did happen?" asked Jeffrey.

"Her car broke down. I stopped to help. She had me over to dinner to thank me."

"And that's all? Everyone in Brixton's got their own theory of the evening's events," said Jeffrey.

"That's because they don't have anything better to do," said Martin.

"Everyone's talking about the two hours you spent at her place without her stepfather around. Inquiring minds want to know," said Jeffrey.

"We had dessert," said Martin. "And we talked."

"Uh-huh. What did you have for dessert?"

"She baked a rhubarb pie," said Martin.

"She did what?"

"She baked a pie," said Martin. "Everyone told me she's a lousy cook, but it was really good."

"I'm sure it was," said Jeffrey. "You're sticking with this rhubarb pie alibi?"

"I'm hanging up now," said Martin. And he did.

🥄 🥄 🥄

"Now, Lee, we hear a lot about the physical evidence: the interlaced but undamaged stalks, the lack of tracks leading in and out of the sites, the magnetic resonance, as well as the frequent reports of aerial lights, but for me, the most compelling part is the obvious communication inherent in all crop circles. Each holds such precision, such insistence, such a lack of subtlety, that it's impossible that they have no purpose."

"Are there commonalities to suggest that all these occurrences are linked?"

"Many commonalities. I've studied hundreds of circles in dozens of countries. It appears that the physical process that creates them is similar everywhere. And we see many recurring graphic motifs, if not nearly identical designs."

"In your books and on your website, you come down firmly on the side of what you term 'purposeful instigation,' that they are made by an intelligence. How do you respond to those who suggest that crop circles have natural origins? Particularly Diderot's equations that suggest localized crystallization of water vapor?"

"Diderot's fractal weather theory is, in my opinion, deeply flawed. He based his theory off observation of early morning frost crystals at very few sites. It doesn't hold up. I debated him about this issue a few months ago in Brisbane."

"If there's a video of that debate, we'll get a link up on wakernation.com. Let's take a call. Sarasota Springs, you're Beyond Insomnia."

"Oh, hi. Lee? This is Vern from Sarasota Springs."

"Welcome, Vern. What's your question for Tom Burlingame?"

"Yeah. These crop circles freak me out, man. I agree with you totally. I mean, they're so clearly, I mean, aliens are totally trying to tell us something. Have you ever talked to anyone at the NSA where they got all them really smart code-breakers? Seems like they should stop listening to all our phone calls and figure out these messages instead. Sure be a better use of my tax dollars."

"Thank you, Vern. Tom, what about using technology to decipher the circles?"

"It's clearly the goal, but we're still a few years away. I've been writing program algorithms to analyze the data. Many of these patterns are so complex that it's going to take significant super-computer time to sort it all out."

"Best guess, Tom: Who is sending these messages, and what are they saying?"

"Who? Good question. But we can make a few observations. They are mathematically oriented, and communicative, but also very shy. The meaning of individual circles may be elusive, but the overall message is, I think, one of peace. The designs are so beautiful. The messengers certainly understand that we appreci-ate beauty. If the messages were warnings or threats, I think we could discern that from the context. Someone out there is not only saying hello, but telling us that we belong with a larger community."

"A wonderful thought. I hope you're right. Can you stay with us through the break and take a few more calls?"

"Certainly, but if a report comes in, I may need to leave. The time window for study on circle phenomena is very small."

"We all understand. Stay up with us through this short com-mercial break, Insomniacs. We'll be right back."

♪ ♪ ♪

Martin's phone waited on the hotel room desk next to the most precious piece of paper he had ever held. Nothing else, not his birth certificate, not his first driver's license, not his passport, had come close. It held all the promise of an unsigned Declaration of Independence, an unblessed Magna Carta, a ticket that matched the Powerball. The phone's dark screen reflected the desk lamp's bulb like a single eye.

What's the problem here? Pick me up and dial, it seemed to say.

What if she gave me the number of the Chinese takeout place in Lewistown?

She wouldn't do that. She knows you'll be coming back to Brixton.

You're right. Everything's fine.

Of course I'm right, I'm a smartphone. Now, call her already. If it gets much later it'll be creepy. Come on. Pull yourself together. No excuses.

Okay. But maybe I should be somewhere else, so it sounds like I'm having fun.

You have talked on a cell phone before, right? Fun sounds are distracting. The only acceptable background noises for this kind of phone call are ocean surf, you preparing a meal in a noncommercial kitchen, or a hospital PA paging you to the OR.

Maybe I should change my shirt. I remember hearing once that your clothes make a difference in how you sound on the phone.

Oh, good grief. Are you wearing pants? Then let's do this.

I need to think out what I'm going to say.

Put the pen down. You are not writing a script. She wants a confident human being to invite her to an experience that will allow you to get to know each other as people. Period.

Confidence. Experience. People. This sounded right. He knew he needed a smartphone. He took a deep breath and dialed.

But what if she doesn't answer? Should I hang up?

Everyone—and I mean everyone—has Caller ID. If you hang up, she'll think you're a coward, a buttdialer, or that you've moved on to the next number in your disgusting little black book.

I don't even have a little black book.

She won't know that if she never gets to know you. Now man up and leave a message at the tone.

. . .

"Hi, Cheryl. It's Martin Wells. I'm coming into Brixton next Tuesday afternoon. Wanted to see if we could get together that evening. Or the next. I'll be working the area through Thursday. If you don't want to go out in Brixton, which I would totally understand, I'd be happy to drive us somewhere, or meet in another town. Let me know. My number is 406-555-6871. Look forward to hearing from you. Oh, and I have your pie plate. I'll bring it with me."

. . .

"Hello, Cheryl. I left you a message a couple of days ago. I'm still planning on being in Brixton tomorrow and Wednesday nights. And bringing your pie plate. Thanks again for that, by the way. It was really good. Anyway, give me a call. 555-6871."

. . .

Martin yanked back the shower curtain and lunged, splashing water across the bathroom, but found his phone inert, and now lathered. He'd been hearing phantom rings all day.

Would he really have answered the phone naked, with the shower still running? He rinsed the soap out of his hair. He feared that if the phone rang for real, he might not have the will to stop himself. Yep, that's my only fear, he thought. Nothing else to fear.

. . .

"We're back with Asmir Falenta, journalist, amateur pilot, and the author of 'The Disappearance of the Bermuda Triangle,' the lead article in the May issue of *Awake*, the official magazine of *Beyond Insomnia*. Subscription and membership information on wakernation.com. Now, Asmir, for this article, you flew your plane around and through the Triangle itself. Were you ever afraid?"

"How could I not be, Lee? The documented accounts, Coast Guard records, and the Lloyd's of London registers make clear that something happens in the Triangle. The majority of these incidents are much odder, much stranger, than other losses at sea. Sudden mechanical or instrument failure, unusual radio communication interference, and changes in temporal perspectives—there are just some things you can't prepare for."

"Now, you spoke to dockmasters, air-traffic controllers, fishermen, a Coast Guard crew, even a DEA interdiction officer. According to the people on the ground, those who deal with it on a daily basis, are there fewer unexplained disappearances or events in the Triangle today than there have been in the past?"

"We've been documenting travel in the Triangle since Columbus. So as a journalist, I wondered at first if incidents were simply no longer widely reported by the media. Instead, I found a consensus that this past decade has seen the fewest strange occurrences by far."

"What could account for this?"

"There are several working ideas. One is related to the natural gas bubble theory, that perhaps the release of those gases has subsided for geological reasons. But the gas bubble theory has never explained certain common phenomena, like the temporal alterations and magnetic disturbances. Some theorize that technology has improved navigation and communication: GPS systems, weather tracking, and more robust radio technology, for instance. However, that doesn't account for the reputation of this very specific area of the sea. Technology treats the symptoms. It's not the cure. Travelers reported strange events well into the last decade. It's like something has subsided."

"Let's cut to the chase. Do you believe we're talking about a natural occurrence?"

"There's no known natural phenomenon that explains all the strangeness. I agree with Buckner and Stone that there is an artifact, or ruin, beneath the ocean floor. That this artifact was the source of some kind of energy, and that recently, within the past ten years, that power source has weakened or run out."

"Atlantis or aliens?"

"That's the $64,000 question, Lee."

"We'll talk about that, and take your calls, with Asmir Falenta after this break. You're Beyond Insomnia on the Weirdmerica Radio Network."

🌙 🌙 🌙

On Wednesday morning, Martin weighed down the end of the hardest mattress in the universe. A twenty-second walk to the breakfast room or a two-hundred-second drive to Herbert's Corner? At least someone there would make him a waffle. None of this pour-the-batter-yourself crap. And they'd have warmed syrup in a nice glass pitcher. He shouldn't be hungry anyway. He had eaten an entire can of Pringles during Letterman, and that Snickers around two in the morning. Plus, the co-op opened early. He could get in there, get done, and get out of town long before Cheryl arrived for her afternoon shift.

He closed the door of his room and paused at the rail of the second-floor walkway. The roof of his truck was useless white space in a mostly empty parking lot. The sun rose over a dying town, huddled in the midst of desolation. A truck grumbled by on the highway. A meadowlark trilled much more shrilly than necessary. A mournful side of beef lowed in the distance. Martin went down to the lobby.

Come on, Big Man, said the breakfast bar. *She's right there in the storeroom. Yep, you heard her, she just opened that box. Let's see you make a waffle. You can't even make toast. Oh, a blueberry yogurt? You know what a real man would have for breakfast? Not blueberry yogurt.*

The griddle beeped as she emerged from the storeroom. Martin scraped his mangled waffle onto his plate, pretending he meant to do it like that, and then turned to face her as if he had never called her. Twice.

"Good morning," said Vonnie.

"Oh, hi," said Martin. "I thought you were…Where's Cheryl?"

"Oh, she quit," said Vonnie. "A couple weeks ago. She called Brenda in the middle of the night, said she was moving to Boise. Charlie promoted me to breakfast."

"Boise?"

"We were all shocked," said Vonnie. "Leavin' her stepfather and all."

"Yeah," said Martin. "Okay, thanks."

"Enjoy your breakfast."

"Did she say why?"

"What?" asked Vonnie.

"Did Cheryl tell anyone why she was leaving?"

"Everyone's saying she met a man on the Internet," said Vonnie.

Wake Up to the Perfect GOLDEN SUNRISE™ Waffle!

Step 1: Snap plastic knife off sawing through the GOLDEN
SUNRISE™ Waffle and Styrofoam plate.

Step 2: Toss it all in the trash in disgust.

Caution: Your fingers will get sticky. Do not do this in public.
Do *not* add alcohol. Suck it up and go to work. Those screws
aren't going to bin themselves.

CHAPTER
7

Somewhere at the edge of his unconsciousness, Martin sensed a presence in his apartment. He listened, not breathing, but heard nothing. Must have been the neighbors. They always came and went at weird hours. He checked the clock. He had to be up at half past his ass to be at an account in Harlowton by seven. But as he tried to bring sleep back, he heard it again, or felt it.

Lying still, Martin stretched out his other senses and found fear. Was this the paralysis all the abductees talked about on BI? Who was there? An ax murderer or a gray alien, with the shiny, teardrop eyes, no taller than a seventh-grader and twice as dangerous? It crept closer. If this was a dream, he'd have awoken by now.

Martin willed himself to wiggle a toe, to adjust his tongue, anything, but couldn't. He heard a strained exhalation. A hiss and a whiff. A wheezing suck. One breath. Then another. Move, Martin. Move. It's not here to hug you and take you to an intergalactic love-in. It's here to probe you in all the ways you'd rather not be probed. Because that's what they do. Haven't you ever listened to the stupid show? Get up.

Suck. Hiss. Wheeze.

Suck. Hiss. Wheeze.

A clammy paw of flesh clamped over his mouth, and a retina-destroying light stabbed his eyes.

"Where is she?" a vicious whisper rasped. Martin screamed into the flesh over his mouth, fearing the end, or a really bad beginning. "You have no right, you bastard."

Martin's muffled scream ran short of breath, but ended abruptly when the light flicked away and he recognized, in a half-second, the stubble on the unshaveable jowls, the nostril hair poking into the holes in the cannula.

Martin fought free of the hand and his sheets, tumbling to the safety of the far side of the bed. "What the hell? Stewart?" The flashlight blinded him again as he got to his feet. Martin fumbled for the bedside lamp and knocked it over getting it on. The resulting shadows were as strange as the unlikely presence of Stewart Campion in his bedroom. He was wearing the enormous sunglasses, the ones he'd put on that evening before dinner.

"Where is she?" Stewart demanded again. "I don't know who you are, but I want her returned. She doesn't know anything."

"What are you talking about?"

"Cheryl doesn't know the recipe. She never did." Stewart struggled pathetically with a pocket until he yanked an object free and brandished it at Martin—a FastNCo. Model 25-C. Stewart had probably bought it, and its PIC #6598 three-quarter-inch staples, at Lester's co-op.

"That's a staple gun," said Martin.

"You wanna test that theory?" Stewart breathed hard but kept the gun up, his trembling hand wrapped around the trigger handle.

"I'm going to call the police now," said Martin.

"You're not like the others, but I'm not going to fall for it. What have you done with Cheryl?"

"She never called me back. They said she went to Boise," said Martin. Martin's skin shrank. Was he being blamed for something?

"You don't think I see what's happening? I...wrote...the god-damn playbook...on this." Stewart's labored breathing filled the gaps between his words, and the gun hand drifted.

"You're going to pass out. Why don't you go out in the living room and sit down? Let me put on some pants, and we'll talk."

"I'm not letting you out of my sight," said Stewart.

Martin edged around the bed, letting Stewart hold onto his illusion of fearsomeness. He pulled on a pair of khakis and yesterday's T-shirt. "I'm going out to the living room." He half-expected a staple to the back, but Stewart followed, wheezing hard.

"How did you get in here?" Martin asked.

"Anyone can pick a lock, boy," said Stewart.

"How did you know where I live?"

"I followed you. What do you think?"

"Look, I'm not actually calling the cops. But sit down. I don't want to have to call an ambulance." Martin waved to the La-Z-Boy.

Stewart held the staple gun out for a few more seconds, then shuffled to the chair. He lowered himself to a seat with a groan, took off the sunglasses, and tucked them in a shirt pocket. He sucked in several deep breaths. "Who are you? Where are you from?"

"Stewart? I'm Martin Wells. I'm from Billings. I'm the FastNCo. rep. We met about a month ago when I came over to your house for dinner."

"I'm not senile, Martin. I want the truth," said Stewart.

"Who do you think I'm supposed to be?"

"Your dermis beats the glasses. Something new?"

"I don't know what you're talking about," said Martin.

"Don't give me that," said Stewart. Then he coughed, coughed again, and then couldn't stop. He dropped the staple gun. As Stewart bent forward, hacking spittle and phlegm onto his lap, Martin feared to upset him even more by leaving the room. But then, as much to keep his own stomach from turning, he fetched Stewart a glass of water.

"Thanks," Stewart managed between the lingering coughs. Stewart took a few sips, coughed a few more times. Then he leaned back in the recliner, the fight gone.

"Should you be in a hospital or something?" Martin asked.

"I'm fine," said Stewart.

"Why don't you tell me what's going on?"

"I was so sure," said Stewart.

"You think I'm to blame for Cheryl leaving town?" asked Martin.

"She baked you a pie."

"What does that have to do with anything?" asked Martin.

"It's everything," said Stewart.

"You're not making any sense," said Martin.

"I tried to protect her from all this."

"All what?"

"The pie. The rhubarb pie. No…"

"Stewart?" asked Martin. But Stewart was asleep, his rasps irregular and not quite deep enough.

☙ ☙ ☙

The smell from the Mr. Coffee hadn't woken Stewart, so Martin slammed the microwave door on the Jimmy Dean sausages and set it going with as many beeps as possible. That did the trick. Stewart stirred under his blanket, lowered the recliner's footrest, and rose into a patch of thin sunlight. Martin poured a mug of coffee and set it on the kitchen table next to the staple gun, recovered from the floor. Stewart shuffled in, considered the gun, considered Martin, and then sat.

" 'Coffee is the only cure for Monday,' " Stewart read from his mug. He considered the orange cat. "It's not Monday."

"Just drink the coffee," said Martin.

After the toaster popped, Martin set a plate in front of Stewart and then sat down with his own. "Eat," he said. He'd hoped the breakfast would give Stewart the chance to offer an apology, an explanation, or even his thanks, but their plates were almost empty when Martin broke the stalemate.

"Is Cheryl in trouble?"

"Never you mind about that," said Stewart.

"Is it something to do with the guy she met on the Internet? The guy in Boise?"

Stewart finished off his toast.

"I mean, she doesn't seem like the type to run off like that. But you tell me. I barely know her," said Martin.

"She's—" Stewart broke off. "It's not your problem."

"Certainly seemed to be my problem last night," said Martin. Stewart sighed a growling breath and shoveled in a bite of scrambled eggs. "You were going on about the rhubarb pie."

"I was upset, not thinking clearly. I've been sick, you know," said Stewart. "It was a mistake to come here."

"I'm sorry you think I would do anything to hurt your daughter," said Martin. "Sorry. Stepdaughter."

"It's okay."

"If you think she's in trouble, why don't you let me help you? We can talk to the police. I could go to Boise and look for her."

"I don't need your help," said Stewart.

"And you're in any condition…?"

"That's none of your business." Stewart sawed at a sausage

with the side of his fork, but before he ate a bite, he picked up his oxygen pack and squinted at the dial. "Jesus," he hissed.

Martin found a fresh tank on the floor of Stewart's Skylark, parked out on the street. "You're driving home?" Martin asked as he helped Stewart switch the tanks on the regulator.

"Where else am I going to go?"

"You're sure there's nothing I can do?"

"I'm sorry for busting in on you," said Stewart. "And for blaming you."

"Hey, it's forgivable. You love her," said Martin.

Martin waited until the Skylark's blue exhaust had dissipated to worry about being late for work.

♪ ♪ ♪

Martin flopped on a bed of the Holiday Inn Express in Belgrade and kicked off his shoes. All he could see behind his eyelids were two-inch galvanized nails, seven-sixteenths-inch stainless steel lock washers, three-eighths-inch zinc-finished hex nuts, and a variety of Phillips pan head screws. Vaguely satisfied customers in Harlowton, White Sulphur Springs, Townsend, and Three Forks had been duly restocked for another forty-odd days. Tomorrow, Belgrade, Bozeman, Livingston, and Big Timber would be sated in their never-ending lust for hardware. What did people use all this stuff for, anyway? What did they build? What was so important that it had to be fixed? Had any of them ever given a second thought to the person who fills all those little bins?

Martin found the energy to lift the remote. On-demand movies. *The Tonight Show. Baseball Tonight.* The Weather Channel. Fox News. Some cookie cutter rom-com. *House Hunters.* Martin paused for a while on *Man v. Food* and a burrito that could have fed an entire Somali family for a week.

"What are you doing, Martin?" he asked himself as he put on his shoes. He asked it several times more as he bought gas and a giant cup of Diet Mountain Dew. The GPS gave him three hours, but he could do it in two.

🐾 🐾 🐾

"Bangor, Maine, you're Beyond Insomnia."

"Hey, great to be on again, Lee. This is Patrick from Bangor. I don't know if you remember me. I called in a couple months ago about the location of the Pentagon and its correlation with a nexus in the Earth's force lines."

"Oh, sure, welcome back."

"Yeah. Let's see, I've been awake for a long time. Renewed my membership last month."

"Glad to hear it. Do you have a question for Guest X?"

"Oh. Absolutely, man. This kind of thing is right in my area of study. How it's all connected—Roswell, the CIA, the United Fruit Company, all that. It's amazing to talk to this person. I have a pretty good idea who it is, but I won't say. Don't want to out someone who's a big hero of mine."

"I'm sure he'd appreciate that. What's your question?"

"Yeah. It's an honor to talk to you, sir. You mentioned the memo that President Kennedy sent out a few days before Dealey Plaza, asking the CIA for all the information about Roswell. You know how he asked for them to pretty much hand the data over to NASA, and how Kennedy tried to excuse it all by claiming that he needed to know about UFOs in case the Soviets figured out what we were doing in their airspace and all…"

"Yes. What's your question?"

"Well, they killed Kennedy to keep the truth from coming out about Roswell, but who is 'they'? Who actually had the most to lose? Of course it's the aliens. The CIA is just a bunch of men. The aliens didn't want to be outed. So even if a human pulled the trigger, it must have been the aliens that gave the order. But this means that aliens held positions of power, and probably still do."

"Thank you, Patrick. Well, Guest X? Could JFK's assassination indicate that there are aliens active in the United States shadow government?"

"There has been some speculation of this kind. I'm personally not convinced, although there have been many strange occurrences involving known members with Majestic clearance over the years. Beginning obviously with Forrestal's supposed suicide. While the reports of dead or dying EBEs in the Roswell craft are credible and corroborated, the reports of living EBEs interacting with officials are less so. But your concern for motive is valid. Why would the government care so much to keep the aliens secret? Especially when such a secret can never hold. National security means something very different today than it did during the Cold War. Especially when the war on terror is—and forgive me if I'm not being politically correct—but it's a religious war. It's long been assumed that proof of alien life would significantly alter citizens' religious worldview. Why not drop the A-bomb, then, so to speak? Why not release the proof of extraterrestrials and destabilize organized religion, weakening bases of terror? If the shadow government doesn't do this, it means one of two things: One, there are valid reasons for keeping the truth hidden, or two, they are being compelled to publicly deny the truth. I don't like either of those alternatives, because they point to something potentially very nasty going on."

♪   ♪   ♪

Herbert's Corner floated like a mirage in the night. The gas pumps gleamed. The neon flashed. Insects swirled and collected around the buzzing lights as if trying to rescue, or join, their perished brethren inside the plastic. Gary, the overnight clerk, sat an uncaring guard over the embarrassment of prepackaged riches in the convenience store. Patsy Cline lamented to an empty diner from the jukebox.

Eileen looked up from a magazine as Martin took a stool at the counter. "Martin? Whatcha doin' here? You know what time it is?"

"I know," said Martin.

"Coffee?"

"Please."

"You lookin' to eat, too?"

"Came to see you, actually," said Martin.

"Well, if you've come to find out what happened with Cheryl, you've come to the wrong place. Surprised us all when she left town."

"You still haven't heard anything? Because I'm having a hard time accepting this story about an Internet romance. I'll admit I'm practically a stranger, but it doesn't seem like her," said Martin.

"People do strange things," said Eileen. "And this town can do strange things to people."

"But Cheryl?"

"You think you know people, but you really don't," said Eileen.

"She gave me her phone number that night I had dinner at her place."

Eileen slid a bowl of creamers and the sugar shaker within reach. "How about some pancakes?"

"I could use some pancakes," said Martin.

"Luis, tall cakes," Eileen called through the window.

"Is anyone looking out for Stewart?" asked Martin.

"Laura and Milton have been looking in on him," said Eileen. "A couple other neighbors."

"I think he's sicker than he lets on," said Martin.

"Why do you say that?" asked Eileen.

"Cheryl said he won't go see a doctor." Martin ached to tell her about Stewart's visit but shut himself up with a gulp of coffee.

When Eileen set his pancakes down, the scoop of butter slid off the top and began to dissolve into a foamy pool on the side of the plate. She added a little pitcher of maple syrup to the counter. "You need anything else, my dear?"

"What can you tell me about what happened to Cheryl's mother?"

"Oh, you don't need to worry about all that," said Eileen.

"Please," said Martin. "Did you know her?"

"I met her after she came back to town. I started here in 1986. I was her replacement, in fact."

"Eighty-six? That's when she disappeared?"

"Right after Cheryl was born. Right after Herbert Stamper was killed, too."

"He was killed?"

"Yep, shot. Right there in the store. Holdup, I guess. Weren't more than a hundred bucks in the till."

"This all happened about the same time?"

"Linda had her baby. Then Herbert got shot. Then Linda ran off."

"Linda was Cheryl's mom?"

"Her name was Linda Laughlin."

"I've heard that Cheryl's grandma worked here, too."

"I didn't know Margie. She died before I moved to town," said Eileen.

"And they made the rhubarb pie?" asked Martin.

"Now, where'd you hear about the rhubarb pie? We ain't had that since…"

"Since Cheryl's mom disappeared?"

"What are you getting at, sweetie?" asked Eileen.

"What was the deal with the rhubarb pie?" asked Martin.

"That pie built Herbert's Corner. Used to be signs fifty miles out in every direction. Don't know how it was that good, but people would drive miles out of their way for a piece. They said truckers would eat an entire pie in one sitting and then ask for more. Story was that Margie and Linda had some secret recipe. I used to think that it was just one of Stamper's tall tales, but then after Linda left, no one could make the pie. The new owners took out the bakery anyway."

"Who were the new owners?"

"Some corporate group. They own a bunch of truck stops from Texas on up."

Martin didn't realize he was tapping on his plate until Eileen glanced at his fork and said, "You've got a Columbo look in your eyes. What are you thinking?"

Martin sank his fork into the last pancake. "I shouldn't have come. I'm going to drive myself crazy."

Eileen peered into his eyes. "Something happened to you. What do you know?"

"Maybe I listen to Lee Danvers a little too much," said Martin.

"All right, finish up," said Eileen.

"What?"

"I'm not the one you need to be talking to."

CHAPTER
8

Gary barely looked up from his *Soldier of Fortune* magazine when Eileen called across the store that she was stepping out. She led Martin out the back door to her Dodge Shadow. As she turned out onto Highway 15, she lit up a cigarette. Martin cleared his throat, and she muttered an apology and rolled down the window.

Eileen didn't slow up through Brixton. She waved her cigarette at the lurking deputy, who flashed his lights but didn't pull out after her.

"Shouldn't we call ahead?" Martin asked.

"She'll be up. She listens to that blamed show all night, just like all you drivers."

A couple of miles out of Brixton, Eileen turned onto a dirt lane, then another, then one more. They approached a lonely orange light clinging to a pole outside a mobile home in a barbed-wired half-acre. The front door opened before Martin had a chance to shut his car door.

The woman in the doorway must have been about a hundred. She wore a housecoat and sported a shotgun that would probably have put her back through a wall if she ever fired it. "Eileen," she yelled. "Scared the bejeezus out of me pullin' up this time of night."

"Evenin', Doris. Care for some company?"

Doris Solberg studied Martin from head to toe. "Little young for you, ain't he?" she said.

"Get your dirty mind back inside before you catch a cold," said Eileen.

Doris's double-wide had wood-paneled walls and shag carpet. The furniture wouldn't have been out of place on *That '70s Show*. Lee Danvers's voice drifted down the hall from a bedroom.

"Can I get you anything?" asked Doris. She shuffled into the kitchen, flipped on the light, and set the shotgun on the turquoise laminate counter. Martin declined. "Sit down," she said, waving behind her to the little round table as she opened the refrigerator.

Doris clanked a six-pack of Rolling Rock in the middle of the table. "Been saving this for company," she said and pulled three free. Martin took one. Couldn't hurt to be polite. Doris's frizzled, silver hair was a fright, but her face was bright and alert. "Now what's going on?" she asked, taking her can. Her finger looked like it would snap as she pried the tab, but the aluminum yielded first.

Eileen introduced Martin as "the young salesman who was after Cheryl Laughlin."

"I thought Cheryl ran off with you," said Doris. Martin shook his head insistently.

"No, Doris," said Eileen. "Remember, she met some man on the computer."

Doris smacked her lips at Martin after a long pull of beer and said, "Must piss you off."

"He came to the Corner tonight asking about Linda and the

rhubarb pie and Herbert. Thought he should be talkin' to you," said Eileen.

"Long before your time, son," said Doris. "You aren't even from Brixton. Where are you from?"

"Billings," Martin said.

"Billings," Doris scoffed. "That town killed Brixton. They put in the Walmart and the Price Club. Don't get me started on Billings. Awful place. The traffic…"

"Was anyone after Linda's secret recipe before she disappeared?" Martin asked. The women looked at him as if he'd grown antlers.

"Now, what would make you go and ask a question like that?" asked Doris.

Martin studied his motives in the faces of two of Brixton's, if not the state's, most notorious gossips. Was he indulging a fantasy? Had he misunderstood Stewart? Had he misread Cheryl? He had to be back at work in Belgrade in five hours. The beer tasted about two months past its sell-by date. But he couldn't help himself. He set the beer aside. "Stewart Campion broke into my apartment last night and said some very strange stuff."

Doris pursed her lips. "You don't even know this," she said to Eileen, "but a company did want to buy Linda's recipe. When she was pregnant with Cheryl."

"In 1986?" Martin asked.

Doris nodded. "She told me the recipe was no big deal, but that if some big corporation wanted to pay her for it, she wasn't going to say no. She wouldn't have to work as many hours. Maybe stick to baking and stop waitressing. Maybe put away some money for the baby. Herbert helped her make the deal, but they kept it real quiet. He didn't want the corporation revealing where they'd gotten the recipe. Wanted to keep his little world-famous gimmick."

"How do you know all this?" asked Martin.

"Doris was sleeping with Herbert Stamper," Eileen told him.

"Yes, and you've done no better," said Doris. Eileen frowned. "But it all went to hell. She gave them the recipe, but when they went to make it for themselves, it wasn't the same. The corporation demanded to know what she'd left out. Herbert was furious. He stood to get a good chunk of the money. I remember him and Linda shouting at each other up in his office. Then Cheryl was born, Linda was gone, and Herbert was dead."

"Stewart thinks Cheryl was kidnapped. And that it's connected to all this," said Martin.

"Now that you say it, it doesn't surprise me," said Doris.

"But that's ridiculous. No corporation would kidnap someone for a stupid pie recipe," said Martin.

"Depends on the corporation," said Doris, then added, "or the pie."

"So there was a secret recipe?" asked Martin.

"All I know is that after Linda left, no one was ever able to make the pie again," said Doris. "Lord knows I tried."

"Cheryl made a pie for me," said Martin.

"Now, that is interesting," said Doris.

"But I didn't tell anyone. I kept my mouth shut about the whole evening," said Martin. "But it still doesn't make any sense. Food companies have chefs and food scientists to develop recipes. They don't need to rough up small-town bakers."

"Unless they do," said Doris.

"All right, enough with this enigmatic crap," said Eileen. "Out with it, already. Tell us what you want to tell us. I gotta get back to the diner sometime this century."

"I don't want to tell you anything," said Doris. "And you don't want to hear it. 'Cause you know it's all true."

"I certainly do not know that," said Eileen.

"Then why'd you bring this boy out here tonight?" asked Doris. "You knew exactly what I'd tell him. You want me to tell my crazy story so you can go back and tell him to pay no mind to old lady Solberg."

"Just tell him, Doris," said Eileen.

Doris narrowed her eyes. Martin shivered. "Twern't no human corporation interested in Margie's rhubarb pie," said Doris. "You get my meanin', son?"

A new hour of *Beyond Insomnia* began down the hall. "From Virginia Beach to Yreka, from the Rio Grande to…"

"The…truckers…Herbert's…?" said Martin.

"That's right," said Doris. "They been comin' since Herbert opened the place in '46. And they loved nothin' better than that infernal pie."

"Do they still….?"

"I suppose they do," said Doris. Eileen gave Martin a wide-eyed glance, committing to nothing. "But nowhere near as many as when Margie and Linda were bakin'."

"Cheryl," said Martin. "Then where is she?"

Doris captured Martin's eyes. "Eighty-six was a long time ago. Five'll get you ten that she's run off with some slab to Boise. But if that ain't the case, there's not a blessed thing you or I can do about it."

Eileen let Martin blink, then said, "Come on. Let's let Doris get back to her show."

As her headlights found the way back to Brixton, Eileen took a deep drag on a fresh cigarette and blew a cloud out her window. "Aren't you going to ask me if I buy it?" she asked.

"I don't know what to ask," said Martin.

The blinking yellow at the center of Brixton warned of something, but Martin couldn't imagine what. Back at Herbert's Corner, his FastNCo. truck waited like a long-lost memory.

"Why did you take me out there?" Martin asked after she shut off her engine.

"Because you care," said Eileen. "Am I wrong?"

.ↄ. .ↄ. .ↄ.

From the FastNCo. procedural manual for area representatives who've been up all night (among other distracting issues):

1. Make contact with the account holder. He/she may be an alien. If account has invoices outstanding, do not grab anyone by the collar and try to peel his/her false face off.

2. At FastNCo. installation, take a general survey. What the hell are you doing? Does your already-piddling job retain any shred of its significance when aliens have probably abducted your girlfriend? Can you even call her your girlfriend?

3. For each drawer:

    a. Scan product code into FASsys. Scan it again. You're not doing it right.

    b. Stare at PIC card until you remember what you're supposed to be doing. Remove inappropriate items and put them anywhere. Shoppers' kids will mess it all up again anyway.

    c. Weigh contents. (For products 1264-2350, hand count must be taken.) You'll get right on that.

    d. Record weight (or count). A kindergartner could do your job.

    e. Restore inventory. Why are you on your knees in a hardware store while real live beings from another world are prowling around?

    f. Confirm restoration of inventory with FASsys. You're still using a PDA running on Windows C? This whole species is doomed.

4. For bulk products...

♪ ♪ ♪

Martin struggled to steer the truck toward Billings and not a ditch, the wrong way down the interstate, or back to Brixton—all equal and viable options.

Brixton. It was no destination. Not even now. At best it was a place to eat and use the restroom on the way to somewhere else. At worst, it was a place to start. Like Cheryl had, Martin thought, not for the first time that day. He couldn't ever get to the next thought.

Whether Cheryl was being probed by an alien or an Idahoan, there was no getting around that somehow this was all his fault. If he'd left well enough alone, she'd probably be helping Lester close up the co-op and heading home with some broasted chicken for Stewart right about now.

Martin hated the seed of uncertainty that had been planted, fertilized, watered, fertilized, and watered again. It had grown into a noxious weed worthy of its own desk at the state agriculture office. How long would it take me to get to Boise? he wondered. He wouldn't even have to talk to her. It'd be enough to see her working or shopping, or hanging on the arm of some—very nice, I'm sure—online predator. That, somehow, was worse than aliens.

Martin's phone rang. He thought about ignoring it but decided he couldn't cope with one of Rick's Homeric epic voicemails. Or worse, Rick would ping the locator in the truck. Martin had found out about that the hard way. He had ignored a call one day, only to have Rick call the manager at the next store.

"Were you asleep?" Rick asked when Martin answered.

"I'm driving," said Martin.

"According to FASsys, you visited four accounts today. I thought we were trying to make it at least five," said Rick.

"I got to everyone I could," said Martin.

Rick harrumphed, and clicked on a keyboard. "I'm coming out to see you, Marty," he said.

"When?" Not now. Please not now.

"Soon. I'm about to send you an email. There's a memo from corporate attached. Going out to all the account reps. A new program they're rolling out."

"Why doesn't this sound good?" Martin asked.

"No, this will streamline your workflow," said Rick. Martin rolled his eyes. "The goal is to transition much of the product ordering and inventory maintenance to the stores themselves. Accounts will be able to log into FASsys through a web app. It'll even link up with their existing point-of-sale system. Real slick."

"A lot of my accounts don't even have a computer, let alone Internet access," said Martin.

"Then we'll provide them with a FASsys PDA setup," said Rick. "They'll only need a phone line. I assume they have telephones."

"This sounds like corporate's trying to phase out the account reps," said Martin.

"We'll never do without account reps. Don't even worry about that. But the service cycle can be stretched out. We may even be able to consolidate some territories. You might have a bigger region but actually spend less time out on the road. How's that sound?"

There's no way the math added up on that. "This kind of thing won't be easy for a lot of my accounts," said Martin. "These are little places, understaffed and fighting for their lives. They appreciate someone coming in every month to maintain things."

"We're confident that the price incentives will be persuasive," said Rick. "Okay, I've sent out the email. I'll let you know when I'm coming. We'll spend a few days pitching to a dozen or so accounts, and then you'll be off and running."

Thanks for the shovel, Rick. I'll just dig my grave right over here, shall I? Specifications for graves could be found on Page 392 of the FastNCo. employee handbook. And…call waiting.

"Are you there?" asked Rick.

"I'm here," said Martin.

"I'll need you to reply back and acknowledge that you received the memo," said Rick. Call waiting.

"Got it," said Martin.

"Everything else going okay?"

"Going fine," said Martin. Except for…well…you know…

Finally rid of Rick, Martin answered the other call.

"Thought I was going to have to leave a message," said Jeffrey.

"Talking to my boss. What's up?"

"You still in the job market?" asked Jeffrey.

"Does a bear crap in the woods?"

"Good. Now, it's not a sure thing yet, but I might be getting a transfer. The Denver region might be opening up, and I'm on the short list. That, of course, would leave a handy little void up here."

"Wow," said Martin.

"I mentioned you to my regional manager. They'd love to have someone who knows the territory," said Jeffrey. "You interested?"

"Yeah. I mean, I can't make any commitments, but I'd be happy to talk to someone," said Martin.

"Cool. I'll let him know," said Jeffrey. "How you getting on with that girl from Brixton? You her shining knight yet?"

Martin opened his mouth to tell Jeffrey about Cheryl but stopped. He would find out soon enough. Eileen and Lorie's gossip-senses would start tingling next time Jeffrey got within ten miles of Herbert's Corner. "You aren't telling people about her and me, are you?"

"Who would I tell, Screw Man? Nah," said Jeffrey.

"Thanks. It's just kind of personal, you know," said Martin.

"Candy Man's got your back," said Jeffrey. "Where you going to be this week? Anywhere where we could grab a bite?"

♪ ♪ ♪

"You're in for a real treat tonight, Wakers. We've been working on this for a long time, ironing out the legal issues, and it's finally time. A BI exclusive. Tonight, in the always-on-the-move BI Bunker, we have Chris Tethers, the man who cracked Area 51. Chris is a self-professed nobody, but he's a hero to many, and a great friend to this program. Welcome to *Beyond Insomnia*, Chris."

"Thanks a lot, Lee. I'm happy to be on."

"I'm sure you are. You just completed your prison sentence."

"I'm very glad to be out."

"Before we get into your story, I need to inform everyone in the Waker Nation that Chris's actions were dangerous and, as much as we may not like it, illegal. You should not attempt to emulate anything you hear tonight. Sorry, Chris, my lawyers tell me I've got to say that."

"Kiddies, don't try this at home. I'm with you. I did this so you don't have to."

"But you paid a price."

"I did. A $25,000 fine, twelve months in federal prison. And I lost my job, my apartment, and worst of all, my girlfriend. Hi, Sandra, if you're listening. I'm sorry. No hard feelings, though."

"Let's get into it. What drove you to do this?"

"Well, Lee, I'm the type of person who can't let things go. I was always the kid with my hand in the cookie jar. I spent the night in my hometown library more than once because I just knew they kept secret books in the back. So you put a place like

Area 51 out there, and I've just got to know. I studied everything about the place, paying close attention to the security, and to the mistakes others have made trying to get in."

"And that's how you decided to hike?"

"I didn't have much choice. It's restricted airspace, and they have all the approach roads lined with vibration sensors and under audiovisual surveillance. The trick was figuring out how to accomplish it."

"Now, we can't go into the technical details, like the exact gear you prepared or the route you took. But we can discuss some generalities. You had to prepare for several days and nights in a very harsh environment."

"It took over a year to prepare. I got desert survival training, learned stealth and evasion techniques from a former Army sniper, and I trained my body for the strenuous walking, crawling, and deprivation. I disciplined myself to stay still for hours under very uncomfortable conditions."

"What did you hope to achieve?"

"I am not a spy. I am a U.S. citizen and a patriot. But what disturbs me are the lies, the secrecy, the denials. The government spends over fifty billion a year out there, paid mostly to Lockheed, Raytheon, Bechtel, and other major defense contractors, with little accountability. That ethic might have been appropriate during the Cold War, but it doesn't fly in this Internet age. I planned to get in, transmit as much video and audio as possible, and get out."

"You transmitted the data live?"

"I had adapted a satellite phone to upload everything straight to a secure server. I didn't want to be caught with any recordings on my person."

"What was your intention for all this data?"

"I could have streamed it all straight to the Internet, but I would have been caught a lot faster. So I collected it. I wanted to use that information to campaign for a new openness from the U.S. government and the defense industry. They need to acknowledge that we are not simpletons to be protected, but that we have a right to know. I'm not talking about needing to know the alloy formulas for new aircraft frames, but I want to know that the tax dollars spent in my name aren't being wasted—or worse, used to develop unethical weapons systems, like the next Manhattan Project. Or even worse than that, used to protect me from myself."

"You're talking about positive knowledge of extraterrestrials and the use of alien technology."

"In so many words."

"I'll ask the question that everyone wants to know: Did you see evidence of aliens or alien technology?"

"If I did, Lee, it was already folded into the designs of the aircraft I saw. But, no, I didn't see anything conclusively alien. However, I never entered any of the buildings or underground facilities. I stayed on the surface and never got closer than about half a mile from any infrastructure, runways, or radar stations. But I still witnessed some pretty amazing stuff."

"We're all anxious to hear about it. After this break, we'll find out more about Chris's amazing few days and nights inside Area 51, and the harrowing story of his eventual capture. You won't want to miss a second of this. Stay up with us. *Beyond Insomnia*."

🌢 🌢 🌢

Martin pulled the truck onto the side of the dirt road under a pink sunrise. Across the cattle guard, and down the lane, the tail of the Skylark peeked out from the trailer's driveway. Martin gave himself one last chance to bug out, then shut off the engine. A neighbor's mutt scampered out to the cattle guard to greet him, and after a couple of barks and a pat on the head, it accompanied Martin to the porch.

The door hung open behind a screen door. Inside, in the shadows, a man lay feet up in the recliner.

"I wondered when you'd show up," said a voice unused to talking. Stewart cleared his throat, and then said, "Heard you were in town night before last."

"May I come in?" asked Martin.

Martin expected Stewart to be squatting in miserable piles of dirty dishes and festering laundry, but things had been pretty squared away. Whether due to the kindness of neighbors or Stewart's own competence, Martin was relieved not to have to feel that extra layer of sorry for the man.

"Can't decide if you're too smart or too stupid for your own good," said Stewart.

"Probably too stupid," said Martin, taking a seat on the couch. "I can't sleep. I don't know if I'm responsible or even if there's anything wrong, but I feel like I need to put things right."

"That's the stupid talking," said Stewart. "Especially if you found yourself out at Doris Solberg's place."

"You came to me first. Don't forget."

"I was distraught, not in my right mind," said Stewart.

"I don't believe that," said Martin. "I think you have a pretty good idea of what Doris told me. And after what you asked the other night…"

Stewart laughed, a cynical, mocking laugh that quickly turned to coughing. "You have no idea what you're talking about," he sputtered as he recovered.

"You don't think Cheryl went to Boise, do you?" said Martin.

"Get out of here."

"Please," said Martin.

"Leave now," said Stewart.

"Dammit, you need my help," said Martin.

Stewart snapped the recliner's footrest down with alarming force. He rose to every inch he could muster of his once-formidable height. "Don't you think you've done enough?" he asked.

"I only want to help Cheryl," said Martin.

Stewart's eyes flicked to the front door, then settled hard on Martin.

CHAPTER
9

Martin jerked and snuffled awake at the sound of brakes. The semi had come from the south on 360, and its blinker signaled a turn west onto 15. Green truck, white trailer. Tri-Mountain Freight, not that that meant anything to Martin. It turned out under a blast of black exhaust. Martin guessed the truck would continue into Brixton, but it veered into the far entrance of Herbert's Corner, the one past the diesel pumps.

Martin scooted up in the bucket seat of his Subaru and watched the truck disappear around the building into the truck lot. He wiped the sleep out of the corners of his eyes and started his car. He parked in one of the spots on the side of the building with a view of the lot, got out, opened the hatchback, and pretended to rummage.

The driver of the green semi was a broad-shouldered, narrow-hipped man with enough facial hair for two broad-shouldered men. He hoisted up the waist of his pants as he neared the diner door.

Since Martin had arrived in Brixton on Saturday night, every driver had gone straight to the restroom, first thing, without exception. About half had used a stall, and the others had ignored Martin as he used a urinal alongside them. Martin cringed at the noises this new driver made behind the partitions, but they sounded more or less human.

Lorie rolled her eyes as Martin took a seat at the counter. "Another one? Why don't I give you my dress and you can go take his order?" she said.

"I don't have the legs for it," said Martin. "Here he comes."

The driver strolled in, hitched up his pants again, and took a seat at a free table.

"Have you seen him before?" asked Martin.

"Be right there, hon," Lorie called, then to Martin said, "A couple times. I think."

"What do you think? Is he?"

"I don't know. But I'm beginning to have my doubts about you," said Lorie. She poured him a cup of coffee and left to take the driver's order.

"What did he order?" Martin asked as she hooked the slip on the rail at the kitchen window.

"None of your business," said Lorie.

"Did you ask him if he likes rhubarb pie?"

"For the last time, I am not askin' anyone that. What would you suggest I do if they try to order some?" She waved over to the display case of muffins, cobblers, cream pies, meringues, and a few melancholy fruit pies. As she had pointed out before, it contained decidedly no rhubarb anything.

Martin nursed a coffee and a side of hash browns as the trucker ate. He tried not to get caught staring as the driver paid at the till and then strolled out into the sun. Martin tossed a five on the counter and waved to a disapproving Lorie.

The truck rolled out of Herbert's Corner toward Brixton, filling the blue sky with its own personal thunderclouds of exhaust.

Martin counted to sixty and followed. He stayed back at least a quarter mile, following his self-imposed rules. Heading west on 15, he'd go only as far as the county line, Hansers Road, about twenty miles. East, he'd go to the wind farm. North on 360, he'd drive as far as the Placer's Homestead historical marker. He hadn't followed anyone south yet, but he guessed he'd go as far as the turn to the Kiln Lake National Wildlife Refuge. Roughly the boundaries of Big Thunder Valley.

The truck stubbornly headed west. Five miles, and then ten. At Hansers Road, Martin put on his blinker and let this one go.

A few minutes later, he was back by the Herbert's Corner propane tank, where he could watch the junction inconspicuously. He shook his Diet Mountain Dew cup; even the ice had deserted him a long time ago.

On his way into the store, he counted the trucks. The orange one was still there, and the blue one, and the black-and-red one. But he had missed the yellow one leaving.

"Martin, what do you think you're doing?" Eileen called, and flicked ash off her cigarette onto the ground by the back door.

"When did you get in?" asked Martin.

"Lorie says you've been here all night chasing drivers."

"It's my day off."

"Hell of a way to spend it," said Eileen.

"I went back to talk to Stewart a couple days ago," said Martin.

"I heard," said Eileen.

"If he thinks Cheryl's in trouble, he's not doing much about it."

"Maybe there's nothing he can do," said Eileen.

"I can't believe that," said Martin. "I'm going to find one of these…" He lowered his voice. "…these aliens, and I'm going to do whatever I have to do to get her back from them."

"Even if you find one, what makes you think he'll know what you're talking about, let alone have anything to do with it?"

"I don't know, I thought…"

"I know I took you out to Doris's. Maybe I shouldn't have. But what she didn't tell you—if you want to believe it—is that no one could tell them apart from humans, except Herbert Stamper. They say Herbert would point at one guy or another and say, 'Yep, he's one,' or 'Nope.' Same with the trucks."

"How could he tell?" asked Martin.

"Doris'd tell you it's because he was one of them."

"Didn't you say she…and he…were…you know?" He twirled a finger.

"They were," said Eileen.

"Do you believe it?" asked Martin.

Eileen considered her nearly finished cigarette, dropped it in a five-gallon bucket of sand, and blew out one last breath of smoke. "I didn't know Herbert that well, but I admit, after a while I got a feelin' that things were a little weirder 'round here than they had a right to be. Don't know how else to explain it."

"But if there are…alien…truckers, why wouldn't they know about Cheryl?"

"You said it yourself," said Eileen. "They're truckers. They aren't all in cahoots. The reason we can't tell them apart from people is that they're no different. They come in here to eat, rest, visit a spell, have some coffee, do their paperwork, and get on their way. Nothing sinister, nothing special."

"You're saying that Herbert's Corner is just a truck stop?"

Eileen smirked. "I gotta help Lorie get ready for the breakfast rush."

"One of them might be willing to help me find Cheryl, maybe give me a ride."

"I think you oughta be careful," said Eileen.

❧ ❧ ❧

That evening, Martin hurried back to his Subaru with an armload of snacks and more Diet Mountain Dew, as much to hear the start of *Beyond Insomnia* as to make sure he didn't miss any trucks coming through the junction. But there wasn't much chance of that. Trucks were few and far between on a Sunday night.

Martin wondered if after all this was done—when Cheryl had returned and everything was put right again—if it would qualify him to be a guest for Lee Danvers. He had always liked to imagine the "always-on-the-move BI Bunker" to be some sort of tricked-out RV with military-grade stealth technology, but Lee probably broadcast from some studio back East somewhere.

From the outside, it probably looked like any other anonymous office in a business park. He'd be met at the door by a producer who would lead him down a hall lined with framed promotional posters into a softly lit green room with potted plants, a couple of couches, and maybe a counter with a tray of cookies, bottled water, and a pot of coffee. One of the evening's other guests would be there. Maybe someone who worked for NASA who had been ordered by men in black to keep the true nature of Jupiter's moon Europa a secret. Or maybe a Wiccan priestess who claimed that the rocks of Stonehenge had been levitated into place. Maybe there'd be chocolate chip cookies, good ones almost as big as your face.

Lee would sweep into the room like a benevolent lord to introduce himself. With him would be X-Ray, BI's notoriously anonymous, but extremely competent, broadcast engineer. Lee would graciously spend a few minutes chitchatting like an old friend, and X-Ray would make sure Martin knew how to talk into a microphone.

A few minutes later, he'd be in the studio having a pair of headphones fitted over his ears and a microphone boomed a couple of inches from his lips.

"Look around at where you are right now, Waker Nation," Lee would begin, "because you'll never want to forget where you were and what you were doing when you heard this interview. The man in our studio tonight is soon to be a household name. He's a former account representative for a second-rate hardware concern, but now a renowned expert on extraterrestrial hunting and author of the upcoming books *Snaring ET: How to Build the Mother of All Mousetraps* and *Among Us: A Love Story*, soon to be a Lifetime original movie. Martin Wells, welcome to the Bunker."

"It's a pleasure, Lee. As a longtime Waker, there's no greater honor."

Martin would tell his story in a way that—despite its being about rhubarb pie and alien truck drivers—made him sound perfectly reasonable. It would start right here, with him waiting by the Herbert's Corner propane tank, and end with Cheryl at his side as the aliens declared a civilization-wide holiday in his honor for solving the riddle of the pie.

After a break, Lee would take calls.

Ruth from Des Moines would ask, "Your story is fascinating, but I've always wondered: How does a regular person get themselves abducted?"

"I wasn't abducted per se," Martin would answer. "I found an alien willing to help me and arranged to travel with him."

"But that's not to say that abduction doesn't take place," Lee would add.

"Absolutely," Martin would reply, "and that's an important part of my upcoming book."

"Which will be next month's must-read recommendation at

the wakernation.com bookstore," said Lee. "Now, Ruth, do you really want to be abducted?"

"I do. I can't explain it. I feel this pull, this calling."

Martin's tone would become sympathetic. "I understand what you're feeling, Ruth. Alien abduction is a serious personal choice. However, the experience can leave lasting psychological and physiological scars. It may be difficult for your family and friends to accept. So if you really want to, you must understand the risks."

"Ruth, have you had experiences before?" Lee would ask.

"When I was a little girl, I saw lights over the lake at my aunt and uncle's cabin. I remember them as vivid today as then."

"Ruth," Martin would ask, "what kind of aliens are you hoping to get abducted by?"

"I don't know. Maybe the little ones with big eyes."

"It's an important subject to consider, because there are many different species. It sounds as if you're familiar with the Grays, who are responsible for the majority of reported abductions. They can alter time and manipulate matter with light, which might provide interesting experiences. But they are also infamous for, shall we say, sticking hilariously metal objects in unmentionable places on your person. So consider: Reptoids, spirit beings, angels, Annunaki, Men in Black, Log Cabin Republicans, to name a few. It's important to know what species of alien suits your lifestyle, to know who they're looking for in an abductee, and where they commonly are found. My book provides a guide on making this choice."

"And I suppose that this choice depends greatly on what you hope to achieve."

"It does, Lee. Many simply seek the thrill of the unknown. But others have loftier ambitions, such as the search for proof."

"Hasn't it proved very difficult to do actual science in abduction scenarios?" Lee would ask.

"It has proved notoriously difficult. Aliens resist collection of evidence by carefully controlling the circumstances, leaving abductees with nothing but vague memories. But far be it from me to discourage anyone."

"Ruth, are you searching for scientific proof of your abduction?"

"I'm just looking for the truth."

Martin would nod knowingly to Lee and say, "Ruth and others may wish to communicate, and to become messengers. It's a laudable goal. Obviously we hope that any message will be one of universal peace. But, Ruth, if you find yourself writing a cookbook, or articles of surrender for the United Nations, please inform the authorities right away."

"Excellent advice. Now, Martin, what would you say to people who want to be abducted for fame or recognition?"

"It's not a good idea. I can personally attest to the fact that there are quicker, and much safer paths to fame. Ruth, if fame is your goal, I might suggest picking up a video camera and getting a dolphin to whack your husband in the balls…"

"Or drop angry squirrels on him in a hammock," Lee would add.

"Those are easily worth a couple million YouTube hits each."

"Well, thank you both so much for your help. And Mr. Wells, congratulations to you and Mrs. Wells. It's such a beautiful story. Will you be expecting soon?"

"As a matter of fact, we are. You heard it here first."

"Break out the cigars, Waker Nation." Lee would reach across the console and shake Martin's hand. "We'll be back with more questions for the indomitable Martin Wells. Our sponsor this hour is the Pajama-of-the-Month Club. If you're searching for a one-of-a-kind-gift for your pregnant wife, your mom, or even your boss…"

♪   ♪   ♪

Martin let the GRT Logistics truck go at the wind farm as Lee Danvers wrapped up the last hour of the night's broadcast. The taillights faded away around the bend. By the dashboard clock, he had to be back in Billings and heading to work in a few hours.

If any of the trucks had been alien, there was nothing to distinguish them. Nothing floated or flew. None had strange lighting, or plasma exhaust. Martin had sneaked through the parking lot, knocking on panels and kicking tires. They all smelled like fossil fuels. They all had the license plates, regulatory stickers, and debris in the cabs that one would expect. The trailers all had the battle scars of the road: mud, scratches, dents, stains, and missing rivets. Either all were alien or none were.

The drivers had ranged from heavy-set Bible readers in coveralls and lined flannel shirts to lanky dudes with iPads in T-shirts and shorts. This one chewed tobacco in little pouches, that one put Worcestershire sauce on his scrambled eggs. That one had an eye twitch, this one kicked his left shoe off under the table. Some kept to themselves, some knew the other drivers or were simply sociable. They all spoke English—at least Eileen and Lorie never had a problem getting their orders. Maybe the waitresses…? He didn't let himself finish that thought.

When Martin rolled back into Herbert's Corner, Eileen emerged from the diner and crossed to the pumps. "I'm getting gas, then going home," Martin called.

"You should," said Eileen, and then handed him a cell phone as she stepped up by the squeegee bucket.

"What's this?" he asked, taking it cautiously. "Hello?"

"Martin? It's Doris Solberg."

"Hello, Doris. What can I do for you?" Martin asked, looking at Eileen.

"Eileen tells me you been drivin' around after trucks all weekend."

"I'm heading home now."

"Well, I wish you'd talked to me. I could've saved you a heap of trouble. Herbert always told right where they come from. Not that they come 'round much since they took the pie off the menu."

"What? Really?"

"Sure. Now, I never saw it myself, but Herbert said they came from that bluff up from Deaver Creek. About seven miles south on 360. Toward Billings. Where the highway got cut through the hill in '52. You know the place?"

"I think so. You come up that hill from the creek, the road narrows. There's rock on both sides?" He'd driven through that gap and back eight or nine times in the past twenty-nine hours.

"That's the place. He said they would appear in there and roll right on up here to Brixton. Then when they'd leave, they'd roll right back and go off."

"They'd just leave? They didn't have any other business on Earth?" asked Martin.

"What other business would they have?" Doris asked.

"I don't know. You tell me." Martin gave her a moment to respond, and in the silence could imagine her chewing her lips at him. "So if I just go hang out down there, I'll eventually see one come out?"

"You might be waitin' till you're as old as I am," said Doris. "But I ain't gonna tell you not to 'cause I'd just be wastin' my breath. You be careful. Now I gotta go. It's my bedtime."

"Yes, ma'am. Goodnight," said Martin. He handed the phone

back to Eileen. She listened for a moment, but Doris had hung up. "Did you know about that place?" Martin asked her.

"I didn't," said Eileen. "But you should probably get on home and think hard about what you're doin'."

"How can you say that? Cheryl's in trouble. And some of your customers are real-life extraterrestrials. Nothing else matters if that's true."

"You're wrong about that. Nothing changes. I still gotta eat. Still gotta pay my bills. Gotta put gas in my car. Death and taxes and all that. And you're no different. You've got a job and a family somewhere, like everyone else. There's no getting around that."

Martin topped off his Diet Mountain Dew. On the way out, Eileen called to him. "I know it won't do any good, but you should pass that gap right on by."

❧ ❧ ❧

A knock startled Martin awake. He squinted into the sunlight. A looming figure outside his car resolved itself into a roughly humanoid shape. Martin scooted up in his seat, swore silently, and rolled down the window.

"Good morning," said the highway patrolman from under the rim of his Smokey Bear hat. "Is something wrong with your vehicle, sir?"

"Uh, no. I got really tired. Needed to pull over," said Martin. The patrolman glanced up and down the highway. To his right it sloped down around the corner to the Deaver Creek bridge. A hundred meters up the hill yawned the gap. The Gap. "Well, you couldn't have picked a worse place to do it, sir. There's very little shoulder and limited visibility for vehicles coming up behind you."

"Oh?" Martin asked, and glanced over his shoulder. "Sorry. It looked better in the dark."

"License and registration, please."

As the patrolman returned to his cruiser, Martin checked the time and swore to himself again. By the time he got back to Billings, got the truck loaded, and cleaned himself up, he'd be lucky to get three accounts in today. What was he thinking?

He took a sip of his flat and watery Diet Mountain Dew to clear the goo out of his mouth. Then he took another sip; it might have to be breakfast.

The patrolman returned a few minutes later and returned Martin's documents. "Mr. Wells. Next time, I suggest you find a rest area or a motel."

"Yes, sir. I will. Thank you," said Martin. The patrolman glanced up the hill to the Gap. But with no traffic coming, nothing to draw attention that Martin could sense, part of him wanted to believe that the patrolman was in on it, even as the man walked away. Martin head checked, pulled out, and some more sensible part of him said, "Martin. Martin. Martin. Martin."

CHAPTER
10

"Pittsburgh, Pennsylvania. You're Beyond Insomnia."

"Great to be on, Lee. This is Benjamin. Been awake for a long time. I used to listen to you back when you were on WXGR. Great show tonight. Anyway, I have a question for Dr. Cunningham."

"Sure, go ahead."

"If I could interrupt, Lee. I'm not a doctor. I appreciate the respect, but I don't have a Ph.D. I wish I did. But I'm plain old Dick Cunningham."

"Oh, sorry, sir."

"Go ahead with your question, Benjamin."

"Yeah, so NASA's sending all these rovers up, and they always claim to be searching for evidence of life. They're scraping rocks, putting sand in mass spectro-thingies, and sniffing for water. But they've got the Cydonia complex right there. The Face, the pyramids, everything. If there was a civilization on Mars, they'd need water, right? Wouldn't the best place to look for water be near the ruins?"

"Good question. Yes, Dick, why hasn't NASA, or the Russian

Space Agency, for that matter, landed a rover or a probe at the Cydonia complex to put the questions to rest?"

"Two possibilities. A—they don't want to. Or B—they don't want to. Let me explain. A—They truly might not consider Cydonia a scientifically viable site. Or it might be too logistically difficult to land there with our current entry technology. Or it might have a surface geology that they've already studied on another mission. Or B—they might not want to because there may be answers there they aren't allowed to find."

"But that doesn't make sense. Sorry. Can you hear me?"

"We hear you."

"Great, my phone was a little…anyway. It makes no sense. I understand the science and logistics and all. But NASA's always crying about their budget being slashed. If a rover discovered pyramids, man, they'd have more money than they knew what to do with overnight. Everyone would be demanding that we go and see what the aliens built."

"Of course, part of Cydonia is the famous Face on Mars. I'm sure all your listeners are familiar. NASA drug their heels, but finally reimaged it in detail. The new images suggested that the Face might be only a trick of light. But I agree, the delay itself is telling."

"Thank you, Benjamin. Next up, Roseburg, Oregon. You're Beyond Insomnia."

"Thanks, Lee. Quentin in Roseburg. Hi, Mr. Cunningham. Read all your books. I listened to that last call, and I gotta say—NASA's reimaging of the Cydonia Face is not convincing at all. They had to say it isn't real. We can't trust anything that NASA shows us. These are the same people that faked the moon landings, and that was with sixties video technology. Hell, my nephew could do a better job with these pictures on Photoshop."

"That's exactly what I've been saying. The data is there. The satellites are in place. A new rover is almost ready to be launched. But decisions have been made to avoid Cydonia. We need to ask harder questions and hold them accountable to do the research and the science that we're paying them to do. Now, I've talked to scientists at NASA—I can't give you their names; their jobs would be in jeopardy. But they tell me, 'Dick, we want to go to Cydonia. We find the imagery as compelling as you do, but it's not going to happen.' "

"They've been told not to go to Cydonia?"

"That's what I take away from that, Lee."

"Amazing. Quentin, what's your question for Dick Cunningham?"

"Sure. Mr. Cunningham, I wanted your opinion of the theory floating around the web that the Cydonia site structures are actually a better analog to the constellation Lyra, rather than the Pleiades, as previously thought. I'll hang up and listen to the answer."

"Thanks, Roseburg. Dick, has the Lyra-Pleiades controversy figured into your recent research?"

"Not to disappoint the caller, Lee, but I find the constellation analog far less interesting than the analogs we find here on Earth. Overlay the schematic of the Cydonia site on an area map of the Avebury Stone Circle in England. Or compare the shield volcanoes on Mars's Tharsis Bulge—perfect alignment with the Giza pyramids and Orion's Belt. Or the Teotihuacan pyramids. We're finding parallels with ancient Peruvian ruins, Native American burial sites, and even sites now underwater, near Australia and in the Mediterranean. With every one of these discoveries, it becomes more and more undeniable that an ancient civilization capable of great feats of engineering, and who revered the stars, lived on Earth and Mars. Were they human or alien? It's impossible to say. But it's clear that a certain part of their knowledge and will to construct monuments has passed down to us. We are driven to build bigger and bigger structures and public works, often for little reason. Could it be some of this racial memory that drives us? It's the goal of my research to try to connect those dots."

✿ ✿ ✿

Why had the Montana Department of Transportation cut Highway 360 through the eastern slope of this unnamed bluff? Was it simply a civil engineering decision? Or were the engineers influenced to make something perfect for an alien purpose? Or were they aliens themselves? Martin waited for answers in a folding chair on a hillside, reeking of bug spray. At sundown, Martin had parked his Subaru about a mile to the south on a rough gate-access track, well out of view from the highway. He hoped it wouldn't annoy the rancher whose land he'd trekked across.

Martin dug a Snickers out of his backpack, and as he took his first bite, headlights appeared from the north. Binoculars. An SUV. A Chevy Suburban, maybe. The headlights blinked out of view at about the moment that the sound of the car reached Martin. The SUV appeared again on the hill. Then, as it entered the Gap, its high beams lit up the ragged rock to an unnatural brightness. And then it was gone.

Martin strained, listening. Did it disappear? He held his breath until the slashes of white light, chased by red, reappeared over the hill, continuing south.

Martin took another bite of candy and slapped at an insect on his elbow.

A tuft of grass rustled a few dark yards away, and Martin felt a bit of adrenaline. The incessant wing fluttering and leg rubbing of the insects he could deal with, but not the other noises. A prairie dog might as well be a mastodon. Was that a wren landing on some sagebrush or a herd of pissed-off pronghorn? Worse were the things he would never hear. His primate brain conjured up wolves or a stalking lion. Get to a tree, it urged. Get in the car and shut the doors. Nothing will get you in that little nest of leaves you call an apartment. But as no attacks materialized, fear soon subsided into complacence.

A few cars passed through the Gap. And fewer trucks. Martin took video with the camera he'd picked up at a pawnshop a few days ago—a pretty good one, a Sony. He hoped it hadn't been stolen. Martin stuffed the Snickers wrapper into his backpack. Pack it in, pack it out. Two cars, a Volvo and a Saturn, rolled through in quick succession. Martin cracked open his bottle of Diet Mountain Dew, took a swig, and as he settled it into the chair's cup holder, he felt the effect of all the liquid he'd had on the road up here.

He scanned north and south. Empty road. The nearest tree was probably a cottonwood a mile away down along Deaver Creek, but it wouldn't be needed. The spattering under a future tumbleweed sounded unnaturally loud in this immense dome of nature. He felt at once large and insignificant. The stars didn't care. Nor did the Earth. He was simply another little part of the fresh water cycle.

A bright light and a truck filled the Gap. Martin swore as he dribbled the last of his business on his pants. As he zipped up, he glimpsed a sky-blue sleeper cab and a trailer from a company called Cal-Can Trucking, with a red maple leaf in the logo. Where had it come from? Martin froze, unsure, as it headed north toward Brixton. When it was out of sight, he grabbed up all his gear as if his body had made up his mind without him. He snatched up his chair and ran to his car, faster than he should have for his cardiovascular health, his ankles, and his minuscule flashlight.

Martin rolled to a stop at the junction, and although the crossing was clear, he waited. Herbert's Corner waited. This might be it, Martin thought.

All week, he'd thought about what he'd say.

"Hi, are you an alien?" No.

"Welcome to Earth, can I buy you a cup of coffee?" Maybe.

"Rhubarb pie?" Shudder.

"I know this may sound crazy, but…" Stop right there.

"So, where're you from?" Gah. Should it be this hard?

Martin crossed Highway 15 and drove around the back of Herbert's Corner. He crawled to a halt on the far side of the truck lot, out of reach of the lights. He turned off the engine. The truck had parked among the others.

Martin treaded as quietly as possible on the gravel. The sky-blue Peterbilt had a chrome grille larger than his kitchen. The engine popped and pinged as it cooled. The Cal-Can trailer had those aerodynamic flaps hung between the front and rear sets of wheels. The back doors were padlocked. Martin checked for anyone coming from the truck stop and then grabbed the handhold and hoisted himself onto the cab's footstep. In the dim parking lot light, he couldn't see much more than a steering wheel, a giant pack of sunflower seeds on the dashboard, and a Burger King bag in the passenger seat. A CB radio hung from the ceiling. The door was solid, the glass was glass. The cab rocked under his weight.

"Hey," called a voice, "what're you doing?"

Martin stumbled down and scrambled toward the end of the truck. The voice called again. Flight said to get back to his car as fast as possible. Fight agreed and curled up into a little whimpering ball.

Martin sneaked around the next truck and crouched behind

a set of tires. The trucker checked the driver's door, circled the rig, and then jogged back to the building.

Martin got the hell out of there. About a quarter-mile south on 360, he turned onto Birdbath Road, where his binoculars would provide a pretty good view of the Corner.

About five minutes later, Martin watched as a sheriff's vehicle arrived and took a slow circuit around the gas station. A deputy got out and strolled inside. He emerged a few moments later with Gary and the truck driver. The driver indicated someone about Martin's height lurking near his rig. The deputy walked the perimeter with his giant Maglite flashlight and returned to Gary and the driver with his verdict. They all shrugged, shook their heads, and headed back inside.

🐞 🐞 🐞

The next afternoon, Martin reprovisioned himself and arrived at the ranch access road near twilight. He followed his own foot tracks up the hill to the vantage point and set down his chair. The western sky was a tapestry of orange and yellow under wisps of clouds rarely seen off a canvas. The first stars and planets twinkled in the east over the Gap, with a bright quarter moon. The bugs buzzed around his cloud of Off! as if to welcome him.

Thank you, Subway, for making breakfast sandwiches all day long, Martin thought as he munched his flatbread. He let the insects have the lettuce that fell out. An offering.

Martin supposed that the relatively heavy northbound Sunday evening traffic was people coming home from a day shopping in Billings. Not too many people came south from Brixton. And few trucks came from either direction. But after a couple of hours, even the northbound traffic slowed to a trickle. He'd videoed only four trucks by the time he'd finished his second Diet Mountain Dew and opened a third.

It cracked and hissed, and the insects fell quiet.

The hairs rose on the back of Martin's neck. Diet Mountain Dew overflowed the cap and ran over his hand. He felt something in his gut, like when a car with a month's salary worth of subwoofers in the trunk pulls up next to you in traffic—but not audible, more ethereal. He missed the chair's cup holder, and the foaming bottle fell onto the dirt. He groped for his camera, not taking his eyes off the Gap. He hurriedly pressed buttons until he got it on. A single cricket chirped twice and stopped.

Martin awoke, his face in the dirt a few inches from an ancient cow pie. He got to his feet to find the camera still wrapped around his hand, still recording. With sticky fingers, he fumbled with the playback controls. His whole life narrowed to that two-inch screen in the middle of the dark Montana rangeland.

He had recorded his muttering efforts to find the Gap in the view; then the camera had settled, shakily, onto the moonlit arc of crumbling rock. Then the view blurred again, and stopped a moment later, tilted and half-blocked by a tuft of grass and a rock. The autofocus ratcheted back and forth, searching for something of significance. A minute later, a bright light flared the screen white. The light turned blue, and the lens focused on a yawning electric mouth. A uvula of light spat out a boxy form. The light sucked away in an instant, leaving the blurred object and streaks of running lights. It left the frame in a half-second. Martin rewound clumsily, failed to freeze on the moment in the first attempt, but then got it: a blur of a red tractor pulling a blank trailer.

Martin ran back to the Subaru and floored it to Brixton, gasping, sweating, with his heart trying to claw its way out of his chest.

CHAPTER
11

While last Sunday there had been three trucks in the Herbert's Corner lot, tonight there was only one. The One. It had to be. A red Freightliner, its trailer blank on both sides. The only identifying markings indicated that the load might be corrosive, and that both the truck and the trailer were licensed in Kentucky.

Martin managed to get into the Herbert's Corner restroom without being seen. He washed his dirt-encrusted hand, then swiped at the smudges on his face and clothes with a wet paper towel until he was relatively presentable.

The man at the counter was about Martin's height and size. He sported a Freddie Mercury mustache and a pork pie hat. His shirt bragged that he been to the Harley-Davidson store in Omaha. He had the heels of his cowboy boots hooked over the stool's footrest.

Martin took a stool a couple down, and they exchanged friendly nods.

The driver had ordered a club sandwich, french fries, a Pepsi, a pickle wedge, and a side of potato salad. Eileen emerged from the kitchen and raised one eyebrow at Martin.

"What happened to you?" she asked, reluctantly pouring him a cup of coffee.

"I was hiking," said Martin. He flicked his eyes over to the other diner, and she rolled her eyes. "Fell down."

No, she mouthed. "What can I get you?"

He nodded discretely. Yes. "You got any of that rhubarb pie?" he asked.

Eileen eyed him coldly. Martin grinned and forced himself to keep his gaze on her. In his peripheral vision, he thought he saw the driver stop chewing.

"Now, you know we don't have any of that," said Eileen. "I got peach, pecan, chocolate cream, banana cream, and I may still have a slice of apple."

"The peach sounds okay," said Martin. "Warm, with a scoop of ice cream."

Martin stirred Sweet'N Low into his coffee. "They used to have the best rhubarb pie in here," he said. The driver acknowledged him with a nod. "My dad used to bring me in here just for the pie. I was only a kid, but I still miss it." The driver chewed thoughtfully. Martin thought he might speak, but he took another bite of his sandwich.

"You ever come here when they had that rhubarb pie?" Martin asked.

The driver stared for a moment, then nodded slowly. A chill rode up Martin's back.

Eileen returned with a little white plate. She'd topped the pie with Reddi-wip, but no ice cream. "You better eat quick and get home. Ain't you got work in the morning?"

Martin shrugged. "We were just talking about the rhubarb pie you used to serve here. Long time ago. Seems…sorry, I didn't get your name."

"Glen," the man said.

"Seems Glen remembers having it, too. Good stuff."

"You ever getting that on the menu again?" Glen asked. He spoke in a surprising accent. Texas, maybe? An odd choice for an alien, but so was the hat.

"We get our pies from a big bakery over in Great Falls now. Don't think they do rhubarb," said Eileen.

"That's too bad," said Glen. He turned back to his meal.

That's enough, Eileen mouthed to Martin. "Enjoy your pie."

Martin waited until Eileen returned to the kitchen. "Quiet tonight."

Glen nodded and chewed.

"Where you headed?" Martin asked.

"Wherever the company sends me," Glen replied.

"I heard that," said Martin.

Martin finished his pie at about the same time Glen scraped the last of his fries through a swirl of ketchup. Glen took a long sip at the dregs of his Pepsi, got up, and looked over the check Eileen had left tented on the counter. He licked his teeth behind his lips as he dug in a back pocket for a wallet.

"You heading out again?" Martin asked.

"In a few," said Glen. "Thought I'd clean up while I got the chance." He nodded toward the ceiling and the second-floor showers.

"You have a safe drive," said Martin.

After Glen paid, Eileen took Martin's coffee away. "This stops now," she said. "You've got no business comin' in here and doin' this."

"I talked to him," said Martin. "What's the big deal?"

"So he remembers the pie. Don't mean he's…"

"An alien? You didn't see what I saw down on 360," said Martin.

"And what exactly did you see?"

"I blacked out, but I got it on video. Well, sort of. There's a bright, kind of swirly light, then poof, the truck appears."

"So you didn't see it? You need to let that poor man be. He's probably got a long drive comin', and he doesn't need you freakin' him out."

The back door jingled, and Glen headed upstairs with a black gym bag. Martin tossed a five on the counter.

"That was you sneakin' around last night, wasn't it?" Eileen asked. "I will call the sheriff."

"Thanks for the pie."

In all respects, the red Freightliner appeared to be a perfectly normal truck, one of the newer models with aerodynamic styling. Other than being a bit cleaner than a truck had a right to be this far from civilization, there was nothing immediately amiss. Martin hunkered down for a peek under the trailer. Everything felt solid and freakishly normal. It was roadworthy, but he wouldn't call it spaceworthy.

Martin checked that the coast was clear and climbed up between the tractor and the trailer, almost certain that he'd cross through some sort of force field, or bump into a disguised hull. A set of snow chains, real enough, hung on the all-too-solid back wall of the cab. The air smelled like a blend of oil, diesel exhaust, and hydraulic fluid, as it should.

There were handholds inside the rig's aerodynamic cowling, and for a moment, Martin considered hiding there, trying to hang on to the next destination. He wondered if he'd have the stamina to keep his grip, and to endure the exposure, like that guy who sneaked into Area 51. Then he remembered where space-ships went. It didn't matter how much ninja sniper training he had, he'd end up a floating Martinsicle to be splatted and swiped across the windshield of the next ship to come along. Great plan.

Martin hopped down. Still no sign of Glen. On a whim, he

checked the driver's door handle. It opened. This might be the only chance he'd ever get. He stepped up on the running board to poke his head inside the cab.

A lumbar support pad had been strapped to the high, bucket captain's seat, and the cab was full of all the expected paraphernalia: a CB, a couple of transmitters, probably to talk to interstate weigh stations. But no slimy, chitinous, or biological surfaces. Nothing squelched or oozed. Nor was it a Buck Rogers cardboard interior with washing machine dials and oscilloscope screens.

An odd smell—something musky but tangy, like a ferret-and-pineapple smoothie—gave Martin his first real evidence. Then he traced the odor to the Playboy air freshener hanging from the radio dial.

Martin poked at the bed in the sleeper and checked under the tangle of dark sheets, a flannel-lined sleeping bag, and a crocheted throw blanket. Toolboxes and a few plastic grocery bags choked the narrow floor space. Glen had a penchant for Funyuns.

Martin studied the dash in increasing desperation. It couldn't be just a truck. This truck, or ship, or whatever, had been spat out on a tongue of plasma. Martin wondered how someone would draw a graphic for a control knob that changed a semi into a spaceship and back.

Martin sat in the driver's seat knowing he had squeezed every drop of luck out of this situation. He could make out the shape of his Subaru in the dark. The coast was still clear. But what then? What if Glen drove right back to the Gap and into the alien vortex? How would that help Cheryl? All Martin would have would be a nutty story and some blurry video to sell to the Discovery Channel. Martin dug out his keys and clicked the fob toward his car. The lights flashed and the horn squeaked once as the doors locked. Martin climbed into the bed in the back and concealed himself under the pile of bedding.

With every breath, the air under the sleeping bag smelled more and more like hamster cage and failure. Every second he stayed made it more dangerous to give in to good sense. When he heard the footfalls on the gravel outside the truck, Martin almost threw up his peach pie. The cab rocked, and a door opened. Glen grunted and harrumphed as he settled into his seat and closed the door. He began to hum an unidentifiable tune. He clicked, plunked, and shuffled, and then the engine rumbled with a torqued roar that settled into a bladder-trembling vibration.

Every second the truck idled, Martin felt his resolve melting away. He gave himself to the count of three to throw back the covers and cry uncle, when, with a healthy growl, the truck lurched into gear. Martin followed his inner ear out across the lot and through a right turn onto 360. The truck's brakes squeaked them to a stop at the junction. If Doris was right, Glen would drive his disguised spaceship straight, back toward the Gap. What if that didn't happen? Martin hated to think. Damn you, Stewart. Why did you have to come to my apartment? And Doris and Eileen, you ridiculous busybodies. Where would I be without your guidance? Oh, yeah, safe in bed.

Another truck grumbled by, and the cab rocked in the buffeting wake of wind. Go straight, Martin willed. Go straight. A bit of static and unintelligible chatter crackled over the CB, but Martin didn't hear a blinker. Then another roar and buffet of wind.

The cab lurched and gears engaged. The rig rolled forward slowly, too slowly. Martin feared it would turn, but it picked up speed and bounced straight across the junction onto 360 southbound proper. Martin bit back a cheer. Then he remembered that in a few minutes he'd be sucked into the Gap's electric maw. He probably should have thought this through a little more.

Who would even realize that he was gone, let alone dead?

His rent wasn't due for a couple of weeks. A few accounts might wonder why he hadn't shown up, but they'd shrug him off for at least a week. The next FastNCo. shipment was due at the storage unit—when?—he couldn't remember. No one in Brixton would give him much thought. They'd think he'd gotten on with his life like he should have in the first place. He'd be dead in less than five minutes, and no one would care.

Then he stifled a groan. Rick would care. He'd check FASsys and start calling and pinging him. Wonderful. He'd be known in the papers as Marty the missing Screw Man. Screwed Man was more like it.

Was he going to be blasted into another dimension? Wormholed to the other side of the galaxy? Get up, you idiot. Say something. Groan and pretend you've been beaten up and forced into the truck. More chatter crackled from the CB, not alien but distant, staticky, meant for other ears.

Martin eased his cell phone out of his pocket and checked the time. Almost midnight. Another minute clicked by. They would be there soon.

A heavy object landed on Martin's gut, and he couldn't stifle a surprised cry. And then the world let Martin go. He tumbled off the mattress onto the Funyuns. His head struck a toolbox cushioned by the crocheted blanket. The truck shuddered, and Martin felt himself being tossed about the floor by physics and his own stupidity.

Everything stopped, still and quiet, except for the vibration of the idling engine. Martin untangled his head from the blankets to find a shiny switchblade six inches from his face and a black duffel bag on his lap.

"Don't move a muscle," said Glen, groping behind him. He kept his eyes on Martin as he found the CB handset and keyed the transmitter.

❧ ❧ ❧

The reddish-brown stain on the concrete floor resembled three, maybe four, tarantulas squashed together with an iron. Martin didn't want to know how it got there, and yet he empathized, found it kindred. The man on the far bench had been snoring since Martin had arrived, but he woke with a nasty, phlegmy cough. He was dressed like he'd had a long day's work at the chicken farm and had the worst hat hair Martin had ever seen.

"What the hell time is it?" he asked. The reek of liquor wafted across the cell.

"The sun's up," Martin said, nodding up to the barred window near the ceiling, which had been light now for a couple of hours.

"That sucks. I'm supposed to be at work," the man slurred. He staggered to the gate and shouted, "Derrick. Derrick. I gotta get to work." He banged on the bars, then turned around. "What you in for?"

"Reckless driving," said Martin.

"I didn't even drive," said the man, then shouted through the bars. "You hear me? I wasn't going to drive."

A door buzzed and a deputy strolled into view. "Wells," he said.

"What about me?" said the drunk. "Come on, Derrick. I gotta get to work. Norm's gonna fire my ass." The deputy opened the cage and let Martin out.

"Sally's on her way," said the deputy, clanging the door shut.

"You didn't call Sally. Dammit, Derrick. She's gonna kill me."

The drunk's shouts echoed after them. At a counter, someone handed Martin a Ziploc bag containing his wallet, cell phone, keys, belt, and shoelaces.

Stewart waited in the lobby of the sheriff's office.

"Thanks for coming," said Martin. "I didn't have anyone else to call."

"What the hell were you thinking?" asked Stewart.

"Can we just get out of here?" Martin asked, and led the way out into the late morning sun. Stewart's Skylark backfired twice before it left the county seat and headed toward Brixton.

"At least you didn't have to pay bail. They're not going to press charges," said Martin. "I'll pay you for the gas."

"Damn right, you will," said Stewart, hitching his oxygen tank onto the seat beside him.

"You talk to Eileen?" Martin asked. Stewart humphed. "I suppose everyone's heard by now."

"You're gonna get yourself killed. Or worse."

Worse? Martin didn't ask. "You don't know what I saw out there," Martin said. "I know you don't want to talk about it, but I know you believe it. That driver was not a human. He may have looked human. His truck might fool a Freightliner mechanic..."

"So what? What did you think would happen? What did you think he was going to do for you?"

"I thought he might take me to Cheryl, or show me the way," said Martin.

"You're a fool," said Stewart.

"I never said otherwise," said Martin. The passing mileage markers and Stewart's wheezes punctuated a long silence until Martin said, "Someone has to do something, Stewart."

"You think I haven't done everything that can be done?" asked Stewart.

"What does that mean? What can you do?"

"I've left messages on Cheryl's phone. Either she's listening, or they're listening. Either way, if we haven't heard back it's 'cause whoever's on the other end doesn't want to talk. I don't have what they want."

"You're talking about the secret recipe," said Martin.

"Of course I'm talking about the goddamn recipe. You happy now? All that crap Eileen and Doris been filling your head with is completely true. Cheryl's been taken for the godforsaken rhubarb pie, just like her mother. There wasn't a thing I could do about it then, and there's not a thing I can do about it now."

"You told them in the messages that she doesn't have the secret?"

"Of course I told 'em."

"What are they doing to her?" Martin asked.

Stewart glared, and Martin made a mental note to never ask that again. But Linda had come back. Mentally ill, but back. What had they said? A couple of years later? Cheryl had only been gone a few weeks. She might still be okay, out there, somewhere. Was that consolation?

"Why don't you just give them the recipe?"

"It isn't that simple," said Stewart.

"Why?"

"For one, no one knows it. It died with Linda."

"Then why don't we call and tell them that we have the secret recipe and want to trade it for Cheryl?"

"Think, Martin. They'll want proof. Can you bake such a pie? Cheryl told me you'd never even had rhubarb pie. You think you'll be able to fool them? Besides…"

"Didn't Linda leave behind recipe books? Cards? A diary? A shopping receipt? Anything?"

"Don't you think I've looked through it all a hundred times?"

"Couldn't hurt to have a fresh pair of eyes on it," said Martin.

Stewart took Martin straight to Herbert's Corner and rolled up alongside the Subaru. Martin handed Stewart all the cash in his wallet and got out. He unlocked his doors as Stewart drove away. Then Stewart backed up and rolled down his window.

"Will it keep you from hijacking semis? If I let you see Linda's stuff?" he asked.

"Scout's honor," said Martin.

"You were never a Boy Scout," said Stewart.

"No, I wasn't."

"Follow me home. I'll give you what I got."

CHAPTER
12

Handwritten on a loose scrap of paper stuck in a worn ring-bound copy of The Iowa Homemaker's Cookbook, published 1956, by the Iowa City First Methodist Church Ladies' Circle.

Mom's Pie

Fill
4 c chopped rhu
¾ c sugar
2 Tbsp flour
Crust
3 c flour
1 c Crisco
1 c cold water and crushed ice
1 tsp salt
Sugar and cin to sprinkle on top
425 for 15 min, 350 for 35 min

Martin held the piece of paper up to his living room lamp, flipped it over, even inspected the edge. It had the ragged top and green tint of a page torn from a steno pad. The author, presumably Linda, had used a blue ballpoint pen. Her scrawled handwriting was hurried, unheeding of the lines, as if written for herself, and not for the pastor's wife to include in the church cookbook.

Martin had dug through the entire Black Velvet box, and this was the only thing that came close. Nothing in the box of recipe cards, nothing in any of the cookbooks, nothing even on that scrap could turn a non-pie maker into Mrs. Smith overnight.

Why had Linda even written this down, only to tuck it into a book full of recipes for covered hot dishes, potatoes au gratin, meatballs, and Jell-O salads? Surely she wouldn't have needed the recipe. She could probably have made this pie easier than he could pour milk on Frosted Flakes. Cheryl hadn't followed a written recipe. She had gone from garden to pie—filling in from memory all the technical details of its fabrication that this scrap of paper left out. She'd had the tools at hand.

Martin considered his own kitchen. His oven had never cooked more than frozen pizza and chocolate chip cookies from a tube. Rolling pin? No. Measuring cups? Doubtful. Knives? He had a couple that could probably cut it—rimshot. He had Cheryl's pie plate, clean and empty, never returned, waiting on her kitchen towel, laundered and neatly folded.

♪ ♪ ♪

"No, we don't have that," said a Walmart worker emptying a box of bagged lettuce. "Don't know that we've ever carried it."

Martin studied his cart. Flour, Crisco, sugar, cinnamon, a rolling pin, and measuring cups. Salt and ice he had at home.

"Try Albertsons," said the worker.

Martin thanked him and almost abandoned his cart.

Beep. "Making a pie?" asked the cashier. Beep.

"Trying to," said Martin. Beep. "You don't know where I could find some rhubarb, do you?" Beep.

"What's rhubarb?" asked the cashier. Beep.

At Albertsons, a produce stocker spent several minutes in the back, then returned with a shake of his head. "You should try the farmer's market on Saturday," he said.

"I need some tonight," said Martin.

"I don't know what to tell you," said the stocker.

At home, Martin set his bags on the counter next to Cheryl's pie plate. He opened the freezer, took out a pint of Brownie Batter Ben and Jerry's, found a clean spoon, and collapsed on his couch.

He pushed aside the cookbooks to make room for his feet on the coffee table. All those recipes. All those hours spent perfecting dishes to share with the church ladies' circle. And what could he do? Burn frozen pizzas and epically fail to buy ingredients for a simple pie. The only person who could have taught him was Cheryl. He remembered her hands in the floury mixture, rolling the dough with those deft strokes, and crimping the crust. He could probably figure it out, but there was no time for a learning curve. She was the only one, thought Martin, and then stopped with a spoonful of ice cream halfway to his gaping mouth.

♪ ♪ ♪

"In example after example, we find that ancient cultures revered water for its healing properties. I don't think it's any accident that the Greeks associated Mnemosyne, the muse of memory, with a pool of remembering. Long before the Greeks, the ancients knew that water from certain sources healed, restored, and brought life. These carvings that have recently been unearthed in Syria clearly show ancient visitors preparing, offering, and administering water to humans."

"Do you have pictures of these carvings up on the web for the audience to see?"

"We don't yet, but we're working on it."

"We'll put a link on wakernation.com when those come available. Now, do you think that the visitors—extraterrestrials, if I'm to understand your assertion?"

"That's correct."

"Do you think the extraterrestrials simply exploited local, Earthly water sources with healing properties? Or did they add something to the water to create these elixirs?"

"That's an excellent question, Lee. And it's an issue to which we are devoting a great deal of time. If it is true that certain elements in these springs and water sources have naturally occurring healing properties, that's an amazing discovery and a real validation for the homeopathic community. What a wonder to have Gaia herself confirm what we've witnessed so many times before. On the other hand, if the visitors used homeopathic techniques, and added their own compounds to the water, that's also very significant. It means that certain sites, like Lourdes, Bethesda, Chilca, the Ganges, and many others were perhaps seeded with healing compounds by the visitors. We may be able to reconstruct these alien elixirs from the water's own memory."

"We're up against a hard break, but when we come back, Sandy, I'd like to hear how, exactly, you read the memory of water."

"I'll be happy to stay with you, Lee."

"Great. Wakers, we may not know the secret ingredient for the alien elixirs yet, but I have the ingredient to heal your portfolio. Gold. Now, I've been investing in gold through TheYellowHoard. com for several years now, and I can tell you…"

※ ※ ※

"No need to get your gun, Doris. It's Martin Wells. I came the other night with Eileen."

Doris answered the door in her housecoat and shotgun.

" 'Don't get your gun,' " she said. "You think I'm a fool?"

"I need to talk to you about the pie recipe. And…"

"And what?"

"I wondered if you could teach me to bake a pie." She raised the barrels, and he put up his hands. "I've got all the ingredients in my car. Except the rhubarb."

"Well, get 'em and get in here 'fore all the bugs do," she said.

Doris didn't put her gun aside until Martin set his Walmart purchases on her kitchen table. She peeked in the bags and said, "You keep comin' around in the middle of the night, people gonna talk."

"I'm sorry to impose, but Eileen said you stay up late. I'm a big BI fan, too."

"So, you're gonna try your hand at the pie?" Doris asked.

"If they abducted Cheryl for the recipe, the best way to get her back is to give it to them. Maybe then they'll leave everyone alone."

"Bring those muscles of yours," said Doris. She shuffled across her living room, down a dark hall, and into a sparsely furnished guest bedroom. She slid open the closet and pointed to a footlocker. Martin carried it out to the living room.

From her easy chair, Doris opened the clasps and lifted the lid. Martin got a whiff of ancient mothballs. She extracted several manila envelopes, a pile of stiff lace doilies, and a few photo albums, handing them all to Martin to set on the coffee table. Then she presented him with a little black book.

"That's the pie diary," she said. "From 1986 through 1992, I baked pies every day I could get good rhubarb. Tried to do it like Linda each time, but changed a little bit of this, a little bit of that.

Kept track real scientific-like. I'd seen her and Margie make 'em hundreds of times. You'd think I'd have gotten it, but I never did."

Martin thumbed through the diary. More sugar, less rhubarb, cinnamon in the filling, only red-skinned rhubarb, only the green, crusts baked separately from the filling, a wide range of times and temperatures. First one variable, then combinations. Then she'd tried odd ingredients. Carbonated water. Pineapple juice. Brown sugar. Maple syrup. Crystal Pepsi.

"This is incredible," said Martin.

"There were a couple other gals tried it some, too, but don't worry 'bout poundin' on their doors tonight. You'll be knocking on headstones."

"None of these worked?" asked Martin. "How did you know?"

"Oh, Herbert had introduced me to some regulars. They'd taste 'em for me."

"Can I borrow this?" asked Martin.

"I don't have much more use for it," said Doris. "But if it makes you rich, you count me right in for half."

"I promise," said Martin.

"Let's make a pie," she said, and slapped his knee, hard.

"I don't have any rhu…" Martin began, but Doris waved him off.

"Oh, I got rhubarb coming out my ears. Cut from the same plants Linda grew."

As Doris held the flashlight, Martin cut the stalks exactly as she commanded. She started barking out orders even as she hauled herself up her steps and back into the house. No Hell's Kitchen wannabe chef would have left Doris's kitchen without deep emotional scars.

Doris slapped Martin's hand away from the knife as he

chopped the rhubarb. "Didn't your pappy teach you how to hold a knife?" she scolded.

"I've seen those Ginsu infomercials," said Martin.

She pointed the tip of the knife at his nose. "You gonna backtalk, you can get out right now," she said.

Martin had to measure everything exactly right, which was to say not at all. "Linda Laughlin never used a measuring cup in her whole life, and you ain't gonna either," said Doris. "Now, feel the weight of that, pour it back in there, and try again."

Martin kneaded the wet dough like a sissy-man. He used a rolling pin like a deficient chimpanzee. He handled the crusts like Jimmy Carter. This he didn't understand, but her tone suggested that it wasn't a compliment.

"God gave you fingers, didn't he? Why don't you use 'em for something other than pickin' your nose?" she scolded, making him recrimp the edge.

Martin set the pie in the oven, closed the door, and flopped into a kitchen chair. Doris took one can of Rolling Rock from the refrigerator, popped the tab, and said, "This kitchen ain't gonna clean itself, boy."

With more than half an hour left on the second bake, Martin folded a faded kitchen towel, embroidered with a crowing rooster, and set it on the counter.

Doris rocked in her recliner, listening to Lee Danvers interview an anonymous intelligence officer about UFO sightings near the HAARP antenna in Alaska.

"Do you mind if I take a look?" Martin asked, pointing to the stack of photo albums on the coffee table.

"Go ahead," said Doris.

The first album was filled with aunts, great-grandfathers, cousins in Army uniforms, babies in their baptismal finery, women in horn-rimmed glasses, and men wishing they were fishing in

Norman Rockwell paintings. In the second book, shaggy-haired dudes leaned on muscle cars, three cousins in Toughskins rode one shaggy horse, women in bell-bottoms visited Carlsbad, and Herbert's Corner held a company picnic. Summer 1983, according to the hand-painted banner strung between two cottonwoods behind the picnic tables.

"Is this Linda?" Martin asked. Doris leaned forward.

"Looks just like Cheryl, don't she?" said Doris. "Used to think for a while that it was her everyone came for, not the pie."

"She looks sad," said Martin.

"Eighty-three? Margie, her mother, had passed not too long before, I recall," said Doris. "And there's me. I was pretty hot stuff, even standing next to Linda. I had my share of indecent proposals over the years. Don't mind sayin'. You'd hit that, wouldn't you? Isn't that what they say these days?"

Martin laughed. "Is that what they say?"

Doris chewed her lips and turned the page. Then another. "Here we go," she said, tapping a page of shots of Linda and others in a kitchen. "That other one's Corrie. She didn't last too long." Evidence of baking surrounded them, but nothing hinted at a secret ingredient. Linda had a smudge of flour on one cheek.

"Is that Herbert Stamper?" Martin asked. A pear-shaped man with thin hair combed over a spotted scalp had joined the women for one of the shots. He wore a pair of thick, black sunglasses, the kind that fit over prescription glasses. Martin felt a chill. Stewart had worn ones just like them at dinner and again in his apartment. Indoors. After dark. "Eileen told me that you think Herbert was an alien," said Martin.

"Think? Woman don't share a bed with a man for ten years and not know something like that," Doris replied.

"So he was?"

"Well, of course he was. How do you think he knew all about them?" said Doris.

"Those sunglasses. Did he wear them all the time?" Martin asked.

"Never went without 'em. That's how he could see who was and who weren't like him. I told him they made him look like Truman Capote, but he never worried about appearances."

"What happened to the glasses after he died?"

"Why?"

"If it's alien technology…" said Martin. Maybe Stewart got ahold of them somehow.

"I have 'em," said Doris. "But they don't work anymore. They got all busted up when he was attacked. They knew to stomp on 'em."

"You don't think he was killed in a robbery?" asked Martin.

"Never did," said Doris. "But what can you tell the sheriff? He ain't gonna put down the truth in no report."

"I'm sorry," said Martin.

"Long time ago," said Doris.

"Do you have any more pictures of the kitchen, them baking pies?"

"Maybe a few," said Doris. She pointed and snapped her fingers at an album still in the trunk. Martin handed it to her.

"That's Linda with her hand in the dough. That's Margie, her mom, there next to Herbert." Margie, shriveled from years of smoking and work, stood proudly behind an enormous pile of leafy, fresh-cut rhubarb. "First pies of the season. I don't know what year. Late seventies, I'd guess."

"Didn't they ever stop smoking?" Martin asked. Both Margie and Linda had cigarettes dangling from their lips.

"Never," said Doris. "I used to warn 'em that those things would put them in an early grave. Look at me now. Was I wrong?

Both them gals died of the cancer. I'm lucky I didn't get it from all the secondhand fumes I breathed in over the years. Wish they had the smoking bans back then."

"Weren't there Health Department rules or something?" Martin asked.

"Health Department? In Brixton? Herbert hated the smoke, too. It'd make him wheeze and cough. I told him a thousand times to make them quit, or at least take it outside, but those gals were his golden goose. They could do no wrong."

Martin stood, staring a million miles through Doris.

"Restroom's that way," she said.

"No," said Martin. "Book."

"Book?"

"Black book," said Martin. He found it on the table with the Walmart bags.

"What's gotten into you?"

He leafed through its pages, and managed to speak. "Did you ever…?"

"Out with it already, before they publish my obituary," said Doris.

"Smoke?" asked Martin.

"I told you. I never smoked a coffin nail in my life," said Doris.

"But don't you see? They did. You said they always smoked. They smoked while they baked the pies."

"You don't think…?"

"What else could it be?" asked Martin.

"Now, why didn't I ever think of that?" asked Doris.

CHAPTER
13

Gary didn't look up from his *Soldier of Fortune* magazine until Martin cleared his throat. "You? Out harassing truckers again?" Gary asked from his stool.

"I need to buy some cigarettes," said Martin.

"You don't smoke," said Gary.

"I'm looking to start," said Martin.

"Start? People don't start smoking. Is this another phase of your spiral into complete lunacy?"

"Look, Gary, are you going to help me or not?" Martin checked over his shoulder for Eileen.

Gary tossed his magazine on the back counter with a sigh and slid off his stool. He bellied up to the counter, framing himself in front of a hundred choices on the back wall. Red, green, blue, white, brown, yellow, black, lites, menthols, 100s, naturals, filterless, slims. Stacked like a wall of Lego bricks. Martin wondered how he'd choose if he really had wanted to start smoking. One pack of each to find his favorite? Did taste actually matter, or something else? Should he pick the brand least likely to get him beaten up in the nearest bar? Should he pick the one with the advertising model that best fit his demographic? Was he Kool? Did he belong in Marlboro Country? Did he have American Spirit? Or—why a Camel, exactly?

"Okay, first-timer, what kind do you want?"

Martin held out one of the pictures from Doris's photo albums and pointed to Linda's face. "This kind," said Martin.

Gary snatched the picture. "Who's that?" he asked.

"She's dead," said Martin. "The cigarette."

"Just 'cause I sell them, I'm supposed to be some kind of expert?"

"Come on," said Martin.

"Fine," said Gary. He tossed the picture on the counter. "It's your funeral. Those would be Pall Mall. You can tell because the filters aren't tinted; there's the stripe and logo."

"You're sure?" asked Martin. "It's an old picture. You think they looked like that in the eighties?" Gary glared under his brow. "Fine, a pack of Pall Malls. The most normal kind."

Without looking, Gary reached back, selected a pack, and dropped it on the counter. Under the shiny wrapper, it glittered as red and gold as Christmas. "Anything else? And before you ask, no, I do not know any crystal meth dealers."

"Just that," said Martin.

Gary plucked a little blue tube with a chrome top from a flimsy cardboard rack in front of the till and set it on the pack. "I assume you'll need one of these," he said.

"Is there anything else I need?" asked Martin. "Never done this before."

"Cigarettes. Over eighteen. Lighter. Death wish. I think you're good to go," said Gary.

Martin slapped a bill on the counter. Gary handed him the change. Martin dropped the coins in the take-a-penny bowl.

"Oh, thanks," said Gary.

"Any way I could ask you not to mention this to Eileen?" asked Martin. Gary smiled, but not in any kind of pleasant way. Martin put another bill on the counter, but kept his hand on it. "Please."

Gary smirked at the paltry bribe. Martin retracted the offer.

The Pall Malls somehow seemed no more deadly than all the candy, gum, snacks, beer, energy drinks, and packaged foods peddled in front of the counter—and definitely more honest. Instead of "Nutrition Facts," the pack displayed an easy-to-read label warning him of his imminent demise. Twisted, government-mandated candor—the clause that refreshes.

"You have a good night now," called Gary.

♪ ♪ ♪

"So how would this work?" Martin asked.

"You tell me. This is your harebrained scheme," said Doris.

"I think one of us should smoke the whole time, very near the whole process," said Martin.

"Well, don't look at me," said Doris. "If anyone's doing any smokin', it's gonna be you."

"You're sure you're okay with smoking in here?"

"Won't be the first time," said Doris. "Besides, I want to be here if this works."

"Okay, but I think you should do most of the baking. The pie should be as authentic as possible."

"Deal," said Doris.

"Ready?" asked Martin.

"Quit your stallin' and light up already."

Martin tore away the cellophane. He tamped the pack against his palm, sure he'd seen people do that before. He opened the hinged lid and gave the pack a little shake. One cigarette put its head up a little higher than the others. Martin sealed its fate and put it between his lips. One easy strike on the lighter, and he got a flame. He touched the fire to the tip of the cigarette, got a little flare, then smoke.

"Try again. You gotta suck in a little, give the tobacco some air," said Doris.

Martin lit it again, and this time got a mouthful of acrid smoke. He coughed and his eyes watered.

"That's it," said Doris.

"Wonderful," choked Martin, checking the smoldering tip. "Are you going to start?"

"I'll get started after you do. Come on. Obama's in the White House, not Clinton. I guarantee you that Linda and Margie both inhaled."

Martin took a deep breath, exhaled, and then drew a lung-ful through the cigarette. He expected nausea and barfing—the usual after-school-special consequences—but the smoke arrived surprisingly easily. Martin felt an instant sort of buzz, but he couldn't call it pleasing. More like oxygen deprivation.

"Bake fast," he said. And a few minutes later, he found himself cutting rhubarb in the dark, a cigarette dangling from his lips. Worst Steinbeck novel ever.

♪ ♪ ♪

The pie cooled on Doris's counter as the first light of a new day crept through the kitchen window.

"One more," she said.

Martin groaned. He had already kicked his eight-cigarette-a-pie habit after retching onto Doris's driveway forty-five minutes ago.

"You never know," she said. "It could need to happen now,

blend with the steam, work its way into those bubbles in the vent…"

Martin lit one more. He sucked the smoke down his raw throat into his swollen, resistant lungs, and then exhaled onto the pie, as he had during every other step. His smoky breath had been stirred with the filling, kneaded into the dough, even blown under the top crust before Doris crimped it shut. He took a second puff, then a third. He couldn't feel his face.

He stubbed the vile thing out among the ashes and wreckage of its martyred brethren in a heavy amber glass ashtray. "That's enough," he said. She chewed her lips for a moment, then agreed.

"You think we did it?" she asked.

"Are there any other variables we might have forgotten?" asked Martin.

"I woulda said we should make it in the kitchen at the Corner, but they took out the bakery back during the remodel."

"The flour, the water? Maybe Crisco changed their formula?"

"They used all kinds of flours, different brands of sugar. Herbert'd buy rhubarb from anyone. That's why everyone's still got it in their gardens around here. There wasn't nothin' consistent about them."

"What was consistent?" asked Martin.

"Margie and Linda. And I suppose the smoke," said Doris. She grabbed his upper arm with a hard grip. "Boy, you might just have saved Cheryl. Except how're we going to test it? You gonna chase down another trucker? Highway Patrol been told to keep an eye out for you."

"I don't think we need to do that," said Martin.

🥧 🥧 🥧

Martin offered Doris a hand up the front steps, but she slapped it away.

"Don't you drop them pies," she said.

Martin knocked. After a long minute, Stewart answered the door. "Martin. Doris," he said. He glared at the objects, covered with kitchen towels, in Martin's arms. "What can I do for you?"

"Smells like you're makin' coffee," said Doris.

"So what?" asked Stewart.

"Well, invite us in already, you old goat," said Doris, and pushed past Martin.

"By all means," said Stewart, getting out of her way.

A few moments later, Doris cut into the first pie. She set a slice on a paper plate and put it on the table in front of Stewart.

"I don't know what this is all about," said Stewart.

"Try the damned pie," said Doris.

"You can drop the charade," said Martin.

"I don't know what you're talking about," said Stewart. Doris handed him a fork.

After a quick, falsely thoughtful chew, Stewart said, "Rhubarb pie."

Doris cut a piece from the other pie, slid it onto a fresh plate, and handed him a fresh fork.

Stewart took the next bite just as skeptically, but before he swallowed, Martin thought he detected a tiny tremor, the slightest tilt of the man's head. Stewart cleared his mouth with his tongue and said, "They taste the same."

Doris checked Martin and then pursed her lips at Stewart. "Thought we had it," she said. "Or maybe the boy's wrong about you."

"Or maybe both," said Stewart. "You remember when I was born, Doris Solberg. Now you think I'm like Herbert?"

Doris shook her head. "He had me convinced," she said.

"You knew Herbert was an alien?" asked Martin.

" 'Course," said Stewart. "Most everyone knew. Though some chose to pretend otherwise. Why did you think I was?"

"The sunglasses you wore in my apartment the other night. Herbert Stamper wore a pair just like them to identify aliens," said Martin.

"Don't know why that'd make me one," said Stewart. He waggled his prescription glasses over his nose. "Sensitive eyes."

"Well, this is a bust. And it's way past my bedtime." Doris grabbed Martin's forearm in another bony vulture grip. "Take me home, young man."

"Take your pies with you," said Stewart.

"You keep 'em," said Doris. "Doctor's doing a poor job of keeping me off sugar as it is."

"You know I don't care for it much. Not since Linda passed," said Stewart. "I guess they're yours," he said to Martin.

⚲ ⚲ ⚲

The day had more than officially begun as Martin rolled through Brixton below the speed limit. Doris had been dropped off at home, and the pies and the pack of cigarettes sat in the passenger seat in her stead. One pie was as normal as a rhubarb pie could be. The other could be Cheryl's salvation. He may have been wrong about Stewart, but the jury was still out on the cigarettes. Martin coughed, and phlegm scraped at his trachea. His lungs felt like a hippo with a bottlebrush had sat on his chest for an hour.

He put on his blinker as he neared the junction. He should have left Billings an hour ago to get to his day's calls. Another day of binning screws, sorting nails, assuaging complaints from assistant managers, and driving. More driving. Over roads he'd traveled a hundred times. Probably more.

From the FastNCo. procedural manual for area representatives who find their lives, beliefs, purpose, and health in utter shambles and haven't had anything to eat in the past twelve hours but ice cream and cigarettes:

1. "Hi, Rick…yeah, I know. Not feeling very good. Bad cold or flu or something. Felt it coming on yesterday, but thought I was going to be able to shake it. I was up all night. Won't go into the details. But I don't think I'm going to be able to make my appointments today…Yeah. I'm calling them right after I talk to you…Hopefully tomorrow…Send a revised schedule, check. Writing it down…Thanks, Rick."

He hung a U-turn in front of Herbert's Corner. The Brixton Inn was three minutes away. If he checked in now, maybe he could get a waffle before crashing.

PART II

1986

They arrived in two identical black cars.

The tires rolled silently across gravel. The engines' hum blended with the breeze and the insects. They traveled dark, no headlights, no brake lights, no glow from the dashboards. The cars braked in unison, and three figures emerged. As they gathered on the road, wind and moonlight passed right through them and continued on their way across the prairie.

A dog barked in the distance.

Though silent as shadows, they strode awkwardly, as if unaccustomed to the ground beneath their feet. After they wobbled across the cattle guard, one tapped at a device on his wrist, compelling the only potential witness to fall asleep in front of a late-night movie. A half-drunk beer fell to the floor and dribbled onto the carpet. The others nearby, already asleep, moved into a dreamless state.

The three beings turned into the third driveway on the left, mounted a little porch, and entered a trailer. One located a set of keys on the kitchen counter, acknowledged the others, and left. He backed the Ford Pinto out of the driveway and drove away. The night fell quiet again.

They found her in bed. One being set an object on her forehead. After a moment, it melted, sending insectile tendrils trickling around her ears and through her hair. Her body stiffened as if in pain, and her breath shortened. Her mouth opened in silent terror, and then she relaxed.

They pulled back the covers.

"She's naked," said one.

"So?" said the other.

"So, we can't take her naked. She'll get cold."

"What do you suggest?"

"I don't know. This is the first time I've ever done this."

"Oh, and I'm an expert? Come on, I'll get her legs."

"Wait," said the first being. He opened a couple of drawers and found a flannel nightgown. The second checked the time and sighed. "Help me," said the first.

Together, they yanked her up like a rag doll. The first gathered up the nightgown and fit her head through the neck. They each wrestled an arm into a sleeve, and then she flopped back onto the bed.

"Are you happy now? Can we get on with it?" said the second. "She stinks really bad."

"I think it's because she smokes," said the first, tugging the gown down.

"That wasn't in the dossier," said the second.

"So what?" asked the first.

"How can they breathe those toxins into their bodies?"

"I don't get it either, but shut up. It doesn't matter," said the first.

Her hips and elbows banged against the doorframe and the walls as they carried her down the narrow mobile home hallway.

"Watch it," said the first.

"Give me a break," said the second. "She's slippery."

Her legs slumped on the floor as the second opened the front door.

"I can't believe they're this heavy," said the second as they shuffled down the driveway.

"Quit complaining; we're earning our bonus," said the first.

"If you have to work for it, it's not really a bonus, is it?"

The first stumbled on the cattle guard and lost his grip on the woman. Her bare bottom fell onto the cold metal grating. She moaned, and the second being fell forward, folding her in half and cursing as he caught himself.

A minute later, they had her in the trunk of one of the black cars. As per the plan, the first being watched the car go and then returned to the mobile home. He searched the kitchen and thought he had found what they had come for—but realized immediately that the scrap of paper contained no new information. He tucked it back into the flimsy book where he'd found it and continued looking. He dug through every cupboard and every drawer, checked every container in the refrigerator, and even pawed through the refuse receptacle. He searched the shelves and cabinets in the living room, flipped through every book and magazine, and examined every object. He checked the time before he rummaged through the hall closet. The neighbors' sleep induction would be wearing off soon.

As he searched the dresser in the tiny second bedroom, he sensed a presence. A brush, a breath, something alive. He froze, trying to recall anything in the dossier about an animal. The woman was supposed to be here alone.

A dangling art object of crescent moons and pointed stars hung over a piece of furniture—a miniature bed with four high sides. He edged forward, drawing his weapon. He peered into the bed to find a tiny, pudgy human. Two arms. Two legs. Nearly bald. Eyes closed. Its chest rose and fell in a gentle rhythm. It was so small, so helpless. It jerked an arm and grunted, and he nearly pulled the trigger in surprise. He put the weapon away. Why did they even issue me this? he wondered. He barely knew how to use it.

What would happen when this infant woke, probably needing food or mental stimulation? From what he knew of humans, he guessed it would make noise. If that noise led the neighbors here, and they found it alone, it would undermine the cover story set up by the handwritten resignation letter on her boss's desk and the notes to the other waitresses, already in place. He suspected that a human mother wouldn't abandon her child on a whim. At least her messages would have made some mention of it, begging another to take over its care, or providing some apology.

He checked the time again. Someone might already have found her farewells. The car would already have been searched and destroyed. The woman already taken off world. Why hadn't the dossier mentioned the infant? Was it an oversight? Sloppy intelligence? Or did they intend for the team to find the little creature and deal with it? He cursed. They had forced him to point his weapon at the innocent thing once. He would not do it again.

A car door slammed. The being froze, listening. Heavy, clumsy footfalls tromped up the steps, and the front door opened.

How had this gone so wrong? the being wondered. He was a product market development analyst, not a soldier. Not a spy. He'd stupidly taken this responsibility, assured of promotion, bonuses, and recognition.

An adult human male passed the second bedroom and continued into the main bedroom, leaving a reek of barley-based alcohol in his wake.

"Hey, sugar lips," the man said in a slurred half-whisper. "Came by for some of that delicious pie you bake up." The being heard cloth handled, two heavy thumps on the floor, and the man snuffing and huffing. "Linda? Hey. Where are you?"

The bedclothes rustled, and then the man stumbled past the second bedroom again, this time wearing only a pair of tight white undershorts. "Linda?" he called into the bathroom. He headed out into the living room and the kitchen, calling for the woman.

Then he returned, filling the doorway of the second bedroom. "Who...?" he said, and crumpled to the floor.

The being stared at the weapon in his hand. When had he drawn it?

He studied the body lying in a grotesque heap in the hall. Who was this man? The dossier about this woman was obviously a botched job. He should never have trusted the work of another department. Some logistics manager had probably handed it to his most worthless flunky and had transmitted it on without even bothering to proofread. But his manager had assured him it would be okay, and had convinced him of the need to expedite the program. No sense delaying the entire product development chain, he had said. They'll get all the relevant information.

All the relevant information except for the part about the male who visits for inebriated nocturnal reproductive liaisons, now deceased, and the still-living likely result of one of those liaisons. The being closed his eyes. He uttered a curse so long, so profane, that he imagined the entire pantheon of old gods coming back from obscurity for this singular chance to be blasphemed.

The infant stirred. The sleep induction had lapsed.

He opened his eyes and decided.

He stepped over the dead human and hauled him onto his back. The man's hair was graying, and he had a bit of a gut. The being held a device over the man and pressed an indentation. Then he rolled the man onto his back and did it again. Then he swore to himself again, less profanely, and pulled the man's underwear off. He repeated the procedure with the device.

The being removed his own clothes. Then he inserted the device into a fold in his dermis. His first humanoid form faded and flickered. The bathroom mirror reported the results. He inspected his new face, ran a human hand over his stubble, and felt his teeth with his tongue. The dangly bit between his legs explained the tight underclothes. His navel suggested a mammalian-style birth. His hair was wispy, but thick enough.

The being dragged the body into the bathroom and wrestled it into the shower. The slumped body was a pathetic thing. Elements that once had life and utility had been rendered a waste. He adjusted the setting on his weapon. No bonus was worth this. The being fired once more, and the body dissolved. He turned on the water and rinsed the nameless man down the drain.

The infant began to squall.

The being dressed in the man's clothes. They fit perfectly, having so recently held his shape, but stank of smoke and fermented grain. He returned to the infant's bed, still working out the belt buckle.

Nothing in his brief training had prepared him to hold this infant, to feel it squirming, to hear its cries. He carried it into the kitchen and attempted to feed it various foods. Bread, a slice of meat, a conical vegetable. He dripped water into its mouth from his fingers, but this only made the infant scream more obstinately.

The being knocked on the neighbors' door. A man in pajamas answered, along with a woman in a nightdress, her hair in roller devices.

"Stewart?" asked the man. "What's going on?"

"I think Linda up and left town," said the being. "With that fellow from California she's been talking about." It was what the letter on Herbert Stamper's desk and all the notes to her coworkers said. "I came over and found a note. She's left"—he held out the child—"and I have no idea what to do with this one."

They invited him in, baby and all.

CHAPTER
14

Martin knew he had been asleep. After breakfast, he'd said goodnight to Vonnie, had asked Brenda to spread the word to everyone to let him be, and had hung the "Do Not Disturb" sign. He shouldn't be awake. Whatever had woken him hadn't been loud enough for him to open his eyes. But he remembered hearing something. A rattling, perhaps. A key sliding into a lock? Had there really been a brief bright light, quickly extinguished?

Suck. Hiss. Wheeze.

Suck. Hiss. Wheeze.

Of course, Martin thought. I should have fastened the chain. And then he rolled over into the barrel of a FastNCo. staple gun.

"Really?" Martin asked with a voice of paste and gravel. "We're going to do this again?"

"I have to," said Stewart.

"I suppose you followed me, and picked the lock, and all that," said Martin, clearing his throat.

"Vonnie leaves her passkey hanging on her cart," said Stewart. Martin scooted up on the bed, pulling the sheet with him.

"I was right about you, wasn't I?" he said. "And I was right about the pie, too."

They both looked at the pies on the table, and Stewart nodded.

"I knew it. Want another slice?" asked Martin.

"I have to do this," said Stewart. The staple gun trembled.

"You don't have to do anything," said Martin. "Besides, what are you going to do? Staple me to the sheets? Can I put on some pants first?"

Martin eased out of bed toward Stewart, forcing him to back up. Stewart bumped into the table and turned for a split second. Martin snatched the stapler and held it away. Stewart growled and lunged, but Martin dodged, and Stewart nearly fell on the bed.

"Sit down before you fall down and can't get up," said Martin.

"You don't know what's at stake," said Stewart.

"It's a stupid rhubarb pie," said Martin.

"You don't understand," Stewart gasped. He collapsed into a chair by the table.

"So where are you from?" asked Martin.

"A long way away," said Stewart.

"What's the next step? Do we call them? Arrange a trade?" asked Martin.

"We can't do that," said Stewart.

"What? Why?"

"And I don't even want to know the secret," said Stewart. He picked up one of the pies and dropped it, foil plate and all, into the trash can behind him. "I don't want to know how you figured it out. Nothing." He dropped the second pie in with the first. "And I'm advising you, right here and now, to forget this, and go back to your life. Walk away now. And never speak of it again." Foam flecks appeared at the corners of his mouth, and he wheezed and sucked air as he spoke.

"It's too late for that, Stewart," said Martin. "If you don't help me, I'll leave a message on Cheryl's phone. I'll hijack more trucks. I'll make as many pies as I need to. We're talking about Cheryl's life here."

"Don't you think I know that? But under no circumstances can you let anyone know that recipe. Not even me."

"You were going to kill me?" asked Martin, and waggled the staple gun. "What about Doris? Were you going to staple her to death, too?"

"If I had to."

"There's no way this pie is worth that."

"You don't understand anything."

"Then explain it to me, Stewart."

He began at the beginning.

🐾 🐾 🐾

Stewart excused himself to use the bathroom, where he had a coughing fit that carried through the thin wall. Several minutes later, he returned to the table as if his oxygen tank weighed on him like Catholic guilt.

"Are you okay?" asked Martin.

"Do I sound okay?" asked Stewart. He set a miniature ping-pong paddle of beveled glass on the table. He tapped the surface several times. Icons and words flashed by, but in no alphabet Martin had ever seen.

"Is that like an iPad?" asked Martin.

"Trust me. It's no iPad," said Stewart.

He scraped at the glass, and a long, narrow plane of light, covered with gibberish, appeared in the air a few inches over the device. Stewart swirled three fingers on the plane, and the markings resolved into a page of English.

INTERNAL MEMORANDUM
XXXXXX Snack Food Company

From: XXXXXXXX, Vice President, Retail Marketing Division

To: XXXXXXXXXX, Director, New Product Development Department

Re: Project Rhubarb

Samples have garnered the highest consumer rating ever for a test product, near 100%. Economic analysis is positive in 95% (+/-3%) of markets. Consumer repurchase probability is near 90% over two XXXXXX in nearly all markets, an unprecedented statistic for a product below the addiction threshold. Therefore, the product has been up-queued for immediate market positioning.

Production procedures and resource allocation plans have been approved and forwarded to Logistics. Fabrication of production facilities is proceeding. Marketing is developing a strategic campaign and has begun design of the packaging and ancillary materials.

Research and Testing has still been unable to recreate the exact formula. It is to be your top priority to obtain this formula from the local environment using all necessary means.

"What is this?" asked Martin.

"It's the death warrant for your species," said Stewart. "You have to know what the terms mean. 'Production' involves setting up processing and baking facilities at strategic locations on your planet. 'Resource allocation' means turning every possible inch of Earth into managed farms for wheat, palm, canola, sugar, cinnamon, and rhubarb."

"That's preposterous. If this is some kind of sick joke…" said Martin.

"I wish this was a joke. A huge amount of money was spent to prepare for this product, and when it didn't deliver according to the timeline, heads rolled. They're still rolling."

"But a whole planet?" asked Martin. "To make pies?"

"Wouldn't be the first time," said Stewart. "A small, productive planet in a minor solar system? No problem."

"But, if you hadn't noticed, there's seven billion people using this planet right now," said Martin.

"Now do you understand why we can't give them this recipe?" said Stewart.

"Then why in the world did you give me all of Linda's cookbooks and stuff?" asked Martin.

"Because I never thought in a million years you'd actually figure it out."

"What happens if they figure it out themselves?" asked Martin.

Stewart threw up his hands. "They've failed so far. We can only hope that they'll eventually cut their losses and abandon the project. But as you read in that memo, the potential for profits is huge, and…never mind."

"Don't you clam up now," said Martin. "Speaking as the sole representative for humanity, I'm a big boy. I can take it."

"That automated production facility has been waiting on the edge of your solar system since 1987," said Stewart. "And the first step of the logistics plan is the atmospheric release of a targeted neurotoxin. Every human would be dead in a matter of hours."

"That's monstrous. Who does that?"

Stewart sighed and continued. "The fabrication facility can't be retasked. It's designed for this job and this job only. That means that they're not going to sell it for scrap, recycle it, or pay to transport it somewhere else. It's waiting up there. All it takes is the press of a button, and it's on its way. Fully automated, completely unrelenting. You won't even have time to ask why. Or who."

"Can't you see that we're sentient?" asked Martin. "I mean, we like rhubarb pie, too."

"Not like this you don't," said Stewart. "And anyway, you're a few measly billion. There are trillions of us on thousands of worlds. You may register as sentient, but no one knows about you. No one will even notice that you're gone, or were ever here. And even if they did, they'd probably consider this pie to be the pinnacle of your species' achievements."

"But you changed your mind about us," said Martin. "Why?"

"I think you know the answer to that."

"Cheryl," said Martin.

"I know it doesn't make sense, given what we planned to do to your planet, but I felt responsible for her."

"So you raised her," said Martin.

"I fell in love with that crying, spitting, drooling, peeing, pooping little thing. So I quit," said Stewart.

"Then why can't you go to them and tell them about us?"

"I'm a nobody, Martin. A low-level marketing functionary. I was on a fast track to management—that's why they picked me to lead the recipe acquisition—but I was never a decision maker. And now? I'm less than a nobody. I'm not part of the company, or any company, now. And if I went back, no one would listen. You have to understand how my people think."

"They're capitalists who eat snack food. How different can they be?" asked Martin.

"I'm sorry," said Stewart.

"So your plan is to sit here and hope they can't figure out the secret recipe? Doris Solberg is an old bat, and I'd never baked a pie in my life until last night, and we figured it out in a few hours."

"What exactly would you suggest we do?" asked Stewart. "If you even hint to them that you have the recipe, you'll be in as much trouble as Cheryl. So go ahead and call them if you want. You'll only have to live with the guilt for a few hours." A rustle of foil and wet plastic came from the trash can—the ruined pies mocking him for all his efforts.

"I barely know her," said Martin.

"What?"

"Cheryl. I don't even know her," said Martin. "That one dinner, a few mornings at the breakfast bar, a few words at the co-op. That's all I have."

"I'm sorry," said Stewart.

"I've been in love with her since almost the first time I saw her, but I don't really know her," said Martin. "I don't know what I'm trying to say."

"If it's any consolation," Stewart said, "I've never approved of any man for Cheryl—not that she needed my approval. But I think I approve of you."

"Thanks," said Martin. "But I can't believe you're just going to give up on her."

"This isn't giving up. I know she'll come back. She may not be the same person who left, but she'll be returned sooner or later. We're going to have to be patient."

"They'll return a single person, but they'll murder an entire species?"

"Company procedure, I'm afraid," Stewart replied.

"Is this why that wormhole, or whatever it is, down on Highway 360 exists? So you can come kill us all to put your snack company in the black?"

"No. The portal's nothing more than an off-ramp. Your solar system is simply another node in the network. My people have been stopping here for centuries." As Stewart spoke, Martin followed his gaze to the staple gun in his hand.

"I'm going to keep this," said Martin. "I'm tired of waking up with it pointed at my head."

"But…" said Stewart.

"No. You want another one, go on down to the co-op. Lester keeps two or three in stock," said Martin.

"Fine," said Stewart. "But be careful with it. Remember what we've talked about here. And don't do anything stupid."

CHAPTER
15

"Lake Havasu City, Arizona. You're Beyond Insomnia with Lee Danvers and guest Marilyn Pringle-Carlson."

"I'll get right to the question. Marilyn, is this the end of the world?"

"I'm sure you get asked that a lot."

"I do, Lee. At almost every talk I give, it's the first question. People feel helpless, dragged along by forces they cannot control. Fear is a natural state. But is it the end of the world? My favorite way to answer that question is to say that it will be the end of the world as we know it. But will it be the cataclysmic apocalypse we see in the movies? No. Caller? Sorry, I didn't get your name."

"This is Sheila."

"Why do you think you're afraid?"

"I been hearing so much about it, and I don't know what to believe. I want to protect my family, but it's so hard with so little information. You'd think the government would put out announcements about how to get ready, but when I see that they aren't, it scares me that maybe there's nothing I can do."

"I in no way want to belittle your fears, Sheila, but I hear worries like yours all the time about the coming alignment. I'm saddened that all the hype tends to breed instead of quell fear. Most people—sorry to say that many of them have been guests on your show, Lee—don't view these calendars through the correct lens. And until you understand the original authors, you can't understand the intent."

"Who were the authors?"

"Before I answer that, I want to look through the lens of who we are now. Our society has been steeped in a culture of Western religions. And those religions—Christianity, Islam, Judaism, and all their offshoots—prophesy an end brought about by their gods as a fulfillment. Those ends are nasty affairs, in which many suffer. Say the phrase 'the end of the world' to most Americans, and they will imagine colossal wars, devastating earthquakes, piles of plague dead, zombies, the sky ripped open. Need I go on? And it's all a bit ironic, because the Western calendar is completely open ended. What are our Westernized minds to make of a calendar with an apparent end?

"But the authors of this calendar did not hold such a bleak outlook on life, nature, or the course of history. They viewed cycles as the natural order of the universe. Lunar cycles, seasonal cycles, solar cycles, cycles of life, death, and rebirth for plants, animals, and people. But—and this is getting to an answer for Sheila—they also observed critical galactic cycles that we are only beginning to relearn as a civilization."

"Why are these galactic cycles important?"

"These calendars demonstrate a sophisticated understanding of the cosmos not possible through direct, unaided observation of the stars. Pre-Olmec cultures first recorded the calendar as an attempt to interpret the universal cycles described to them by visitors. The pre-Olmec people believed these visitor beings were gods, but you and I might have a different name for them."

"In other words, we should read the calendars through the combined perspectives of these visitors—technologically advanced aliens, if you will—and the pre-Olmec culture?"

"Exactly, Lee. And neither held an apocalyptic view of the world. They celebrated the ends of ages, welcomed them, even though each new age brought change and fresh challenges. Sheila, I hope that this can put your mind at ease. I know through my past-life regression that I personally have lived through a similar time in history. When I was Teoronuc, I was a celebrant in the temple. The people were not fearful, but came out to worship and greet the new age. If you want to prepare yourself, prepare yourself for something beautiful, something wonderful."

"That's so great to hear. My husband will be happy. I've been worrying him to death about this. Thank you."

"Thank you, Sheila in Lake Havasu City. I'd like to know more about these galactic cycles, but first, let's go out to the Waker Nation for another call. Billings, Montana, you're Beyond Insomnia."

"Am I on?"

"Yes. Go ahead, caller."

"Oh, I'm so glad I got through. This is Martin."

"Hi, Martin, do you have a question for Marilyn Pringle-Carlson?"

"I don't know. It may be a little off topic, but it is about the end of the world."

"All right. Go ahead."

"You had another guest on a month or so ago who talked about UFO sightings and alien visitation in Brixton, Montana. Do you remember that, Lee?"

"I do."

"I have to tell you that it's all true. And it's still going on. I've talked to these aliens. I've even got video of them arriving. I can show you right where their vehicles appear and disappear."

"What's your question, Martin?"

"I have to warn everyone that some of these aliens are planning on killing everybody and taking over our planet. I didn't know who else to tell. If we do something, we might be able to stop them. Please don't hang up on me. I know how this sounds, but I'm not making this up. Like your guest said, they've been coming to Brixton for years. They eat at the Herbert's Corn…"

"Thank you, Billings, Montana. After this break, we'll be back with more from researcher and former ancient Mesoamerican priest Marilyn Pringle-Carlson."

"Don't hang up," said a voice that was not Lee Danvers.

"Hello?" asked Martin.

"Stay on the line, Billings," said the voice, a young man's. Was this X-Ray, the engineer? "Lee's going into commercial, but he wants to talk to you."

A few seconds later, the line clicked over. "Martin?" asked Lee Danvers.

"Hi?" said Martin.

"Sorry to have to cut you off. It's not that I don't want to hear your story, but I've got to keep the show on topic. Hope you understand. Now, you said you have video of their ships coming and going."

"Well, coming," said Martin.

"And you took this video near Brixton, Montana?"

"About seven miles south," said Martin.

"Are you a professional photographer, videographer, computer graphics specialist, or anything like that?"

"I'm a salesman," said Martin.

"Good. Have you shown this video to anyone? Put it on YouTube? Anything?" asked Lee.

"No," said Martin.

"Excellent, don't. Do you have a pen? I'm going to give you a number. I want you to call it tomorrow. Not tonight. Tomorrow after 9:00 a.m. Eastern time. You're going to ask for Alicia. She's one of my producers. If your video's good, we'll issue you a contract for exclusive rights. It'll get put up on wakernation.com, where everyone can see it, and you might get up to five hundred dollars. How does that sound?"

"I don't care about the video," said Martin. "I'm trying to tell everyone about the…"

"The invasion. Sure."

"It's not an invasion. They're going to extermin…"

"I appreciate you listening, and I'm sorry, but I don't have time to be anything but rude. I get about a dozen alien invasion calls a week. Ring the number in the morning and tell your story to Alicia. If it's worth a segment, we'll get back to you. I've got to get back on the air. Got your pen ready?"

✿ ✿ ✿

The complimentary breakfast at the Lone Pine Inn in Sidney had a different waffle setup than the Brixton Inn. The batter had been pre-poured into little cups and set in a special plastic tray. But no insightful red-and-yellow placard told Martin what to do next. So they don't trust me to dispense my own batter, but they expect me to instinctively know how to operate a griddle? Martin wondered.

As Martin poured his chosen cup of batter into the black grooves, a heavy hand fell on his shoulder. He dropped the cup and had to fish it out of the pooling batter.

"Our man in Sidney," said Jeffrey. "If I'd known you were here last night, I would have given you a call. We could've gone out for a drink or something."

"I got in late, had to park the truck around the back," said Martin.

"I'll bet you did," said Jeffrey.

Two minutes and thirty seconds later, Martin joined Jeffrey at a table. "I never heard from anyone from your company," he said. With everything else going on, Martin had nearly forgotten that Jeffrey had all but offered him his job. "Did your thing in Denver not pan out?"

"You know how these things go; always takes longer than you think," said Jeffrey. Another man wandered into the breakfast room with a USA Today tucked under his arm. Jeffrey waved.

"Morning, Mark," said Jeffrey. Mark was a greeting card guy. Not Hallmark or American Greetings, but folksy sorts of cards. Wacky cowboys, shriveled grannies, and farm animals with their tongues up their noses wishing for you to get well or to have a happy birthday. If you threw a Santa hat, a Bible verse, or few pink hearts on them, the drawings worked for any holiday. A spinning rack of them lived in most Montana stores, never too far from Jeffrey's candy.

Mark gathered his complement of breakfast and joined them.

"Mark, you know Martin. FastNCo.?" said Jeffrey.

"Sure."

"Good to see you again," said Martin.

Mark chewed a bite of donut and swished it down with orange juice, all the while pointing at Martin. "That," he said and finished swallowing, "wasn't you I heard on BI last night?"

"What?" asked Martin.

"No? It's funny you're here, because I thought of you when I heard it. Caller was named Martin. From Billings," said Mark.

"What did he call about?" asked Jeffrey.

"The show was about all the Mayan end-of-the-world junk, but this guy, Martin…"

"Not me," said Martin.

"…goes completely off topic. Starts babbling about how aliens are coming to Brixton—yeah, Brixton, Montana—and how they're going to kill everyone on Earth. Oh, and he has video proof of all of it. Danvers pretty much shut him down."

"You see why I don't listen to that show," said Jeffrey. "Bunch of nutcases. Listen to it long enough, and you start to believe it all, too."

"Too bad Danvers hung up on him. I like it when he lets the kooks on," said Mark.

Martin had tucked his overnight bag behind the driver's seat of his truck when he heard his name. Jeffrey had left the back door of the motel with his own bag.

"You okay?" Jeffrey asked, shading his eyes from the morning sun with his iPad.

"Yeah, why?"

"Not to be rude, but I think maybe Mark had you pegged. Are you calling into Beyond Insomnia now?"

"What do you mean?" asked Martin.

Jeffrey waggled his iPad. "Listened to the podcast of last night's show—the bit Mark told us about, anyway. And it really does sound like you. And it's about Brixton. I know you've been spending some time over there lately."

"What've you heard?"

"I know that girl who baked you a pie left town. And I heard you got arrested for scaring the crap out of a trucker," said Jeffrey. "What's going on, Martin? Are you in some kind of trouble?"

"I'm fine," said Martin. "Wait. How do you know about the pie?"

"What are you talking about? You told me," said Jeffrey.

"I didn't tell anyone," said Martin.

"You told me as we passed each other on Highway 12. Remember? I called you. You told me my driving sucked," said Jeffrey. "It wasn't that long ago. Are you sure you're okay?"

Martin dove into the cab of his truck, brushed a couple of paper bags from yesterday's meals onto the floor of the passenger seat, found what he needed, and slid back out onto his feet.

"Hey, whoa, FastNCo. issue a permit for that thing?" Jeffrey laughed.

Martin kept the staple gun pointed at the ground. "Who else did you tell?" he asked.

"About what?"

"About me and Cheryl? About the pie?"

"Are you off your medication?"

"Who did you tell?"

"No one. What's the big deal?"

Martin raised the staple gun. "Where is she, Jeffrey? Or whoever you are?"

"Holy crap, that was you on the show," said Jeffrey.

"She doesn't know anything," said Martin.

"And you are nuts."

"Don't move," said Martin.

"You're delusional," said Jeffrey, not stopping. "That's a staple gun. I can see the FastNCo. logo on the side."

"Then why are you backing away?" asked Martin.

"I'm leaving now. Stay away from me."

Martin aimed just to Jeffrey's right and squeezed the trigger handle. The staple gun clicked and popped like a staple gun should and, as if coincidentally, the trash can by the back door of the motel exploded.

Jeffrey stumbled away from the shower of shrapnel. Martin felt a brief, hot concussion, and debris peppered the back of the truck. The staple gun still felt perfectly normal.

Jeffrey straightened, unhurt but changed. No more indignation and false fear. His eyes were no longer casual, lying things, but sinister, focused.

The desk clerk burst out the back door and swore at the wreckage.

Jeffrey bolted.

"Hey," the desk clerk called.

Martin tossed the staple gun into the truck and chased Jeffrey around the side of the building in time to see him dodge between two cars. A few seconds later, the Lincoln Town Car lurched out. Its tires squealed as it braked, then again as it raced forward. As it bounced out onto the street, a pickup truck slammed on its brakes and skidded sideways.

Martin stayed in town long enough to give both the fire chief and the sheriff Jeffrey's full description. He told everyone how he had witnessed Jeffrey drop an object into the trash can a few moments before it exploded. Homeland Security FBI types liked to hunt mad bombers, didn't they?

CHAPTER
16

The truck's headlights swept across an all-too-familiar Buick Skylark parked on the street outside Martin's apartment building. His apartment was dark and locked, but that didn't keep Martin from saying, "Make yourself at home, why don't you, Stewart?" before flipping on a light.

"Where the hell have you been?" Stewart asked from the recliner. A wind-up radio, Lee Danvers recommended, played BI at a whisper on his lap.

"Trying not to lose my job," said Martin.

"What was the last thing I said to you?"

"Just say what you have to say," said Martin. "It's late, and I've been on the road for three days."

"I told you not to do anything stupid," said Stewart. "What possessed you to call the show?"

"I don't know. Maybe I'm not content to sit on my ass while your friends kidnap my girlfriend and exterminate my species."

"She wasn't your girlfriend," said Stewart.

"Oh, fine, let's argue semantics right now," said Martin. He tossed his bag in his bedroom and called, "Have you been sleeping here?"

"I couldn't stay home, and you didn't come back," said Stewart.

"Get out," said Martin.

"They monitor the show, Martin. And it's not going to take them long to figure out how you learned about the production plan. They left me alone as long as I kept my mouth shut. But now…"

"So you came here?" asked Martin. "It probably won't take them long to figure out where you went. In fact, I ran into one of them a couple of days ago."

Stewart furrowed his brow. "Who?"

"A candy salesman named Jeffrey Scarborough. He was in Sidney the morning after I called the show."

"Why do you think he's…one like me?"

"Because he's the only one I told about Cheryl baking me a pie before she disappeared. I'd forgotten I even mentioned it to him. He drives all over the state, knows every little diner, bakery, breakfast joint everywhere. Always seems to be in Brixton. And you should have seen the look he gave me after I shot at him."

"You shot him?"

"I fired a warning shot with your little staple gun."

"What happened?"

"A trash can blew up," said Martin. "After that, he pretty much gave up the pretense."

"You better get packed," said Stewart, waving Martin back toward his bedroom. "It's not safe here."

"Forget it," said Martin. "Besides, I'm a crackpot. Lee Danvers wouldn't even believe me. You know what he said? He told me he hears a dozen alien invasion stories a week. I even told the gist of it to a producer of his. Don't worry, I didn't mention you or Cheryl or the pie. She thought I was crazy, too. But she heard me out because they wanted to buy my video before I put it on YouTube."

"What video?"

"I got a rough shot of a truck, or ship, or whatever coming through the gap thingy, down on Highway 360," said Martin.

"Did you give them this video?"

"Emailed it this morning. They're paying me five hundred dollars for it," said Martin. "But do you see what I'm saying? I'm no threat to your friends, even if I know their preposterous plan. No one's going to take me seriously. It's not like the Pentagon's going to nuke Highway 360 on the word of a Waker."

"That's why no one will care when you disappear," said Stewart. "I used to be one of them, Martin. I know how they think. There may be a thousand other nutcases out there, but you're the one with the right information. They won't want to risk anything."

"They let you live here as a human," said Martin. "Why risk that?"

"You don't think I've asked myself that a million times?" asked Stewart.

"You aren't some kind of deep cover agent, are you?"

"I could have already told them about you," said Stewart. "You'd be out there with Cheryl right now."

"You know where she is?"

"If I had to guess, I'd say she's out on the production facility."

"And where is that?"

"Through the portal," said Stewart. "Out in the Kuiper Belt."

"The what?"

"That's what your astronomers call a big ring of small icy bodies outside Neptune's orbit," said Stewart. "There's a minor trans-stellar network branch terminus out there."

"The off-ramp?"

Stewart nodded. "And that's where you'll go if you don't get packed and get the hell out of here with me."

"I'm not leaving," said Martin. "If they want me, they'll get me one way or another. Now, I'm going to take a shower. Then I'm going to drink a beer while I upload my orders, if you haven't been raiding my fridge, too. And then I'm going to get some sleep. We can talk about this in the morning."

Stewart gave his radio a few cranks and turned it up. Martin found two beers still in the fridge. He took both back to the bedroom with his laptop.

Half an hour later, Martin closed the bedroom door to fall into bed, but he stopped on a sigh. He dug a spare pillow and blanket out of the closet and tossed them onto the living room couch. "You take the bed, Stewart," he said.

As Stewart used the bathroom, Martin snuck down to the truck and found the staple gun. "Say hello to my little friend," he said as he settled in on the couch. An hour later, the front door remained unmolested, and down the hall, the tinny mumble of Stewart's radio clicked off.

🐾 🐾 🐾

Martin awoke with a sore back and the hope that the last few days were nothing more than a late-night-spicy-burrito-induced hallucination. But he still had the FastNCo. staple gun that didn't fire FastNCo. staples. And none of the memories had faded like dreams should. Nope, they were as real as the coughing and wheezing old man who took his own sweet time in the bathroom.

"I'm really not supposed to have passengers," Martin said as he dug Stewart's spare oxygen tanks out of the Skylark's trunk.

"So, if anyone asks, you're my uncle and you got kicked out of your assisted-living place for groping one too many nurses."

"Who's going to ask?"

"I'm just saying I'm not real comfortable with this," said Martin. Stewart started to reply, but Martin cut him off. "Right. I know. It's better if we stick together until this blows over."

"I was only going to offer to buy breakfast on the way out of town," said Stewart.

Martin chuckled. "Well, then. Mount up."

With a Croissan'Wich in one hand, the steering wheel in the other, and the staple gun hanging from his belt, Martin merged onto I-90 West. Pixar-perfect clouds salted the expanse of Big Sky. On the southwest horizon, the Beartooth Mountains floated like a chunk of New Zealand had been digitally transported out of the *Lord of the Rings* movies. The fully loaded truck handled sluggishly but soon got up to speed. And for once, the radio stayed off. It had become half armrest, half table, where Martin's cardboard tray of French Toast Sticks waited with the little pack of syrup.

"This is what I do," said Martin. "Ninety percent of my job, right here."

"I had to do a bit of travel for my job," said Stewart. "They'd send me to different planets, and I'd sample the local delicacies, determine which ones had market potential."

"Was it you who found the pie?"

"No," said Stewart. "We heard about it through our distribution division."

"Truck drivers," said Martin.

"You could call them that. The field report and the samples were sent to my division. But they only brought me in when the first formula acquisition attempts failed."

"Why you?"

"It usually wasn't that difficult. Bring a few samples to the lab, and they'd break it down," said Stewart. "But with this pie, we found strange inconsistencies in the samples, and nothing indicated what gave it that kick, that special ingredient that made it so good."

"Is it really that good? It didn't taste any different to me than the other," said Martin. "I tried them both that morning before you threw them in the trash."

Stewart grunted, annoyed, and continued. "It's satisfying and stimulating, and then you crave more right away. I've never eaten anything like it. And of course that's perfect for a snack food and restaurant concern like ours."

"So that's why you figured Linda had some secret," said Martin.

"Not me, but yeah. They couldn't duplicate the pie in the lab. They brought me in to deal with the abduction."

"You'd had experience doing it before?"

"Not really. No one had. There's only a few sentient species out there, and we're the only interstellar travelers that I'm aware of. They brought me in because I'd trained under the last guy who had dealt with primitive species. He had died a few years prior, so I became the go-to guy."

"If there's only a few sentient species, wouldn't the enlightened thing be to keep us alive for study or cooperation or something?"

"Perhaps, if anyone knew about you. But when the explorers and the surveyors, the ones who assembled the network, first came by, your ancestors still lived in trees. And you're not on the beaten path. Almost no one comes out here but independent haulers trying to avoid the tolls on the primary links. The branch terminus, the off-ramp, isn't here for you. The surveyors simply noticed a habitable world in the system that someone might take an interest in someday. And now someone has. But the company's more interested in profits than anthropology."

"Surely there's some government, some rules against this kind of thing," said Martin.

"There's a government," said Stewart. "Run by and for the corporations. File the right forms, and a corporation can do pretty much whatever it wants."

"There's no recourse? I mean, we travel in space. We've sent probes. We have big-ass radio dishes. Can't you give us the coordinates and translate a message for us?"

"You're aware that light has a speed limit?" said Stewart.

"You seem to get around the galaxy pretty quick, so obviously that can be circumvented," said Martin.

"Different principles," said Stewart.

"You don't have a clue how the portal works, do you?"

"Not the faintest."

"But I assume you know how to use it. Help us get up there. Hey, I almost hijacked one truck; I can do it again. Then we'll go plead our case."

Stewart shook his head. "Anything you do risks them pressing that button."

"Maybe we should destroy the portal," said Martin.

"They'd just wait for the network to sense the damage and recalibrate itself on a new target location," said Stewart. "There's nothing special on Highway 360 to destroy. It's just nice and remote. But near the Corner."

Martin dripped syrup on his pants and swore. Stewart dug in a bag and handed Martin a napkin. Martin cleaned himself the best he could, holding a French Toast Stick in his mouth like a cigar. The syrup left a dark stain.

"You have an answer for everything, don't you?" said Martin.

"I've spent every moment of my life as Stewart Campion

trying to figure out how I can stop this. I'm convinced that the only thing we can do is wait."

"Can we make a deal with your corporation? The recipe and a certain amount of land, in exchange for…"

"They would never make any agreement that cut into profits," said Stewart. "And who are you to make that deal?"

"I've got the secret recipe, and without it they make nothing," said Martin.

"Give it to them and they'll delete whatever pact they might have signed with your president or secretary-general, release the neurotoxin, and sleep well that night.

"Your people are jerks," said Martin.

"Not all of us," said Stewart.

♪ ♪ ♪

YAHOO! ANSWERS
Ask! What would you like to ask?

Resolved Question
How do I get to sleep in a cheap motel room shared with the stepfather of the woman I love but haven't established a relationship with, who (the stepfather, not the woman) is an aged extraterrestrial with respiratory problems, while knowing that other aliens might burst in at any moment to at best kill me and at worst torture me for a secret pie recipe and then kill every human on the planet, while individually coiled mattress springs poke me in the back and there's nothing to stop an intruder but a loose doorknob and a flimsy safety chain? Also, I drank about 4 gallons of Diet Mountain Dew today and have to get up early to drive 100 miles for work. And what is that smell?
6 hours ago

Best Answer—chosen by asker
Hahahahahahahaha. Loser. Get a life and stop gunking up teh internets with your stupidness. Sleepin with your girls dad is sick. Go on Jerry Springer. Your worse than Hitler.
2 hours ago
Asker's rating: *****

Other Answers (3)
Are you sure he's an alien? I mean, have you actually seen proof that he's an alien? Pics or it didn't happen.
4 hours ago

You should probably see a doctor, and a psychiatrist, and a psychologist. No offense.
43 minutes ago

Um…you need to read this book… billionbooks.
com/title/5738204/Yates Field Guide to Mushrooms/
review/7198277…I think you've been foraging in the wrong part of the forest, my friend.
3 hours ago

"You look terrible," said Stewart.

"Shut up," Martin replied and poured himself another cup of coffee—the reason he had driven straight to Perkins for breakfast without even asking what Stewart wanted. They put that pitcher of coffee on the end of the table and let you pour your own. No waiting for the waitress. Never an empty cup. And it never seemed to run out. Martin stirred an individual serving of International Delight Hazelnut Creamer into his coffee. The French Vanilla would be next. Then the half-and-half. He felt prepared to slap Stewart's hand away if he tried to take any of them.

The waitress also looked willing to swat Stewart's hand away if necessary.

"Very smooth, Stewart," said Martin, after she had taken their order.

"What?"

"Restaurant servers these days do not like to be ogled, winked at, or called 'sugar.' I don't know how they do things back on your planet, but can you please maintain a low profile here?" said Martin.

"Just playin' my part," said Stewart. "Remember, I'm the guy who got thrown out of his nursing home for grabbing the nurses."

"I take it back," said Martin. "But you're going to put me off my breakfast."

"So I'm required to smile while you leer at my stepdaughter, but you get to throw up if I wink at a pretty waitress who's going to bring me pancakes?"

"I never leered at Cheryl," said Martin.

"Then tell me, how come all of Brixton knew you were after her before anyone but Lester knew your name? Don't tell me to behave myself. At least I have the guts to talk to 'em and look 'em in the eye while I objectify them."

The waitress returned as Stewart spoke, and Martin turned to apologize. But it wasn't the waitress.

"Objectify who?" asked Jeffrey. "Oh, close your mouth. And scoot over, old man."

As Jeffrey slid into the booth, Martin wanted to pull out the staple gun Han Solo style, but Jeffrey narrowed his eyes and gave him a little shake of the head. "Relax. I'm here to talk, and to get some breakfast. Now where's that waitress? She's kind of a perky little thing, isn't she?"

CHAPTER
17

Jeffrey ordered without a menu, and the waitress left, unaware of the tinderbox to which she had just agreed to bring an omelet and a muffin.

"You didn't ask about their pie," said Martin.

Jeffrey sniffed a laugh. "A little early in the day for pie, don't you think?" He poured himself a cup of coffee and helped himself to the French Vanilla creamer.

"How'd you find us?" asked Martin.

"You have a cell phone. The Screwmobile has a locator transmitter. Plus…" He mimed a telephone at his ear. "Hello, random store manager. Setting up my schedule for next week; what would be a good time? Oh, and have you seen Martin Wells from FastNCo.? Been trying to get ahold of him. I owe him some money." He hung up his thumb and pinky finger. "It's not rocket science."

Stewart slipped his sunglasses out of his shirt pocket, put them on, and gave Jeffrey a once-over. "I don't know you," he said.

"No, you don't," said Jeffrey.

"You're my replacement?"

"I'm the one they brought in to fix your mess," said Jeffrey.

"Bang-up job you've done," said Stewart.

"You know, I deserve that," said Jeffrey. "I really do."

"What do you want, Jeffrey? Either bring back Cheryl or get out of here," said Martin.

"Ah. Cheryl."

"She never learned how to make the pie," said Stewart.

"I really want to believe that," said Jeffrey. "But I don't have the luxury to make assumptions."

"You've had her for weeks now," said Martin. "Don't you think she would have told you if she knew?"

"Not necessarily," said Jeffrey. "Not if she knew the production plan. Which given Stewart's apparent willingness to share with just about anyone…. She's such a noble girl. Why wouldn't she resist to save her pathetic species?"

"You bastard," said Martin. Stewart put up a hand.

"What have you done to her?" asked Stewart.

"Phase I and II probes and scans. What? Are you squeamish about that? They weren't kidding when they said you'd gone native. Oh, and she bakes. We set her up a nice little kitchen, with gravity and everything. But we're going to have to ramp up to Phase III soon, if she doesn't give us what we want."

"Can I call him a bastard now?" asked Martin.

"Why? Why move to Phase III so quickly?"

Jeffrey said a word. It sounded like "Chumpdark," but with bits of punctuation and a little squish in it. "I fully intend to hand him the recipe when he arrives."

"Who's this Chumpdark?" asked Martin.

"The CEO," said Stewart.

"The CEO?"

"You understand the term, don't you?" asked Jeffrey.

"Why's he coming here?"

Stewart answered. "Because this project has gone on for too long."

"Something like that," said Jeffrey. "And I don't intend on being the scapegoat."

"Why tell us?" asked Martin.

"What makes you think you're relevant here? I'm talking to the old man."

"Well, out with it then," said Stewart.

The waitress chose that moment to arrive with a tray of everything. Plates of eggs. Plates of hash browns and bacon. Plates of sourdough toast. Plates piled with pancakes. A plate for Jeffrey's enormous muffin. A rack of syrup. Heinz ketchup. Tabasco sauce.

"Can I get you anything else?" she asked.

Jeffrey peeled the paper off his muffin. "I can't say I won't miss eating on this godsforsaken planet. Look at this thing. It's as big as my head. Thanks, sweetheart."

The waitress gathered her tray with an eye roll.

"Out with it," Martin demanded.

"I won't miss the manners. Relax. Eat," said Jeffrey.

"I could shoot you," said Martin.

"Please. Jackie Bauer. This isn't *24*," said Jeffrey.

Martin's glare had no effect, so he unrolled the napkin from his silverware and ate.

A few minutes later, Jeffrey finished his muffin and wiped his mouth. "You know," he said, sucking the chocolate and caramel out of his teeth. "I should thank you, Martin. If not for you, I never would have gotten authorization to abduct Cheryl."

"I'm surprised you needed authorization," said Martin.

"We're not savages. We're doing a job like everyone else," said Jeffrey.

"What gives you the right? To take Cheryl? Her mom? To

take our planet? Any of it? I mean we're sitting right here. Why don't you just ask? We could be business partners. We could be customers. Hell, with the unemployment in the world, we'd happily set up factories for you."

"Thanks for the offer," said Jeffrey. "But it's much harder to make money with a non-automated labor force."

"You can't make a dime if you don't have a product," said Martin.

"Astute," said Jeffrey.

"Which you don't have. So why don't you go home?" said Martin.

"Pushy creatures, aren't they?" Jeffrey said to Stewart.

"You have no idea," said Martin.

"Give me a break," said Jeffrey. "Okay, old man, here it is: I'm willing to cut you a deal if you're willing to come back."

"I don't have the recipe," said Stewart.

"That may be, but you might have some insight now that you didn't have then. You might be able to help the lab guys. Or perhaps you can persuade Cheryl to cooperate," said Jeffrey.

"Are you making me an offer?" asked Stewart.

"I am. And here's the fun part: Name your own terms. If I solve this problem, I can write my own ticket. And if I have to bring you along, so be it. Imagine it. Reinstatement, your benefits restored, your pension upgraded, a job in any market you want. We could arrange for Cheryl to join you, and maybe a few others if you're feeling generous." He turned to Martin. "How's that sound? You and Cheryl repopulating your species on another planet. Isn't that some kind of fantasy for you male mammals?"

"I really wish you would stop talking now," said Martin.

"What makes you think any of that sounds appealing?" asked Stewart. "You think this"—he yanked at his oxygen cord—"is part of the disguise? You think I can leave this planet and have a long, healthy life anywhere? I've been here too long. I've breathed too much secondhand smoke and fossil-fuel exhaust. Do you know how many chemicals they put in their air? Pesticides. Herbicides. Fungicides. The only thing that's holding me together at this point is this infernal dermis."

"Oh, cry me a river. Fine, then. If you don't do it for yourself, then do it for Cheryl, and poor Martin here," said Jeffrey.

"Give me one reason I should let you walk out of this Perkins," said Martin.

"Because the next development analyst they send might not be as easy on Cheryl," said Jeffrey. "Yeah. That's what I thought." He pushed his empty plates away, downed the last of his coffee, and slid out of the booth. He picked up the bill and zipped it through his fingers. "This one's on me, gentlemen. Oh, and, Stewart? He'll be here in…" Jeffrey checked his phone. "…let's say, a few days. So don't take too long making up your mind. Have a nice day."

When Jeffrey had paid the bill and left, Martin poured out his fury in the form of way too much syrup on his pancakes.

"You know, Martin," said Stewart. "He made that offer to you, too."

"Yesterday, you said I'd be dead if I gave it to him," said Martin.

"Perhaps, but if you give the recipe directly to the CEO, you might be able to win a solid deal for yourself. And Cheryl," said Stewart.

"How can I even consider that?" asked Martin.

"I'm just saying," said Stewart.

As they left, Martin tossed a few bills on the table. "Bastard probably didn't leave a tip."

🐜 🐜 🐜

"It is no accident of history that gave the Rothschild family controlling ownership of the Federal Reserve Bank. They control it because they're allowed to. And the CFR, the Bilderbergers, the Trilateral Commission, the Club of Rome—they're only the middlemen to whom the Rothschilds answer. These organizations mask themselves in public as think tanks or policy research cooperatives, but those are only fronts. They perform tasks and affect policy to shield the truly important organizations that cannot afford such exposure: the Freemasons—and I don't mean your little neighborhood lodge down the street—the Vatican, and the Illuminati."

"And those are the organizations that communicate with the Reptoids?"

"The Freemasons learned their secrets from the Reptoids during the building of the Egyptian pyramids. If you deconstruct their rites, they're about preparing the human mind for meeting with an actual Reptoid, as well as preserving the knowledge for preparing the world's infrastructure for the Reptoids' arrival. Think of the Freemasons as hardware, whereas the Illuminati are the software. The Illuminati manage the preparation of politics, economics, and propaganda."

"What of the Vatican?"

"It's strange, Lee, but there have been no reports of Reptoid visitations to the Holy See in many years. The last rumored visit might have coincided with the death of Pope John Paul I, who, if you remember, held the office for only thirty-three days in 1978. This suggests that the Reptoids may have been involved with his death. With no known contact since, we have to wonder why the Reptoids have severed relations with the Vatican. Did they fall out of favor? Or did they complete their preparations for the arrival?"

"Can you describe what might happen during the arrival? And what preparations are being made?"

"Given the population-control measures that are being devised, I think we can safely assume they're not coming to eat us. Ha ha ha. Seriously, though, they are preparing the world economies and the minds of the human population. I believe that we are intended to be servants, or slaves, if you will, but willing ones. It's about mind control. We'll wake up one day in a familiar but alien world. There will be no more freedom. We will essentially be breeding stock."

"What of those who are helping to prepare the way? The Illuminati and others?"

"Conspirators will be retained in positions of power and maintain certain privileges, but they're delusional if they think that the Reptoids will tolerate their freedom for long. After several generations, human intercessors won't be necessary."

"I suppose the questions are these: What can we do? Is this inevitable? Has the countdown already begun? What hope do we have?"

"Those are exactly the questions, Lee."

"Indeed. A wakeup call for the Waker Nation if I've ever heard one. We'll be back with your phone calls and more questions for our guest, Raymond Erickson, after this short break. Stay awake and stay with us."

Martin turned down the commercial. "Is any of that true?" he asked.

"No," said Stewart.

The tires thrummed along the road surface. The reflector posts slipped by in time. The high beams stretched out, but blinded Martin to all else beyond the dashboard and the few yards of pavement ahead.

"Then why do you listen to it?" asked Martin.

"To keep informed," said Stewart.

"So some of it's true?"

"Nah. It's all bunk. But if you're hiding in plain sight, it's good to know if anyone's looking in your direction."

"I'm sorry if I've put you in danger," said Martin.

"I'm surprised it's taken this long. You should have seen me when I first took over Stewart Campion's life. I had no idea how to be human. Luckily, he was a bit of a drunk. Everyone assumed that having to take care of the baby shook me straight. I got to be a new man, sober and getting my act together. Everyone was more than happy to excuse my faults and quirks."

"When Linda got back, did she…?" asked Martin.

"She figured it out pretty quick," said Stewart.

"But she let you stick around, even after what she'd gone through?"

"I promised to take care of Cheryl, and that was good enough for her. She knew she wasn't right."

"Did you love her?"

"Linda? I don't know if I'd call it love. I did what I needed to do for Cheryl. If that meant taking care of Linda through her spells and then through the cancer, so be it. I felt responsible."

"You're a good human, Stewart," said Martin. Stewart laughed, but his laughter turned to coughing. When his coughs subsided, Martin asked, "So what are you? I mean, if it's not rude to ask. Are you a Gray? Or one of these Reptoids?"

"If I had to describe us in Earth terms, we're something more akin to squid or octopus," said Stewart.

"You're aquatic?"

"Part of our lives. We're hatched underwater. Many return to the oceans later in life. We often vacation there."

"Aliens take vacations?"

"Why does that surprise you?"

"I don't know. I guess I never thought about it."

"We sleep. We dream. Some of us are artists and storytellers. We have extended and complex families. For instance, I have 386 brothers and sisters. One of my sisters is a well-known dramatist."

"A dramatist? Wow," said Martin. "So you're not all genocidal purveyors of packaged food?"

"It was a job," said Stewart.

A mileage sign flashed by. Still seventeen miles out of Havre. Martin hoped the motel had held his room—their room—this late. He took a long, sputtering drag on the last of his Diet Mountain Dew.

"You know," said Stewart, "I've been thinking about what you asked yesterday, about destroying the portal."

"You said it was pointless," said Martin.

"It is," said Stewart. "That's why maybe we need to think about the production facility instead."

"Destroying it?"

"Or disabling it," said Stewart. "It'll be big."

"You haven't seen it?"

"I saw a few drawing-board sketches on my way here. It's mostly a transport for all the bots that will do the work. They're self-replicating, so there's just the bare minimum, but still…"

"How big?"

"Bigger than a city, smaller than a county," said Stewart.

"Could you be a little more specific?"

"I wish I could," said Stewart.

"And how would we destroy such a massive thing? This staple gun doesn't have a hydrogen bomb setting, does it?" Stewart sneered. "Plus Cheryl's up there. I presume we'd like to get her out first," said Martin.

"I'm aware of that," said Stewart.

"If you have an idea, out with it already," said Martin.

"I don't want to get your hopes up," said Stewart. "It's a wild-assed notion."

"And the first step is…?"

"We go back to Brixton."

CHAPTER
18

"Why? What's in Brixton? A spaceship or something?" asked Martin.

"More or less," Stewart replied.

"What do you mean?"

"Just that," said Stewart.

"You mean, you've had a spaceship this whole time and it didn't seem relevant to mention that until now?" Martin couldn't believe he'd just uttered that sentence. He felt like whiny Luke Skywalker dithering about after the princess while Obi-Wan Kenobi wasn't telling him the whole story. But this wasn't *Star Wars*. Or who knows—maybe it was.

"You have to understand how it works," said Stewart.

"By all means, explain it to me then," said Martin.

"Vehicles, like the semi you tried to stow away in, are nothing more than shuttles. They can't operate far from their mother ship. They're able to travel through the off-ramp portal, and on the roads here on Earth; I wouldn't even call them spaceships. They're equipped with bits of technology that make a temporary bubble, good for a few minutes of heat and air to get you through space.

Another bit talks to the portal and the mother ship dock, which pulls the vehicles in."

Caught in a tractor beam. Of course, thought Martin. Why not? He'd barely slept since he'd shot at Jeffrey, and all he had to look forward to tonight was another motel mattress and an audio tour of Stewart's sinuses. This is my descent into madness. Why fight it?

Forget Luke. WWHSD? What would Han Solo do? "So let's go hijack another truck and get Cheryl." Either that or hide under the floorboards.

"That would only get us onto the truck's mother ship, not the production facility," said Stewart.

"How does that help us get her?"

"It doesn't," said Stewart.

Damn fool, I knew you were going to say that, thought Martin. "I'm not getting this, Stewart."

Stewart took a deep, wheezing breath. "I have the vehicle I was issued in 1986. It has the devices installed that have the access codes. That's what will get us onto the production facility."

"Do they know you have this ship?"

"Of course," said Stewart.

"Then what makes you think they haven't changed the codes in twenty-five years?"

"Jeffrey's propped the door open for me. He doesn't want to shut me out now," said Stewart.

Who's the more foolish, the fool or the fool who follows him? "Okay. I'll buy that for the moment. But Jeffrey's not just going to turn Cheryl over," said Martin. "And you said it yourself—anything we do risks him pressing the button and heading for Earth, or hurting Cheryl."

"All true," said Stewart.

"And he's probably not there alone," said Martin.

"Actually, he might be."

"Really?" asked Martin.

"There'd only be one or two others, maximum. Maybe a laboratory guy, maybe a trainee. Have you ever seen Jeffrey with anyone, like he's working with them?"

"Never," said Martin.

"Probably not a trainee then," said Stewart.

"What's this plan of yours? You're still being vague."

"That's because I haven't worked out all the details. It's a variation on a contingency plan I came up with years ago—something to put into action if I ever got wind that they'd gotten the recipe. I was going to hijack a truck, kind of like you did, take it back through the portal, and crash its mother ship cargo vessel into the production facility before it could get through the portal to Earth."

"Sounds like a suicide mission," said Martin. Han Solo would have noted that right away.

"It might be," said Stewart. "Although I was kind of hoping to be able to set an autopilot and get back onto the shuttle vehicle before I had to resort to that." Just like Beggar's Canyon back home, eh, Stewart?

"Are these cargo vessels large enough to destroy the production facility?" asked Martin.

"Should be. Like I told you, the facility's mostly a big dumb warehouse. You crash into the engines or destroy the control section, it's not going to go anywhere."

"And they wouldn't shoot it down or anything?"

"It's a factory, not a battleship," said Stewart.

"I thought it might be armed."

"This ain't *Star Trek*; this is real life," said Stewart.

"What's to keep them from coming back to repair it, or building another one?" asked Martin.

Stewart shrugged and harrumphed. He coughed a few times, then a few times more. "Sorry," he said when the fit had subsided.

"Let me get this straight," said Martin. "Your plan is to hijack another truck, then for us to take that *and* your company spaceship up there. Get on board the facility and rescue Cheryl, while—what?—distracting Jeffrey with an imminent cargo ship collision?"

"That's the general gist of it," said Stewart.

"There's about a billion things that could go wrong with that," said Martin.

"I know," said Stewart.

"It would take really precise timing," said Martin.

"Never said otherwise," said Stewart.

"It's completely crazy."

"You said you wanted to do something. You got a better plan?"

I could get two motel rooms in Havre so I don't have to listen to you snore all night. "So where's this spaceship of yours?" asked Martin.

"Hank's junkyard," said Stewart.

"Let me guess, Hank's an alien, too?" Brixton, Montana. You'll never find a more wretched hive of scum and villainy.

"Nah, he's just my mechanic," said Stewart.

We must be cautious.

❧ ❧ ❧

Martin and Stewart left Havre long before the motel put out the complimentary breakfast, and long before the sun began to rise. But when it peeked over the horizon a few miles out of Brixton, Stewart checked his phone for a signal and called ahead.

"He's an early riser," Stewart told Martin as he waited for an answer.

Hank met them at his gate and swung it aside for Martin to roll the Screwmobile into the tight quarters of the parking yard outside his house and Quonset hut shop. Hank greeted them with a Thermos lid of coffee in one hand and a lip full of chew. He was an old-timer, but healthier than Stewart, less curmudgeonly than Lester, and seemed, all in all, content with his life of fixing cars and tractors and chewing the fat with anyone who came a-scavenging in his junkyard.

He rambled past his shop to a wide gate in a high, crooked slatted fence. A few glassed cabs of harvesters and the yellow dome of a school bus were the only occupants tall enough to see the sunrise. Hank held the Thermos cup in his teeth as he unlocked the massive padlock and shoved the gate sideways.

Martin felt like he'd wandered into some secret elephant burial ground. Decades, if not centuries, of rusting hulks had fallen and died in the few fenced acres of tall, dewy grass. He pitied the farmer who might still need parts for these ancient machines. His heart ached for the young kid desperate enough to have to hack his way through this caged metal prairie for a cheap part to get his hand-me-down car running. He mourned the accounts in Havre that he would have to call soon and beg for a later appointment.

They had almost reached the back fence when Hank said, "Here she is." He nodded at a tumbleweed-tangled, car-shaped tarp sandwiched between a sun-bleached, windowless Wagoneer, and a hoodless Firebird, and then ejected a brown splat of tobacco spit into the dust.

Martin frowned at the tarp until he realized that the old men were staring at him. "What?" he asked.

"That tarp ain't gonna move itself," said Hank.

A quarter-century of dust and bird poop awaited Martin as he found the edge of the tarp in the weeds. Stagnant water had pooled in the folds, and something rustled in the grass, but he struggled the tarp back over the hood, the roof, and off the back of the trunk. He let it fall and brushed off his hands.

"What a piece of junk," Martin said.

"It's a 1986 Lincoln Town Car," said Stewart. "Only got about a thousand miles on it, too." The corroded paint sketched an odd map of weathered archipelagos on pristine seas. The delaminating vinyl on the rear of the roof probably wouldn't last past twenty miles per hour once the car got a new set of tires.

"You've got to be kidding me. I had accounts scheduled, Stewart."

"Everything okay, Stew?" asked Hank.

"We're fine. Can you give us a few minutes?"

"No problem. Just holler."

"I thought you said…" said Martin.

"I said not to get your hopes up," Stewart interrupted. "Things aren't always exactly what they seem."

Martin checked over his shoulder to make sure Hank was out of earshot. "How long has this been sitting here?"

"Hopefully everything still works," said Stewart.

"Still works? Oh, that's just great."

The driver's door opened with the creak of metal on metal. Stewart produced a key and turned the ignition but got nothing. "Too much to hope, I suppose," said Stewart.

Martin's stomach growled. All he'd had to eat was half a box of powdered donuts from the gas station several hours ago. If his morning appointments in Havre couldn't be rescheduled, he'd have to think up a new excuse for Rick. Death in the family? Overslept? Food poisoning? Or maybe something positive this time. *Yep, I walked into the grocery store this morning, and I was their millionth customer. Free shopping spree and everything.*

Stewart popped the hood. The engine looked surprisingly clean. A few spider webs, but no visible corrosion or damage, except for a few coral blossoms of acid around the battery terminals. Stewart poked around at some of the hoses and cables.

"Run up to the garage and ask Hank to borrow his jumper," said Stewart. "Oh, grab a fire extinguisher, too. Hell, just get Hank back here. He'll know what to do."

🐾 🐾 🐾

The good news was that Hank preferred to give them the bad news over breakfast at Herbert's Corner. He even drove them there in his homemade tow truck.

"Well, bless me, it's Stewart Campion," said Lorie. "I ain't seen you in here in forever. How are you?"

"Hanging in there," said Stewart.

"You're lookin' good. You heard from Cheryl at all?"

"Nope. Still no word," said Stewart.

Lorie clicked her tongue and shook her head. "Such a shame. After all you did for that girl. Anyway, what can I get you?"

"So what's it going to take?" Stewart asked after Lorie had left with their orders.

"Might be easier to tell you what don't need fixin'," said Hank. But he rattled off a list of nearly every major engine component anyway. Apparently a car, even a new one, shouldn't sit under a tarp for a quarter-century. The fluids leak out or turn to sludge. Parts freeze up. Hoses and lines clog with gunk.

"What was that smell?" asked Martin.

"Think some raccoons been birthing a quiverfull up under there somewhere," said Hank.

"How long?" asked Stewart.

"Three weeks minimum," said Hank. "Longer if Billings don't have all the parts."

Martin shook his head at Stewart, and stirred more sugar into his coffee.

"I don't know what to tell you," said Hank. "Gordon brought his Dodge in yesterday, and he's got all those cattle to water. Sheriff's got a couple vehicles need work. I won't take it personal if you do the work yourself."

"Don't look at me," said Martin. "I can barely change the wiper blades."

"I ain't worked up any costs, but…." Hank shook his head. "It's a tough call. She'd be a good car if you can clean her up. Told you twenty years ago she shouldn't sit like that."

🐾 🐾 🐾

Back at the junkyard, Stewart insisted on one last look at the Lincoln. "Help yourself," Hank said and sauntered to his shop.

"Can I officially call this a dead end?" Martin asked. "We don't have time to futz around. Can't we steal another semi? Force our way on board the facility?"

"Won't work," said Stewart. "It needed to be this one."

"Maybe we could get Hank to tow us up there," said Martin.

"We'd still need to get the battery and alternator and all that electrical stuff working," said Stewart. "And I don't even know if the portal would work if we weren't moving. I've only ever traveled through it at speed. And I don't know how we'd get off the facility without a working car. But, hell, it's all moot now."

Martin hated this weed-grown altar to futility. Screw the tarp, he thought. Roll down the windows and let the weather in. Let the raccoons make themselves at home. Let it rust and crumble.

Maybe someday some squiddy archeologist will dig it up. Its V8 engine might prove that humans were sentient. Whatever's left of its dated but stylish design would declare that we didn't deserve extermination. What will they make of their own technology embedded within this hunk of junk? Will that indict our executioners for their crimes? Maybe they'll erect a monument right here to the sentient species lost to hubris and greed. Or maybe they'll throw their tentacles up in ambivalence.

"It's a shame we can't just pull out those devices and put them in another car," said Martin.

Stewart nodded, and then said, "What did you say?"

"I said it's a shame we can't just pull…"

"You got a toolbox back in that truck of yours?" Stewart asked.

"Really?" asked Martin. "That's all it takes?"

"Yeah," said Stewart. "Sorry."

"You're here from another solar system. You'd think you could be the one thinking outside the box," said Martin.

A few minutes later, three chunks of black plastic rested on the dusty upholstery of the front seat. Two were identical, cylindrical things with a pair of long wires trailing out of one end. The other resembled a Wi-Fi hub, but without the blinking lights and RJ-45 jacks. It, too, had a pair of wires, but it also had a set of flexible arms that Martin assumed were antennas.

"That's the communicator?" Martin asked, as Stewart touched the wires of the hub to the handle of his little glass pingpong paddle non-iPad.

"And these two make the bubble," Stewart said and tested their wires. "They all seem to work."

"And these wires connect into a car's electrical system, like they were here? Or do we have to do something special?"

"Should work on any 12-volt system. They made it all simple

enough for guys like me to set up," said Stewart. "Thought maybe we'd put 'em in my Skylark."

"We're not going to the Kuiper Belt in your Skylark," said Martin. "My Subaru's a 2009. If I'm going to die in space, I'd rather do it in a car built in this century." He picked up one of the pieces. "It's so light," he said.

"Everything my people build is light," said Stewart. "Less mass, less energy to get it off a planet, less energy to move it. You'll see when we get up to the production facility. It's not just us. Parts of your Apollo moon landers were foil thick."

"Didn't know that," said Martin.

Martin found a cardboard box in the back of his truck and secured the alien parts in a drawer emptied of its staples. When he hopped out, Hank was there. "Decided not to buy her?" he asked Martin.

"Nah, too much work," said Martin.

"I tried," said Stewart.

"Real shame," said Hank.

𝅘𝅥 𝅘𝅥 𝅘𝅥

"Where are we going now?" asked Stewart, as Martin pointed the Screwmobile back toward Brixton. "Your Subaru in Billings?"

"I'm heading back up to Havre. I've got work. But I'm taking you home first," said Martin. "We're not in danger anymore, and besides, you need to stay here and figure out how we're going to steal a truck."

"That's just a matter of waiting for one to show up," said Stewart.

"It's that easy?" asked Martin.

"You could've done it that night you got arrested."

"Can you do it?"

"I'll need my trinket back."

"Your what? Oh," Martin touched the staple gun, but he kept it on his belt.

"You need to take me back to Billings anyway," said Stewart.

"What? Why? I don't have time," said Martin.

"My car's still at your place," said Stewart.

Martin groaned. Rick was not going to be happy.

Two and a half hours later, Martin carried the oxygen bottles, mostly empty, to the trunk of the Skylark. "You got someone to fill these for you?" Martin asked.

"Milton and Laura will help me out," said Stewart. He grabbed his little duffel bag from the back of the truck and shuffled to his car.

"Okay," said Martin. "You got my numbers?" Stewart patted the business card in his shirt pocket. "You call me the second a truck shows up, and I'll be on my way."

Stewart nodded, and Martin took his bag. "Thanks," said Stewart. Martin dropped the bag in the trunk and closed it.

"Are we kidding ourselves?" Martin asked. "I mean, do we have any hope? Are we already too late for Cheryl?"

"Can't think like that," said Stewart.

"I feel like I'm going to wake up any second. Probably in a straightjacket." Martin sighed. Then he forced himself to hand the staple gun to Stewart. "Are you going to have to kill anyone?"

"I hope not," said Stewart. "I'll set it on stun."

"I thought you said this wasn't *Star Trek*."

CHAPTER
19

It was a quiet night in Shelby, Montana, after the hardware stores had closed, but not as quiet as Martin's cell phone. It had been two days since he'd left Stewart to steal a truck. Martin would have welcomed a call from anyone now, even Rick, to prove that his phone still worked and that he still existed. In his motel room, Martin let a sitcom laugh track chip away at him. Then the baseball highlights. Some strutting crime scene investigators had their turn next. How many talking heads did one TV need?

The Sandra Bullock movie on HBO was the final straw. Martin turned off the TV, but the soundtrack continued, muffled, on the other side of the wall. He doubted that Neil Armstrong had ever felt this pathetically unprepared, or Yuri Gagarin, or Alan Shepard, or even that Saudi prince who went up on the space shuttle. Should he be training? Sitting in some mock-up simulator of his Subaru? How many gees could he stand? Martin got off the bed, peeked through the curtains, and considered jogging in the fading twilight. Followed by a quick trip to the emergency room for resuscitation. Waiting for Stewart to call was going to be worse than an eternity of Sandra Bullock movies.

The uncertainty almost made Martin want to call Jeffrey and make a deal. If the aliens shipped the two of them off to another world, Cheryl need never know that he had traded her for the rest of humanity. Besides, what could be more romantic?

He had to do something.

Out in the motel's parking lot, the red and green neon of the Mexican restaurant next door beckoned with the promise of one of those Slurpee machines full of margarita. That was probably a better choice. But Martin unlocked the back of his truck anyway, telling himself for the hundredth time that he shouldn't.

Nothing screamed "alien"—or even "foreign"—about the plastic gadgets from Stewart's Town Car. There were no markings, etchings, odd protrusions, or a sense of anything living inside. None of them had any obvious openings or fasteners, except for the rubbery nipples from which the wires extruded. The fine-gauge wires appeared to be copper, not so different from the ones he'd used to connect his XM radio to the truck's electrical system.

Hoax. Fake. Setup. A camera crew was surely about to emerge from a motel room doubled over with laughter. Martin enjoyed these few moments of doubt. Cheryl really had moved to Boise. Jeffrey and Stewart, Doris and Eileen—they had all concocted some small-town episode of *Punk'd*. The video of the truck emerging from the Gap had been faked, and so had the exploding trash can in Sidney. Even Lee Danvers must be in on it, providing the fake history of Brixton and Big Thunder Valley. "Big Thunder Valley." Someone must have had a good laugh when they thought up that one.

"What are you doing, Martin?" he asked himself. But no one answered as he removed the back of the plywood box, disconnected the radio's wires, and twisted the feeds of Stewart's devices into their place.

"This is all in your head, Martin," he told himself. Perhaps

Brixton didn't even exist. Maybe Cheryl was only a pipe dream. *Beyond Insomnia* had driven him insane—that, or too many miles on empty highways, too many days counting nails and screws, too many nights sleeping alone in front of motel televisions. How much Diet Mountain Dew did one have to drink before hallucinations took hold?

Martin started the engine. He closed the door to let the cab go dark and checked the devices. No glow. No indicators. No vibration. No sound. He rechecked the connections.

Martin considered calling Stewart, but he froze when a high-pitched whine slipped out of hearing range and a glowing plane appeared in space between the steering wheel and the speedometer. A hovering rectangle of light—he'd call it blue if it had any color—dotted with three icons: a yellow, car-shaped one with a grayed-out oval around it, a green hourglass with the two bulbs separated by a lightning bolt, and something that looked like a garage door being violated by a thick, red arrow.

Martin checked the parking lot for onlookers. He honestly didn't know if he'd shut off the engine to hide the phenomenon or call a stranger over to confirm that he saw the panel, too. He touched the side of the square but felt nothing. The pale blue light surrounded his finger as it neared an icon, but he pulled back before he did something stupid.

That oval icon probably toggled the bubble, that hourglass one must activate the portal, and the one with the arrow maybe communicated with the mother ship's dock. Any of them might signal Jeffrey that Stewart's company car was back from the dead. Hell, connecting the devices might have sent the signal already. Anyway, what did he know? That icon could put a radioactive crater in the middle of Shelby. That one could whisk his fragile mammalian body into the vacuum of space. That one could start the invasion of the self-replicating killer robotic bakers. Choices, choices.

He turned off the engine, and the panel blipped away. Martin breathed—he hadn't done that in a while—and wondered what he'd have told Rick if he'd accidently vaporized the Screwmobile with alien technology.

♪ ♪ ♪

"Waker Nation, it's time to put on another pot of coffee. I'm Lee Danvers, and let it never be said that I don't deliver for you. Tonight we have something very special: a guest with the most amazing story and with the most amazing video, which will be shown for the first time in a few minutes. This story is so incredible that we're co-broadcasting this conversation live on wakernation.com. If you're on the road, you're going to want to pull over and log on. This has got to be seen to be believed. So without further ado, via Skype, Thomas Worthington, you're on *Beyond Insomnia* and wakernation.com."

"Thank you, Lee."

"Thomas, why don't you tell us a little about yourself?"

"Certainly. I'm thirty-two years old. I'm a videographer and photojournalist, based in Oakland, California. I've worked in broadcast television and done freelance work for my whole career. I've shot everything from weddings to Super Bowls."

"What exactly has brought you to the Waker Nation?"

"Well, Lee. A little over a week ago you had on a caller who claimed to have video of a UFO or some kind of vehicle appearing out of nowhere on a road in Montana."

"Yes. It's up at wakernation.com. And—oh—we've got the video playing right now. Nice work, X-ray."

"Exactly; that video. Now, the caller…"

"Martin from Billings."

"Yes. He sounded a little over the edge, but the video intrigued me. I'm a professional. I know all the tricks. I know all the software out there. I can usually spot a fake in a heartbeat, but not this time."

"And that's when you contacted the show."

"I called and asked to get a look at the raw file of the video. And one of your kind producers took me up on my offer to see if it had been edited, graphics added, colors or details enhanced. Debunk it, if you will."

"And what did you find?"

"Lee, I was amazed to find pristine video. I expected to find cuts, such as when the camera fell to the ground, or to find editing artifacts along the edges of the rock and grass along the left side. I expected to see problems of scale or lighting, shadow angles and such, with the truck object itself. But, Lee, I found nothing. It appeared to be a completely authentic capture of an event."

"Incredible. That's when you decided to go to Montana?"

"I had to get there and see if this could have been faked somehow. I packed up my gear, got in the car, and drove almost straight through to Brixton, Montana."

"What kind of gear did you bring?"

"I couldn't be sure of the conditions I'd find, so I brought everything. Several video cameras and mounts, microphones, extra batteries, weather cases, lenses, all the usual stuff."

"What did you do when you got there?"

"A lawyer buddy of mine found out who owns the land from where the original video was taken, a very nice rancher named Norman Young. He hadn't seen the video, but he didn't seem too surprised. He told me this stretch of Highway 360 has had a long reputation for weird sightings. He also said—and I thought this was interesting—that his cattle avoided the area. He gave me permission to set up on his land."

"Had he ever seen anything happen on the road?"

"He said he hadn't, but something in his voice told me that he might have."

"Okay. When we come back, more from videographer Thomas Worthington and the world-exclusive first look at his incredible images from Brixton, Montana, on wakernation.com and *Beyond Insomnia*. Tonight's broadcast is brought to you by…"

"Are you listening to this?" asked Martin. Martin had practically run off the road trying to call Stewart and turn the volume down on the commercial at the same time.

"This video guy on BI?" asked Stewart. The commercial on Stewart's end was delayed a few seconds over the phone.

"Of course 'this video guy,' " said Martin. "Did you see him?"

"I never saw anyone with a video camera," said Stewart. "But I've been watching Herbert's Corner, not the portal."

"Well, it sounds like he got video of a truck coming through."

"It might have come while I was asleep or something. I asked Eileen to call if she ever got a feeling about someone," said Stewart.

"A feeling? Dammit, Stewart, how could you miss one? Where are you now?"

"Parked at the Corner, where I've been damn near every waking moment of the last few days."

"You know we're running out of time," said Martin.

Stewart coughed. "If it's so important, why aren't you here, too?"

"I have a job," said Martin. Because it was so critical that Shelby and Great Falls got restocked with FastNCo. hardware before the coming apocalypse. Never fear, Lewistown, I'm coming for you. You'll have your screws and nails in time to die.

"I had a job to do, too," said Stewart.

"Don't spread the hero stuff on too thick. You were pretty much on board with exterminating all humans until you met baby Cheryl." After a long, wheezing silence, Martin said, "I'm sorry, Stewart. I shouldn't have said that."

"Show's coming back on," said Stewart.

"…easy to find. I can attest that the landscape of the original video is accurate. The highway runs southeast along the north side of a bluff, rising in elevation, and then passes through an excavated cut in the top of the hill—there's rock on both sides— and then makes a sharp turn to the southwest, descending the other side of the bluff. I found the exact location 'Martin from Billings' used to record the original video. The ground had been disturbed recently, and I found a plastic bottle. Mountain Dew, I think."

"A wake-up call there. Don't litter while watching for UFOs."

"Exactly. I set one camera there, and then I set up three more. Two on each side of the cut in the hill. That first evening, I drove through the gap several times to give myself a benchmark for the lighting conditions."

"Is this a well-traveled road?"

"During the day, I'd say it gets a vehicle passing through there every three to five minutes, but at night it's more like every ten to fifteen minutes. That location is about seven miles south of Brixton, which is a pretty small town. The only traffic light is a blinking yellow, if that gives you an idea. And from this bluff, you can't see a single electric light. Not a ranch house, not a farm, nothing. The stars were incredible."

"You captured video right away?"

"I'd given myself seven days, but I honestly thought that I'd get a recording on the first night. I figured one or two trucks would drive through and their headlights would recreate the effect, proving that the original video wasn't what it seemed."

"But that's not what you found."

"The first two days and nights, I got plenty of footage of vehicles coming through the cut. The Montana Highway Patrol might be interested to know how many drivers take that curve way too fast. But nothing unusual. When semis come through that section of road, their headlights make a definitive, recognizable sweep across the rock. I can tell you now that it is not the same light as we see on the original video. I ran the footage through processing software and tried to recreate the bloom of light, but it never looked close. I began to believe that something had really happened there."

"Tell us about the third night."

"He was there for at least three nights," said Martin. "When, do you suppose?"

"Couldn't have been more than a couple of nights ago," said Stewart.

"Did they say where he's calling from?"

"Didn't hear."

"You're not watching this on the website, are you?"

"Website? I'm parked at the Corner," said Stewart.

"I'm trying to get to my motel as quick as possible," said Martin.

"…got very quiet. Eerie. All the insects went silent. And then I woke up. I'd fallen asleep, slumped over in my back seat. At first, I thought I was exhausted, but then I remembered the insects. I'd been unconscious for only about ten minutes. I gathered all the footage from the cameras, synched all the images together on a split screen, and I couldn't believe it. The south side of the hill stayed dark. No trucks came or went that way. But on the north side, the Brixton side, a bright pinpoint of light appeared above the road surface in the cut. This point bloomed into what I can only describe as a sideways fountain of blue light. It shot out a few meters down the road, and suddenly a semi popped out of nowhere. But a regular truck like you'd see on any highway in America. It descended the hill and headed north toward Brixton."

"And now, the world premiere of the video of this event, shot by Thomas Worthington, two nights ago outside of Brixton, Montana."

"I wish I was seeing this." Martin tapped his cruise control a whisker faster.

"Maybe it didn't stop in Brixton," said Stewart.

"You think it was delivering dishwashers to Helena?" asked Martin.

"You're right. You're right," Stewart replied.

"Did you follow the truck?"

"I didn't. By the time I had woken and synched the playback, it could have driven to the junction at Brixton and gone any direction. I decided to wait out the night in case it returned."

"Oh boy, Wakers. You have to stay with us. After this break, we'll hear more of his story and see more exclusive video of this incredible event. Stay awake with us. Now, when I'm out on a lonely highway, it's always comforting to know that I'm heading the right way. Our friends at Garmin…"

.ꙮ. .ꙮ. .ꙮ.

Martin paid lip service to the speed limits in Lewistown, and bounced, tires squealing, into the motel's parking lot. He ran into the lobby with his laptop. As it booted, Martin checked the ceiling for any indication that he would get Wi-Fi, and saw only a wagon-wheel chandelier. But the twenty-first century came through for him.

Martin logged into his wakernation.com account and watched the videos. First, the truck arriving. Then, in the next clip, the same truck, at least one with the same logo, leaving, about two hours later, according to this videographer guy. Long enough for a restroom visit, a breakfast special, and a little chit-chat with Eileen. The clip replayed the four synched images in slow motion, two dark and two of the truck being sucked into the portal. Then Martin clicked to the main event, the shot that Lee had dragged out the first two hours of his show to present. It began with the four familiar images of the Gap, but this time a car, not a truck, materialized out of the bloom. "A black car," Thomas Worthington had called it. "And I never saw it return. That means that whoever, or whatever, it was might still be out there somewhere on Earth. It was possibly a Cadillac or a…"

"A Lincoln Town Car," said Martin.

"Hello, Martin," said Jeffrey.

CHAPTER
20

"You have got to stop doing that," said Martin. "Scared the crap out of me."

"I needed to see you," said Jeffrey.

"You could have called."

"Watching that video Lee Danvers got? Nice looking Town Car, eh?"

"What do you want?"

"To talk to you," said Jeffrey.

"You made yourself pretty clear at the Perkins," Martin said, snapping his laptop shut. "So unless you're returning Cheryl unharmed and getting the hell off my planet..."

"Spare me the dramatics," said Jeffrey. "Come on, let's get some coffee or something."

Martin wished he'd taken a decoy staple gun out of the back of the truck. Even if Jeffrey realized it wasn't the real ray gun, Martin bet that a three-quarter-inch staple to the neck might do some damage. "I need to check in first," said Martin.

Jeffrey scanned the lobby with a raised eyebrow. "You're checking in here?"

"Shut up," said Martin, heading to the front desk.

"They don't even serve breakfast," Jeffrey called after him.

"Is everything okay, Mr. Wells?" asked the desk clerk.

"Oh, just peachy," Martin replied.

"Shall we take my car?" asked Jeffrey, when Martin returned with his key.

"How about I follow you?" said Martin.

A few minutes later, Jeffrey parked diagonally in front of a tavern under a banner that said, "Welcome Bikers."

"I thought you said coffee," said Martin.

Jeffrey tossed his suit jacket across onto his passenger seat. "They'll have coffee," he said and shut his door.

If Lynyrd Skynyrd wasn't playing on the stereo, Martin knew he wouldn't have to wait long. The few patrons, surely regulars all, looked their direction before returning to their conversations. For some reason, a women's tennis match was playing on the TV behind the aged bar. The bartender didn't blink when Jeffrey ordered and soon enough provided two steaming mugs of black coffee.

Martin followed Jeffrey to a table.

"You came all the way back to Earth just to talk to me?" asked Martin.

"I did," said Jeffrey. He kicked his legs out straight and leaned back in his chair. "You know, I wanted so much to ask you about Cheryl's pie before. How she made it, what it tasted like, all that. But I couldn't. Then Stewart spilled the beans, and you and I kind of got off on the wrong foot."

"What could possibly be the right foot?"

"I've watched her make dozens of pies in the last few weeks—she's quite the baker—but I don't see anywhere in the process where she's leaving anything out. There's no hesitation at any point. No little quaver where you can see her thinking, 'Skip that ingredient,' or 'Don't mix it this way.' I'm beginning to think that she really doesn't have the secret."

"That's what we've been telling you," said Martin.

"But yet she baked you a pie. And I'm thinking that for a special occasion, for the right person, she might have baked it the right way."

"You think I was watching what she was putting in the dough? All I was thinking about was getting into her pants," said Martin.

"Oh, knock it off. I know you well enough to know that that's the first time in your life you've even thought the phrase 'getting into her pants.' "

"So what? Even if I did notice something unusual, what makes you think I would tell you now?"

"I could abduct you, and we can find out."

"Go ahead," said Martin.

"Don't have authorization," said Jeffrey.

"That shouldn't stop a go-getter like you," said Martin. "You don't want to upset CEO ChipmunkFart."

Jeffrey laughed, took a belt of coffee, and then pointed at Martin. "They didn't send me here because I was the last egg hatched. And my intuition tells me that you know something."

"Jeffrey, I've known you for just as long," said Martin. "This isn't some kind of friend-to-friend chat. You're panicked."

Jeffrey chuckled again. "Now I know that you know something."

"Think what you want," said Martin.

"What can I offer you to change your mind?"

"I don't have anything to tell you. Even if I did, I wouldn't do it."

"What if I told you that I could have the operational plan altered?"

"Altered?" asked Martin.

"Changed. Edited. Rewritten. Revamped."

"How?"

"With the recipe in hand, I'd be able to make recommendations to my CEO."

"Recommendations aren't a guarantee," said Martin.

"We could negotiate with your leaders for part of the planet. Build domes on Mars for the rest."

"Wow. Sounds like a sweet deal. Where do I sign?" said Martin. "How can you be doing this? Don't you have any guilt at all? Can't you see that we deserve the right to exist unmolested on our own planet?"

"I'm not a monster," said Jeffrey. "But I've staked my whole career on this."

"Your career?"

"Driving your truck of screws around, you might not understand what it means..."

"Oh, we're going to go there? My job is stupid, Candy Man? Or does the candy company even exist?"

"At first, no, but now we sell candy in forty-eight states. Plus Canada, and we would be expanding into Mexico, but..."

"So you're willing to sacrifice your candy concern if you get the pie?"

"Chump change. So what if we sell a few million bucks of tooth rot to humans every year? Do you know how much that pie recipe is worth? Trillions of customers buying several a year, or even every month, all at the equivalent of a couple bucks apiece. You do the math. Even if demand flattens or slopes off in a couple of years, it's still a fortune."

"Well, when you put it that way, by all means, murder all of us then," said Martin. "I'm so sorry that we're even in your way."

"You know, she thinks you're part of it," said Jeffrey.

"What?"

"She thinks you're one of us. She thinks you sold her out."

"She'll know the truth someday," said Martin.

"Maybe."

"What does that mean?"

"If you don't tell me what I want to know right now, I'm going back up there to start the next stage of interrogation. And if she doesn't tell me what I need to know, your breakfast princess is going to be eating Jell-O in a padded room for the rest of her life."

Martin lunged. The table tipped, spilling the coffees. Jeffrey tumbled back, mouth open. A mug smashed. Martin fell on Jeffrey, hands around his throat.

Jeffrey swatted at Martin and pushed up under his chin. Martin let go with one hand to slap at Jeffrey's face, but a hand, the bartender's, caught his wrist. The bartender shouted, but Martin heard nothing but the blood rush in his ears. He twisted his arm free and punched Jeffrey under the eye. Jeffrey bucked him off into a pool of coffee spiked with the shattered mug and struggled to his feet.

Martin followed, shoving the bartender aside, and tackled Jeffrey. "He's going to kill us all," Martin shouted to anyone who cared to hear.

Jeffrey kicked at him and gained the door on his hands and knees. He pulled himself to his feet on the crash bar.

"He's crazy," yelled Jeffrey. "Call the cops."

Martin was out the door a half-second after Jeffrey, and punched at the back of his head. Jeffrey stumbled and then turned, setting up in some kind of martial-arts stance. He laughed, backing to the Lincoln Town Car.

The bartender and the Lewistown tavern regulars spilled out onto the sidewalk.

Martin started forward, but Jeffrey touched something on his left wrist. And Martin collapsed into the gutter.

❧ ❧ ❧

Martin awoke in a heap in Jeffrey's empty parking space. He lurched up, his legs and arms on pins and needles, his clothes stained brown with cold coffee. He brushed bits of gravel from his palms and the side of his face. The bartender and the other patrons were heaped in undignified piles on the sidewalk. One had cut his head. Martin stumbled to the Screwmobile, scrabbling in his pockets for his keys. He backed out as one of the patrons got to his knees.

Martin guessed Jeffrey had had only a few minutes' head start. The mostly-empty Screwmobile roared easily up into the please-step-out-of-the-car-sir range of the speedometer. Jeffrey had to have come this way. Highway 15 made practically a beeline to Brixton, and the portal.

"Pasco, Washington, you're Beyond Insomnia."

"Evening, Lee. My name is Clark. I've been awake a long time, but I ain't heard nothing like this. Gives me chills. But I have a question for your guest."

"Thomas Worthington, yes. Go ahead."

"Yeah, Thomas, you said you fell asleep every time, and then woke up a few minutes later. What was that like? And did you dream?"

"I'll first let you know that I am not narcoleptic, and I have no history of sleep disorders. I didn't dream. And it wasn't scary. The first time, it caught me by surprise. The second and third times, when I heard the insects go quiet, I immediately lay down wherever I happened to be. And then I'd be out. Like falling asleep at night. I don't know if it's a protective effect of this phenomenon, something to keep witnesses from seeing things, or if it's a natural effect of the technology. It surprised me that it didn't disrupt the recordings. Perhaps whoever set it up didn't care about technology, only eyewitnesses."

"Do you think these trucks are actually alien?"

"I can't answer that question. I'm only a journalist and videographer. For all I know, the phenomenon might be teleportation technology that the government has kept secret. Maybe it's how they haul nuclear missile parts around that area. The truck that emerged, and the car, were clearly recognizable as human objects, not alien."

"Thank you, Clark from Pasco. Thomas, were you aware of the history of sightings and visitations around Brixton before this?"

"I hadn't heard of Brixton, but your producer filled me in on the area's history."

Taillights appeared in the distance, but it turned out to be a pickup truck. Martin passed it as if it were going backward—hopefully too fast for the driver to read the number on the "How's My Driving?" bumper sticker.

What would he even do if he caught Jeffrey? Run him off the road? Get in another ridiculous slap fight? Martin had the alien parts. With a few minutes of work, he could follow Jeffrey right through the portal. Jeffrey would never expect it. But then the rest of the plan would be right out the window. Besides, Jeffrey might not even be going through the portal. Could he send a signal up to the facility to start this next phase on Cheryl? Surely he had some device to do that? Probably his stupid iPad. The damned things did everything else.

Stewart.

Martin wrestled his phone out of his pants pocket, swerving. He kept the car half across the yellow line as he dialed so he wouldn't veer into a ditch.

"Hey, Martin. Where you been? What's this black car Lee keeps talking about?" Stewart asked.

"Listen to me. Jeffrey's heading your way east on 15 from Lewistown right now. I'm a few minutes behind him. We need to stop him. He's going back up there to move Cheryl into the next interrogation phase thing."

"How do I stop him?" asked Stewart.

"You've got a car and your FastNCo. Model 25-C staple gun. You figure it out," said Martin. "He's driving a black Town Car."

"How'd you meet up with him?" asked Stewart.

"He found me. Tried to make a deal. I didn't tell him anything, but he suspects I have the secret."

"That's not good," said Stewart.

"Not for me," said Martin.

"But maybe we can use that somehow."

"How?" asked Martin. "He's holding all the cards. What can I threaten him with? Put the staple gun to my own temple and tell him to bring back Cheryl or it's back to the drawing board?"

"When do you think he'll get here?" asked Stewart.

"Any time. I left Lewistown about an hour ago and haven't caught him. He put me to sleep somehow, but I don't think I was out more than a few minutes."

"Okay, I'll do what I can," said Stewart.

"Baton Rouge, Louisiana. You're Beyond Insomnia. Hello, you're on the air."

"Oh, am I on?"

"You are. What's your name and question for Thomas Worthington?"

"I'm MaryAnn. I'm wondering how close Thomas got. It looks like the cameras are a hundred yards away or so. Did he get closer personally?"

"I drove through the spot more than a dozen times during the day and night and can report nothing unusual. I walked through the area during the day. I even climbed on the walls, but they were pretty crumbly, and I didn't want to fall into traffic. There are real plants growing out of cracks in the rock. If there's some kind of object or mechanism there, it's buried or well camouflaged. I walked around the site, too, but found no signs of excavation, construction, no odd manholes or structures, nothing to indicate that anyone had ever built anything but a road there."

"Can I ask another question?"

"Sure, go ahead, MaryAnn."

"Is Thomas single? He sounds real nice, and he's so handsome, too. I can't imagine a woman letting him run off to Montana all alone."

"Fair enough. So, Thomas, what's the verdict? Are you on the market?"

"Not to disappoint, but I have a longtime girlfriend. Stacey. Hi, Babe. She's wonderful, and very supportive of my career, which she knows can take me to strange places at strange times."

"Sounds like he's taken, MaryAnn."

"Oh, that's too bad, Lee. And I know you're never going to leave Mrs. Danvers."

"I'm in it for good with the amazing Mrs. D, but I'll take this moment to remind you that premium wakernation.com members get full access to the Insomniacs Forum, including the Not Sleeping Single pages. I get email every day from people who've made connections with fellow Wakers there. Good luck, MaryAnn. Let's go to Queens, New York…"

☙ ☙ ☙

Martin slowed to pass through Brixton. Twenty-five miles per hour felt like standing still. The town slept unaware. Even the deputies had abandoned their vigil by the market. Martin sped up.

There were no cars filling up at the Herbert's Corner gas pumps and only a couple of trucks in the back lot. Stewart's Skylark wasn't parked by the propane tank. Martin flicked on his blinker, started to turn south at the junction, but then stomped on the brakes.

Across Highway 360, taillights filtered through the grass on the side of the road. A plume of exhaust rose like a smoke signal.

Martin's feet crunched on shattered red plastic as he ran across the road.

"Stewart?" he called.

The Skylark idled at an unnerving angle in the shallow ditch. The passenger's-side tail end had been mangled. Stewart was hunched over the steering wheel. Martin called again, wading through the grass.

"He hit me," Stewart said, after Martin opened the door.

"Are you all right?"

"I think so," said Stewart. "Trying to catch my breath." Martin helped Stewart out, taking his oxygen tank for him. "Got off a shot at the car, but I don't think it did any damage. I'm sorry."

"It's all right. How long ago?" Martin held Stewart's arm as he took the embankment one step at a time.

"A few minutes."

"You want to go to the hospital or anything?"

"Are you kidding?" asked Stewart.

🌒 🌒 🌒

As they approached the base of the hill, Martin hit his brakes. Cars, pickups, SUVs, and RVs lined the road. And people, laden with cameras and phones and flashlights. Was that a shotgun? Some conferred in excited little knots. A teenager ran past them down the hill.

Martin rolled down his window. "What's going on?" he called to a group.

"Another one just came through," said a man. "The car. The black car. One of the men in black. We all just woke up."

"The one on the radio," said another man. "Haven't you been listenin' to *Beyond Insomnia*? There's honest-to-god aliens comin' and goin'. Right up there. And we just seen one."

The first man waved to another, who brought over a camera, flipped out the screen, and let Martin and Stewart watch. The one-eyed Town Car roared toward the camera. Jeffrey's motion-blurred face appeared momentarily through a ragged hole in the shattered windshield. Martin glanced at Stewart. The staple gun had inflicted some damage after all. Jeffrey didn't slow down for anyone, or anything. The few people visible had slumped over, or had crumbled to the ground.

"I don't think he's coming back," said Stewart.

CHAPTER
21

Martin awoke to a buzzing, metal and plastic on wood, in a sideways world. Some small part of him knew exactly what, even if the rest didn't understand why or where. He sat up, wiped drool off his cheek, and answered his phone.

"Martin Wells?" asked a chipper voice. Martin grunted his assent. "I'm sorry. Have I called at a bad time?"

"No. Who is this?"

"Alicia McLanahan, producer for Lee Danvers and *Beyond Insomnia*. We spoke a couple of weeks ago about your video."

"Yeah. Hi. Didn't get much sleep last night."

She laughed politely. "Did you hear last night's show?"

"Some of it," said Martin.

"Then you probably won't be surprised to hear that Lee is coming out to Montana to do several nights of special shows."

"Okay?" said Martin.

"And of course he'd like to meet you and have you on the show," said Alicia. "Would it be possible for you to come to Brixton either tomorrow night or the next evening?"

"I think I'm in Brixton now," said Martin. His surroundings

had resolved themselves into the living room of Stewart's trailer. Cheryl's home. The sunlight that found its way around the curtains regretted it. This was Stewart's couch, Cheryl's couch. The crocheted blanket he'd thrown aside might have been handmade by Cheryl, or Linda, or maybe Margie, the grandmother. Or it could have been made in Taiwan and bought at Kmart.

"Oh, that's great, then," said Alicia. Is it? Martin wondered as he swiped at a pool of drool he'd left on the upholstery.

"We have a field producer, Brian, landing in Billings this morning, and we're making arrangements to broadcast from Herbert's Corner. Do you know where that is?"

"Have you ever been to Brixton, Montana?" Martin asked.

Alicia hesitated. "I'll take that as a yes. Can I confirm to Brian that you'll be available either tomorrow or the next day?"

"Sure," said Martin.

"Thank you, Mr. Wells." She typed for a moment, and then said, "One more thing. Lee is very much looking forward to meeting you but would like to talk exclusively about the video and how you obtained it. On your original call you made reference to an alien invasion. We would like to downplay any discussion that may cause unwarranted fear or panic."

"Unwarranted?"

"Unnecessary…"

"I know what it means, I just—you know what? Fine. The video," said Martin.

"Brian will explain more when he arrives," said Alicia. "Including the appearance contract and stipend. It's not much, I'm afraid, but it should compensate you for your time."

"Fine," said Martin, not sure what he had agreed to. Behind the curtains, he found the Screwmobile parked where Stewart's Skylark should have been, or Cheryl's Pontiac. It all flooded back.

Punching Jeffrey, chasing him down 15, Stewart's wreck, the assembly of Wakers on the bluff.

Martin checked the time. He had two accounts expecting him in Lewistown. And maybe the police, too. Then he needed to go back to Billings for another load. He couldn't remember his schedule past that. Except that he now had to come back to Brixton to be interviewed on the radio by Lee Danvers. Was that a good idea? And with all those people camped out there now, how were they going to steal a truck? The stupid CEO could be in the solar system any minute.

Martin heard his name as he looked into Stewart's bedroom. The "Mar" sounded like the whisper of tearing paper. The "tin" more punctuation than syllable. Suck. Hiss. Wheeze.

The dingy gray light revealed the old man on the bed exactly where Martin remembered leaving him. Martin rearranged the blanket over Stewart's socked feet and checked his oxygen. "How you doing?" he asked.

"I've been better," said Stewart. "I'm sorry."

"What are you sorry for?"

"That I didn't get us a…" Stewart coughed and sputtered. He moved strangely, as if part of him didn't work any longer. Martin found a Kleenex and tried to put it into Stewart's hand. His rough skin felt cold and looked unnaturally purple, as if bruised. Martin wiped the flecks of spit from Stewart's lips when the coughing subsided. Stewart let out a gruff but miserable moan. "…get us a truck when I had the chance. Jeffrey'll be warning everybody. There won't be another."

"Don't worry about it now," said Martin. "Let me change your oxygen."

"That wreck did a little more damage than I thought," said Stewart. "Can't really move too well."

"Can you take off the skin thing you're wearing?" Martin asked.

Stewart shook his head and closed his eyes. "Won't last long like that."

"What do I do?" asked Martin.

"I know you probably have appointments."

"That's not what I mean," said Martin. "I mean what do we do? Are we finished?"

"I've been thinking about it all night, but…" He coughed a few more times and then continued. "I don't know. But no sense you losing your job 'cause of me. Go on."

"I can't leave you like this," said Martin.

"The hell you can't. I'll call you if I think of something. Go next door," Stewart wheezed. "Laura and Milton'll look in on me."

"Are you sure? They'll probably want to call a doctor," said Martin.

"It'll be…okay," said Stewart.

Martin hesitated in the driveway, then climbed the steps and knocked on Laura and Milton's door.

☙ ☙ ☙

"Martin. You look terrible," said Eileen.

"A number five, to go, as fast as possible," Martin replied, taking the only free stool in a diner full of unfamiliar faces. People up from Billings or over from Great Falls or wherever. Bleary people, in yesterday's clothes, not exactly the tinfoil-hat crowd, but the practical fringe smart enough to come down off the hill and find a place for breakfast, probably—hopefully—on their way home.

"Anything else?" she asked.

"Stewart's not doing so well," he said.

She pursed her lips. "Deputies talked about findin' his car in the ditch. He injured?"

"Didn't seem so last night," said Martin. "I got him home. Laura and Milton are looking after him now."

"You know who hit him?" asked Eileen.

Martin nodded. "No deputy'll catch him," he said. "I don't know what to do."

"I know you and Stewart were cookin' up something," said Eileen. "Stewart Campion refused to set foot in Herbert's Corner for twenty-five years until a few days ago. Why don't you go ahead with whatever you all were plannin'?"

Martin shook his head.

"You were going to go after Cheryl," said Eileen. Martin nodded. "It's a long way to Boise." She glanced at the other break-fasters. "But the last thing you want to be is stuck here in Brixton with nothing but regrets. Take it from me."

"What do you regret?" Martin asked.

"Oh, that's too long a story," said Eileen, backing away to fetch an order off the kitchen window. "Besides, I got a houseful here."

"You a regular?" asked the man on the next stool. His mutton-chops segued expertly into a Def Leppard T-shirt. His friend leaned over like a second head on the man's shoulders.

"What?"

"You know the waitresses."

"Oh. Yeah."

"Have you seen any aliens here?"

Martin had, in fact. He'd seen Jeffrey over in that booth, he'd seen Stewart at that table, and he'd talked to at least one truck driver who had sat right here. Heck, the whole darned place had been named after an alien. But at least they belonged here, he thought.

"Nope," said Martin. "There's no aliens. The guy who built this place made it all up."

"Then what do you think's happening down the road?" asked the friend.

"On behalf of the Chamber of Commerce, thanks for spending money in Brixton," Martin replied and gave them a wink. Hopefully they'd think he was an alien.

☙ ☙ ☙

Martin plodded up the vaguely familiar stairs to a distantly recognizable door, and was surprised when a key in his possession let him inside. These objects in this few hundred square feet of carpet and painted drywall couldn't be his, couldn't be relevant. But Martin got his laptop on, uploaded the orders from the last couple of days, hopped in the shower, and tried to let home soak in anyway. The sense of place returned ten minutes later, hot water gone, when he couldn't find a pair of clean underwear.

After jamming several quarters into the commercial Maytag in the complex's laundry room, Martin checked in with Stewart. Milton answered. Stewart had slept and he'd eaten a little, and had gotten into the bathroom a couple of times. A deputy had come by to ask questions about the wreck. Laura had recruited a couple of other neighbors to keep an eye on him. Martin promised to get back and help as soon as he could. Almost as soon as he'd hung up, his phone rang.

"Hey, Marty. Did you get my email?"

"Rick? Email? No," said Martin.

"No? I sent it yesterday."

"The motel…" Martin paused to give his brain a moment. "Their Wi-Fi wasn't working."

"Explains it. I didn't see any orders from you yesterday," said Rick.

"Uploaded them a few minutes ago," said Martin. "What's the email about?"

"I'm flying in tomorrow morning. You'll pick me up bright and early at the airport. I'm going to work with you for a few days, train you on pitching the on-site account ordering application. Corporate's got a name for it now: FastLink."

"Snazzy," said Martin. He was being usurped by a microwaveable sausage. "Tomorrow?"

"My flight lands at 6:30 a.m. I've already set up the appointments. We'll spend the first day in the Billings area; then we'll head out of town for a couple days. The itinerary's in the email."

"I just spent the last three hours loading up the truck for accounts out east," said Martin. "Do I need to restock for these different accounts?"

"No, don't bother. We won't be restocking or writing orders. Shake 'N Bake sales calls," said Rick.

"Understood," said Martin. Shake 'N Bake sales calls? Was that even a thing?

"Great. I'll see you in the morning. Bright eyed and bushy tailed," said Rick.

"What time will we be done tomorrow?" asked Martin.

"Why? You got a hot date?" asked Rick.

The producer Brian had called earlier that afternoon and scheduled Martin as an official guest on *Beyond Insomnia* tomorrow night. With any luck, Martin could get to Brixton, do the show, and get back to Billings the next morning without having to tell Rick about it. "No, just wondering," he said.

Someone had tacked Papa John's coupons on the laundry

room bulletin board. Martin ripped them down and made the call. Time for someone else to do the driving for a change.

🐾 🐾 🐾

The next morning, Martin's phone rang as the airport rose into view. He winced but answered.

"Where are you?"

"Two minutes out," said Martin.

"Are you sure you can find me at this bustling international airport? I'm on the sidewalk outside—what is this?—Door 4? And I don't think there is a Door 5."

Rick was a beer keg of a man with graying red hair, squeezed into a department-store suit, towing a too-small carry-on—a Viking emasculated by the times. He stuck out his thumb as Martin rolled up to the curb.

"Truck looks good," he said, opening the passenger door. Martin breathed a sigh of relief that he had pulled himself together enough last night to go wash and vacuum out the Screwmobile. He had stowed the radio box and otherwise made everything fleet inspection-worthy. "Driving okay?" Rick asked as they put his bag in the back.

"Well enough," said Martin.

"Yep, had good luck with these Fords," said Rick.

"Where are we going?" asked Martin.

"Thought we'd get some breakfast. We'll go over the pitch and the materials, and then head out. Oh, but change of plans. No Billings today. Got a call from the Shipton's people. Got to do them later. We're going to Bozeman. Then up through Helena and Great Falls the next couple of days. We'll do Billings later this week."

"I'm not packed," said Martin.

"Then I suggest you get packed," said Rick.

❧ ❧ ❧

"And that is how we do that," Rick said as they emerged through the sliding glass doors of their first account in Bozeman. Martin agreed dutifully, but something told him that Julius had already signed his store up for FastLink long before Rick walked through the door. "It's all about playing up the incentives."

"Will corporate really sustain these kinds of discounts?" asked Martin.

"They will as long as everyone's making money," said Rick.

Martin gave corporate twelve months before they started rolling back the incentives. Someone had it all worked out. Step 1: Offer deep discounts to get stores to have minimum-wage stockers do the work of the account reps. Step 2: Scale back the number of account reps, get rid of the fleet of expensive trucks in exchange for freight services, and pass freight costs on to the customer. Step 3: Creep the prices back up to pre-discount levels. If done slowly enough, the stores wouldn't even notice that they'd been shafted. Plus, with the high turnover at most stores, soon people wouldn't even remember a time when a FastNCo. rep replenished the stock, or even that one had ever existed.

At the next store, Rick told the same lies to a different store manager. And then another. The last one pulled Martin aside after the meeting, while Rick used the restroom.

"Sounds like they're putting you out of a job," she said.

Martin paused to decide whether to toe the party line. "FastNCo. will always need a rep in Montana," he replied.

"But will Montana always need a FastNCo. rep?" she asked. "They start jacking the prices back up, and I'll be shopping for a different vendor."

God, I need a new job, thought Martin.

Rick returned, rubbing his hands together. "Time for some lunch," he said as they left. "Bozeman's a college town. They got a Hooters, don't they?"

"I think so," said Martin.

"Good. Nothing beats an owl-themed restaurant." Rick guffawed and, in the truck, poked at Martin's GPS for directions.

Martin's phone rang as he was pulling out of the store's parking lot.

"Stewart?" he asked, answering.

"Martin." Stewart's voice was breathy and strained.

"Are you okay?" asked Martin. He gave Rick a shake of the head that it was nothing he needed to worry about.

"Laura won't stop trying to feed me," said Stewart.

"What's going on?"

"Did Jeffrey call you?" asked Stewart.

"No," said Martin. "Is he back?" The GPS told him to turn, and so did Rick. Martin turned.

"He's still up there. But he called me," said Stewart. "Gave me one last chance to give myself up and get my job back. I told him to go screw himself. But that's it, Martin. He's desperate. Chumpdark's there, or close."

"But with everyone out there, we can't get through the..." Martin checked himself. "...out of Brixton without..." He couldn't finish the sentence with Rick in the cab. "Right?"

"I know," said Stewart. "I'm sorry, Martin. I should have listened to you. We could have figured out this plan a long time ago." His voice quavered. Martin heard a woman's voice in the background and imagined Stewart waving Laura away with those giant, thin-skinned hands. "I'm afraid it'll be too late. I'm afraid of what they'll do to Cheryl if they can't send her back. I have to try and get her. You have to come back. You have the devices."

"I don't know when I'll be able to get back up to Brixton," said Martin, glancing at Rick.

"If we don't get through the portal in the next twelve hours, Cheryl…" Stewart began to cough.

"I understand," said Martin. "Okay. Leave it to me. I'll see you soon."

The GPS lady said, "Turn right in one thousand feet."

But I don't want to turn right in one thousand feet, thought Martin as he pulled up to a stoplight. Oh, all-knowing goddess of the dashboard, you who can direct me to any Hooters on the planet, I beg now for your wisdom.

Where do you want to go?

Brixton, Montana.

Location found. Brixton, Montana. In 2.3 miles, make a left turn onto I-90 West.

It's not that easy. My boss wants to eat hot wings and stare at college girls in orange hot pants.

Location found. Hooters of Bozeman. Turn right in one thousand feet.

Maybe Rick would be reasonable if I explained the situation to him.

Location not found. Where do you want to go?

Brixton, Montana. And it's very important.

Location found. Brixton, Montana. In 2.3 miles, make a left turn onto I-90 West.

Rick will never let me go.

Recalculating. In five hundred feet, explain how this destination will boost profits for the company in the long term.

That's not why I have to get to Brixton.

Location found. Hooters of Bozeman. Turn right in one thousand feet.

I absolutely cannot go to Hooters of Bozeman.

Location found. Montana Department of Labor and Industry—Unemployment Division. Make a legal U-turn.

Soon enough, but first I need to get to Brixton, Montana, as fast as possible. It's a life-or-death matter.

Location found. Brixton, Montana. In five hundred feet, turn to your right and tell Rick the truth.

I can't tell him the truth or I'll look like a lunatic.

Recalculating. In five hundred feet, change lanes and then lie. You have arrived.

"Change of plans," Martin said as the light turned green. "We really need to go to Brixton. Right now." He tapped the dashboard clock for effect, head checked, and got out of the lane that would take them to Hooters.

"Brixton?" asked Rick.

"It's a couple hours northeast. Little town," said Martin.

"I know what it is. I'm wondering why we have to go there," said Rick.

"That was someone from the co-op. I had talked to Lester, the manager, last night about you being in the area, and about the FastLink system. He's very interested, but he's leaving town for a few days, so if we want to pitch to him, it has to be today."

"I have appointments set up," said Rick.

"I know. I'm sorry. But, listen, he knows every manager of every store in the northeast part of the state. So if we can sell him on this system, we're in everywhere. Trust me. I know this territory." And we can get on with putting me out of a job some other time.

"Turn right now," said the GPS. Martin checked the gas gauge, and what remained of his Diet Mountain Dew. Both marginally adequate.

"But…" said Rick, looking back at the Hooters sign.

"Recalculating," said the GPS. All that space-age technology wasted trying to get Rick back to Hooters, thought Martin. "Make a legal U-turn in three hundred feet," it insisted.

Martin turned it off.

CHAPTER
22

There could be only one reason why someone was towing a Winnebago camp trailer to Brixton, Montana. Five other cars ground along between Martin's truck and the camper, most with out-of-state license plates. Oregon. Washington. British Columbia. Nevada. No one was ever going to get by the camper on these hilly curves.

Rick drummed his fingers on the door, watching the scenery for now, placated by the promise of a welcome ear to pitch and a good little diner for a late lunch. Not so many owls at Herbert's Corner, but you got a lot of food for the money. And they had good pie.

The gas light popped on with a friendly ding.

"It's only a few more miles," said Martin. What was he going to tell Rick when they got to Brixton? Martin couldn't think of anything Lester wanted less than a PDA and a bunch of extra work. Lester probably kept a fifty-five-gallon drum of tar and a bag of feathers ready for salesmen who came 'round suggestin' newfangled gadgets. There might even be a splintery rail and a couple of stout men at the ready. Martin wondered how quickly he could conjure up a convincing case of food poisoning, or Ebola.

A few minutes later, Highway 15 slowed to a crawl as they reached the edge of town. The Brixton Inn parking lot sagged under the weight of all the cars. A line trailed out the door of the market. "A motorcycle rally?" Rick guessed, pointing to the countless bikes outside the bar.

"I don't know," said Martin. He parked the Screwmobile around the back of the co-op, blocking the loading dock like no Waker had yet dared.

"Something's definitely going on," Rick called around the truck, pulling on his suit jacket as they dismounted.

"Lester'll know," said Martin.

People weren't waiting in line to get into the co-op, but Geraldine, Cheryl's replacement, had a queue a dozen deep buying everything from dog food to tarps. Jeffrey's candy rack had been picked bare of everything but black licorice. Lester wasn't at his desk in the second-floor office window.

Martin left Rick at the FastNCo. racks, ostensibly to find Lester, but possibly to bolt for the door, and broke into the line at the register to interrupt Geraldine.

"He's not here," she said. "They've been setting campfires down at Deaver Creek. The volunteer fire department called in all the reserves."

Martin thanked Geraldine, and then the city-folk Wakers, who didn't know any better than to build fires in a dry grassland.

"Bad news," Martin told Rick.

Rick jabbed his thumb at a couple down the aisle. "They're talking about extraterrestrials. What's going on around here?"

"I don't know, but Lester's been called out. Volunteer fire department."

"When's he going to be back?" asked Rick. Martin shrugged. Rick rolled his eyes. "Let's at least get some lunch."

They stopped in a bumper-to-bumper crawl that stretched all the way to the junction, where the Highway Patrol had set up some kind of roadblock. Pedestrians streamed past. Some wore shirtsleeves and flip-flops. Others had geared up for a night out in the mountains. A Montana Highway Patrol car had parked at an angle in the middle of the road, lights flashing. The patrolman was making sure drivers stayed in their lane. Martin rolled down the window as they crept by, but Rick leaned over and shouted his question first.

"What's going on?"

"Lee Danvers has got the whole Waker Nation convinced there's aliens coming to Earth down Highway 360."

"Who's…? What?"

"It's a late-night radio show," said Martin. "Can we get down 360?"

"I'm not going to stop you from walking, but nobody's driving down there until everyone goes home," the officer replied.

"We're trying to get to Herbert's Corner," said Martin.

"Good luck with that." The officer turned his attention to a car a few lengths back attempting to get out of line.

"Why do you want to go down 360?" asked Rick.

"That's the way back to Billings," said Martin. He checked his mirrors. Pedestrians on both sides, the patrol car, and as much traffic behind as ahead.

Twenty minutes later, Martin used the bulk of his loaded behemoth to forge a path across the highway into Herbert's Corner.

Welcome to Herbert's Corner Food and Fuel.

Step 1: That Toyota pickup is pulling out, and you're much bigger than that Acura. The gas pump is yours.

Step 2: Ignore honks and stared daggers. Exit vehicle as quickly as possible and Select Pay at Pump/Credit or Pay Inside/Cash.

Step 3: Swipe card.

Credit, Debit, or Charge to the Company About to Phase You Out?

Would you like a receipt for the expense report you might never have to file? Y/N/HELL NO

Step 4: Select grade. Pick something and pick it now, because gas might get pretty scarce pretty quick in Brixton.

Step 5: Lift handle.

Step 6: Begin fueling. No smoking. Top off with every drop you can. Ignore shouts from driver angry that you're blocking the driveway.

Herbert's Corner had been turned into a first-world refugee camp. RVs and vans, pitched tents, stretched tarps, coolers, and barbeques. On the roof of almost every RV, people stood vigil with cameras or telescopes, binoculars, spotting scopes, and even rifles—all on tripods, all trained south. The usual distant rumble of truck traffic and the song of grasshoppers were overwhelmed by engines, horns, shouts, scanner static, and Lee Danvers's voice over a hundred scattered radios.

"Gonna go get us a table," said Rick, but he returned before the pump clicked off.

"Crowded?" asked Martin.

"Ha. Some old bird gave me the brush-off, told me they're out of food," said Rick. "The store was about cleaned out, too. This was a hell of a mistake, Martin. We've lost a half a day here. You got gas? Then let's get back to Bozeman." Rick slammed his door.

Martin maneuvered through the melee out to 15 toward Brixton. At the junction, a phalanx of Highway Patrol vehicles, barriers, and flashing construction message boards informed travelers that no way in hell should anyone expect to drive south on 360 today.

"I've got to make a stop," said Martin.

"If you had to go…" said Rick.

"I need to see a friend. He's sick."

"No, we need to get back to Bozeman. I'm going to make a couple of calls—if we can even get cell service out here—and see if we can salvage any of this afternoon."

Martin squeezed out into the line of traffic trickling toward Brixton. The bulging, infested town rolled closer and closer. As Rick made new plans with Bozeman, Martin heard sound and tone, but no meaning. The turn to Stewart's crept nearer and nearer. Nearer and nearer. And then they were there.

I didn't refill my Diet Mountain Dew, Martin thought, and then jerked the Screwmobile through a nonexistent gap between two oncoming cars. Finding an open lane ahead, he floored the accelerator.

Rick swore. "I told you we're going back to Bozeman," he said. "Martin?"

"It's only a mile up here," said Martin.

"Fine. Ten minutes," said Rick. "I mean it." He got back on the phone. "Pete? You still there?"

Milton came out onto the steps as Martin rolled into the driveway.

"How is he?" Martin asked, and followed the neighbor inside.

"Laura's been with him all day," said Milton. "Tried to call him a doctor. But he refuses, and with everything going on in town…"

Laura had opened the curtains and the windows. Fresh air

and sunlight found their way in but managed to avoid the bed and its occupant.

"Martin," said Stewart.

"He's been asking for you," said Laura, turning down the radio chirping talk out of Billings.

"She took my phone away," said Stewart.

"I couldn't really talk anyway," said Martin. "I was with my boss." Stewart's eyes landed on the doorway behind Martin.

"That him?" Stewart wheezed.

Rick filled the doorway like he planned to solve this problem once and for all, but seeing Stewart, he deflated.

"Stewart, Rick. Rick, this is Stewart," said Martin.

"Hi," Rick grunted.

"Jeffrey never called me," Martin said. "What do you think that means?"

"Not sure," Stewart said, then winced and wheezed hard. He swore.

"Tell me what to do. Please," said Martin.

"Give us a minute," said Stewart.

Rick protested, but Laura shooed him out and closed the door.

"You've got the devices?"

"They work. I hooked them up in my truck and got some kind of control screen," said Martin.

"Good enough," said Stewart. "Simple interface. Tap the icons. Can't tell you more. I haven't seen the darn thing since '86."

"But I can't go…"

"Who else, Martin?" asked Stewart.

Martin hung his chin for a moment, and then sighed and nodded. "What am I going to find up there?"

"Jeffrey might still be there alone," said Stewart. "Unless

Chumpdark's arrived. He'll come with a little entourage. You'll need this."

Stewart dug an object out from under a blanket. The staple gun. He fumbled with a catch, made some adjustment, reset the catch, and set it on the bed. "Don't point that at anything you value," he said. Martin set a hand on it but didn't pick it up.

"There's another problem," said Martin. "They've closed 360. Is there a back way up to Deaver Creek?"

"You got your truck?"

"Yeah, and it's fully loaded, too."

"I doubt you'd make it with that," said Stewart. "It's all pretty rough ranch land down that way. But I've been thinking." He nodded to the radio. "Lee Danvers is in town. Been hyping a live show from Brixton tonight."

"I know. I'm supposed to be on it," said Martin.

"You get over there and convince him, he might have some pull to get you through the roadblock."

"His producers have already warned me about talking to him about this stuff," said Martin. "They're not going to let me near him if I start talking crazy."

"Then take me with you," said Stewart. "I think I can convince him."

When Martin opened the door, Laura gasped to see Stewart on his feet. He put one loafered foot in front of the other, with an arm draped hard over Martin's shoulders.

"Are you taking that man to a hospital?" asked Laura. "That's the only place he should be going."

"Do you need anything else?" Martin asked Stewart. Stewart shook his head once, firmly. Martin ignored a demand from Rick.

On the steps, a coughing fit stopped them for more than a minute. "Is he going to try to climb into your truck?" Milton asked.

"Have to," Stewart managed between coughs.

"Uh-uh," said Rick. "That's a company truck. You can't take passengers."

"We can take my car," said Milton.

"We're taking the truck," said Martin.

The coughing subsided, and Stewart wiped his sleeve across his mouth. "Let's go," he said.

"He's not getting in that truck," said Rick, now out on the little porch. Rick repeated his ultimatum and raised a trembling hand like a substitute teacher. Poor Rick. All those useless management-training retreats. There had been no bubbly consultant's lecture on combating civil disobedience. No ropes course had taught him how to face down active defiance. He had nothing left but his bureaucratic bluster.

"You take that truck, and it's your job," said Rick.

Martin shut Stewart's door and rounded the front, thanking Laura and Milton.

"You take that truck and I'm calling the police," said Rick. "Grand theft auto. You'll be held accountable."

"Put it in my performance evaluation," said Martin. He slammed the truck into reverse, backed out, and then headed toward the cattle guard in a cloud of dust.

"Did you just quit your job?" asked Stewart.

They rumbled faster across the grating than the taxed suspension liked, and Martin skidded the tires as he turned back toward town. "It might be a good thing if I die in the Kuiper Belt tonight," he said, giving Stewart a sidelong glance. He chuckled. The old man laughed, too, then leaned his head back in pain.

CHAPTER
23

Martin and Stewart waited to turn right onto Highway 15 for so long that Martin turned his blinker off. Vehicles still flooded in from the west, and to the east, the inundation had backed up in an unforgiving snarl. A constant stream of Wakers waded past on foot as if Lee Danvers was presiding over the Second Coming of Oprah Christ Presley at Herbert's Corner.

"Could you walk to the Corner?" asked Martin.

"Doubt it," said Stewart. "Can you cross 15? Come at Herbert's from the north? Maybe Trappers Road over to 360?"

"Maybe. If I could force our way across," said Martin. "Or maybe I could get Lee Danvers to come to us."

"You have his number?"

"I've got his producer's number," said Martin. "But where would we even meet him?" Martin made the call.

Brian was glad to hear from him. "As you can guess, it's been crazy. We've had to change the location of the broadcast," he said. Martin's stomach sank. Lee probably hadn't made it into town because of the road closure. Martin's anger swerved into guilt when he remembered that this was kind of all his fault. Telling

Jeffrey about the pie. Calling BI and selling them the video. What had he been thinking? Stupid butterfly wings spinning eddies off into the air. "Company that owns Herbert's Corner said no to the broadcast, so we're at the Brixton Inn. You know where that is?"

❦ ❦ ❦

Martin had never before seen the Brixton Inn turn on the "No" of the vacancy sign, yet the lobby was strangely deserted. Martin lowered Stewart into a chair at a table in the breakfast area, and Stewart slumped forward. His back rose and fell with the Herculean effort of sucking in his own breath. Martin felt inches taller after finally releasing the man—or man-like being, or being in a man suit. He'd supported Stewart for several hundred yards—which was as close as he could park, even on the meager back streets of Brixton.

Brenda was leaning on the front desk as if she'd been there for a month, but she helped Martin get Stewart a cup of water. "Do you want me to call someone? A doctor?" she asked.

"No, thank you," said Martin, dialing Brian's number again.

A few minutes later, the lobby door chime binged for a slim, gym-toned man in a button-up shirt and expensive slacks. "Martin?" he asked, and offered his hand. "I'm Brian Buchheit. Pleased to meet you. Is this your father?"

"This is Stewart. He's a friend," said Martin.

"Oh. I'm glad you found the place. Now, it's only…" he checked the time on his iPhone, but Martin interrupted.

"We need to talk to Lee right now."

"I'm afraid that's impossible," said Brian. "As I was saying…"

"It's very important," said Martin. "Is he here?"

"And I'm telling you it's not going to happen," said Brian. "Now, if we're going to have a problem, we will simply cancel your interview. Lee Danvers maintains a very high professional standard for content on his broadcasts, and he is pleased to offer you a chance to be on the show. He also appreciates his fans. However, he does not have time to deal directly with every listener or guest with a question, a grievance, or even a compelling story. If you have an issue, I would be happy to hear it. But that's as far as it goes."

Martin gripped the staple gun tucked in his belt, but Stewart grunted and shook his head.

Stewart sucked in a deep breath and pulled himself as tall as he could in the chair. "Brian. What if I told you that we held physical evidence of extraterrestrial visitation, right here, right now, in this room?"

Brian laughed. "I've heard this one before, guys. I get six calls a day from people who say the same thing."

"Not like this, you don't," said Stewart.

"What is it? Show me," said Brian.

"Lee has to be here," said Martin. "I need him to get me up to the Deaver Creek bluff. Once there, I can show him how the portal works and where the vehicles come from."

"Is this some ET-phone-home crap?" asked Brian.

"My stepdaughter's up there," said Stewart. "Through the portal. They have her."

"Your stepdaughter? They? Aliens? Your stepdaughter has been abducted by aliens? Come on, guys. You can't do any better than this?" asked Brian. He slid a piece of paper from a folder and set it on the table. "This is the appearance contract, Martin. We'll need your signature on that prior to..."

Stewart's hand landed on Brian's wrist, and Brian made a sound that might have begun as an English word in his brain, but didn't escape his throat as such. "Please," said Stewart.

"Let go of me," said Brian.

"Brenda?" Stewart bellowed.

"Yes, Mr. Campion?"

"Come over here, please." Stewart's eyes were blazing.

"What do you need?"

"Lee Danvers's room number."

"I…I can't…" said Brenda.

"You and I both know that Cheryl didn't run off to Boise," Stewart said to Brenda, but staring down Brian. "Now, in order to help her, I need to talk to Lee Danvers. If I don't, she'll most likely die, and we'll never see her again. Now, I'm going to ask you again, what room is he in?"

Brian shook his head at Brenda, but he couldn't wrench his wrist free. Martin gave her a reassuring nod.

"They're in Rooms 209 and 210. They've got the adjoining doors," said Brenda.

"Thank you, Brenda. Now, listen producer boy, you have two choices. You can take us up there nice and friendly-like. Or Martin and I will go up alone, disintegrate the doors, and talk to Lee without you."

Stewart let go of Brian's wrist, and the producer backed up to the breakfast bar, dark and wiped clean for the day. The waffle maker closed and cool. The cereal rack empty. The icy bowl of juices and yogurts gone. The toaster unplugged. As if it were all waiting for Cheryl to return. "Please," said Martin.

"Fine," said Brian. "Five minutes max. Less, if Lee doesn't like what he hears."

☙ ☙ ☙

Lee Danvers was shorter than Martin expected, so much smaller than life, with thinner and less coiffed hair than in all the promotional photos. The photographers had been good. Lee had a nose for radio, not overly large, but somehow cavernous. It was probably what gave his voice its resonance. Martin had always pictured Lee in a suit and tie, but he wore a polo shirt with a wakernation.com logo. Lee took off a pair of reading glasses to examine Martin and Stewart.

Stewart recovered enough from the stair climb for a last push to a seat on the nearest bed in Lee's motel room.

"You're Martin Wells?" asked Lee.

"Yes, sir. And this is Stewart Campion. Thank you for seeing us."

"What can I do for you? Brian tells me you have proof of extraterrestrial visitation."

"Yes, sir," said Martin. "But what we're really asking for is help to get a vehicle up to the bluff on Highway 360. We have to get through the portal."

Lee glanced at Brian and laughed. "Through it? You're serious? What makes you think I can help with that?"

"Sorry. I'm not explaining. We can get through the portal with our truck, but we can't get *to* the portal with the road closed. We assumed that you'd have some kind of access arranged," said Martin.

"You can actually get through this…portal?" asked Lee.

"You don't believe it's real?"

"I don't know what's going on up there," said Lee. "What's this proof of yours?"

Stewart folded over into a coughing fit.

"Should he be in a hospital?" asked Lee. Brian checked his iPhone, and Martin felt their patience slipping away.

"Some water?" asked Martin. Brian returned from the bathroom sink with a plastic cup of tap water and a handful of Kleenex. Martin pressed them into Stewart's hands as he continued to cough, and then faced Lee. "I've been told you don't want to hear about it, but everything I told you that night I called is true. There are aliens on the other side of the phenomenon down the highway, ready and willing to destroy every human on the planet. They've kidnapped this man's stepdaughter, and we're trying to rescue her before they kill her, and trying to stop them from moving ahead with their plans for Earth."

"Plans for Earth?" asked Lee.

"You wouldn't believe me if I told you," said Martin.

"Oh, don't hold back now," Lee said and gave Brian a nod. Brian moved to grab Martin's arm, but Martin shook him off.

"They're going to turn the Earth into a giant factory to bake rhubarb pies," said Martin.

"Get them out of here," said Lee. "And he is not coming on the show." Brian shoved Martin toward the door.

"Wait," Stewart bellowed. Everyone froze. "I'm the proof," he said.

Brian resumed manhandling Martin toward the door. Lee shouted for them to get out. Martin shoved Brian and turned to see Stewart pluck the cannula out from under his nose.

"Stewart?" called Martin.

Stewart groped inside his shirt, even as Brian tried to yank him off the bed. Stewart let Brian pull on one arm, but he clutched a small object in his other hand. Stewart's eyes met Martin's for a moment, and then he pressed the object with his thumb.

Stewart's skin began to slip off like a silk sheet, migrating toward the little device. Brian staggered back in revulsion. Stewart's shoes lifted off the floor and then dropped away as the appendages changed shape. His pants twisted, bulged, and then were pulled away by a pair of tentacles with articulated suckers on their wide pads. Another pair deftly unbuttoned and sloughed off Stewart's shirt. The socks and underwear were peeled away and tossed to the floor on the far side of the bed.

The glistening body, as gray and translucent as any netted squid, and nearly twice the size of Stewart the man, flopped onto the creaky mattress with a squelch of flesh. Far apart, near the middle of the bulbous, cylindrical body, blinked a pair of glassy, wide eyes, foreign but communicative. A few inches lower, a pair of slitted nostrils swelled open and clamped shut laboriously. Stewart pushed himself to a more comfortable position on the bed and sagged in relief.

Another man—X-Ray the radio engineer, judging by the headphones—strolled through the pass door from the other room. He screamed and collided with the doorframe trying to back out skeleton-first. Stewart's black eyes swung in his direction, watched the man leave, and then swept back to Lee Danvers.

His rough, aged voice emerged from the open nostrils but originated deeper within the mass of his body. "Do you want to hear my story now?" he asked.

*　*　*

Brian had locked himself in the bathroom. X-Ray had edged back into the room, having lost his ability to blink or close his mouth. Lee Danvers remained rooted to his spot at the foot of the bed, perhaps by two decades of broadcast experience, although he had dropped his reading glasses.

As Stewart told his tale, Lee studied Stewart in parts, as if trying to find the zipper. Stewart didn't have a face to read, as such, but Martin sensed emotion in his wriggling tentacles and hoped Lee noticed it, too. Martin couldn't get over how much Lee Danvers made three-dimensional flesh was not the Lee Danvers of his mind's eye. Lee shouldn't be this bald, nor so much less masculine than his voice. His pants bulged out with a spare tire under his belt. His body pinched to narrow shoulders, and a shadow over his upper lip said he'd spent most of his life with a mustache. Lee began to fidget and open his mouth to speak. He's too good an interviewer, thought Martin. He knows Stewart's avoiding all the details.

"Where are you from?" Lee blurted out.

"That's not important," said Stewart.

"I think it's pretty damned important," Lee said, as if he often interviewed squiddy aliens in motel rooms. Which, for all Martin knew, he did.

"My species lives on many worlds around this galaxy," said Stewart.

"How did you get here?" asked Lee.

"A transportation network. The portal's part of it," said Stewart.

"And what do you want with us, with Earth?"

"We told you," said Stewart.

"The rhubarb pie?" said Lee.

"Yes."

"And your daughter—or, sorry, your completely human stepdaughter—has this secret recipe?" asked Lee.

"No, but the others think she does," said Stewart.

"And if they get the recipe, they'll kill us all?" asked Lee. "So who does have this recipe?"

"No one. The only people who knew it died," said Stewart. Martin thought one of Stewart's eyes flicked in his direction.

"That's good, isn't it?" asked Lee.

"If anyone had it, we probably wouldn't be here talking right now," said Stewart.

"I suppose that's true," said Lee. "I've heard a lot of stupid stories in my time, but this one is so...blisteringly stupid, I really don't know what to believe. No offense."

"It's no joke, I assure you," said Stewart. "You have my word."

He raised a tentacle toward Lee. Lee backed slightly, then extended his right hand as if Stewart's tentacle was a frying pan of live scorpions. The suckers on Stewart's palm flexed open, then hissed shut, leaving a flat blade of pale gray skin. The two appendages met. Stewart's tentacle wrapped gently around the heel of Lee's hand. "Everything I've told you is the absolute truth," he said. Then, the tentacle wilted, limp and drained.

Martin stepped on the oxygen line and picked it up, wondering if Stewart still needed it, or where he'd even position the cannula. It might serve one nostril, or gill slit, or whatever, but not both.

"You don't believe me?" asked Stewart.

"I don't know what to believe. You're…pretty believable, but this whole thing is preposterous."

"Why preposterous? What's a sensible reason for my species to come to Earth?" asked Stewart.

"I don't know. Exploration? Scientific discovery? Contact?" suggested Lee.

Stewart made a sound. Laughter, Martin supposed. "A hundred thousand years ago, maybe," he said. "These days, we come when the numbers add up. The truck drivers take the most economical route, and they like a bit of foreign food. My company's here because they can make untold profit on a novelty sure to become a dessert staple in trillions of homes. Why did you come to Montana?"

"I…" said Lee.

"I'll tell you why," said Stewart. "You came to Montana because you could charge your advertisers prime rates for a show done live from an unexplained phenomenon before it becomes yesterday's news. Which, because you're a jaded broadcaster used to dealing with such things, you're sure has a perfectly reasonable explanation or is an elaborate hoax. You don't care about the truth.

You like the cash. You like the attention and the new members dropping twenty-five bucks a pop for annual memberships to the Waker Nation for the exclusive footage. You don't care that your listeners are trampling this town to death in search of a truth that you never intend to give them."

"We're both big fans," said Martin. Lee looked at Martin like he'd forgotten about him and then collapsed into a desk chair.

"Are there any more of you?" asked Lee. "Or others?"

"No. I'm the only one on the planet right now. As far as I know. And there aren't any others. No Grays. No Reptoids. Only me," said Stewart.

Through a long quiet, Lee studied the carpet, then the horrible pattern of the bedspread, then a focal point a million miles past. Then he found Stewart again.

"I'm glad you came to me, but..." said Lee. He looked at X-Ray, then at Martin, then at the bathroom door where his producer was probably shivering fetal in the tub.

"You can't put this on the radio," said Stewart, stating a fact, not a demand.

"That's right," said Lee. "I have a section in my contracts, my company's insurance documents, in every deal with my sponsors. My lawyers call it the 'War of the Worlds' clause."

"You can't start a panic," said Stewart.

"I even have a—let's call it a verbal agreement—with certain representatives of the United States military, that if I am ever in this exact situation, I'm supposed to call them immediately. Do not pass go, do not collect two hundred dollars."

"We're not asking for publicity. We only need your help getting up to the portal," said Martin.

"And what makes you think I can help?" asked Lee.

"We figured you'd be going up there later to do the show.

That you'd have a deal with the Highway Patrol to get past the roadblock," said Martin.

Lee laughed a sad little chuckle. "I hate to tell you, but I don't have any such deal. We're not exactly the Montana Highway Patrol's favorite people right now."

CHAPTER
24

A piteous, burbling, low-frequency moan emanated from deep inside Stewart. Then he began to cough. His body contracted. Hot air and flecks of phlegm spurted out his nostrils. He bent near his middle and rolled over to cough into the bedspread, tentacles flailing with each spasm.

"Stewart?" Martin put a hand on his back.

X-Ray said, "He's going to die. Aren't you going to call anyone?"

"Who do you want me to call exactly? 911?" asked Lee.

"911. The government. You gotta know someone who can…"

"Who can what?" asked Lee.

"What's wrong with him?" asked X-Ray.

"He's old," Martin fired over his shoulder. "He's been squeezed in that skin since the eighties, and this isn't exactly his home environment."

"He can't die here. He can't die here," said X-Ray. "You have to call…"

Lee grabbed X-Ray's collar. "You think the United States government is going to nurse him back to health and let him get back to shuffleboard at the retirement home? I'm not calling anyone."

"Martin," Stewart choked out.

"What? Everyone, quiet." Martin climbed onto the bed to get nearer. Stewart coughed a few more times, then his body relaxed.

"Martin," he said again.

"Yes, Stewart. I'm here."

"You can't waste any more time. If he can't help you, you have to go. Get Cheryl," said Stewart. "Save her."

"I can't do it by myself. I don't…"

"Martin. I can't," said Stewart.

"What do I do?" asked Martin.

"I don't know," said Stewart. "But you're the only…"

"Stewart?"

"Oh my god, he's dead," said X-Ray.

Stewart's body swelled and deflated, and the nostrils slapped open and sucked closed with sticky effort. "He's not dead," said Lee.

Martin got off the bed and found himself face to face with Lee Danvers. "I have to go," said Martin. "And I have to leave him…"

"No," said Lee.

"What? I can't move him," said Martin.

"I mean, wait," said Lee. He grabbed X-Ray by the arm and dragged him toward the bathroom. He pounded on the door. "Brian, open this door right now. Or you can kiss your job goodbye."

Lee pounded again, and then the doorknob clicked. Lee pushed the door open before Brian had second thoughts. Martin felt a welcome waft of cool air. Brian must have opened the bathroom window but found it too small to escape through. Lee shoved X-Ray in before him and closed the door.

Stewart stirred with a rill of tentacles. "What's going on?" he asked.

"They're arguing," said Martin. "Trying to decide what to do about you, I think. Are you sure you can't move? Maybe get that skin thing back on?"

Stewart moaned and waved a tentacle. The device whacked against the wall and bounced on the floor. "It's useless now," said Stewart.

"I'm sorry," said Martin.

"What for?" asked Stewart.

"Making you come here. Everything, really."

"It was my decision to take off the dermis," said Stewart.

"Are you going to die?"

"Probably." Stewart's nearest eye noticed the oxygen line in Martin's hand. "That still putting out oh-two?"

A few minutes later, Lee emerged from the bathroom with his team, Shaken and Stirred.

"I'm not dead yet," Stewart told them. He was holding the cannula under one of his nostrils with several tentacles.

"I'm coming with you," said Lee. X-Ray squeezed around Martin and disappeared into the other room.

"Really?" asked Martin.

"Brian and X-Ray will watch your friend until we get back, and they're not going to call anyone," said Lee.

"I don't understand," said Martin.

"You said you couldn't do it alone, so I'm coming with you," said Lee.

"Um…and you know what we're about to do?" asked Martin.

"We're going to drive through the portal down the highway, pop out on the other side, and rescue his daughter from a couple of aliens."

"Stepdaughter," said Martin.

"Oh, you think that's the salient detail I need to get right?" asked Lee.

X-Ray returned with an open backpack. He fished around, checking the contents. "Okay, your iPad, a camera, an audio recorder. Everything's charged," he said.

"And you're set up to broadcast a call from my cell?" asked Lee.

"Should be. Call and I'll run a check," said X-Ray.

"You're putting this on the radio?" asked Martin. "We did mention that we might end up out in the Kuiper Belt with some pissed-off squids and no way back. How's that going to sit with your lawyers?"

"I didn't come to Brixton to sit in some fleabag motel room." Lee zipped the pack shut and slung it over his shoulder.

"I don't know about this," said Martin.

"You came to me. You want my help or not?" asked Lee.

"Martin," said Stewart. "Take him with you. He can help."

Side by side with Lee under the motel's carport, Martin said, "It's not a fleabag."

"No?" asked Lee.

"They have a good breakfast," said Martin.

"Great," Lee said.

As they walked along the parking lot that was Highway 15, Martin worried that someone would recognize Lee and delay them, but Lee was a radio star. "Which one is yours?" Lee asked as they turned down the side street.

Martin pointed. "The FastNCo. truck."

"Not exactly what I was expecting, but okay," said Lee. "You a salesman?"

Was he? It seemed like a lifetime ago since he'd picked up Rick at the airport, or even since he'd abandoned him at Stewart's house. "Account rep," said Martin. "Nothing to do as I drive around but listen to you. I got XM so I could hear your show 24/7."

Lee smirked. "You know, I always figured that if I did this show long enough, something would eventually be true. But honestly, I didn't think it would be this one."

"None of it's true?" asked Martin.

"I can't help that my audience takes it all a little too seriously," said Lee.

"But then why do you keep spreading it all around?"

"Because I've got an ex-wife and two kids in college, a new wife and kid, a mortgage, and a staff of thirty-two to keep paid," said Lee.

"Oh," said Martin. "Is that why you're coming along? For ratings? More blurry video for wakernation.com?"

"This is what I do," said Lee.

"I suppose," said Martin. "But that's not why I'm going."

"I won't get in your way," said Lee.

Martin climbed into the back of his truck and dug out the radio box, cringing as he moved Rick's overnight bag out of the way.

Lee whistled, and said, "Lotta hardware."

"Here." Martin handed the box down to Lee and turned to find his tools.

"What's this?" Lee asked.

"It's you," said Martin. "They wouldn't let me put XM in the fleet truck, so I had to improvise."

"But they're going to let you take their truck to the Kuiper Belt?" asked Lee.

"This probably won't fall under the 'incidental personal use' section in the FastNCo. employee fleet manual, no," said Martin.

"Even though it's an emergency?" asked Lee.

"Don't remember," said Martin, hopping down. "Don't care anymore."

A few minutes later, as Martin lay on his back under the passenger-side dashboard, Lee asked, "Have we figured out how we're going to get out to this portal thing?"

"Been thinking about that," said Martin. "We have to assume that they'll have all the roads blocked, even the dirt ones, anything on the GPS maps. But there's got to be some kind of back way."

"So we're just going to head out in that direction?" asked Lee. Martin shimmied out from under the dashboard and turned on the ignition. Lee gaped when the plane of glowing alien icons slid into existence behind the steering wheel.

"Mount up," said Martin. "I thought we'd talk to someone local first."

．．．

"She's going to be happy to see you," Martin said as he opened the screen door. He knocked, then called, "Doris. It's Martin Wells. I'm not going to tell you not to bring your shotgun this time."

"Shotgun?" asked Lee.

Doris answered the door, wearing a simple dress, a loose cardigan, and a double-barreled shotgun thicker than her forearm. "Martin? And who's this with you?"

"Doris Solberg, this is Lee Danvers," said Martin.

The barrels rose a few inches. "That ain't Lee Danvers," she said.

"Good evening, Miss Solberg. It's a pleasure to meet you," Lee said in a smooth, familiar baritone that made Martin's eyes widen along with Doris's. "May we come in?"

"Of course. Where are my manners? My, oh my, Lee Danvers in my house," she tittered as she stepped aside.

"We can't stay long," said Martin.

"Can I get you anything?" she asked. She scuttered into the kitchen, then back. She slapped at Lee's hand. "You're not tall enough."

"So says my mother," said Lee.

"Probably makes up for it in other ways," Doris said to Martin. Martin cringed.

"I made another pie," Doris called. "I been makin' them every couple days."

"Found that secret ingredient yet?" Martin asked.

"Now, you know I haven't," said Doris. "I was saving this one for Wanda's grandkids, but…"

"This is the pie?" Lee asked.

"Not *the* pie," said Martin. "But close."

Doris herded Lee to the head of her kitchen table with a piece of pie on her best china. She served one to Martin and then, heedless of their protests, hurried away to put on a pot of coffee. "You're going to be up all night. I ain't lettin' you leave here without a cup of my coffee. I got a Thermos around here somewhere. I'll make you some for the road. You all heading down to Deaver Creek and all the commotion?"

"That's what we came to talk about," said Martin.

"Excellent pie, ma'am," said Lee.

"Ma'am?" said Doris, blushing. "Now, you call me Doris."

"Doris it is," said Lee.

Doris giggled and muttered to herself.

Does she know…? Lee mouthed to Martin, waving his fork at the ceiling. Martin nodded. "I have to tell you, Doris," Lee said, "it's very good—but is, was, the special pie so much better?"

"Does he know…everything?" she asked Martin, waggling a pie server at the ceiling.

"Oh, he knows," said Martin.

"Good. I could never imagine leaving Brixton, because I'd sound like a ravin' loon anywhere else. Anyways, I couldn't taste any difference, but the aliens…? They'd shiver and quiver and order up another slice."

"But you don't know the secret?" asked Lee.

"Lord, I've tried to figure it out," said Doris, shaking her head. "Eat up."

"We hoped you might know a back way to Highway 360 from here," said Martin. "The Highway Patrol has it all blocked off, and…I'm trying to help Lee get up there to do his show."

Doris chewed her lips in Martin's direction, then turned back to her burbling coffee pot. "It's worse than that," she said. "Eileen called a bit ago. Said they're bringing in the National Guard. They're lining up trucks near the Corner." She looked squarely at Lee. "Now, you know that whoever that is, it ain't the National Guard."

"How long ago was this?" asked Martin.

"A few minutes before you knocked," said Doris.

Outside, the sun was setting. "We'd better get going," Martin said to Lee, and then asked Doris. "Can you help us?"

CHAPTER
25

Directions from Doris Solberg's house to somewhere about a quarter-mile north of the Deaver Creek bridge on Highway 360.

"First, you go about three, maybe four miles south on this road right out here. You'll pass the Mitchell place. Then the old drive to the Lazy W. You'll want to go a little ways more to Juniper Road. There's no sign, but Edgar Wilcox has got a No Trespassing sign there. Ignore it, he's harmless. He just don't like people much. And watch out for his bull. His boy's always leaving the gates open. Juniper'll go east for a while, then bend north, then back west, but soon you'll be heading east again. Now, here's where it gets tricky…"

🐾 🐾 🐾

"Are we there yet?" asked Lee.

Martin stopped the truck about twenty feet away from a gate at what appeared to be the end of the road, and rechecked his hastily sketched map. "This should be the last one, or second-to-last," said Martin. "360's right over there somewhere." The next gate, theoretically a half-mile away, on the other side of this pasture, opened onto a minor turnout along the highway.

Martin's arms felt like jelly from handling the truck over washboard roads ruined by rain, and from navigating tracks worn by ranchers on four-by-fours and trailing herds. Martin put the truck in park, and reached over Lee for the shake-up flashlight in the glove compartment.

Martin rattled the flashlight as he and Lee waded through the grass to the gate, then switched it on. Lee groaned when the feeble light landed on the latch, and the chain, and the lock.

"I hope you've got a pair of bolt cutters back in the truck," said Lee.

"You'd think so, wouldn't you?" said Martin.

Lee checked his cell phone for the thousandth time.

"Still no bars?" asked Martin. "I told you, it'll get better as we get near the highway."

"Could you ram through?" asked Lee. "It's almost broadcast time."

"No," said Martin.

"Then what… What's that?" asked Lee. "A staple gun?"

"We should probably step back by the truck," said Martin.

From behind the driver's door, Martin aimed the staple gun over the hood. He squeezed, and earned a snapping ka-chunk. He'd hoped there'd be a beam of light in the dark, that the morning sunlight had washed out the special effects when he'd shot at Jeffrey, but nothing came out. No cohesive bolt of blue, or red, or green. Not even a staple.

The fence post exploded. Lee and Martin ducked but couldn't help but watch as barbed wires twanged loose like razor-thin kraken arms in a cloud of splinters. The gate twisted away, ripping grass and metal alike. A narrow fifty-yard strip of grass and brush beyond the gate erupted in a wall of flame. A sage bush blasted out of the ground, roots and all, and landed charred and flickering a hundred feet away.

"Whoa. Ho. Ho," Martin laughed.

"Holy crap. I thought you were joking," said Lee.

"It's Stewart's." Martin handed it to Lee for inspection.

"It's a FastNCo. brand," said Lee.

"He was hiding in plain sight," Martin said, taking back the gun.

The padlock and the chain were still intact, hanging limp from the bent, relocated gate. The post had been reduced to a shattered, charred stump. Little flames still flickered along the strip of burned grass.

"We might be able to squeeze through here," said Martin. He pushed on the gate, but it would have taken more strength than he possessed to move it farther. He looked back for help, but Lee was already in the truck, checking his phone again. That's why they call them bumpers, Martin supposed.

The loaded truck bottomed out more than once. Grass and sagebrush kept up a constant scraping sweep under the floorboards. For one stretch, Lee had to get out and walk ahead, picking their way around an impassable patch with the flashlight.

"How much farther?" Martin asked as they climbed what seemed like the third rise too far. "I feel like we should be in North Dakota by now."

Near the crest of the hill, Lee said, "Stop." About a half mile to the south, Highway 360 rose up the side of the bluff. A galaxy of lights had descended onto the hillside, framing and pointing the way to the gap. The Gap. Lee rolled down the window. Martin turned off the headlights.

"What do you think?" he asked.

"I think we need to know what we're up against before we get any closer," said Lee.

"Do you have time?" Martin asked.

"I've got a few minutes, and…" He held his phone up for Martin to see. "Two bars."

"Told you," said Martin. He killed the engine and rolled down his window, letting in the murmur of a crowd, not very far away. He couldn't see the road at the nearest point, or the promised gate, but it couldn't be more than a few hundred yards east. Staple gun in one hand, flashlight in the other, Martin met Lee in front of the truck, and they set off.

"Remember where we parked," said Lee.

Their walk took them up a gentle slope that, after a few moments, peaked, and Martin let out a low whistle.

"Oh, wow," said Lee.

A Super Bowl of people, at least for the middle of nowhere Montana, lined the road from the top of the bluff and down the hill, breaking only at a brief dark gap for the Deaver Creek bridge. Like an aerial view of a river through a city at night, the banks of the road twinkled with thousands of flashlights, headlights, iPhones, and cameras. Two narrowing columns trailed off to the north, steady parallel streams of faithful pilgrims, wide awake in the night.

"Is this your fault or mine?" asked Martin.

A Highway Patrol car rolled cautiously down the middle of the road, lights flashing but with no sirens.

"Oh, definitely yours," said Lee. "Is that the gate?" At the base of the dark slope, and to the north, there might have been a thickening of the fence.

"Only one way to find out," said Martin.

They found the gate a few minutes later, at the bottom of an increasingly well-defined set of tracks rolling down the slope. The roadsides were compacted with people. And some early-bird Waker had neatly parked a six-figure motor home on the pullout, stretching like a castle wall from ditch to crowded ditch on the other side of the gate. The roof of the RV bristled with people manning cameras and telescopes.

"What do we do?" asked Martin. "We can't blast our way through that."

"I could ask them to move," said Lee. "Besides, it's time. I've got to get on the air now."

"You go over there and you'll be mobbed," said Martin.

"Maybe not," said Lee.

"Maybe there's another gate farther north," said Martin.

"You really want to waste more time searching for another gate?"

"No," said Martin.

"Then trust me and get that truck of yours down here," said Lee, dialing. He waded away through the grass with his phone to his ear. When he looked back and noticed that Martin hadn't moved, he said, "Hurry."

🐛 🐛 🐛

When Martin finally reached the Screwmobile, he hung on the hood for more than a minute to catch his breath, his gut heaving. Martin stripped off his sweat-soaked FastNCo. polo, longing to be free of the polyester. He put his hands on his head and paced, stumbling, his breath returning slowly.

In his bag behind the seat, the only other shirts he could find were more FastNCo. polos. He struggled one on over his clammy skin, hating his flab, hating the rasp of the stitched logo.

Martin started the truck. As he waited for the plane of icons to appear, a cheer rolled up from the road. Martin switched on the AM/FM radio, already tuned to the station out of Billings. As he set off for the top of the hill and the easy track down the other side, he recited with the broadcast, "From Virginia Beach to Yreka, from the Rio Grande to the Upper Peninsula…"

As Martin crested the hill, people were clamoring off the roof of the RV as if late for a Black Friday sale. They handed their tripods down to a forest of waving hands. People spilled out onto the road, making way for the RV. Some of them had linked hands, and were stepping back slowly, keeping the crowd in check, clearing a path.

The show intro ended, followed by a few seconds of silence. And then Lee, Lee as he should be, but breathless and clipped by the cell phone's range, spoke to Martin through the truck's radio. "I'll be right with you. The danger of live radio is that sometimes things don't go as planned. I beg your patience, Waker Nation."

Familiar pan flute and synthesizer bumper music toodled out in place of Lee. And over that, a prerecorded announcer's voice said, "Please stay tuned. We are experiencing technical difficulties. *Beyond Insomnia with Lee Danvers* will return shortly on the Weirdmerica Radio Network."

The RV's lights glimmered on, and it maneuvered back and forth in the tight pullout. It soon squirmed free onto the road, and backed north, leaving the lane clear for Martin to make a turn south toward the portal. A solitary figure in the middle of it all waved and pointed, directing the crowd like a conductor. The recording repeated.

Lee lifted his arms as if for a finale, and through the magic of radio, the gate opened. Several men had lifted it off its hinges and swung it into the field, pivoted on the chained end.

Lee hustled through his own personal Red Sea up the hill toward Martin with his phone still pressed to the side of his head. "This is amazing," called Martin, when they converged about a hundred yards from the gate. But Lee put a finger to his lips. He opened the passenger door but didn't get in. The pan flute toodling ceased and was replaced by a rustling and air buffeting into a microphone.

"Waker Nation, welcome to Montana," said Lee, and a few seconds later the radio repeated it. A cheer erupted across Big Thunder Valley.

"Folks." Lee waved frantically at Martin to turn off the truck's radio. "I can't tell you how excited I am about tonight's show and to be able to share this unprecedented, potentially historic, moment, not only for *Beyond Insomnia*, but for our planet and very species, with you. Since the discovery of this phenomenon, top scientists, in cooperation with the Weirdmerica Radio Network and wakernation.com, have been analyzing the collected video evidence, as well as completing geologic surveys, magnetic resonance scans, studying satellite thermo-photography, and…"

Oh my god, thought Martin. He just makes this stuff up.

"…believe they have determined the properties of the phenomenon. Today, at an emergency symposium in…in…"

"Great Falls," Martin suggested.

"…in Great Falls, Montana, these scientists assembled a package of instruments that are designed to activate, study, and potentially pass through the phenomenon to communicate with whatever is on the other side. I have been given the distinct honor of riding along for the delivery of this instrument package to the phenomenon itself. And I can't tell you how thrilled I am to bring you all with me. It's time for the rest of the world to wake up and see that the Waker Nation is the smartest audience of any radio show in the world!"

After a few seconds of delay, the crowd roared. Lee stepped away from the truck and took it all in. He gave Martin a grin. "Tonight," he said as the cheers faded, "we—not a government, not a military, not NASA or the ESA, no church, or secret cabal—yes, we, We The People, will be the first to reach out our hands in friendship to an extraterrestrial intelligence, to knock on their door and welcome them to our world as one!"

Another thunderous roar.

He was Mick Jagger.

"Are you ready?"

He was Barack Obama.

"Then let's get started!"

He was William Shatner.

He climbed in the cab. "Wakers, I'm here with a very special guest. George Henr...in...son, from the University of New Mexico at Las Cruces. George is a physicist who worked with JPL on the Dawn Probe to the asteroids Vesta and Ceres, and has been selected by his colleagues to deliver the instrument package to the phenomenon. Let's wake up and welcome him to the show."

As the assembly cheered, Lee fumbled with his phone. It beeped and he held it out on his palm.

"Welcome, George," said Lee, then nodded to Martin.

"Um. It's a pleasure to be with you tonight?" said Martin. Lee shook his head, chewing his lower lip, and gestured for more. Martin shrugged. "We are excited to be able to study this phenomenon with so many from your audience."

Lee gave Martin a thumbs-up. "So much of science is done in a lab, with few witnesses. It's a unique opportunity for people to see the work that you do. Can you tell us a little bit about what we can expect to see tonight?"

"Um, yes." Martin threw his hands up, but Lee egged him on. "We will approach the phenomenon, or the portal, as some call it, from the northwest, coming up the hill from Deaver Creek. We will need everyone to stay back, off the road. There is no danger from the portal itself, but we don't want to run over any of your guests."

"I'm sure we all thank you for that," said Lee, then waved for more.

"We will activate the…instruments…which repeat the frequency ranges we've obtained from our scans. This will activate the portal. Then we'll send in the probe."

"If it works, it should be quite a show," said Lee, "so everyone have their cameras ready. George, will the photographic evidence collected here today be valuable to your research?"

"Absolutely?" Martin shrugged. "We are setting up a database for photos and videos to be submitted to the research project, all through wakernation.com."

Yes, mouthed Lee and gave Martin another thumbs-up. "Excellent. Also, tonight we'd like to welcome a new sponsor who's woken up and smelled the coffee. FastNCo. hardware has graciously provided the delivery vehicle for the instrument package tonight. FastNCo.'s fastening hardware can be found across the nation, so be sure and follow the FastNCo. trucks to fine retailers for the best-quality products for the professional, the do-it-yourselfer, or the visitor from another world. Let's hear it for FastNCo."

Before the resulting cheer, Martin heard a rumbling, more distant than the Screwmobile's engine. Oh my god, thought Martin. The portal. But he stayed awake and no swirl of light appeared.

"Folks, I think we're about ready," said Lee. "George? Are we a go?"

Martin opened the door and stood on the doorframe to get a better view.

"George?" Lee asked again.

A line of red and blue flashing lights was approaching from the north, followed by even more lights. Not the streams of hiking Wakers with flashlights, but headlights, bright and high. A convoy of lumbering trucks.

"We have to go, now," said Martin.

"We've been given the green light," said Lee.

Martin headed west as fast as the field would let him, but kept an eye to the north. Lee grabbed onto the door and almost dropped his phone. "Let's have a countdown, Waker Nation. T minus one minute."

"Too long," Martin cried. The crowd across the road, blocking 360 to the north, began to thin. Martin heard a whoop and a bloop of a siren, and an unintelligible PA announcement, and floored it. The last thirty yards were smoother than the rest, but the compacted gravel of the pullout was a welcome sensation under the truck. Martin barely braked as he bumped out onto the road—and shouted until he knew they hadn't flipped over and murdered a bunch of Wakers.

"Ten…!" called Lee.

The open-mouthed crowd raised their arms and voices as the truck raced by. Flash. Flash. Flash. Cameras from every direction. Constellations of supernovas lit their path.

"Nine…!"

One patrol car squeezed through the Wakers in Martin's rearview mirror, then another. Lee stopped counting, seeing the chase. Objects in mirror may be closer than they appear. "Go. Go. Go," he said.

"I'm going," said Martin.

A third patrol car broke through.

"Wakers. They're trying to stop us…they're trying to stop you from knowing the truth," said Lee.

The speedometer climbed, but not nearly fast enough. Martin hoped to be more than exceeding the legal speed limit by the time they reached the bridge and the base of the hill. He couldn't let the patrol cars catch him on the slope.

The crowd counted off three, or maybe four, as they thumped across the bridge. The patrol cars neared, but then backed off. People had begun to crowd the road. Whether stepping out to hail their guru's passage, or deliberately trying to slow the evil government vehicles in the cause of scientific justice, the Screwmobile gained ground.

"Hold on," Martin called as he made the corner. He could make out the individual faces of the people he would kill if he took the curve a whisker too fast.

Martin whooped when he hit the bottom of the hill at eighty-three miles per hour, leaving a slipstream of cheering, waving, flashing Wakers in their wake. The patrol cars gained the hill, but the crowd still bogged them down.

"You know what you're doing?" called Lee.

"This one to seal us in, and this one to activate the portal," said Martin.

"Shouldn't you do that now?" asked Lee. The Gap loomed closer and closer.

Martin tapped the icon to activate the environmental field, partly hoping nothing would happen. This dampened the crowd noise, but not much. "The windows," Martin screamed. "Roll up the windows."

They cranked frantically, shutting out even more of the crowd's roar. Then Martin stabbed the portal icon. A single patrol car raced up in his mirror, having beaten the crowd.

"Did it work?" asked Lee.

On both sides of the road, as if in slow motion, people slumped, falling into piles of humanity. The patrol car slowed.

A singularity flickered into existence in The Gap. In a millisecond, a maw gaped open, swirling like an electric toilet bowl.

Martin's scream, and Lee's, and the Screwmobile's straining roar melded in the swirl and chaos.

Light shot out like a chameleon's tongue and yanked them in.

CHAPTER
26

Disconsciousness.

Extrusion of life and light.

Existence snapped back into darkness. The myriad flashes and flashlights had been replaced by the dashboard lights and a swath of stars so thick it would have made Martin want to run the windshield wipers, if he hadn't still been so busy screaming.

He separated from the seat, weightless, but forced himself back in place with both hands on the steering wheel. Lee braced himself against the ceiling.

The RPMs raced toward the red. The empty Diet Mountain Dew cup drifted out of the cup holder. The radio box wanted to float away, but Martin elbowed it against the seat.

They both stopped screaming at the same time, as if in rehearsed agreement.

"Are we dead?" asked Martin, letting his foot off the gas.

"God, I hope not," said Lee. He checked his phone, then showed it to Martin. "No Service," it said. "I guess I'm off the air."

"Could be worse. They could be charging you roaming fees," said Martin.

Lee laughed. "I'll probably get better ratings with this dead air than I've ever had. Where are we?" The Milky Way spread out ahead of them, but an object loomed in the mirrors—not so much visible, more an absence of stars.

"I suppose I press this now," said Martin, and tapped the docking icon, even as Lee raised serious wordless doubts.

They accelerated, but backward. In unison, Martin and Lee zipped their seat belts across their shoulders. The truck turned, slowly, to face their destination. An asteroid, or some kind of roughly natural body, hung nearby, dwarfed by the unnatural, scale-defying object.

The Screwmobile's headlights illuminated the thing like a firefly over an aircraft carrier. Parts, for it couldn't all be taken in at once, resembled shopping malls stuck onto hives of aircraft hangars, and not the little ones, but the Goodyear Blimp-sized ones. Those clusters were glommed fractally onto a drunken parade of airports, convention centers, and domed stadiums. Every facet, large and small, too many to count, had been decorated with a logo, the sight of which made Martin's mouth water. He felt a nascent sense of desserts, indulgent but at the same time wholesome.

"This has got to be the place," said Martin.

"I probably should have asked this earlier, but what's the plan when we get in there?" asked Lee.

Martin felt for the staple gun. "Find Cheryl and get out," he said.

"That's it?" asked Lee.

"Sue me. I'm a little out of my element here," said Martin. "I thought you were going to get some blurry footage."

Lee unzipped his bag and extracted his iPad. He held it up to the windshield and scanned the view. Martin leaned over to watch the screen.

"It's 10:23 Mountain Time on…I can't remember the date…"

Lee narrated. "And we've passed safely through the portal. I don't know where we are, but there's an asteroid or ice body close by. I'll try and get a shot of it. We are approaching, by the apparent use of some kind of tractor beam, a large ship or space complex. As you can see…" Then he shut it off.

"What?" asked Martin.

"Screw it," said Lee. "No one's ever going to believe us anyway. That's if we make it home." He looked as if he wanted to toss the iPad out the window as so much fodder for Native American tears. But he stuffed it back in his bag and zipped it all shut.

"What about the proof?" asked Martin.

"No one wants proof," Lee replied. "The truth's never interesting."

"Profound," said Martin.

"We're going to die, aren't we?"

"Okay, shut up now," said Martin.

"Are we speeding up?" asked Lee. Within the radius of the towering clusters, the stars vanished, replaced by constellations of logos. "I think we're definitely moving faster." Lee edged away from his door as they neared a nasty protrusion—a couple of dozen flame-broiled Burger Kings stacked, pagoda-style, on top of a petrified Staples Center. Lee let out a little noise as they sailed past, ridiculously close.

They had cleared the spur, but were definitely approaching an all-too-solid surface. The speedometer belied the view. Logos blurred by like billboards on the freeway.

"Martin," Lee prayed through clenched teeth.

Martin stomped on the brake pedal and nearly peeled the steering wheel cover off under his sweaty grip. They only flew faster. Martin shivered, and his breath steamed, and he smelled the acrid choke of exhaust. The brakes didn't work, so Martin's right foot instinctively went to the gas pedal, as if trying to kill them faster.

Lee wailed, and Martin tensed as their lane narrowed, crowded by structure. Ahead, a lit logoed aperture split open, as welcoming as a Venus flytrap, but less alien, and revealed a docking bay of some kind—an open void with a solid floor, a solid back wall, but sized for a thousand Screwmobiles. An object inside resembled a linked pair of taxidermied whales. It bore the same logos as the facility and hovered a few meters off the deck. Dwarfed nearby—Martin would recognize it anywhere, especially now that it had one front corner crunched in—waited Jeffrey's Lincoln Town Car. Martin doubted he'd come here to peddle candy.

The hangar swallowed them whole.

Lee screamed Martin's name as they touched down on a solid surface. Martin stomped the brake pedal with both feet, but too late. The speeding tires had bit, but bounced on the floor. Some force that wasn't gravity wanted the truck to stick, but its mass in motion clearly had other ideas. The radio box crashed against the windshield and rebounded hard onto Lee. The back wall hurtled toward them as no wall ever should.

Martin closed his eyes and thought, I knew I would die in this stupid truck.

Then, as if plunging through the branches of a high canopy jungle, the truck rent through the wall. Shreds smeared cleanly across the windshield. Solid tubes shattered against the bumper and shuddered the frame of the truck. They plunged through chaotic darkness and then unforgiving light, sometimes in the same second. Some unseen obstacle left a spider's web crack in the windshield in front of Lee, way bigger than a dollar bill.

They rattled through a long stretch of jostling, pounding, shredding dark, and then they tore through a wall and fell into a dimly lit blur of machinery, pipes, tanks, and conduits. Everything shattered in front of them, but each collision slowed them a little bit more. A wall, or floor, or ceiling, neared, as if time itself was grinding down. And then, with a final renting, the Screwmobile stopped.

A pasty amber light seeped into the cab. Everything around them diverged at wrong angles. Martin pried a hand off the steering wheel, and turned off the engine.

Ding. Ding. Ding.

Martin removed the key from the ignition.

Ding. Ding. Ding.

Martin turned off the headlights and everything fell quiet.

Martin felt a laugh rise from his belly. Lee, too, began to laugh, even as he cradled a bloody arm. When their eyes met, they both laughed out loud. Martin whooped and pounded against the ceiling and the steering wheel. Lee grabbed Martin's shirt with his good arm. "We're not dead," he said, shaking Martin. "We're not dead. We're not dead."

"My boss is going to be so pissed," Martin laughed.

"You totaled the crap out of this thing," Lee declared. "I mean like no one's ever totaled anything."

"Dear Allstate?" Martin said, miming a phone.

"Triple-A? We need a tow," said Lee.

When their laughter subsided, Lee said, "We're screwed, aren't we?"

"Quite possibly," Martin replied with a final chuckle.

"How are we going to find your friend?" asked Lee.

"I have a feeling it won't be hard," said Martin. "We didn't exactly sneak in here."

"What do you…?"

Martin made sure he had his staple gun. "Come on. Let's get out of here before…"

They heard a crash, distant, but near enough.

"Oh, crap," said Lee.

"Speak of the devil," said Martin.

꘎ ꘎ ꘎

Stewart may have looked ungainly on a Brixton Inn double bed, but his species clearly thrived in microgravity. The three squids who hauled Martin and Lee through the 3-D maze of corridors and junctions—a king-sized Chuck E. Cheese playground—swam and swung with an enviable grace. When their suckered tentacle pads couldn't reach, they ejected spurts of air from unseen sacs to hoist themselves across the voids—with sounds that would incapacitate an entire junior high school with paroxysms of laughter. Martin and Lee, held around the waist by unyielding tentacles, felt the full inadequacy of their monkey appendages.

Jeffrey led the way. Martin had recognized him in an instant, before he had spoken, before he saw the iPad, before he had snatched the staple gun away. Even without his expensive jacket and haircut, he had an air of self-assured competence. Even swimming, he had the swagger.

"Oh, this is rich," Jeffrey had said before grabbing the gun. Martin might have fired, but the other two had held similar devices, certainly not FastNCo. brand, but recognizable enough. "Martin, come to play the white knight. And in the Screwmobile no less." Jeffrey had laughed as he'd held out his iPad in a free tentacle and snapped a picture of the devastated truck. "Honestly, I thought it would be Stewart groveling back here with your unconscious ass in his trunk. But who are you?"

Jeffrey had eyed Lee closely with one, then the other, of his black, blinking eyes and then laughed. "I know who you are. Clever, Martin. Bring them." Then he had jetted off with a resounding fart.

They arrived at a round door that shuttered open for them and entered a not-at-all terrifying place. Part office suite, part control center, it reminded Martin of his visit to the FastNCo. headquarters for his company orientation—but for the presence of two more disconcertingly large cephalopod-ish beings, one svelte, one blubbery. This office's single decoration, besides the prominent corporate logo, had to be the alien equivalent of a human resources legal notice poster.

The skinny squid had a bluer hue than the others, and Martin sensed she was female. She was tapping at several devices displaying charts, graphs, and some kind of three-dimensional spreadsheet. She stopped editing to stare at the captured men, and let out a fluttering, high-pitched quibble. The obese specimen waved his stubby tentacles and glared at Martin and Lee with eyes an arm's length apart. His bulbous head/torso section gave him more of an octopusness compared with the cylindrical squiddiness of the others. He seconded the female's objections to the newcomers with much guttural glurping and eye bulging.

Jeffrey bluttered to him for a moment.

"Where's Cheryl?" Martin demanded.

"Shut up," said Jeffrey, and continued his conversation. Martin tried again to wrench free of the tentacle embrace. Lee hung resigned, cradling his bleeding arm. Little globs of blood dripped off and floated in place.

The fat one—Chumpdark, Martin supposed—shuddered and blustered. Of course, he might have been the happiest CEO in the ocean for all Martin could understand. At a blurb and a wave of tentacles from Chumpdark, their captors hauled Martin and Lee down a short, round corridor and tossed them into a room, more dodecahedral-shaped office than jail cell, and closed the door.

"We're not dead yet," said Martin.

"Oh, good," said Lee.

The door slipped open and, without a word, an alien tossed

in a soft severed-head-sized pack, and closed the door. Martin caught it on the first bounce.

"I think it's a first-aid kit," said Martin, showing Lee the universal graphic on the side of the pack—a pair of healthy tentacles cradling a single one bent at a right angle. Martin found a catch on one side that slipped along a seam, and the pack bloomed inside out with clear rubber pouches. Martin found a roll of tape—slippery and colored somewhere in between the mottled gray of the males and the dappled blue of the female. He picked off the end and found a cottony layer underneath.

"You're not putting that on me," said Lee.

"You want to bleed to death? Come on."

"Is there anything else?" asked Lee.

"Some sacs of putty or something, a plastic speculum thing that I don't even want to think about, and I think this is an eye patch."

Lee took his hand away from his wound. The rough-sawn plywood corner of the radio box had scraped out a chunk of skin and arm meat. Martin wrapped the tape tight under the elbow, then continued wrapping until he'd covered the wound. He searched the kit for scissors but ended up sawing through the tape with the key to the Screwmobile. When the tape separated, Lee shouted and grabbed his arm, fingernails ready to claw the bandage away, but then he relaxed.

"It tightened, like it was alive, but it's comfortable now," said Lee.

Martin pushed off to the door and tried the latch and the panel beside it, but the door had been secured. Seconds later, the door opened, and Jeffrey oozed in, crowding the room.

"I want to talk to Cheryl," said Martin.

"So persistent," said Jeffrey. "You'll see her soon. I'm curious, though. Cheryl screamed for almost a week. But you two aren't surprised at all. Did the old man finally take off his dermis?"

"He's dying," said Martin.

"Yes, probably," said Jeffrey. "A dermis is supposed to be worn temporarily. It can't filter all the toxins on your filthy little planet fast enough. Living with a smoker for all those years couldn't have been good for him at all."

"If you had any compassion, you'd help him, not mock him," said Martin.

"Stewart made his choices," said Jeffrey. "Although I may have to send him a nice fruit basket, or a pie, to thank him."

"To thank him?"

"For sending you to me, of course," said Jeffrey. "I'm beginning to think perhaps he did it on purpose. Maybe I'll have a chat with him after all this is over. Maybe, just maybe, he lied to you to get you to come up here on your own instead of doing something stupid like killing yourself or running off to China."

"What are you talking about?" asked Martin.

"I know you know the secret recipe," said Jeffrey. "It's the only thing that makes sense. And I read it in your eyes the other night in Lewistown."

"I don't kno…"

"Oh spare me," said Jeffrey. "Shut up and listen. I am not going to sit idly by and let you screw up my career. That's the CEO out there, and he is currently very disappointed. I have told him that you know the secret ingredient…"

"That was a stupid thing to do," said Martin.

"I don't think so. So here's the deal. Either you tell me what I want to know, or I will make your life a living hell. There will be a great deal of pain, and you will watch as I torture Cheryl and your new friend here. Neither you nor they will die for a very long time, but I guarantee you will be the last."

Martin lunged but Jeffrey rebuffed him with a tentacle and pressed him to a wall. He opened his eyes and found his own staple gun pointed at his face.

"Oh my god, he means it," said Lee.

"Why, Candy Man?" asked Martin. "Why can't you leave us alone? What would you do in my place?"

"And what would you do in mine?" asked Jeffrey.

"I lost my job today because of this," said Martin.

"Well, aren't you the hero? No wonder you and Stewart got along so well," said Jeffrey. "I'm afraid I can't do that. I've spent too long on this to give up now. And if I fail, my career's over. Do you know how many promotions I've passed up? But this is the big one. If I make it rain profit like no one else…"

He paused for a moment, and it sounded like he cleared his throat. He studied Martin and Lee. Then he continued, quieter, and deeper. "Do you know what I've sacrificed? I haven't been home. I haven't seen my brothers and sisters in decades. I have no life, no reef. Every day I squash myself back into that infernal four-limbed dermis and travel to your planet. Every night I take it off, feeling a little more dirtied by your environment, your lifestyle, your trivial human concerns."

"You're marketing a snack pie," said Martin, "and you're calling me trivial?"

"I've given up everything," Jeffrey thundered. He clutched Martin's collar, drew an eye up a few inches from Martin's, and whispered. "And I intend to get it all back. Plus interest."

He tossed Martin sideways and farted out in a flurry of tentacles. "Five minutes," he called as the door whisked shut.

"Oh, this sucks," said Lee.

CHAPTER
27

"Do you have this secret recipe?" asked Lee.

"You don't want to ask me that," said Martin.

"Jesus Christ," said Lee.

"Exactly," said Martin.

"What are you going to do?"

"What can I do? I'm going to try and cut a deal," said Martin.

"What? Can you do that?"

"They're businessmen."

"They're psychopaths."

"What the difference?" asked Martin. "Besides…"

"Besides what?" asked Lee.

"Let me think," said Martin.

♪ ♪ ♪

A few minutes later, the waist-grabbing goons hauled Martin and Lee to the main office, where Jeffrey was holding court with Chumpdark and the accountant.

"Have you made a decision?" asked Jeffrey.

"You've given me such wonderful choices," said Martin. "Let's see. Easy death or hard death?"

"It doesn't have to be death for you," said Jeffrey. "I'm willing to deal. I'll take care of you, Cheryl, and anyone else you want in exchange. I've discussed it with Chumpdark, and he agrees that we could create a home for you somewhere. Maybe even on Earth."

"With a few dozen of my closest friends?" said Martin.

"Something like that," said Jeffrey.

"What a gracious offer," said Martin. "But before we go any further, I want to talk to Cheryl. Alive. Conscious. Right now."

"Fair enough," said Jeffrey.

🐙 🐙 🐙

As they traveled along a long tunnel, the sensation of up and down returned. Gravity increased until the squids no longer reached out to the walls, but slithered along what could now be called a floor. The goons prodded Lee and Martin to walk.

At a human-sized rectangular door, Jeffrey pushed Martin forward. "Honey, I'm home," Jeffrey said with a sputtering laugh. He blobbered his joke to the others.

"Hello?" Martin creaked the door open, shocked to find a bogglingly perfect replica of Stewart and Cheryl's trailer inside. A crash struck the wall near his head, and showered him with shattered glass. He ducked back, but Jeffrey shoved, and Martin tumbled into the mobile home, falling against the legs of the kitchen chairs.

"Martin?"

He rolled over to find Cheryl standing over him, armed with another glass tumbler and a wicked kitchen knife.

"Cheryl."

"What are you doing here?" she asked.

"Coming to get you," said Martin.

Cheryl considered him through narrowed eyes, and then she shouted at the door. "Is this another stupid ploy, Asshat? I know you're out there." She readied her tumbler for another throw, but the door remained closed.

"I had nothing to do with any of this," said Martin.

"I don't care. Get up," said Cheryl.

"You're not going to stab me, are you?"

"I might, if you need stabbing."

"I'm surprised they let you have a knife."

"I've got a whole kitchen of 'em," said Cheryl.

"Jeffrey told me they make you bake every day," said Martin.

"Jeffrey? Oh, Asshat? Yeah. They've got a whole garden of rhubarb, a big warehouse of flour and Crisco, whatever. I jump through their little hoops every day, but apparently my pie isn't good enough. And it never will be." This last struck the door harder than a tumbler.

"You look good," said Martin. "I mean, considering…"

"Don't start, Martin. What are you doing here?"

"I told you. I'm rescuing you. Stewart was going to come, too, but he's too sick. So I got Lee Danvers to come."

"Lee Danvers?"

"It's a long story," said Martin. "He was in Brixton. We came through the portal and crashed my truck onto the ship."

"What are you talking about?"

"You don't know where you are?"

"It sure as hell isn't my kitchen."

"Do you want to know?"

"Will I like it?"

"No," said Martin.

"I kind of figured that," said Cheryl.

"You're about as far from the sun as you can be, but still be part of the solar system."

"Oh, that's just great," said Cheryl. "So what's your brilliant rescue plan?"

"It hasn't gone quite as I envisioned," said Martin. "Listen," he whispered. "They're threatening to torture us to death unless we give them the secret recipe."

"I don't have it. Do you? 'Cause if you do, let's give it to them and get the hell out of here," said Cheryl.

"It's not that…oh, god, you don't know," said Martin.

"Know what?"

"What they plan to do if they get it," said Martin.

"What do they plan to do?"

He told her.

"You're joking," said Cheryl.

"Ask Stewart," said Martin. "He's the one who told me."

"How would Stewart know anything?"

"Oh, god, you don't know that either," said Martin.

"What are you talking about?" asked Cheryl.

"I'm sorry you have to find out like this, but Stewart is one of these aliens," said Martin.

The blade of Cheryl's knife caught a glint of light. "Liar," she screamed as she lunged. And then nothing.

♪ ♪ ♪

Martin awoke on a brick-red tile floor. As he staggered to his feet, a door swung open and Jeffrey squelched in. "Sorry about that, Screw Man. Couldn't have your girlfriend martyring you back there," he said.

"Where am I?"

"The Herbert's Corner kitchen, circa 1986. In fact, these are the same appliances. We bought them at the auction when they remodeled. Pretty cool, huh? These are the exact ovens where Margie and Linda Laughlin baked thousands of pies. Everything runs off gas. We've even got well water from Brixton. I can tell you're impressed."

"Where's Cheryl?" asked Martin.

"Oh, she'll be along. I've sent her out to collect supplies. You two are going to bake me one last pie," said Jeffrey.

"Go screw yourself," said Martin.

"Clever. No, I'm serious," said Jeffrey. "And before you say anything, it's too late for deals. I'm tired of mucking around, and Chumpdark's getting very impatient."

What would have been the back door of the kitchen banged open, and the two goons forced Cheryl and Lee inside. Cheryl had an armload of fresh rhubarb. Lee had a twenty-five-pound sack of flour. They dumped their loads onto the wide stainless-steel table in the center of the room.

"Are you all right?" Martin asked.

"Oh, just peachy," said Cheryl.

"Hi, Lee. You meet Cheryl?"

"We've gotten briefly acquainted."

"She's not a fan of the show," said Martin.

"Nobody's perfect," said Lee.

"Did you ask her not to stab me?" asked Martin.

"Did I need to?" asked Lee.

"Tell her that you met Stewart, too," said Martin.

"Enough. Time to bake a pie," Jeffrey said, clapping several tentacles together.

"How many times do I have to tell you...?" said Cheryl.

"Yes, yes. You don't know the secret. That's why you're going to bake it with Martin," said Jeffrey.

Cheryl laughed. "Martin? What, do you have a store-bought frozen pie for him to thaw?"

"You've been away a long time," said Jeffrey. "Your paramour's been rather busy."

"Is it true what Martin told me?" asked Cheryl. "Are you going to kill everyone on Earth?" Martin noticed that she didn't protest the use of the term "paramour." He didn't know what it meant exactly, and maybe she didn't either. But he liked the idea that maybe he was hers.

"Details," said Jeffrey. "Start baking. Now."

"Tell me," said Cheryl. "Or I don't bake another pie. Ever. I don't care what you do to us." Lee gasped. Jeffrey slammed several tentacles on the table and grabbed for Cheryl.

"No," Martin shouted. "I do have the recipe."

Martin heard every sucker of Jeffrey's tentacles pop off the stainless steel as he slid back slowly. A single product pan fell from a shelf under the jostled table and rattled on the floor.

"You win, Jeffrey. Get Dork-Chump in here. I want him to see everything." Cheryl tried to protest, but Martin put up a hand. "We'll bake you the best damned pie in the universe. But someone's got to take me to my truck. The secret ingredient is there." Jeffrey glared at him. "What are you waiting for?" asked Martin. "Go get your boss and have one of these goons take me to the Screwmobile."

. *.* *.*

The ragged shaft through which the FastNCo. fleet Ford E-250 Super Duty Cutaway Screwmobile had raged was deep, but not as deep as Martin expected. The hangar opened perhaps two hundred yards away through the sparking tunnel of wreckage.

Stewart had warned him, but Martin marveled at the insubstantialness revealed by the crash. Here, in the microgravity, the facility had been outfitted with paper-thin walls, and hollow, brittle structure. Bird bones.

"You tricks no," the squid goon grunted from the other end of his staple gun and stretched out a tentacle. "Fast get."

"I'd get it if you'd let me," said Martin, pulling against the goon's appendage. "It's right here." The goon let slip a bit of slack, and Martin yanked the driver's door open, tilted the seat forward, and found his bag. He secreted the lighter in his pocket and turned around with the Pall Malls.

"What it?" the goon asked.

"A kind of herb," said Martin. "You know what an herb is?"

"No," said the goon.

"Then stop asking stupid questions and take me back," said Martin.

*. *. *.

The kitchen had been altered. One wall had been slid away, revealing a glassed viewing room full of impatient squid. A battery of dinner plate-sized images—dozens of live video feeds and data streams—dotted the periphery of the glass. A different image cycled onto a prominent central circle every few seconds. Every surface of the faux Herbert's Corner kitchen must have been embedded with sensors and covered with cameras.

"I suppose the doors are all locked," said Martin after the goon had dumped him into the kitchen and left to join the others.

"What are you playing at?" asked Cheryl.

"I'm a little curious about that myself," said Lee.

"We're going to bake them the magic pie," said Martin.

"I won't," said Cheryl.

"Then I will," said Martin.

"You?" Cheryl laughed. "You can barely make a waff…"

"I make a great waffle," said Martin.

"Whatever. If you really have the recipe, you can't give it to them," said Cheryl.

"Yeah, you probably shouldn't," said Lee.

"Actually, I think it'll be okay," said Martin.

Jeffrey's voice boomed over a PA. "If you monkeys are done squabbling, we'd like to see you bake a pie now. Some sort of herb, Martin?"

"It's not what you think, Jeff…Asshat. That name suits you much better," said Martin.

"Sticks and stones," said Jeffrey. Behind him, Chumpdark bellowed and slapped the blade of a tentacle against the glass, with a firm eye on Jeffrey. "Get started. Now," said Jeffrey.

"Fine," said Martin. He turned to Cheryl. "Help me. Please. Last one."

Cheryl closed her eyes. Lee put his hands to his forehead and drug them back through his thin hair.

Martin found a couple of large stainless-steel bowls on a shelf under the central table and banged them down next to the armload of leafy, unwashed rhubarb. A magnetic strip covered with knives hung over a three-basin sink. A rolling pin and several other utensils bristled from a drying rack next to a stack of foil pie plates. Various shelves and cupboards contained the sugar, the Crisco, the cinnamon. As if on cue, an icemaker dumped a load of ice into its bin and began to sluice in another batch. Martin surveyed it all again and still felt like he lacked everything.

He shouldered between Cheryl and Lee to get to the wide commercial ovens. He picked the top of the two, touched the knob, and hung his head, trying to remember.

"Four twenty-five," said Cheryl.

"Thank you," said Martin. He set the temperature, and after a little orange indicator clicked alight, the oven rumbled as the gas ignited deep in its bowels. Martin turned back to the table, and found Cheryl gathering up the rhubarb.

"Wait," said Martin. He put a hand on the rhubarb, and she paused. "Trust me," he said. He dug the Pall Malls from his back pocket but kept them out of view under the table. They probably had a camera there, too, but it felt safer to do it this way. Cheryl glowered when she saw what he had brought, but he hushed her before she could speak. Martin zipped out a single cigarette, returned the pack to his pocket, and then, doing his best black-and-white movie star, popped the cigarette between his lips.

"No smoking," Jeffrey called over the PA, slapping on the glass. "Besides, you don't smoke, Screw Man."

"Do you want your pie or not?" Martin asked out of the corner of his otherwise occupied mouth. Then, shielding his lighter like James Dean in the wind, he lit up.

He took a long first drag and fought back the urge to cough out his esophagus. He let the smoke burn deep into his lungs, and then, eyes watering, exhaled it slowly, first toward the glass and the suddenly apoplectic cephalopods, and then all over the rhubarb.

"What are you doing?" asked Cheryl.

Jeffrey burst through the door with frightening speed. A tentacle lifted Martin off the floor. Another pushed Cheryl back, and another, Lee. A fourth snaked around Martin's neck as Jeffrey drew him close to one of his eyes.

"What do you think you're doing?" Jeffrey asked.

"Put him down," Cheryl shouted.

"Put it out. Now. And stop fooling around," said Jeffrey.

Martin choked a smoky breath directly into Jeffrey's eye. It squeezed shut, and the skin around it browned and shriveled. Jeffrey bellowed and wiped at his eye with a juicy tentacle. Another arm batted the cigarette from Martin's fingers, and another squashed it on the tile floor.

"I don't know what you're playing at," said Jeffrey, holding Martin farther away, glaring with his un-smoked eye.

"Not…playing…" said Martin.

"You're choking him," shrieked Cheryl. Jeffrey's good eye swiveled toward her in time to see the rolling pin. It blunted against his eye and clattered to the floor. He bellowed again, and Martin found himself free, collapsing, not ready to hold his weight. But at least he had air to breathe.

When Martin had recovered enough to look up, he saw Lee standing between Cheryl and a blinking and sputtering Jeffrey.

"Listen to me," said Lee, his commanding, chocolate voice belied by the quivering knife in his good hand. "Martin and Cheryl were only defending themselves. There's no more need for violence. Now, you may not like what you're seeing in here, but you asked Martin to bake a pie. And he's providing you a demonstration in good faith. If you want to know whether he's serious or if he's simply wasting your time, there's only one way to find out. And that's for you to get out and let him work."

After a few moments, Jeffrey relented. He brought a rheumy eye back to Martin. "So help me, if you're screwing with me…" The door slipped shut behind him.

"Thank you," said Martin. "And nice throw."

"I've had a lot of practice the last few weeks," said Cheryl. "What do we do now?"

"We make the pie," said Martin. He slapped the pack of Pall Malls down next to the rhubarb and rubbed his throat.

"Smoking will kill you," said Cheryl.

"Tell me something I don't know," said Martin.

CHAPTER
28

Martin had expected every nuance of the making of the pie to be scrutinized, but he and Cheryl worked virtually ignored but for the kitchen sensors. Even through the language barrier and the muffling glass, the squishy ruckus in the viewing room seemed perfectly clear. Jeffrey argued, waffled, and equivocated. Every breath of secondhand smoke seemed to enrage the accountant more. Her voice was more pointed and precise, as if she had the facts and the moral high ground. Martin hoped she was on his side. Chumpdark thoomed angrily when he could get a word in edgewise.

"I don't think they care for smoking much," said Lee.

"That's what I hoped," said Martin.

"How'd you figure it out?" asked Cheryl. "I mean, unless it's..." *Not real?* she mouthed behind a hand.

"Pie-making 101 with Doris Solberg," said Martin. "She showed me pictures of your mom and your grandmother, always smoking, even while they baked. I put two and two together."

"Is that why your friend is so sick?" asked Lee. "Being around smoke and pollution so much?"

"Are you talking about Stewart?" asked Cheryl.

Martin nodded. "Laura and Milton and I have been looking in on him since you disappeared, but…"

"But?"

"He's not going to be the same when you get back."

"What do you mean?"

"He had to take off the human skin—they call it a dermis—but I don't think he can put it back on," said Martin. Cheryl sighed, and Martin blew another cloud of smoke into the rhubarb and sugar.

Cheryl worked quickly, and Martin had to smoke only five cigarettes before she put it in the oven. After Cheryl set the timer, she slumped onto the floor against a cupboard out of direct view of the arguing aliens.

Cheryl tucked her knees up against her chest and asked, "Where is he?"

"Who? Oh, Stewart?" asked Martin, joining her.

"He's in my motel room," said Lee. He sat where he could keep an eye on the glass and the door.

"The Brixton Inn," said Martin.

"My producer's looking after him," said Lee. "I hope."

"Cheryl, he loves you, and he's been trying to stop all this," said Martin. "Are you okay?"

Cheryl had buried her face in her knees. "I keep hoping that I'll wake up," she said. "That I'll be back in my bed, alarm going off, and late for work. But it keeps getting worse. I don't know what to believe anymore." A squishy tentacle thwacked the glass as if in response. "And maybe I'd be able to think clearly, if those things would quit fighting over there." She grabbed a metal pan from a shelf and hurled it at the glass.

The nobbering ceased when the pan struck and clattered onto the floor, then resumed. Jeffrey took over the discussion, and then several phlegmed objections arose at once. It sounded like the goons had joined the debate.

"And what is he even doing here?" Cheryl asked Martin, jabbing a thumb at Lee. "I'm not some back-of-the-milk-carton national news story on BI, am I?"

"No," said Lee.

"That's good, because I might have to do something to you, and I doubt they'd stop me this time," Cheryl said.

"Everyone knows about the portal, though," said Lee. Cheryl shrugged.

"It's how they get on and off Earth," said Martin. "Wormholish thing up the Deaver Creek bluff on Highway 360. A bunch of Wakers were there when we came through."

"I think we may have topped Orson Welles," said Lee.

"What? This was on the radio?" Cheryl asked.

"A little," said Martin, and then turned to Lee. "What do you make of the National Guard?"

"Probably crowd control," Lee replied.

"Not some kind of UFO squad?"

Lee shrugged and threw up his hands, and then said, "You look surprised."

"I always figured you had people scanning military radio traffic, or had contacts with insiders who tipped you off to this type of stuff," said Martin.

"Oh, good grief," said Cheryl. "You don't take anything on his show seriously, do you?"

"We're on an alien spaceship," said Martin.

"That doesn't mean you…oh, never mind," she said.

"She's right," said Lee. "I'm an interviewer. People show up and I ask them questions. That's all."

"But why all the paranormal stuff if you don't believe in it?"

"I found a niche and filled it," said Lee.

"A niche?" asked Martin.

"I'd done local radio for about ten years. Morning talk, drive time, whatever. But then during the first Gulf War in '91, the Pentagon offered to fly local media types to hang out with local troops for a few days. It sounded like an adventure. So I signed on, and I found myself out on this airbase in Saudi Arabia a few clicks from the Iraqi border. One night, I stumbled on a rumor about strange lights in the sky near the base. UFOs coming to keep an eye on American air operations, they said. So I packaged it all up nice and spooky, tongue in cheek, and sent it to my producer. When I got back a week later, no one wanted to talk about anything else. No one got the joke. The phone rang off the hook, and the ratings…? It didn't take long to figure out that there's a market for this stuff after the sun goes down."

"What were the lights at the airbase?" asked Martin.

Cheryl rolled her eyes. Lee laughed. "See? My point exactly. They were rumors at the end of a long chain of telephone tag. Or a joke—bored soldiers keeping themselves amused in the desert. I was a radio guy living out a bit of military fantasy, not a journalist. I didn't realize that I should be appalled that people cared more about UFOs than the war."

Cheryl returned her forehead to her knees, and Martin wished he could comfort her. But it had begun to sink in that he'd given these sadistic squids the secret they needed. He flushed. What if he'd misread the situation? No, no way I, Martin Wells, FastNCo. Area Account Representative, could have ever misconstrued the intentions and motivations of a completely alien culture. What if they're not arguing about the cigarette smoke? Maybe they're upset that they now have to sacrifice rhubarb-growing capacity for tobacco plantations. He scanned the room for some way to stop it. Too late to destroy the pie; they'd only bake another. Too late to kill himself, although it would be a bit of a relief. Besides, what would an afterlife hold for someone as stupid as Martin Wells? He pictured himself in a dunce cap for eternity. Any human who ever lived could punch him in the face once a day. Twice if you got neurotoxined. Even Gandhi would take a swing every few millennia.

"It's probably a little late to become a journalist," said Lee.

Cheryl knocked her head against the cupboard several times, and then asked, "What are we going to do? We can't let them get away with this."

"I have an idea," said Martin. "But it's not a particularly good one."

"Why?" asked Lee.

"Because it'll probably kill us in the process," said Martin.

Lee turned to Cheryl, who shrugged, then back to Martin. "Well, tell us already," he said.

♪ ♪ ♪

Although every pie had its own fingerprint of crimping, cinnamon and sugar, vent slits, and phrenological lumpiness, the steaming, golden-brown thing that Cheryl removed from the oven seemed too generic. Shouldn't it glow, or levitate? Instead it was a simple dessert on the stainless-steel table among the discarded rhubarb leaves, sloppy dusting of flour, and melted puddles of crushed ice—it couldn't be the most dangerous object in human history. Could it?

"Smells good," said Lee.

The cigarette smoke that Martin blew on the pie's steaming vents couldn't usurp the homey, sweet scent that had filled the kitchen. Martin could almost believe that he could step out the back door into a fine summer morning in Brixton, Montana. There might be a couple of semis warming their engines in the parking lot. He'd lean against the back wall of Herbert's Corner and enjoy the meadowlarks, the blue sky, even the final drags on this last cigarette he ever hoped to smoke.

"Put that thing out," Jeffrey called over the PA, destroying the illusion. "I'm coming in."

Martin stubbed the butt into a coffee cup with the other ashes and stained filters and put his hands up. The door opened, and Jeffrey entered, followed by Chumpdark and the accountant. The goons hadn't come in yet, but the door remained open. Martin had hoped they'd all come in and close the door. Patience.

"It needs a few minutes to cool," said Cheryl.

"Cut it," said Jeffrey, and before she could protest, he added, "It'll cool faster that way."

Cheryl sighed. "Plates are over there," she said, sending Martin to a cupboard. He chose one plate for each of their captors. Cheryl waited until he returned before she touched a knife to the center of the top crust. "It's really better if it…"

"Now," said Jeffrey. The staple gun pressed the point.

Cheryl sank the knife in and cut first one slice, then the rest of the pie into five even wedges. She dug through a drawer, and then another, and then found what she needed on the sink counter. Martin hoped they didn't sense her deliberate delay. She returned with the pie server and carefully set the slices on each of the plates that Martin held out for her. The hot filling oozed out into a puddle around each slice and provided a tangy, citrusy aroma. Lee caught Martin's eye and gave him the most imperceptible of nods.

"Will anyone need a fork?" Cheryl asked.

Chumpdark leaned in to dangle a nostril over a slice and inhaled deeply. His bulbous head bobbled as he lurched back up and grunted a few phrases.

"He says it smells delicious," Jeffrey said.

"What were you arguing about in there?" Martin asked.

"Arguing?" said Jeffrey. "You misunderstand."

"I don't think so," said Martin.

"Think what you want." Jeffrey bent over and took his own whiff. "Just like Mother used to make, no?"

Cheryl's hand hovered over the knife on the table, but Jeffrey waved the staple gun a little closer. "Not much of a sense of humor with this one, Martin. Are you sure you want to spend the rest of your life with her?"

"Oh, I'm very sure," said Martin. He wanted to pull the lighter from his pocket and prove it, but they needed more time.

Jeffrey tested his piece with the tip of a tentacle, smearing off a bit of the filling and curling it up under a gray flap. Jeffrey slurped, and the tentacle stretched out a bit, then snapped free as he quivered slightly. "Tart, but sweet," said Jeffrey. "So far so good." He hurbled to the others and slid his plate closer. The goons entered and took theirs. Chumpdark picked up his plate and deftly inspected it all around on the tips of several tentacles.

The accountant took hers last. She blurted angrily and hurled her plate against the glass. Chumpdark called after her as she slithered out. Martin exchanged a worried glance with Lee, but she had gone. The gray-green filling and shattered crust slid down the glass, even as the unbroken plate rolled across the floor.

"I think she's more of a cake person," said Jeffrey. He slid his slice, plate and all, up under the flap of flesh. He closed his eyes, and smooshed deep in his body. He held still as he drew out a clean plate, and then he quivered, bending his body sideways, returning upright, wide-eyed and laughing. "Martin, my friend. Congratulations."

The goons slurped theirs off their plates. Chumpdark ate his in one slurging bite. His flab and loose head magnified the resulting quiver. Chumpdark tossed up some tentacles and cleaned the crumbs from his sticky fold with others. He jibbled and turned to leave. Martin sniffed the air. Nothing there but pie and cigarettes. Lee shook his head. A few seconds later, the aliens retreated to the viewing room and resumed their argument. The accountant returned, her devices bristling with data. She nudged Jeffrey away to put the information in front of Chumpdark.

"So is it a success?" asked Lee. "The pie, I mean."

"It's right," said Martin.

"There never was a secret recipe," said Cheryl.

"I doubt your mom even knew," said Martin.

"Unbelievable," said Cheryl. "Now what? Our plan didn't work."

"Not yet," said Martin. Lee had managed to extinguish the pilot lights on the stove while Cheryl cut the pie. Natural gas was leaking into the air, but too slowly. "There's still a chance. Maybe we can get them to come back in here."

Martin heard a sound that, hearing once, he never wanted to hear again—like a plummeting blimp of oatmeal crushing a cow. Mucousy gray chunks and thin, pink liquid had been splattered on the glass. The chunks formed sliding dams of horror. They heard a thumperous struggle, and then the horrible sound again, and then again. The fourth time, a fresh splatter of gray gore coated the windows. A clear slip of plastic stuck to the glass and emitted a 3-D spreadsheet into the kitchen.

"Oh crap," said Martin. "Help me, quick. We need a lot more gas, and fast."

Near the stove, Martin smelled the rotten eggy odor. Together they scooted the stove out into the aisle. A metal-wrapped hose stretched between the appliance and the wall. Martin climbed over the stove and tested all the connections. "I need a wrench, or get back here," he said.

Together they pushed, but the hose stayed firm. "Again," said Martin.

"We'll probably blow ourselves up doing this," Lee said even as they heaved once more. Then a third time.

"Come on," Martin said, as much to the hose and the stove as to his companions. "Once more. Give it everything." They backed up to the wall and rushed together.

The oven crashed into the worktable, rearranging everything. Pans banged and clattered across the tiles. The table crashed against the glass and the door. The hose hung loose now, hissing. Martin's taxed respiratory system already ached for better air.

The door slid open, scraping chunky gray slop onto the floor. A pink and sticky Jeffrey burst in, staple gun first. The path closed off, he slithered onto the table, sliding to a stop on the remains of the baking, looming and breathing heavily. His skin browned and puckered in the volatile air.

Martin held up his lighter, thumb on the striker.

"You wouldn't dare," said Jeffrey.

"Why not?" asked Martin.

"You'll die, too," said Jeffrey.

"You're going to kill us," said Martin. "What's the difference?"

"You murdered them," said Cheryl.

"They wanted to shut it down, didn't they?" asked Lee.

"There was some discussion about the ethics of including such an ingredient in the product, yes," said Jeffrey. "Chumpdark wouldn't listen to reason."

"And you couldn't give up, could you?" asked Martin.

"Now I return to the board of directors, single-handedly having acquired the recipe and started production. I'm a hero, and lucky to be alive," said Jeffrey.

"What about them?" asked Martin.

"Unfortunate casualties of a violent, primitive species," said Jeffrey. "History will thank us for ridding the galaxy of you."

"You know we can't let you get away with this," said Martin.

"Please," said Jeffrey. "It's already happening. I initiated the planetary entry sequence right before I came in here."

Martin repositioned his thumb on the lighter's little knurled wheel, digging for the will to snap the striker home. Jeffrey jammed the staple gun against Martin's forehead with a warning laugh. Lee bellowed and lunged, but Jeffrey knocked him back. Tentacles encircled Martin's waist and throat. Another snatched at his hand, but Martin kept a death grip on the lighter. Suckers sucked and clawed at Martin's knuckles and skin. Martin gasped for breath and kicked to get away, scraping at slippery, rubbery skin with his free hand. A tip of one of Jeffrey's tentacles covered the top of the lighter, and Martin flicked the wheel.

If it sparked, it did nothing. Martin's head throbbed, and his lungs screamed for a clean breath of air. And then he collapsed, free, as Jeffrey howled a throaty, spewting growl of pain and rage. The wooden handle of a kitchen knife protruded from his torso a few inches above and behind one eye. No small-handled paring knife, but one of the big ones capable of chopping through a whole handful of rhubarb. Cheryl held her footing on the table amid the flailing tentacles, hauled off with a rolling pin, and pounded the knife home. It sank in, handle and all, with a spray of watery pink goo. Jeffrey tumbled sideways, screeching, clutching at his body, eyes panicked.

"Blow us up already!" Cheryl shrieked, clamoring across the table after him with her rolling pin and another knife.

Martin sucked what oxygen he could into his lungs through his ravaged throat and nearly blacked out. Knowing only that his thumb had to do something, he fumbled it on the top of the object clutched in his fist. A hand clamped over his.

"Don't. Not now. He's gone," said Lee. Martin longed to lie down on the floor, but Lee grabbed his arm. "Let's get out of here."

Lee helped Martin over the table, and they followed the slippery trail of alien blood out of the Herbert's Corner kitchen. The exploded remains of one of the goons coated the vestibule. Lee retched over his squelching feet. Martin forced himself to hold his breath for a few more seconds. A dollop of squid dripped onto the back of his head, and he slapped it away before it dribbled into his collar.

They hung together in the corridor, sucking for air and scuffing gore off their shoes.

"Is everyone okay?" Martin asked as he slumped to the floor with his back on the wall.

"We're not dead," said Cheryl.

"Thanks to you," Martin said. "You were amazing."

"We have to stop him," said Lee.

"He'll be easy to find." Cheryl pointed her rolling pin toward the trail of pink glops and Jeffrey's diminishing howls. "Come on." She offered a hand to pull Martin up.

"No," said Martin. He still needed a few moments to catch his breath.

"What? Come on," said Cheryl.

"We have to stop this ship," said Martin.

"How do you propose to do that?" asked Cheryl.

"Chumpdark's ship," said Martin.

"Chump dar…?" asked Lee.

"The CEO, the fat one. His ship's in the hangar. We fly it out, and then set it on a collision course at whatever looks most like the engines, then get the hell off," said Martin. "It's what Stewart and I planned to do. Also…"

"Also?" asked Cheryl.

"We destroy whatever we can on the way out. You should see the rest of this ship. It's like it's made of cardboard and chalk. We smash anything that looks important. Set fires. Whatever."

"This place is huge. There's no way we'll inflict enough damage," said Lee.

"It's also automated," said Martin. "Sever enough connections, and stuff stops working. From what Stewart told me, this is mostly a dumb warehouse. Where we are is probably the command and control section, so if we do enough damage here, it might kill off huge parts of the ship. But we're running out of time."

"You guys do that," said Cheryl. "I'm going after Asshat."

Martin grabbed her wrist. "No. Please," he said.

"Let go of me," said Cheryl.

"We have to stay together," said Martin.

"You don't know what he's put me through," said Cheryl.

Martin let her go and got to his feet. She took a few steps backward down the bloody corridor. "We have to destroy this ship now, before it gets to the portal," said Martin.

"Then go do that," said Cheryl.

"I agree. We can't waste time hunting," said Lee.

"If the ship gets in the atmosphere…" said Martin.

"He's wounded. It won't take long," said Cheryl.

"Cheryl, I can't destroy this ship if you're still on board," said Martin. "It's why Stewart asked me to come. Not to kill them, or even to save Earth. He wanted to save you." Cheryl stopped. "Stay with us. Please."

"Fine," she said.

"Besides," said Martin, "if we destroy the right stuff, he'll come looking for us." Cheryl had a great smile.

A few minutes later, they gathered outside the door of Cheryl's trailer, on the alien side, free from the stench of alien innards and natural gas. On the human side, they'd opened all the doors, and had broken every natural gas line, even as they'd gathered up what Lee called "utensils of mass destruction." Along with the rolling pin that had nearly killed Jeffrey, Cheryl had rearmed herself with a savage meat cleaver. Lee had a rolling pin and a meat tenderizer. Martin clasped a thick, wooden cutting board with a handle—a shield to go with his rolling pin sword. Their pockets bristled with knives.

Cheryl rolled up an *Awake* magazine and let Martin light one end on fire.

"I hope this works," said Martin.

"There's enough gas in there for another Hindenburg," said Lee.

The magazine burned quickly. "Open the door already," said Cheryl.

Lee opened the door, and Cheryl tossed the flaming magazine in underhand. It unrolled, flipping end over end, and struck the ceiling. It fell, igniting the air around it. Lee closed the door, wide-eyed. Martin stared back at him and blinked twice.

"Um, run now," said Cheryl.

CHAPTER
29

Martin tumbled weightless through the rotating collar of the junction, out of the faked gravity and faked Earthscapes into the ship proper. He collided with Cheryl. A fireball roared down the corridor from where they had come, its flames swirling into balls as the gravity weakened.

A klaxon screeched, and the collar's aperture swirled shut in an instant. A growl ate at the far side, and then another distant shudder rattled the walls.

"That's probably got his attention," said Lee. Martin laughed until he noticed the floating pink globules of alien blood, a trail of breadcrumbs leading them to Jeffrey.

"We have to go this way," said Martin, pointing in the opposite direction.

"Are you sure?" asked Lee.

"They brought me down here earlier. To get the cigarettes," said Martin. He gripped a structural rib and whacked at a conduit with his rolling pin. The pipe shattered, and the wire inside ripped apart. Nothing else happened, but it felt good. "Just like going through the jungle."

Lee hacked at another conduit, but the blow thrust him hard against the far wall. He grabbed the top of his head. "I guess there's a learning curve," he said, taking a second whack, this time braced.

.❦. .❦. .❦.

Martin had envisioned leaving something like the Screwmobile's tunnel of destruction in their wake. They'd broken countless pipes and conduits, had torn through walls to get to infrastructure, and more than once they'd been sprayed with some kind of oily fluid that globbed out of what Martin hoped weren't sewer pipes. In one room, they had managed to puncture several enormous tanks without drowning or gassing themselves. In another they had rendered a Skylark-sized lattice of glowing and flashing crystalline plates to inert shards. Drops in the bucket.

The truck had lodged in a cavernous, machine-laden framework, and Martin wondered if they'd hit the jackpot. Lee whistled. "There's a lot to mess up in here," he said.

"I—wish—we—knew—if—we—were—doing—any—real—damage," said Cheryl, as she whacked at an array of conduit.

"We can't waste too much more time," said Martin. "We've got to crash the ships." He almost pushed off down the tunnel but uncoiled himself.

"You guys go on," he said.

"What?" asked Lee.

"Go figure out how to fly that ship," said Martin.

"I thought we had to stay together," said Cheryl.

"I've got a full load of shrapnel sitting on a full tank of gas," said Martin. "Should carve out a pretty good hole in the middle of this place."

"How are you going to do that?" asked Cheryl.

"I'll figure something out," said Martin.

"How are you going to get out in time?" asked Lee.

Martin sighed hard, and then said, "I've got some slow-burning fuses." The last cigarettes were bent and crushed, but intact enough. "Set one in the right place, burns down, then boom. Should give me a few seconds."

"Martin," said Cheryl, shaking her head.

"This truck's not good for anything else," said Martin. "This isn't up for discussion. Go. I'll be right behind you."

"Be sure and have the engine running. Get the gas flowing through everything," said Lee.

"What? Have you blown up a truck before?" asked Martin.

"No, just seems like a good idea," Lee replied.

"Enough, go. We might be getting near the portal already, so don't spend any more time breaking stuff," said Martin. He watched them float away until Cheryl stopped looking back.

"What are you doing, Martin?" he muttered to himself. There was no procedure in the FastNCo. employee fleet manual for this.

Martin hacked at the wreckage with his cutting board and rolling pin until he could get to the gas flap. He twisted off the gas cap and almost snapped it onto the retaining hook, but tossed it away instead.

Martin returned from the cab with the first pieces of cloth he could find, a couple of FastNCo. polo shirts from his bag. He rolled one tight and fed it as far as possible into the unleaded gas hole, only a few inches at most. Peeling more debris away, he dug into the back of the truck and found the long bolts he'd special ordered for an account in Glendive. He used one to push the polyester a good ten inches down the throat of the gas tank. Martin tied the other shirt in line and tamped in more fabric until he smelled gas. He stretched the wick out to a flat bit of wreckage where he could rest a cigarette. With his rolling pin, he pounded in a couple of two-inch bright-finish eleven-gauge common nails to hold it all into place.

Martin got into the driver's seat one last time. Did he need anything from the truck? The XM radio? Rick's luggage? The Garmin GPS? The last five years of his life? No more road lay ahead for the Screwmobile, only pipes and conduits leading into a labyrinth of tanks and immense machines—hopefully the engine room, the central plant, or something equally vital.

Martin put the key in the ignition and turned it over. The Screwmobile's engine roared to life. He pushed himself out of the cab and right into Jeffrey.

"Going somewhere, Screw Man?" Jeffrey drew Martin close with several unforgiving tentacles. His torso had been wrapped with a swath of blue-gray bandage, but pink goo oozed from the gaps. Was the knife still inside, cutting Jeffrey deeper with every movement? "I'd hate for you to miss what I'm going to do to your planet."

Martin stifled a cry of pain when Jeffrey jammed the staple gun against his temple. He didn't want Cheryl coming back for any reason.

"I never got the chance to thank you for the recipe," said Jeffrey, his usual smarm sounding a bit strained. The tentacles tightened, and Martin groaned. "It's a bit nasty though, isn't it?" Keep talking, Martin thought. He resisted the urge to check down the tunnel and give away Cheryl and Lee's escape. "Secondhand cigarette smoke. Incredible. We never even considered it. But it's blindingly obvious now that I think about it. We'll call it 'natural flavors' on the packaging, of course."

"What will you do when the truth leaks out? Your customers will be furious," said Martin.

"We may have to settle a lawsuit and pay off some journalists. Maybe hire some nutrition scientists to prove it's actually healthier this way. This isn't difficult stuff, Martin."

"You'll be the one held responsible," said Martin.

Jeffrey laughed, then glurked in pain. The tentacles loosened for a moment, and Martin shifted his hands closer to his back.

"Is something wrong?" asked Martin.

"The company will be making too much money to care. And even if they try to make an example of me, some other company will snatch me up. I'll be able to write my own ticket after this."

"You're delusional," said Martin. He strained his wrist to reach his back pocket, but his stupid endoskeleton didn't bend that way.

"Think what you want," said Jeffrey. "It won't matter for long." Martin yanked hard. His hand slipped a little against Jeffrey's suckers. His fingertips brushed against a knife handle, and he strained as if they might grow longer.

"Do you hear that?" Jeffrey asked. Martin hadn't, but he stopped straining for a moment to listen. A vibrating rumble, oddly high pitched, reverberated through the structure. "The engines are coming online. We'll be through the portal in a few minutes." There came a whoosh, like the sound of a thousand college kids flushing every toilet in a new stadium at the same time, and then the rumble thundered into a screaming roar.

As Jeffrey marveled at the ignition, Martin got a knife between two helpless fingertips. It wasn't enough.

"So Mart—" Martin headbutted Jeffrey, right in the bandage. It felt like plopping on a pillow full of eels. Jeffrey squalled. The tentacles loosened. Martin grabbed the knife and hoped it was a big one. He twisted his wrist and sawed into tentacle flesh. Fluid squirted on his hand, and Martin flew free. Jeffrey snarled and flailed as Martin hacked at the grabbing tentacles.

An appendage connected hard against his chest. Martin

sailed backward and crashed painfully through the remains of a wall. Jeffrey scrambled through the hole after him. Martin pushed away, disoriented, shattering a pipe with his forehead to make it through a narrow gap. He found himself on the roof of the Screwmobile. Behind him, Jeffrey tore at the ragged opening; in seconds it'd be large enough.

Martin knew he'd never make it down the tunnel. He found a grip and pulled himself toward the cab. He swung in and clawed for the handle. He yanked, but a tentacle caught the door midswing. Martin pulled again, but another tentacle pad slapped down and then another. The suckers held firm against the metal and glass. Martin squirmed across the bench seat. Jeffrey's eye poked into view, and more tentacles sprayed in. Martin hacked at them with his knife.

His hand landed on the Thermos on the floor, and he threw it. It bounced back ineffectually, so he ripped the lid off and shook the steaming liquid over bare gray skin. Tentacles whirled in a panic, and Jeffrey let out a chilling skree. Doris made a mean cup of coffee.

A tentacle ripped the steering wheel cover off and snapped the cup holder. Another mangled the back support and tore it out. The GPS almost broke through the windshield as it shattered. Martin scrabbled for the passenger door handle and kicked his homemade radio box in the tentacles' path. They smashed it to splinters against the dash. Martin spilled out of the passenger door just as Jeffrey squashed his bulk in from the driver's side. Martin's feet found some purchase. He almost rebounded into the squid-filled truck but caught himself on the door. A tentacle swiped at him. Martin pushed with all the force he could muster against the door and the protruding tentacle.

Jeffrey screeched and Martin readied to do it again, but the door had latched. The pad of the tentacle flailed and grasped at air, each angry sucker gasping like a vicious little mouth. In the air, a few inches away from Martin, hung the staple gun.

Jeffrey fell still as Martin made his way carefully and deliberately around the front of the truck, keeping the FastNCo. 25-C pointed between the wide black eyes behind the windshield.

"Killing me won't stop anything," Jeffrey said over the engine's roar.

"It'll stop you," said Martin.

"I'm the only one who can abort the manufacturing process now."

"Sorry, Jeffrey. I'm not taking any more chances with you."

Jeffrey's body appeared still, but Martin sensed him trying to free his trapped appendage.

"If you open that door, I will shoot you," said Martin.

"What are you waiting for?" said Jeffrey. "Pull the trigger. I don't think you can do it."

"Maybe not," said Martin. He pulled out the Pall Malls.

"What are you doing, Martin?"

"Thought I'd have a smoke." With one hand, Martin opened the pack, shook the tip of a bent cigarette out, put it to his lips, and tossed the pack away.

"You're disgusting. Your whole planet is disgusting," Jeffrey snarled.

"Maybe," said Martin. "But we have really good pie."

Martin found the lighter in his front pocket. Jeffrey blinked once, and then his eye followed Martin's to the wick of FastNCo. shirts, still intact.

Martin flicked the lighter.

It sparked but didn't light. He flicked again. In Martin's brief inattention, Jeffrey struggled to free his trapped limb, but Martin re-aimed the staple gun and Jeffrey froze.

"I guess you'll have to shoot me after all," said Jeffrey.

Martin flicked one more time. Nothing. Nothing again. He didn't want to die of embarrassment.

Jeffrey laughed cruelly.

Zip. Click. A narrow, blue flame spiraled out of the lighter to the ceiling. Jeffrey's eyes flared wide. Martin leaned his head to the flame and lit the cigarette.

"Martin?" said Jeffrey.

"See you around, Candy Man." Martin blew out a smoky breath and touched the cigarette to the end of his gas-soaked FastNCo. shirt. It took the flames in an instant.

Jeffrey's bellows followed Martin into the chewed tunnel, until the explosion.

Martin tumbled end over end in an unbearable heat. He wrapped his arms over his head as he crashed through surface after painful surface. Hot nicks scraped his skin. Just when he thought the pain would never stop, he was floating free in cool air. He opened his eyes to find himself skimming across the hangar a few feet off the floor.

"Martin!" Cheryl screamed.

Martin twisted around and felt a dozen pinching twinges on the skin of his back. His clothes were shredded. His arms bled from countless scrapes. An acrid smell had taken up permanent residence in his nose. Cheryl and Lee stood near Chumpdark's ship a few degrees off his line of travel. He tried to swim toward her, to painful avail.

Cheryl crossed the hangar floor with wide, strange strides.

"What's happening?" Lee shouted. Smoking punctures riddled the hangar wall. The hangar shuddered with a thunderous boom.

Martin strained to reach Cheryl's outstretched hand. She lunged and their fingers locked for a moment, but slipped apart.

He hit the floor and rolled, the floor tugging at his clothes and skin.

"It's sticky," Martin said, finding his feet, not with gravity, but a treatment on the hangar floor.

"What happened?" asked Cheryl.

"I think I blew up the engines," said Martin.

"We can't get into the ship," said Cheryl.

"I'd like to get out of here," said Lee. As if to make Lee's point, another shudder shook the floor, and a large section of the back wall exploded across the hangar in a fiery black ball.

"Jeffrey's car!" Martin yelled.

They lurched wildly, prying each footstep free and swinging their legs forward as far as possible. A few feet from the car, they were peppered with a shower of debris. Martin prepared to smash a window, but Jeffrey had kindly left it unlocked.

"Can you hotwire…?" Martin asked, and then laughed. "Never mind." The keys swung in the ignition. A crash sounded from the direction of the Screwmobile's tunnel.

"Someone else drive," Martin said, pointing the staple gun toward the hole.

"Is he coming?" asked Cheryl.

"Start the car," said Martin.

Cheryl got behind the wheel. The Lincoln's engine purred as quietly and coolly as in any convenience store parking lot.

Martin sensed movement in the crumbling truck hole, and fired. The staple gun clicked and debris exploded, doubling the size of the hole, but leaving solid, not gooey, destruction. Martin felt his hair stand on end as if he were back in physics class touching a Van der Graaf generator.

"Get in," Cheryl screamed. Martin backed up and opened the back door. He fired a few more times, and more of the wall exploded.

"Was that the air bubble I felt?" Martin asked.

"Yes, get in," said Cheryl.

"We're pressing this hangar button now," shouted Lee.

Martin closed the door but rolled down the window, if the staple gun shot through the force field, he couldn't stop now. He aimed at the hole, wreaking more and more damage. As Cheryl reversed and turned them, he fired at anything intact.

"Oh my god," said Lee.

"Martin?" Cheryl wailed.

The hangar door was rising, but no sun, no stars, awaited them at the end of the alien canyon—only a swirling, widening blue-and-black abyss rendered fractally terrifying by the shattered windshield. Plasma flashed silently from point to point. The Lincoln idled.

"Go. Go. Go," said Martin.

Cheryl jammed the car into drive and stomped on the gas. The floor grabbed at the tires like fresh tar, but they accelerated. Cheryl screamed. Martin and Lee screamed, and a few yards from the edge, Lee found the presence of mind to reach over and tap the portal icon.

And then they popped out.

Martin opened his door for a better shot back into the hangar, and stood with one hand gripping the handhold over the door. "Get back in here," Cheryl screamed. He squeezed the trigger over and over. Chumpdark's double-hulled ship exploded. Cheryl screamed his name again. Then blue enveloped him and drew reality into fate's fine thread.

*. *. *.

A moment later, Martin tumbled, crunching and scraping, rolling under his own painful weight and velocity on a very hard surface. He floundered one last time and found himself under a bright blue sky. Crumbling rock rose up on the edge of his peripheral vision. An electric-blue swirl spun silently above him, and then bloomed across the sky like the second Big Bang. Everything hurt, but Martin sensed no agony except the certainty of being too late.

A bristle of long antennas emerged overhead, followed by a black, blunt hulk blotting out the sun. One logo, and then another, and then thousands.

Martin raised his arm, relieved to find the staple gun still in his hand, and fired, once, twice—he stopped counting. Every logo was an easy target. Every shot burst some part of the ship.

The factory continued to slip from the vortex. Each ker-chunk of the staple gun was unsatisfying, but dozens, maybe hundreds, of fires now spurted from the hull. Martin's hand stung from the spring's concussion, over and over, against his palm. The ship kept coming and coming.

Martin didn't remember getting to his feet, but he stumbled forward, still firing, and almost collapsed, unprepared for the pain in one knee, and again as he tripped over a state trooper on the side of the road. People had fallen everywhere, presumably asleep from the portal and not yet neurotoxined. The Lincoln had come to a stop sideways, mostly intact, against a National Guard truck.

Martin found himself stopped by the guardrail and began to shout, forcing his numb hand to squeeze again and again. There was now no sky but the ship.

Martin ducked when finally an inert, pyramid-sized engine bell, one of a dozen, passed overhead and the sky over the gap cleared. Plasma sputtered from only two of the bells, but still the ship inched north, stretching out over the northern horizon toward Brixton. Martin kept firing at the still-working engines.

If the neurotoxin came, he wanted to die as part of the solution, and not part of the problem.

And then Big Thunder Valley earned its name.

The concussion hit his chest; the road, his back. And his consciousness went out for a smoke break.

CHAPTER
30

Martin sat in his usual chair by the window. The one with the good view of the pantry and the breakfast bar. No one had set out breakfast this morning, only a hand-lettered sign that read, "Out of Food—Sorry for the Inconvenience." Brenda had left the first aid kit on the table, having pretty much exhausted its supply of bandages, gauze, tape, ointments, and expired analgesics in individual packets.

Behind Martin, Highway 15 drained Brixton of the flood of once exuberant, now shocked and beleaguered, Wakers. A few milled in the lobby, waiting to check out or for the traffic to thin, speaking in quiet voices—or maybe it was that Martin's ears were still ringing from the explosion. They showed one another video taken on cameras and phones. A few had artifacts, bits and pieces taken from the wreckage before the National Guard had cordoned off the area. Despite their tales, Martin sensed a disappointment, as if the truth wasn't good enough.

The Lincoln waited in the carport outside the lobby doors like a smoking gun, with its smashed windshield and mangled front corner. The passenger side had been scraped up in the landing, and the rearview mirror dangled by a wire. After the factory had exploded, Lee and Cheryl had dragged him to the car, and had picked their way down the hill and into the field on the other side of the bridge before the crowd awoke.

Martin had awoken in the back seat a few miles south of Doris Solberg's place. He had groaned, and Cheryl had given him a weak, pained, smile in the rearview mirror. Lee had stared ahead. Questions had arisen, but lost their way.

Lee, Brian, and X-Ray wandered into the lobby, spoke conspiratorially for a moment, and then Lee joined Martin. His arm had been rebandaged with materials a little more human, and he wore a baseball cap low over his face.

"You okay?" asked Lee.

"How's Cheryl?" Martin asked.

"She's with him now, but…" Lee said, and shook his head.

Martin sighed. What did he expect? To be sitting hand in hand, comforting Cheryl in Stewart's dying minutes? That she'd cry on his shoulder, longing for a comforting kiss?

A few minutes later, the lobby door chimed, and Brenda called Cheryl's name. Martin stood, but Cheryl crossed the lobby, weeping. She ducked behind the counter and disappeared into the housekeeping room. Brenda followed, abandoning her customers.

Martin stuck out a hand to Lee. "Thank you," he said.

"No, thank you," Lee replied. "You're not going to…?" He nodded toward the counter.

"No," said Martin.

Martin left the Brixton Inn on foot. Even if he'd had the keys to the Town Car, the Highway Patrol wasn't letting anyone turn anywhere but out of town. He walked against the flow of the crowd, ignoring them and their plight, all the way across Brixton and out of it again.

The roadblock at the junction had been hardened and reinforced by the National Guard. A colossal wall of smoke billowed from the southern horizon behind the endless line of stunned Wakers streaming north on foot.

Scotch-taped bits of paper fluttered in the breeze on the gas pumps at Herbert's Corner. "No gas," each read.

In the half-lit diner, the chairs had been flipped upside down on tables. Martin feared to talk over the hush of the silent jukebox.

"Martin?" Eileen asked, setting aside a magazine. "Lorie, get out here."

Martin stumbled to a stool and sat heavily.

"My goodness," said Lorie, coming out from the kitchen. "What's happened to you?"

"I don't know," said Martin.

"I don't have anything to give you, 'cept for a glass of water," Eileen said. "We're cleaned out."

"There's still those packs of black licorice in the store," said Lorie.

"That's okay," said Martin. "I don't need anything."

🐛 🐛 🐛

Martin awoke to the sound of whispering and sat up in the booth. He banged a shoulder on the edge of the table, but it hurt no worse than anything else. He squinted across the diner, unsure of how long he'd been asleep. There was no sunlight in the vestibule. The dark Pepsi clock couldn't be trusted. A third person was talking with Eileen and Lorie. Someone in a red hoodie.

Martin rubbed the sleep from his eyes and prepared to stand up, but Cheryl slid into the booth across from him. She'd been crying, and she still had shards of alien conduit tangled in her hair. "Hi," she said.

"Stewart…?" Martin asked. Cheryl nodded and touched the

back of her wrist to the corner of each eye. "I'm sorry. About everything."

"Stewart told me what you've been doing for him, for me."

"He loved you very much."

Cheryl accepted this. "What are you going to do now? Stewart said you lost your job."

Martin chuckled weakly, remembering Rick, maybe still at Cheryl's place. It would probably be best to avoid him right now, likewise the Highway Patrol, and maybe the FBI. "Don't worry about me. What about you?"

"I can't imagine leaving Brixton," said Cheryl. "Even now."

"Brixton wouldn't be the same town without you," said Martin.

"Besides…" said Cheryl. She scanned the diner and blew out a hard sigh.

"What?"

"Stewart owned this place, Martin. After Herbert died, Stewart created a corporation, bought the place, and made sure they stopped selling rhubarb pie. He made them remodel and took out the bakery. And he stopped them spreading all the alien rumors."

"To protect you," said Martin.

Cheryl nodded. "And now, it's mine. He left it all to me."

"What are you going to do with it?" asked Martin. "Keeping in mind that it's the only decent place to get breakfast and coffee in a hundred-mile radius."

Eileen crossed the diner carrying a tray. Without a word, she set a steaming mug of coffee in front of each of them.

"What's this?" asked Martin. "I thought you were out."

"Lorie found a box of coffee up in the office," said Eileen. "It's on the house. This time." She winked, spun away, and called back over her shoulder. "It'll take more than this to close Herbert's Corner."

ONE YEAR LATER

"Order a triple shot in your coffees, Waker Nation. It's Weird Science Wednesday night, sponsored by the University of Phoenix, and in a moment we'll be taking your calls and questions for Dr. Helmut Schwartz, theoretical physicist and the author of a recent paper that explores the relationship between dark matter and dark energy and redefines how they affect the fabric of our universe. But first, a reminder that with us tomorrow night will be our friend and official Waker Nation economist Lawrence Montgomery, a professor at the University of Rhode Island, and the author of the book *Everything You Need to Know About Economics Should Be Taught in Kindergarten*. On Friday, live all night with us in the bunker will be thirteen-year-old prodigy Ayani Anami. You absolutely have to meet this young lady. Not only has she been appointed as a UN goodwill ambassador for children based on her humanitarian blog, but she's completing her medical degree, and her first play opens next week off-Broadway.

"And as always, you can find more detailed information about these topics and the work of all our guests on wakernation. com. Welcome back, Dr. Schwartz."

"Thank you, Lee."

"Now, I'm going to ask you more about what we learn from

the map of dark energy, but I need to do my nightly penance first, if you don't mind."

"Not at all."

"Let's get this over with, X-Ray. Greenville, North Carolina, you're Beyond Insomnia."

"Lee, this is Richard. I can't believe you're not talking about aliens anymore."

"What's there to talk about, Richard? Extraterrestrials exist. We know this for certain now. We know a little about their biology and their culture and are learning more every day. We're preparing to make official contact. And we know that the government did not conspire to keep this from us. Every Thursday we get an update from Pauline Nelson, a member of the international observation and research team. There's still much we don't know, but the speculation is over."

"And you believe whatever they tell you?"

"I believe the things that they have evidence to back up."

"Someone got to you, didn't they?"

"I came to the conclusion that it's time to start living in reality. In other words, I woke up."

"You're a hack, Danvers. And your show is crap."

"I'm sorry you think so…and he's hung up. If you're still listening, Richard, and every other Waker out there, I'm sorry. I will gladly shoulder the blame for the speculation and lies for as long as it takes. Phew. Okay. Let's get back to business. Helmut, you described how if you overlaid the map of a galaxy's dark energy with a map of its dark matter…"

♪   ♪   ♪

The pilot relaxed and let his computer maneuver the rig into the slot. He stretched his tentacles and torso, expelled all the air from his bladders, and filled them anew. When the ship was parked, he activated system standby and then noticed an object near the portal facility on the icy chunk. He glurmed quizzically, tapped his screens, and his windshield targeted and magnified the image—a flat, rectangular, faintly lit object, but readable. A homey amateur logo decorated one corner, a flap-watering picture the other, and familiar and welcome script filled the space in between. He plurbed to himself, pleased, and found his dermis generator in a drawer.

A few minutes later, he blurred into place behind a steering wheel on a familiar road between two walls of crumbling rock. More than a thousand lenses, sensors, and monitors captured his arrival and his descent of the hill. He crossed a bridge, slowing as the new signs directed. A lowered barricade blocked the road, so he turned onto a driveway of freshly constructed concrete.

He rolled down his window as he stopped by a little building, built up on a platform. A window slid aside, and a man said, "Welcome to Earth. Name and destination?"

"Um…Glen," said the pilot.

"You real name, please," said the attendant.

"Mushfronf," said the pilot, but with a little burble in the middle of it all. "Do you need my reef name, too?"

"Please," said the attendant, and Mushfronf obliged. "Destination?"

"Headin' up to the Corner."

The man in the booth handed him a blinking puck of plastic. "Keep this in your vehicle at all times," he said. He handed him another that had a clip on one side. "And that one stays on your person. Return them here on your way out."

"Got it," said the pilot.

"Have a nice day."

"I will. You, too," Mushfronf replied.

He parked alongside several other trucks at Herbert's Corner and headed inside.

"Glen," said Eileen. "Long time, no see."

"Afternoon, Eileen. But forget the 'Glen.' I suppose you can call me Mushfronf now, seein' as." He chose a stool. "Saw your new sign. Says you got the pie again."

"We surely do," said Eileen. "Made fresh every day. You want some now, or do you want somethin' that Mama would want you to eat first?"

"Better bring me a number seven with a side of coleslaw, but make sure and save me a couple slices," he said.

"I'll save you a whole pie," said Eileen.

Eileen put in his order, then headed upstairs to the office. She knocked and opened the door, then shut it as quickly.

She scurried away, laughing.

"What's going on?" Lorie asked her, peering up the stairs. "Let me guess."

"Goin' at it again. At least with their clothes on this time," said Eileen.

A minute later, Martin found Eileen in the kitchen. "Sorry about that. What's going on?"

Eileen nodded out through the kitchen window, and Martin ducked to peek out into the diner. "You're sure?" he asked.

"I can't believe you don't remember that mustache and that ridiculous little hat," said Eileen.

Martin donned the dark glasses to be sure.

Cheryl came in behind him. "What's going on?" she asked.

"The truck driver there. I've had Eileen keeping an eye out for him. I owe him an apology," said Martin.

"He's asked for the pie," said Eileen.

"He probably deserves pie for life after the scare I gave him," said Martin.

"Don't look at me," said Eileen. "The owner'd have to approve that."

"What do you say, Madame Owner?" asked Martin.

"What did you do to the poor man?" Cheryl asked, and then threw up her hands. "I don't care. If you want to give him free pie, go ahead, but it's coming out of your paycheck, Mr. Manager."

Martin delivered the man's meal and set his pie on the counter.

"It's you," said the pilot.

"Yeah, hi. I wanted to say sorry about…everything. Your meal's free today, and anytime you want pie, it'll be on me."

"Thank you," the pilot said hesitantly. "Mighty generous."

"Enjoy," said Martin. The pilot took a large bite of pie and quivered with delight. "As good as you remember?" Martin asked.

"Oh yeah," said the pilot. "I've always said that you could sell this here recipe. Probably make a fortune."

"Nah," said Martin. "It's not *that* good."

ABOUT THE AUTHOR

M.H. Van Keuren quit a perfectly good job to devote his life to writing science fiction. He lives in Billings, Montana, with his wife and two sons.

Find his blog at mhvankeuren.blogspot.com.